BEAR

BEAR

FLIGHT TO LIBERTY

A NOVEL

MIGUEL VARGAS-CABA

iUniverse, Inc.
New York Lincoln Shanghai

BEAR

FLIGHT TO LIBERTY

iUniverse books may be ordered through booksellers or by contacting:

iUniverse
2021 Pine Lake Road, Suite 100
Lincoln, NE 68512
www.iuniverse.com
1-800-Authors (1-800-288-4677)

Because of the dynamic nature of the Internet, any Web addresses or links contained in this book may have changed since publication and may no longer be valid.

Certain characters in this work are historical figures, and certain events portrayed did take place. However, this is a work of fiction. All of the other characters, names, and events as well as all places, incidents, organizations, and dialogue in this novel are either the products of the author's imagination or are used fictitiously.

ISBN: 978-0-595-42558-7 (pbk)
ISBN: 978-0-595-68167-9 (cloth)
ISBN: 978-0-595-86887-2 (ebk)

Printed in the United States of America

To the past, present, and future crews of all the *BEARs*, and especially to those who gave their lives in the fulfillment of their duties over the world's oceans, far from home and their loved ones.

"И познайте Истину, и Истина сделает вас свободными."
Евангелие Иоанна, глава 8я, 32й стих

"And you shall know the Truth, and the Truth shall set you free"
Gospel of John, Chapter 8, verse 32

PART I

▼

CAPTIVES

C H A P T E R   1

▼

After receiving the landing instructions, Captain Mikhail Makarov starts the descent. His mind, however, is busy finding a solution to a more critical problem:

"Yura, how much fuel left?"

"The needle is to the left of the red line. If we still have four hundred liters, that's a lot," replies the Flight engineer, Senior Lieutenant Yuri Yevdokimovich Kazakov, his tense voice betraying a slight trembling.

The airplane swallows fuel like a bottomless pit, and even though now the runway can be seen in the horizon, the Captain knows four hundred liters of fuel is not enough to get his machine there in one piece. "Vasya, we'll have to ditch. We won't be able to reach the runway," Mikhail tells his copilot, First Lieutenant Vasily Aristarkovich Chkalov. Opening the intercom line, he warns the rest of the crew: *"Tovarishchi,* brace yourselves. We'll have to ditch."

Behind the flight deck, the technicians of the electronics team start to clean their consoles of anything that could fly at the moment of impact. Once everything is safely out of the way, they tighten their seat belts.

"Yura, how much left?" Mikhail asks again, in the vain hope of hearing an answer different from the one he very well knows he will get.

"Empty. All gages red in all the tanks," replies the Flight Engineer. His trembling voice reveals the fear inside.

Any moment now the engines will sputter and die one after the other. Looking at the water below, and then at the coast before him, Mikhail fixes his gaze on the runway beyond, which now is so close and at the same time, ironically, seems to be unreachable.

Blyad! *Having come from so far, and when we're almost there, this has to happen! Well, at least there's the consolation of knowing that we arrived.* The altimeter slowly marks the descent of the enormous Tupolev towards the cold waters of Goose Bay, Canada. On its shores starts the runway, and everyone's possible salvation.

Despite that, Mikhail can hardly believe it. Less than two hours ago he was furiously attacked by Soviet fighters, shooting rockets and bullets in their attempts to destroy his plane before he reached his goal: defection to the West.

Now, after an odyssey of more than twenty three hours in flight and more than sixteen thousand kilometers filled with adventures and endless dangers, since he took off from the Soviet Navy airbase at Kuzomen, in the Kola Peninsula, USSR, at last he's in Canadian airspace. CF-101 'Voodoo' jet fighters of that country's Armed Forces escort and guide his plane to a safe haven in their air base at Goose Bay, Labrador.

While descending, Mikhail thinks about the events that gave birth to his escape wish. It all started on June 22nd, 1941, after the German assault on the Soviet Union. He was immediately drafted into the Soviet Air Force as a fighter pilot. From June 1941 to May 1945, he made it through the 1418 furious days and nights of the Great Patriotic War. He flew 486 missions, and fought in 186 dogfights.

After four years of rude combat together with the Red Army, and after having smashed the Nazi war machine through Ukraine, Byelorussia, Poland, and Prussia, he finally reached the heart of the Third Reich: Berlin. Many times cited for bravery in combat, by war's end he was a colonel of the V-VS—the Soviet Air Force—and also twice 'Hero of the Soviet Union.'

During the first months of the Allied occupation of Germany, Mikhail fraternized with the pilots and soldiers of the occupying armies. In those months, he began to see the Soviet world from a new and totally different viewpoint: the individuality, liberty, and degree of initiative of the British and American pilots, as well as their lifestyle, which was much better than his.

As time passed in Germany, Mikhail felt attracted more and more to western independence. After several months in Berlin, he showed his real self. He never was a Communist but always was 'at peace' with the regime. He realized he didn't fight the war for Lenin, the Party, Communism, or Stalin. He fought simply to liberate *Rodina*, the Russian Motherland, from the yoke of the invading Nazi armies.

While the war was raging no one asked him why he fought with such ardor. He was a brave warrior, his exploits showed him to be so, and that was all that mattered then. However, once in Berlin things started to be different. The *Stavka*—the Soviet Army General Staff—did not need him as a warrior anymore. Besides, his relationship with the Allies was causing an embarrassment to the Soviets, who considered it 'too friendly.' The NKVD, represented in the V-VS's squadrons by its Political Commissars, discreetly warned him about the relationship and advised him to end it, for his own good.

Disregarding the warnings, Mikhail continued meeting Allied pilots and soldiers. Since its recommendations were not listened to, the NKVD formally forbid him to visit the Allied airbases, and any other place where he could meet soldiers from any Allied country. By now the Cold War had already started. Berlin had been blockaded, and the Korean war was raging.

This prohibition, however, only increased his negative feelings towards the Soviet regime. He continued visiting the allies, making acerbic criticisms against the Soviet system.

The NKVD, wishing to end these 'harmful' relations once and for all, but not being able to punish him directly due to his rank, his position, but more than anything else, because of his fame, quickly and quietly transferred him back to the Soviet Union as commander of a bomber squadron in Byelorussia.

When the transfer took place, however, it was too late. The germ of the disappointment that would attack him several times in the years to come had already infected Mikhail.

After many years in Byelorussia, and still having the same rank and position he had when he got there, he felt forgotten by the General Staff. He obtained his position and rank during the war, it had already ended, so by then he didn't have opportunities to rake up new war exploits and obtain promotions as before. The fact that he never belonged to the Party also contributed to this. Many more years of this stagnation only fertilized the soil where the germ of disappointment with the Soviets slowly grew.

Due to his inborn pride as well as to his personal integrity, he preferred to be where he was rather than yield to the Party. From his command position, however, he demanded less control from Moscow, a heresy of the worst kind according to Soviet theology. His petitions were, of course, ignored, or in the best of cases, considered only to be flatly rejected later, and without any explanation whatsoever.

Although these demands were made following strict military conduits, they just got him more enemies, many of them with powerful contacts in the General Staff. And those contacts were made to work. He was seen as 'politically unreliable,' too dangerous, therefore, to have the important position of bomber squadron commander. So, on a fateful day, and utilizing false witnesses, he was court-martialed, demoted and sent away. With the less compromising rank of Captain of an airplane, Mikhail was suddenly transferred from the Soviet Air Force to the Soviet Navy and assigned to its air arm, the *Aviatsiya Voenno-Morskogo Flota*, or Naval Aviation.

The Soviet Navy Airbase at Kuzomen, Murmansk Military Region, First Military District Leningrad, some 350 kms. south of Murmansk, located on the southern coast of Kola Peninsula, almost inside the Arctic Polar Circle, at the doorstep of the Siberian tundra, and covered with ice seventy percent of the year, was not a place to spend summer vacations. With winter temperatures way under the freezing point, and surrounded by swamps and spectacular muddles in summer, Kuzomen was the perfect location for anyone to send an enemy and forget him there forever. Here in Kuzomen was stationed the 364th *Otdyel'nyy Dal'niy Razvedyvatel'nyy Aviatsionnyy Polk*, ODRAP in its Cyrillic acronym, or Independent Long-range Reconnaissance Regiment.

Once assigned to the 364th ODRAP, Mikhail knew he'd have to spend the rest of his life and his destroyed career in this inclement side of the world. The opportunities to return to the south were practically nil. There he would never be recognized as the 'Hero of the Soviet Union' he was. He'd be just another pilot. That being the case, he had to get out of there at any price.

In Kuzomen, and after still many more years stuck with the same rank and doing the same job, the germ grew and developed. The political corruption he hated so much was even more rampant there than in the bases in the south. And worse: he was in no position to denounce it as before.

Thus, rather than being a participant and an accomplice of the system, Mikhail chose to leave Kuzomen, the Soviet Union, and its corrupt system. More than anything else, he wanted to reach the West, or any other place where corruption was not the way of life, and where life was not under constant control. In other words, to defect, since that was the only way out of the nightmare.

Any defection is an operation full of risks and a thousand dangers. This, however, did not scare him. If others did it before him and were successful, then it was possible. Although he could die trying it, Mikhail grabbed the possibility.

Engine number three sputtering and steadily losing power in its mechanical agony takes Mikhail out of his thoughts.

"Brace yourselves! We're going down!" he shouts in the intercom. With two of its engines already dead, number three sputtering in its last seconds of life, and number four following close behind, the Tupolev starts to sink like a brick. The crew, their souls on a thread, anguished, their eyes tightly closed, just wait for the impact.

When engine number four dies, only the whistling of the rushing air is heard inside the normally noisy aircraft. The blue waters of Goose Bay below get closer and closer, ready to swallow, perhaps forever, the salvation ark of the bold crew.

In these last minutes before impact, Mikhail cannot help but being amazed at how fast this defection was planned and developed.

Thirty five days before, on the first of July, when returning to Kuzomen at the end of one of his many reconnaissance missions, his mind got a firm hold of the defection idea.

As the giant flying machine descended over the runway, its landing gear and flaps out, ailerons delicately controlling the rate of descent, Mikhail's mind was far from there. He had hardly heard the landing authorization and instructions the control tower had just transmitted, sending him to runway 14A.

In the last few weeks, the obsessing idea had been hammering his mind, pushing, attacking him. As before, he tried to get rid of it thinking about other matters that would make him stay: Irina, his family, and his love for Russia. This time, however, the more he fought the idea, the firmer it stayed in his mind.

"Entering final. Vasya, switch propellers to fine pitch," Mikhail said in a distant, absent, automated voice.

"Understood, Captain. Switching propellers to fine pitch."

The airplane continued its descent, slowly gliding in its controlled fall. The landing gear almost touched the pine, spruce, and birch trees surrounding the airbase. The runway quickly approached. The soft bump, followed by the screeching rubber touching the concrete, indicated they were on land.

"Pitch reversion. Now!"

With their thirty two blades spinning at supersonic speed, the eight propellers growled and indicated their discomfort as they changed their push forward, thus helping brake the plane. After more than sixteen hundred meters of runway, the machine decelerated enough to turn to a secondary service runway.

"Vasya, it's all yours," Mikhail said. Vasily took the controls, entered runway 32B, and continued the run to the dispersion area. Here the maintenance team was already waiting for them.

Captain Makarov took off his ShL-61 leather helmet and dried some sweat drops from his forehead, forever marked by a scar over his right eyebrow. The scar, from his right temple to mid forehead, is a souvenir of the most ferocious accident he ever had as a pilot.

Despite his age, Captain Makarov has an agile, lean, flexible, tall body, fruit of the many years of gymnastics and physical exercise he practiced. Although the long flights had him spending several hours seated in the cockpit, he fought the physical inertia running some eight kilometers a day. Neither rain nor thunder nor lightning deviated him from his daily exercise routine.

Mikhail flattened his hair with his rough hands, then exclaimed: "Well, that's it. Back in base." Despite the fact that the tone of voice he used to say it meant something else, Mikhail asked himself if he should have said that.

"About time! I'm tired of sitting in this flying can," Vasily replied, slowly guiding the plane to the dispersion area, engines one and four turning at slow revolutions.

As the plane advanced, Mikhail once again sank deep in his thoughts, in the same distracted way since the obsession got a hold of him.

He was proud of being the pilot of this plane, or of any other airplane for that matter, but he was not proud of the reasons that brought him here. Trying to find a solution to his problem, he decided to take the first step in his escape plan: recruit the help of Vasily, his copilot.

The plane slowly turned to the left, but Mikhail didn't notice. His mind was searching for a way to tell Vasily his wishes and intentions without creating in him undue alarm or worry.

Although his mind explored all the options searching for a better way, he couldn't find one that satisfied him. So he decided to take the most direct approach: he'd just tell Vasily directly, no beating around the bushes.

Suddenly the plane came to a full stop. Mikhail returned from his thoughts and looked around him. They were already parked in the dispersion area. Outside, the maintenance team had already placed the cockpit access ladder on the nosewheels bogey, and swarmed upon and around the aircraft, in order to check and verify its different mechanisms and systems.

Vasily looked at the Captain, and noting the strange look on his face, asked:

"Captain, something wrong? You seem to be worried."

"No, nothing's wrong. I'm just tired. I'm not as young as you are."

Standing up, Vasily suggested: "Why don't you retire? You have been flying for almost as many years as I am old!"

"No. I don't want to retire, yet. There are a few things I'd like to do before that."

"Such as …?"

"I'll tell you later, after debriefing and some rest." Mikhail stood up and followed the copilot.

The radio operator, Senior Lieutenant Serghey Gheorghievich Molotko, also the political informer aboard the plane—the onboard *'chekist'*—had already opened the exit hatch.

The radio operator exited, followed by the Flight Engineer, Lieutenant Yuri Kazakov. On the ground, the rest of the crew joined them. The group of technicians in charge of the plane's tactical and ECM equipment was already involved in one of their perennial technical discussions peculiar to them. After boarding the ZIL-131 truck assigned to the regiment, the group left behind the rows of parked airplanes and headed to the Debriefing Desk, except Lieutenant Molotko, who very indiscreetly headed to the Intelligence Desk to deliver his report.

Once Mikhail and Vasily had filled and signed the different reports and forms related to the flight, they left the office. A few meters away, Vasily took out of his breast pocket a pack of *papirosy* and offered one to the Captain. Mikhail declined with a wave of his hand.

"I'm sorry, Captain. I forgot you don't smoke."

Vasily took one for himself, lighted it, and between puffs asked again: "Well, Captain. What do you want to do before you retire?"

Before Captain Makarov had a chance to answer, the corner of his eye caught the figure of the radio operator returning from the Intelligence Desk. Quickly changing subjects, Mikhail replied: "I remember I should see Col. Rudenko. If you want, go to quarters and rest. I'll see you there in about an hour."

"Agreed. See you later."

The Captain shook his copilot's hand and departed. Vasily remained in front of the Intelligence Office, looking at Mikhail as he headed to Col. Rudenko's office. They'd been flying together for two years already. However, the friendship developed between them in such a short time was something seldom seen among the pilots there. Those two years seemed to be more like twenty. Mikhail always encouraged him to be a better pilot. Vasily trained to one day occupy the plane's left seat. He saw Mikhail not only as a superior but also as a friend. Also, as the father he never had.

Vasily, the war orphan, a *bezprizornik,* spent his first years with his grandparents, in his family the only survivors from the terrible years of the Great Patriotic War against the Nazis. When they died, and not having any other known relatives, he was sent to a state home for orphans, one more among hundreds of thousands. After obtaining his basic education there, he entered a VTUZ, a technical college. Later he joined the paramilitary organization DOSAAF, where he learned piloting and parachuting.

Flying the gliders and small training planes, he heard the call of the air. Leaving the VTUZ, he joined the V-VS, the Air Force. After completing his basic training, he was sent to the A.F. Myasnikov Military Aviation Academy in Volgograd, where he finished his training as transport pilot. Years later, after a dispute with a superior officer, he was transferred to the AV-MF, the Soviet Navy's Air Force, and shipped to Kuzomen. Here he was assigned to Captain Makarov's airplane as copilot.

When he started to fly with Mikhail, he rarely spoke more than the necessary to fly the airplane. Growing alone, living his life alone—he was still single—Vasily's feelings of independence and isolation were naturally well developed. This made him timid, reserved, withdrawn, and insecure, seemingly fearful of the others' reactions. He rarely confided his feelings to someone else.

As they flew together, he started to show, like a Russian winter, an *ottepel,*' a thaw in his relations with the Captain. Mikhail, being older, his superior, a pilot with long experience, and most important, interested in transmitting that experience to him, Vasily slowly started to get out of his psychological shell. Of course, at the beginning he showed some distrust since he wasn't used to so much openness, as is customary in Mikhail.

Despite his age and the emptiness caused by his years alone, Vasily still looked remarkably young. His dark eyes, never still, always examined his surroundings, seemingly in search of the interesting. Despite his shyness, a smile never left his face, wanting to please others and attract them to him, and thus placate the constant thirst of companionship he always felt, fruit of his many years of loneliness. His short, black hair, always cut in a conservative style, was a perfect match for his thin eyebrows. He never liked to grow a mustache or beard, although they would have made him appear his real age and look more respectable.

Despite it all, the young pilot was content having as his superior a sincere and open man, whom he respected and admired.

*   *   *   *

Mikhail knocked twice before entering. Vasily, *papirosa* in hand, was stretched over his cot in a corner of the small room. Furnished only with their beds, a small desk, a chair, a bookshelf—the 'Life of V.I. Lenin' occupying a place of honor amid the other books there—the room could very well have been considered a perfect example of the Spartan decoration prevalent in all the AV-MF buildings in the area.

A portrait of the founder of the first Communist country in the world, practically obligatory in all the rooms there, hung on the wall. The wall painting, evidently applied many years before, was fading where it wasn't already gone, giving the almost empty room an even more desolate aspect.

Sitting on the bed, amid puffs of a cigarette, Vasily asked again: "Well, Captain. Are you finally going to tell me what are those extremely important things you want to do?"

Pulling the desk chair, Mikhail fell on it astride. "It's something that has been churning in my mind for a few years already. I have spoken to no one about it, but it's something that eventually I'll have to tell if I want to do it. So, today I decided to tell you."

"What is it?" the copilot asked, his mind piqued by curiosity.

"I want to defect."

Incredulity could be clearly read in Vasily's amazed face and popping eyes. He couldn't believe or refused to believe what he had just heard. For a few moments, the astonished lieutenant didn't know what to do or say.

"Captain. Are you serious?"

"Dead serious, Vasya. I've never spoken so much truth as today."

"Captain. Are you sick or crazy? Are you feeling all right? Maybe lately you've been flying too much and desperately need a vacation."

"No, Vasya. Physically I'm not tired, but morally I am. This place makes me sick."

"But, Captain! You're the best pilot here! What made you take that decision?"

"Vasya, have you ever stopped to think that if I'm the best pilot in this base, why I'm here up north in Kuzomen, and not in Moscow, Leningrad, or anywhere else where they have the elite squadrons of the V-VS and the AV-MF?"

"No. I never thought about it like that. Do you feel mistreated here?"

"You'd think I'm out of my mind when I come up with such ideas, but that's exactly the reason. Think about it: All the other commanders of TU-95s here are Lt. Colonels or Majors. Me? I'm just a Captain. Why? Because before I came here, I used to be a Colonel, commander of a bomber squadron. And of a fighter regiment before that. The 'twice Hero of the Soviet Union.' HA!"

For a split second Vasily recalled Captain Makarov's unfortunate career. He also noted that the Captain was transferred to Kuzomen as a disciplinary measure, just as it happened to himself. Thinking about the transfers, he said in a low voice, almost a whisper: "So you want to get out of here ..."

"Yes. To the West, America, Great Britain, Germany. Anywhere! Very far from here!"

Vasily remained silent for a few minutes, deep in his thoughts. He knew as well as Mikhail that the security measures taken in the last few years to avoid those kinds of incidents made them something almost impossible to do in the Soviet Armed Forces.

"Mmm … I don't know what to tell you. However … Why did you tell me?"

"You're the only person in this base that has been with me long enough for me to trust you enough to tell you. You know that just telling you would cost me life in prison. That is if they don't execute me first, of course, which is the most probable outcome."

"Understood …" Vasily replied. He raked his mind for a solution, knowing it will be difficult to find.

Mikhail knew that besides being a matter of friendship and trust, the idea of escaping to life conditions better than those of the cold north had nested deep in Vasily's feelings. Many times before Mikhail heard him complain under his teeth about life in the base.

"And how do you plan to escape?" Vasily asked, matter-of-factly.

"I still don't know. I have to make a plan and recruit somebody's help. Maybe I could escape in one of our planes."

"Our planes! How are you going to fly one of those giant monsters out of here without them noticing it? I think it would better if we stop talking about this matter and you forget everything. It won't work."

"Forget it? Never! Never! There are ways to get one of those planes out of here. It's just a matter of finding them."

"But, how? You need at least four men to fly it. If I go with you, we'll still need two more. Besides, how are you going to avoid the radars, interception by fighters, the leading-lead plane system, and the autodestruct system?"

Vasily's words echoed in his mind repeatedly. The leading-lead plane system: Whenever there was a mission to be flown, the Soviet Navy employed this system to send a pair of Bears. One was the *vyedushchiy* or 'leading' airplane in the flight, the other, the *vyedomyy* or 'led' airplane. Rarely, if ever, they flew alone.

However, the words uttered in the last phrase struck Mikhail the most: The autodestruct system. Every time an airplane took off from the base, that system flew with it, hidden somewhere in its insides like a deadly stowaway, always ready to explode in case of forced landing in enemy territory or—in Mikhail's case—desertion.

"It's not going to be easy, I know. But there must be a way, and I'll find it." Mikhail then looked straight into Vasily's eyes, and dropped the question point blank, like a pitcher of cold water: "Do you want to come with me?"

Vasily remained mute, his gaze lost on the floor. He knew that what he was getting into could cost him life in prison or even the executioner's bullet together with Captain Makarov. He could denounce the whole plot to the base *Komendatura* and come out clean. But, he also had to take into consideration the friendship and trust existing between them. Besides, that could be an opportunity, albeit risky, of getting out of there forever.

"Very well, Captain. I'll help you. I'm going with you," he said, still not too convinced. His loyalty to Mikhail, the only person in his life that treated him as a man, a friend, and a son, made Vasily follow him wherever he went.

"Thank you, Vasya. I knew you'd not disappoint me. Now, rethinking about the matter, I concluded that the best way to get out of here is by air. By land or sea is next to impossible. One might as well forget about those routes. Besides, it has to be in our plane. It's the only one they allow us to fly here, and the only one with range long enough to reach America or Britain."

"In theory that sounds very good, but in practice I still think it won't work. How are we going to fly that plane just the two of us? You know we can't. We'd be discovered immediately, and you know what that would mean."

"Well. First, we won't be flying that plane just the two of us. Secondly, it will be during a routine flight, with full crew."

"During a routine flight and with full crew?! That means we'll have to tell the rest of the guys about the plan!"

"Aha."

"Captain, I don't like this. The more people know about this, the higher the chances of being discovered. Besides, how are we going to get rid of Serghey? He's the radio operator. No plane flies out of here without one of them, so, what do we do? Throw him out of the plane in mid flight?"

"That's a wonderful suggestion, Vasya, and I wish I could push that damn stoolie out of the plane from three thousand meters high. Unfortunately, we can't do that."

"How are you going to convince the rest of the crew? If one of them rejects the idea and calls the *Komendatura*, that's the end of both of us!" Fear, which was already showing in Vasily's mind, could be read in his eyes.

"Vasya, don't be so pessimistic! Think positively. Serghey doesn't have to find out about this. Besides, I think there's a lot we can do to convince the guys. If we make a plan good enough to have a high percentage of success, I think we can make them join us."

"And if we don't convince them?"

"That's a risk we should take."

The copilot raised his eyes to the ceiling. Standing up in one single jump, he threw his cigarette to the floor, then stepped on it. Pulling a cigarette pack from his breast pocket, Vasily took out another one, lighted it, and started smoking again while pacing slowly. After a few silent minutes considering the Captain's proposal, between puffs of smoke, Vasily asked, "Very well. What do we do first?"

"The plan. We should figure out where it would be easier to go, and how. We must look at all possible escape routes, Great Britain, Germany, Canada, America, or any other western country. That's only the beginning."

"And once we've found that out?"

"Then I'll expose the plan to the guys. You don't say a word. Leave it all to me. This way you'll be in their same position. That's for your own protection. If one of them rejects the plan and calls the *Komendatura*, you come clean out of the mess. I don't want you to be punished because of me."

"Thank you, Captain. Very kind of you."

"Once initial reactions have calmed down, if they haven't called the *Komendatura* by then, that's when you start to *like* the plan, and you *carefully* try to convince them to join us, so we all escape together in the plane."

"Captain, there are nine crew members in that plane. We're only two. With Serghey we certainly can't count. That means we still have six more people to convince."

"Yes. I know it won't be easy, but that's the only way of getting out of here."

*   *   *   *

Vasily and Mikhail met again in their quarters. Around them, several maps, navigation charts, and other reference material. The two pilots began to sketch their escape plan.

"Of all the European countries, we could only go to Great Britain, West Germany, France, Belgium or Holland. That's a fact," Mikhail said, pointing on a map unrolled on a table before them to each of the mentioned countries.

"Right. Those countries in Southern Europe we might as well forget about them. There's no way that from here we could reach Spain, Italy, or Greece, for example. However, what about those in Northern Europe? Finland, Sweden, Norway? They're closer to us."

"True. But I wouldn't count them in our plans," Mikhail said.

"Why not? I think it's easier to reach them than Belgium, Germany, or even Great Britain."

"If we head to Finland, Sweden or Norway, we'll be interned there for several months, then we'd be expelled. That is if they do not send us back to the Union. I'm not sure the men would like the possibility of escaping from here just to be imprisoned there. Especially in the West. You know what they say they about their treatment of defectors."

"*Ladno*. Agreed. What about if we fly over them?"

"They'll send fighters to intercept and shoot us down. Do you think they'll let a Soviet airplane fly over their territory without challenging it?"

"How, then, are we going to cross Europe to reach, for example, Germany?"

"I don't know. Frankly, I don't see that many possibilities of reaching the countries in the continent."

"That leaves open only the option of reaching Great Britain," the copilot said.

"I'm afraid you're right. We'd reach it after passing west of Ireland, at the end of our routine flight. Then we'd veer towards Scotland by the northwest."

"Any other possibility?" the copilot asked.

"Yes. Iceland, further north."

"I think we should leave this route open as is, and then ask the guys what they think about it," Vasily said, then asked, "Besides this route, is there any other more accessible?"

"I see only two more routes besides this one," Mikhail said. "The first is reaching Alaska via Chukchi."

"Alaska? Mmm … It's somewhat dangerous that area."

"That's only one possibility. Not necessarily we should fly there."

"Very well. What about the other?"

"Canada. Through the North Pole."

"Canada … Well, agreed. We have three possible escape routes. Now, what about Serghey?"

"Serghey is a problem that needs our immediate attention. I won't be able to say anything to the guys if he's present. Imagine, I'm taking a risk big enough just by telling them about this plan. Do you know what would happen if he finds out about this?"

"I prefer not to know. So, what do you plan to do?"

"Looking deeply into the matter, we have to find the way to gather the guys any place where I can talk to them in peace, while at the same time keeping Serghey out of the scene. Of course, without him suspecting anything."

"Captain, tomorrow we don't fly. It's a day off. Why not bring them here tomorrow?"

"Here? You mean to say this room?"

"Aha …"

Mikhail remained silent for a few seconds, thinking, then agreed, "Very well. But I'll need a good excuse to bring the guys here, and an even better excuse to keep Serghey away from them. I don't mind telling the guys about this plan, but I do mind telling that damn stoolie."

"… A good excuse … What about just a drinking party?"

"A party? And if the *Komendatura* asks us why we're celebrating it here and not in the Lenin Hall, what will we tell them?"

"That's the least of our problems. Any excuse will be good. Tell them that it's only for your crew. Besides, I think no one will complain if we don't make too much noise."

"What do you mean?"

"I mean that if you think that it's going to be a real party, forget it! When you mention your intentions to the guys, if you're not immediately arrested, then this place is going to look like a cemetery, so silent and full of astonished faces it will be. By twenty three hundred hours everybody will be gone."

"Agreed. As an excuse to bring the guys here, that of the party sounds good. Still, what do we do with Serghey? Certainly, I don't want him here, and on the other hand, there's no way I can tell him not to come. You know he's everywhere we are. If I order him not to come, he'll get suspicious, and suspicion is the last thing I need now."

"Yes, Captain. That's true. But we don't have to tell him not to come."

"Explain, please."

"We only have to find a way to keep him away from here, long enough to allow you to explain the plan to the guys. Then he can come and join us."

"That's a good idea, but it's still risky. I don't want him here at all. His sole presence here would be enough to make any one of the guys hesitate and spit everything to him."

"Captain, if we don't have him here, there will be no party!"

"And if we have him here I won't be able to say a word!" Mikhail blurted. Then he looked straight at Vasily, drew a smile, and continued: "Although, on the other hand, we don't have to tell him not to come. He can come to the party."

"I don't understand, Captain. First you say you don't want him here. Now you say he can come."

"That's the key! We invite him to the party, then he'll leave by his own will!"

"By his own will? Mmm … I would like to see that. What are you going to tell him that will make him leave? That his mother died? That sonofabitch doesn't have a mother."

"I agree. Most probably he had her sent to a camp somewhere in Siberia."

"Captain, it has to be an extremely good excuse this time, so good that he'll have to put aside his duties as KGB stoolie."

"I'll tell him nothing. I'm telling you. He'll leave by his own will!"

"How? What will you do to make him leave? Hypnotize him? You're no magician!"

"Simple, my dear Vasya, simple. *You* are going to sicken him."

"*I* will sicken him? Captain, forgive me, but I don't understand. Please, explain."

"Very well. If we sicken him in such a way that he can't be here with us, he'll have to leave, and by his own decision and free will!"

"Understood, but what the hell have I to do with that?"

"Oh! You're the one who's going to sicken him!"

"And how am I going to sicken him?"

"Simple. Listen: tomorrow you'll be 'indisposed.' Your stomach will be giving you troubles. You go to the infirmary and ask whoever is there to give you something for your 'sickness.'"

Vasily remained silent for a moment, thinking. His face shone with a smile, and agreed, "I think I know what you mean to say by 'sickening' him."

"Exactly. Later, in the mess hall, when he takes his usual bowl of *borshch*, you simply empty the contents of the laxative in the bowl."

"And if he catches me doing that? I could be sitting in the shadows for several days!"

"Don't worry about that. I'll call his attention to distract him while you do your part."

"Agreed. Now, what about the interceptors, the radars, and the autodestruct system?"

"About that I have nothing specific. Maybe the guys could suggest something."

"That's if they don't denounce us to the *Komendatura* first," Vasily said, grimacing.

"Very well. I'll call the escape plan 'Icarus,' so we don't have to mention the word 'plan.'"

"'Icarus.' I like that name. It's Greek, isn't it?"

That evening, with its three possible escape routes and all its inherent problems, Icarus was born.

CHAPTER 2

▼

"Comrades, the day of the perfect 'Communist Man' in the world society is not too far." With these words Lieutenant Colonel Ghennady Ivanovich Nikitin, Deputy Political Commander of the 364th ODRAP, started his 'Political Hour' in the Lenin Hall. "All the efforts of our Soviet society to produce such a man have yielded excellent results. Our great Soviet Union already has men like that, worthy representatives of our great Soviet Motherland."

"Comrade Colonel," Mikhail intervened. "That's great, and I congratulate the Motherland for that, but today those men, I think, are the exception rather than the rule. Let's descend to a lower level and let's see what we have here in our own base: drunkards left and right, night sentries caught sleeping at their posts, hold ups and burglaries among the soldiers themselves, smuggling and contraband of any article imaginable, and last but not least, what I think is the worst of all: the black marketing of vodka, wine, and *samogon.*"

"Comrade Captain Makarov," the trembling in his voice betrayed the political officer's indignation and anger. "Those are isolated cases that rarely happen in this airbase. Those that did happen have been duly investigated, prosecuted, and those responsible have been severely disciplined!"

"Isolated cases? Perhaps. But rare? That happens at least three times a week! There's not one week here without at least one hold up!"

The pilots and technicians of the 364th ODRAP followed with evident interest the discussion between the two officers. Many of them had been victims of the burglaries and hold ups. Even if they wanted to discuss them, they were too scared to do it. Reporting them to the *Komendatura* was a waste of time. *'In this airbase there are no crimes,'* that was what the top brass said, so any and all reports about crimes committed were dismissed.

"Captain Makarov, I have a duty to do and that's to instruct the men of the 364th ODRAP in the political matters. Right now I don't have time to get involved in discussions about life in the base. If you wish, after the meeting, you can take your complaints to the Political Commander, to the Regiment Commander, or even to the Base Commander. I'm sure they'll be more than happy to listen to you. But as far as we're concerned, for the time being, please, let's continue with our meeting." The officer took the pleading tone, wishing, more than anything else, to silence Captain Makarov. Before he used to just sit down in the back of the hall, silent, only listening.

Even though one of his duties as Deputy Political Commander was to make sure all personnel attended the political meetings, Lt. Col. Nikitin also knew the political dossier of Captain Makarov. So he preferred to have Mikhail sitting quietly in the back. When Mikhail spoke in a meeting for the first time today, his fears were confirmed right then and there. Nikitin only hoped it didn't go beyond that.

"The Soviet Union is making superhuman efforts in all the fields: culture, education, technology, sociology, etc., so that by the end of the century our peoples can enjoy the comforts they very well deserve. Who's responsible for all these efforts, for all those inventions, for all those discoveries? The 'Communist Man.' He is who, without having in mind any benefit for himself, selflessly does all that for the greater benefit of his beloved Soviet Motherland."

Mikhail, feeling extremely uncomfortable because of what he'd just heard, blocked from his mind the stream of words uttered by the Political Officer. Gavno! *That's all this man and all those like him say: Shit! Pure shit! But soon I'll be able to get out of here forever!*

Immersed in his own thoughts, his mind left the meeting until the 'Political Hour' ended.

The meeting finished, Mikhail and Vasily met by the hall's door.

"Captain, call the guys now."

Having arrived at the spot where his crew assembled, Mikhail invited them: "Comrades, what about a party tonight, in my quarters?"

"A party? And what's the occasion?" Alexey, the navigator, asked.

"Nothing special ... just to kill boredom with something different," Mikhail responded. "You know, at night there's not much to do around here. Besides, I got a bottle of Hungarian wine I'd like to open."

"Not bad. What time should we be there?" Yuri, the Flight Engineer, asked.

"Twenty one hundred. Sounds right?"

"Sounds right to me," Vasily said.

"Yes. Sounds right. About time we did something like that," added Anatoly, the Chief Technician.

"*Khorosho*. See you all there."

Mikhail looked at the radio operator who, as political informer, had as one of his duties the spying on all the activities in the life of the crew he was assigned to. In his turn, the character looked back at the Captain. Eye met eye. Mikhail, cold and firm. Serghey, full of hatred and malevolence.

On a gaunt and emotionless face, a broad Stalin-like mustache covering it, shone two dark, beady eyes, ready to shoot rancor-filled looks. His crooked nose, as crooked as his own feelings, the result of the thousand and one fights he had been in because of his acrid and hostile temperament, completed Serghey's facial description. His voice, cold, grave, and emotionless, always barked harsh words and orders, many of them as absurd as the system for which he so willingly worked.

Since his childhood in Khar'kov, Ukraine, Serghey Gheorghievich Molotko had been the *stukach,* the 'stoolie.' Having grown up under a system that encouraged spying among its citizens, it was natural that for this system, its first task was to train its youngsters in the 'art' of spying.

And trained to spy he was. As soon as he finished school he was conscripted. Once in the Armed Forces, his excellent abilities as an informer called the attention of the KGB, which recruited him for its informers cadres. After a short training in information and espionage tactics, while also being trained in foreign languages—English—and radio communications, he was assigned to Captain Makarov's crew as radioman and informer.

Although being the crew's informer was supposed to be a secret, it was a secret known to everyone in the crew and in the base. For this reason he was despised and feared by all. They knew he could ruin their lives and their careers. Serghey knew the immense power contained in the three letters KGB. So he cynically took maximum advantage of that power for his own personal benefit and convenience. It was not for nothing the intelligence organization was called *Kontora Grubykh Banditov,* 'Office of Gross Bandits.'

He knew that in the party no one would talk to him, but he decided to go anyway. After all, it was his duty as the crew *chekist.*

*   *   *   *

Vasily entered the Mess Hall. The place was almost empty. Since he arrived late, most of the base personnel had already had dinner. Patting his left breast pocket, he made sure the laxative bottle was still there. His eyes searched for Captain Makarov. As previously agreed, the Captain would have located Serghey for him. Taking a dish and some utensils, he placed some vegetables and a few slices of black bread on the plate. Then a *pirozhok* and a cup of hot piping tea from the nearby *samovar*. With the corner of his left eye he finally sighted the Captain at the other side of the hall, sitting in front of Molotko.

Even though he was as hungry as a Siberian wolf, that time he didn't want to waste time getting more food. He had to do his job before the informer reached his bowl of *borshch*. Taking his meager dinner, he headed to the table where both characters were sitting.

"Hearty appetite, comrades!" Vasily greeted as he took a seat next to Serghey, on his left. Mikhail looked at Vasily, and silently questioned him about the results of his mission in the infirmary. He answered with a slight affirmative movement of his head.

Mikhail then started the second part of their plan: "Lieutenant Molotko, Do you know that man? The one sitting on that table over there, to your right," Mikhail said while pointing to a table to his left, two men sitting at it.

Molotko turned around to look in the indicated direction, then asked: "Which one, the blond one or the black-haired one?"

"The black-haired one."

While Serghey's attention was on the table at the other side, Vasily quickly pulled the laxative bottle out of his breast pocket. With both hands under the table, one hand firmly gripped the bottle, the other turned the cap. In one single and quick movement he poured almost the whole contents of the bottle in the informer's bowl of beets soup.

"That character, the one with the black hair, yes, I know him. His name is Ustenko, Anton Borisovich. We're from the same city, Khar'kov, in Ukraine. We went to the same school, we're serving in the same branch, and we're stationed in the same airbase," said the radioman in his typical Ukrainian accent, noted by the guttural pronunciation of the 'g.'

"That means he's a radio operator too. I thought he worked with Intelligence," Mikhail said.

"What makes you think that?"

"Well, every time I go down to Intelligence, for whatever reason, he's always there, sitting at a desk, as if he works for them."

Vasily tried in vain to get rid of the laxative bottle, with no results. Not knowing what to do with it, he placed it back in his breast pocket. Sheer bad luck made the bottle fall upside down. Soon a dark spot grew on the left side of his shirt.

"Captain, you know that we all in this airbase and the people from Counterintelligence, we're all tightly working together for the same purpose: State Security," said Molotko.

For Mikhail it was not coincidental that in his explanation he used the last two words of his employer's name: the Committee for State Security, better known for its Russian initials, KGB.

Molotko pushed aside his now empty dish and decided to attack the bowl of *borshch*.

"In my opinion you Ukrainians all look alike. When I was down there, during the war, at the beginning it was a little bit difficult to get used to your way of speaking. Sometimes using Ukrainian words, changing the 'g' for 'h' and so on. But eventually I got used to that," Mikhail commented.

"The same happened to me with the Russian spoken up here. Anyway. Fortunately we don't have to speak different languages. Everybody here speaks Russian, even though we come from the four corners of the Soviet Union." While speaking, the radioman swallowed spoonful after spoonful of the thick soup in rapid succession, without stopping to taste it. Suddenly, he screamed: "AAAAAKH! We'll have to arrest someone here and punish him for conspiracy against the State!"

On hearing that, Vasily felt goosebumps run the whole length of his body, his face became ashen, and his heartbeat sped up. Mikhail asked himself if Serghey could have seen Vasily pouring the laxative in Serghey's soup. Without showing his own worry, Mikhail asked: "And who should be arrested, Lieutenant?"

"The cook! That butcher must be arrested under the charges of trying to poison a whole airbase with this shit! These people's food usually has a bad taste, but today's cooking is inexcusable! This shit tastes horrendous! I wonder if they used rotten beets to boil it!"

On hearing the informer's explanation, Vasily's heartbeats returned to normal. Mikhail felt relieved. The radioman pushed the soup bowl aside and took a small cup of vodka—it's not supposed to be there, it's against base regulations—and drank it in one single gulp. Clearing his throat, Serghey continued his screaming complaint: "This is ridiculous! They shouldn't let rookies cook for us. One of these days they're going to poison someone! I'm going to file a formal complaint for this!"

Vasily, although still hungry—he never had a chance to eat his food—decided to leave, not only because the dark spot on the left side of his shirt has grown even more, but also because the smell coming from it was already making him feel sick.

"Leaving so soon, Lieutenant Chkalov?" Serghey asked.

"Yes. I really was not hungry. Besides, there are a few things I'd like to do before the party tonight. If I don't take care of them now, I won't have time later."

"Oh, yes! The party. Very well. See you later, Lieutenant."

Taking his jacket, the copilot stood up. *I hope this asshole took enough laxative to kill him. He deserves it!* Vasily thought as he left.

∗   ∗   ∗   ∗

When Vasily came to the room, Mikhail was resting, his body stretched full length on his small bed. Vasily sat at the table. Mikhail stood up and pulled a bottle of Hungarian *Tokaj* wine out of a wooden box he had previously hid under his bed.

"Captain, are all the plans ready?"

"Well. Only up to the point we worked on the last time. I put everything in order. All we've got to do now is wait for the guys to arrive."

"Do you think we could make some improvement to the plans while we wait for them?"

"Now? I doubt it. It's not much one can do in such a short time. It's better to wait."

Resting on his bed, Mikhail sipped the wine—slowly, which was not his usual manner—as he got deeper in his thoughts. *The moment to let the guys know about the plan is nearing. Even though between us exists a good relationship, excepting Serghey, of course, I'm not really sure what their reaction will be. If they accept the proposal, then I'll have to show them a very good plan, which I don't have, anyway. They could also flatly reject the whole thing. I only need a rejection by one of them to spend the rest of my days in a camp somewhere in Siberia. That is if I'm not executed right here in Kuzomen first. And there are plenty people here itching to do just that. Besides, if I manage to convince them, everything will have to be done in the shortest time possible. Many of them are about to be discharged, their two years of service almost over. I don't have an alternative. Either I do it now, no matter how, or I'll be condemned to keep on living the same as now: one more victim of this damn system.* Between thoughts and sips of wine, an hour passed.

At twenty one hundred hours, knocks came from the door. Mikhail ran to open it. "Good evening, comrades. Come in! Come in!"

"Good evening, Captain! Where's that Hungarian wine? I'm dying to taste it," asked the main radar operator, Senior Lieutenant of the Technical Service Anatoly Filippovich Kiprenko.

"Come on, Tolya. Be patient. There's wine for everybody," Mikhail replied.

"Vasya! Man! You're here already!" Anatoly commented.

"Yes! Sit down and try this wine. It's great!"

All the men seated, Mikhail passed around the bottle of *Tokaj.*

"*Chudno!* Best wine I've ever tasted in my life!" exclaimed Alexey, the navigator.

"I knew you'd like it," replied Mikhail, pouring some of the wine in small cups.

When nearing the bottle to the cup held by Serghey, the radioman, Mikhail was surprised to see him still healthy. *I hope that laxative is strong enough to sicken him, otherwise this will be nothing more than a royal waste of time.*

When lowering the bottle to his cup, however, Serghey stopped him: "No, Captain. Thank you. I think tonight I will not drink."

"Are you sure you want to miss this extraordinary opportunity? It's not every day that a wine of this quality shows up around here!"

"No. Thank you again. I'm not feeling well. I think something I ate did not fare well in my guts," he said, then exploded: "It's that cook's fault! I knew they were going to sicken someone with that goo they make. Tomorrow I'll place a formal complaint with the Chief Cook and the Doctor!"

Mikhail masked a smile as best as he could, then suggested: "Lieutenant Molotko, if you're not feeling well, why don't you go back to your quarters and rest over there? I'm sure there you'll feel much better than here."

"No. I don't want to be by myself tonight. I prefer to stay here with you. If something happens to me, you'll take care of me."

The Lieutenant's perseverance made Mikhail feel uncomfortable. *You don't want to be by yourself... Bullshit! What you want is to find an opportunity to spit the beans on someone, so you can get a promotion. Blyad! Snake! I'm not surprised you are what your are: a lackey of the Party. Anyway. You leave now, under your own steam, while you still can ... or you'll leave later, and very hurriedly!*

Mikhail turned to his crew and pleaded: "Comrades, Lieutenant Molotko is not feeling well, so let's be quiet. Now, changing subjects … Someone else wants more wine?"

"Here, Captain. Please," Yuri raised his empty cup.

"Empty already? Hey, people! Take it easy! There's only one bottle of wine. After it's gone, there's only *samogon.* "

"Well, Captain, you might as well start opening those bottles of *samogon.* This cup is already empty too," Anatoly said.

"Captain. Out of curiosity, how did you get those bottles of *samogon,* and especially that of wine?" Alexey asked.

"Well … *blat* … you know, one has connections." With that short evasive Mikhail answered Alexey's question, and the navigator perfectly understood. Although officially it was strictly forbidden to have any kind of liquors in the base, the black market in *samogon* and other liquors was very prosperous. The top brass of the base disregarded the traffic, as long as they were the main beneficiaries of the same.

The radioman had his head nestled in his left arm over the table. His right hand pressing and caressing his belly while he contorted his body on the chair.

Mikhail, seeing the character moaning and groaning, suggested once again: "Lieutenant Molotko, in my opinion, you should leave. As your superior officer, I release you of your duties. Remember that you're more useful to the Party when you're healthy."

"Lieutenant, I think the Captain is right. If you're sick, you should go to your quarters and rest there. It's not much you can do in those conditions," added the Doppler radar operator, Technical Senior Lieutenant Pavel Pavlovich Tsipov. Even though the crew didn't give a *kopek* if the radioman died right there, they preferred to have him do that far away, so they could get drunk without fear of saying something 'politically incorrect' in the ears of the informer, and have tons of problems later on.

"Yes, Lieutenant. You shouldn't be here. You might get worse later," said Alexey.

With his face paper-white, Serghey finally surrendered: "I think you're right. I should have stayed in bed."

Trying to stand up, the sick man fell back on the chair. Mikhail and Vasily, one on each side, got a hold of his arms, helped him stand up, and guided him to the door. Walking in zigzags as if drunk, the character slowly dragged his feet. His face sported a strange aspect, his arms still squeezing his belly.

"Take good care of yourself, Lieutenant! I hope to see you well tomorrow. I'd hate to have to ask for a temporary replacement for you!" Mikhail said, then thought, *and I sincerely hope I will have to do exactly that!*

"Thank you, Captain. Good night!" replied the radioman in a hardly audible whisper.

"Good night, comrade Lieutenant!" replied the whole group in chorus.

Closing the door, Mikhail looks at his watch: *Twenty one twenty five. Good! Twenty five minutes to get rid of him. Not bad. Now I have enough time for the second and most difficult part of my plan: Convincing the crew to join Vasya and I in the escape.*

Vasily, Alexey, and Yuri, each holding a cup of *samogon*, sat at the small table, talking about the details of life in the base. The tactical and ECM operators sat on the bed. All of them were, as usual, involved in one of their technical discussions. *Samogon* flowed like river.

"Tovarishchi," Mikhail exclaimed aloud, "here we are. Lieutenant Molotko had to leave because he was sick, but we are not. So, let's go on with the party!" Saying and doing, Mikhail grabbed another bottle of *samogon*, pulled the cork with his teeth, and drank straight from it.

"Aaah! Just like in the old days of the war!" exclaimed the Captain passing the bottle around.

"Waaaah! This *samogon* is pure fire!" Anatoly exclaimed.

"Da! Most probably they mixed it with *alghidras.* To increase the 'yield,'" said Vasily.

"I wouldn't doubt it. They would do anything to make more money," added Yuri.

In order to obtain more liquid with less work, the makers of the strong vodka moonshine sometimes added *alghidras,* **alkogol' ghidravlicheskoy sistemy.** Also known by its Chemistry name as methanol, the 99 percent pure methyl alcohol was used as fluid in the TU-95's hydraulic system, and as coolant for the powerful radars of supersonic jet fighters such as the MiG-25 *Foxbat.* Thus, *alghidras* was stored at the base by the ton.

Watching over them, Mikhail controlled their drinking. He knew that a group of sleepy drunkards would be useless to his plan. After they had had enough liquor to relax them, he called their attention: "Comrades, I need your opinion about something I have in mind."

"What's happening, Captain?" asked Pavel.

"I need your help in a very important task."

"And what task is that?" asked Anatoly.

"Captain, you know we've always helped you in whatever you asked us. So, what's the big secret?" asked Alexey, slightly bothered by the Captain's hesitations.

"*Khorosho*. I'll tell you. But first you will promise me you'll not make a big scandal because of it." Mikhail chose his words very carefully.

"Agreed," Anatoly replied for the group. "Promised."

"I have plans to ... defect to the West in our airplane."

Yuri stood up in one single jump. His chair fell to the ground, back side first, hitting the floor with a loud thump. The sound was immediately followed by the noise of glass breaking when Ivan let his bottle of *samogon* slip from his hand, spreading liquor and glass all over the floor. Vasily calmly pulled out a handkerchief and quietly cleaned the table of all the *samogon* that Alexey sprayed from his mouth. Then ... silence.

The lively group of before became a collection of astonished faces. Mikhail's words charged the air heavily, made it weighty, hot, uncomfortable. From the bed, Anatoly looked at the Captain with scared, widely open eyes, almost popping out of their orbits.

Having filled his cup and emptied it in one single gulp, Alexey filled it up again, just to empty it in the same way. Pavel and Ivan were wordless, mouths agape. Excepting Vasily, the reaction in all of them was the same: amazement, astonishment, stupefaction, and fear.

"Ha! Ha! Ha! Captain, that's the best joke I've ever heard in my life!" Alexey blurted, nervously. "I think the *samogon* already went to your head! To defect! And in our airplane!"

"No, Alyosha, it's not a joke. I have all the plans ready to get out of this place. All I need is your help to perfect them."

"Captain, are you saying that for real? Would you swear it on your honor, on your family?" Anatoly asked.

"Yes, Tolya. I'm serious. I swear on my honor and on my family."

"You know, that you're saying can destroy you, Captain," Pavel said, deadly serious.

"Are you sure of what you just said? Why do you want to do something like that?" asked Jonas.

"Yes, comrades. I'm sure of what I just said, and of the consequences of such an action. But I also have my reasons for saying it and for doing it."

"What reasons are those?" asked Pavel. Buzzes of approval followed the question.

"First of all, I want to get out of this damn swamp. Secondly, I'm tired of all the politics and of all the restrictions."

"In other words, you're tired of our Communist system," added Vasily.

"Exactly. I'm tired of the system, the Party, the KGB and their informers … and of their autodestruct systems."

When he said these last words, only the wind blowing outside broke the total silence. If in principle the crew did not agree with Mikhail's plan, they also didn't like to fly in an airplane ready to blow up whenever they least expected it.

"I still don't know what to say," Vasily said, breaking the silence. "But I think the least we could do is listen to his plan."

Alexey stood up in one jump, screaming, visibly angry: *"Nyet!* No plan! No nothing! I don't like this! That's treason pure and simple, and I'm not going to betray my motherland! If you continue with this little game of yours for one more second, I'm calling the *Komendatura!*"

"Just a minute, Alyosha!" Mikhail exclaimed with authority. "If you're going to call the *Komendatura*, go ahead, do it. The door is open. But do not involve them in this, only me. I'm the only one responsible for the whole thing."

Seeing the Captain's reaction, Alexey stopped cold and looked at the rest of the crew. They in turn looked at him. Finally, Vasily approached the navigator and, taking him by his arm, said: "Come on, Alyosha! Calm down!"

"Yes, Alyosha. Calm down and sit. I agree with Vasya. We should at least allow the Captain to show us his reasons and his plan," said Anatoly.

Anatoly's solemn face of meditating philosopher, so serious that to some people it looks sad, without mustache nor beard to cover it, is the perfect frame for small brown eyes that seem to be closed, but which in reality are just observing everything in general and nothing specifically. His brain receives this flow of information, where it is meticulously scrutinized and analyzed.

On his forehead, usually frowned, his eyebrows join over his slightly curved nose. All of this is product of the constant mental effort the technician dives in, and in which he finds delight, trying to find the reasons and the whys to everything around him and in the world.

Even though in his analysis Anatoly never before thought about defecting, this constant analyzing caused him to become disappointed with the way Moscow controlled the country. Since childhood he had been a fervent Communist. This feeling, however, experienced highs and lows throughout his life. In August of 1968 it reached its lowest level, when the Soviets invaded a fellow Socialist country, Moscow's neighbor to the west, Czechoslovakia. This incident made him lose faith in the leaders and seriously doubt the system. The solid wall that was his faith in Communism started to crack and open.

If before Anatoly used to find at least traces of legality in similar actions, such as the invasion of Hungary in 1956, by 1976 he considered them to be absurd and enslaving. This last action made him see the errors he always suspected the system had, and convinced him of its uselessness. The finishing stroke was the stagnant economy of the USSR during the Brezhnev years of government. The wall fell totally apart.

Despite it all, Anatoly always kept his opinions to himself. On the one hand, he didn't mix his beliefs with his duties. On the other hand, he knew that by himself he couldn't fight the system. In Mikhail, for the first time in his life, he heard someone willing to fight back. To him, in all truth, Mikhail's offer was very tempting, even though he didn't consider it to be an adequate solution; but as far as he was concerned, it was preferable than to remain with arms crossed any longer.

Once Alexey calmed down and returned to his seat, Mikhail explained his plans. The rest of the group was still too confused to protest.

"… Up to now all I have is just three possible escape routes, and as you may very well suppose, one thousand and one small details to refine, something I can not do by myself. Besides, all this would be done in our airplane. For that I need your help," Mikhail finished exposing his escape plan.

Although Anatoly still was not hundred percent convinced that he wanted to join Mikhail in this adventure, he felt increasingly attracted to it. "Captain, how do you plan to avoid the radars and the interceptors? How do you plan to get rid of the radioman and the autodestruct system?"

"Well, that's why I'm asking for your help, precisely. I can't do all that by myself."

"If we're going to dive into this, then let's do it head first. Let's stop asking questions and let's start planning," Vasily jumped in, feeling calmer and with enough confidence to say that.

Anatoly assented with a nod. Yuri, more than anything else, was curious to know what the plans offered, and what benefits they could bring him. Ivan and Jonas were mute still, just watching the events developing around them. Alexey remained silent. Although in principle he rejected the idea, he was also curious, and like the rest of his friends, in the bottom he also harbored the wish of leaving the Soviet Union, although due to personal rather than political reasons.

Alexey arrived in Kuzomen to escape the harsh and constant watch of his father, Lieutenant General Andrey Andreyevich Kocherghin, a fervent believer of the old military Stalinist school. Literally since he started to walk, Alexey was involved in the military. The very same day of his thirteenth birthday he was taken to the Marshal Suvorov Army Cadet Academy. Needless to say he was immediately admitted on the spot.

Here for the first time Alexey tasted the kind of existence that would be his lot in life. The severe, austere, tiresome, and for him boring routine of the institution made him hate the military. The desire of leaving the Academy was always there. But there also was the omnipresent, omnipotent, and enormous figure of his father, who firmly believed that traditions had to be maintained. His only son had to be a soldier like him, like his own father, and the father of his father before him, and so on and on for several generations back. A severe military tradition that has been respected for almost 300 years, when his ancestors fought under Tsar Peter I 'the Great' against King Charles XII of Sweden in the Battle of Poltava, on June 28th 1709, the most famous of the battles of the Great Northern War.

Alexey knew his father well enough to know what would have happened if he didn't obey his orders and quit the Academy. So, against his will, he remained there, secretly cursing the life he had been forced to carry on.

Not being really interested in an Army career, Alexey took courses on topography and cartography. His father didn't share the idea of having him take those subjects—to him they were nothing more than a waste of time—Lt. Gen. Kocherghin, however, knew his son's feelings towards the military and knew that was a way to keep him happy there. Alexey, on his part, did it with the secret hope of someday becoming a simple civilian and work as a topographer.

The Academy over, he was assigned as cartographer for the Army. After some time in the task, however, he felt that spending the rest of his life drawing maps for the Army was not his idea of living. He was fed up with the military, and still wanted out, but as long as his father lived, he knew he'd be a soldier.

Not being able to leave the military, he decided to make a change. He asked for a transfer to the Air Force. Using his father's influence, he obtained the transfer in a time shorter than the norm. At the beginning, the Air Force was reluctant to take an Army cartographer, however, not wishing to offend his father, known for his temper and his power, they accepted him.

After training in navigation and aerial photoreconnaissance, at his father's request he was sent to a bomber squadron in Byelorussia, near the Polish border. Although being there meant more comfort for him—here were stationed the Soviet troops of the Warsaw Pact—it also meant having his father as protector, functions Alexey always detested, since everything he did was supported by the name and prestige of his father. And always after his approval and consent.

Alexey wanted to go to a place where his father's name wasn't known, or at least, where his influence wasn't so strong. One day he found out that in the Naval Aviation airbases in the north he might find what he wanted. Even though the name Kocherghin was known there, the same didn't happen with its influence. Alexey would be thousands of kilometers away from his father and his circle of power in Moscow. In the north he would find harsh and rude climactic conditions, loneliness and discomfort in a wild, muddy, and swampy land. But it also had an important good side. For the first time in his life, Alexey would be somewhat independent, away from his father's constant watch.

Once again he obtained another transfer. This time, however, without his father's consent. He was shipped to the Naval Airbase at Kuzomen. Here he met Captain Makarov, to whose crew he had been assigned as navigator. From the very first day Mikhail felt great affection for this character, due to his age, which made him the youngest member of the crew.

Being the youngest of the crew, his beardless teenager face and his short black hair, reflected also in his dark eyes, gave him an appearance ten years younger than his real age. This made the other crewmembers feel for him the same affection as that felt for a younger brother. His briskness, however, both physical and mental, coupled to his impulsive, volatile, and explosive temper, ready to burst in screaming tantrums, also made the crewmembers really treat him as such. Although most of the time, especially during the long ELINT flights, all recognized his expertise as navigator, and respected him for that.

Faced with Mikhail's offer, the navigator swayed between several options. He could choose not to participate in the defection plot, denounce the whole affair, and remain in the base suffering the harsh winters, the loneliness and the swamps of the area. All of this he detested but had to suffer, since that was the only way to avoid his father's influence. He could also return to the south, but there he would be back to square one: comfortable, in an airbase with a more benign climate, without swamps, near a big city—Minsk, for example, where he could find more entertainment—and also where his father could watch him better. Participation in Mikhail's defection plot could bring him that liberty and absolute independence he always craved, somewhere in the West. It could also mean prison in Siberia or death before the execution squad if they were discovered.

Realizing that by just listening to Mikhail's plans he had nothing to lose, he decided to do just that. "Very well, Captain. Explain your plans."

Somewhat nervously, Mikhail lighted a *papirosa*, even though it was not his habit. The nicotine in the tobacco calmed him. Then Ivan said: "Comrades, tell me all this nonsense I'm hearing is because of the *samogon* I drank."

"I'm afraid it's real, Ivan Petrovich," replied Anatoly. "We want to go to a better place. If we find a way of getting out of here, we will."

"As far as I'm concerned," Vasily said, "I'm sick and tired of this mudhole and of the long flights. If I could, I would leave right now."

"You must be really anxious to get out of here when you come with ideas like that. You know it's betrayal. And of the worst kind! You could all be executed!" Ivan said.

"Maybe. But I prefer to die rather than spend another year in these conditions," Mikhail replied.

"But, Captain! You can retire soon!" Jonas said.

"That's true. Soon I'll be able to retire. Then I'll be able to sit down on a rocking chair, like an old lady, with a blanket on my legs, until the day I die. Right? No, comrades! No! That's not my idea of retiring. If I get to retire, it's not going to be here."

"Where then?" asked Pavel.

"In the West. America, Great Britain, Canada, Germany. Anywhere I could say: 'Here I am, a free man. I can do my will, not that of the Party.'"

"Here you can do that too!" said Ivan.

"Really?" Mikhail asked, then walked towards the bed where the technician was sitting, and asked him point blank: "Have you ever tried to do something against the Party's rules?"

"No. But I think that as long as you follow its political principles, you could live well. I understand you are not a Party member."

"That's right. I'm not a Party member, never have been, and never will. I can think on my own. I don't need the Party to think for me."

"How, then, could you get to be a captain in one of these airplanes, if you've never been a Party member?" Jonas asked, confused.

"Because twenty years ago I was a Colonel, commander of a bomber squadron. Before that I was commander of a fighter squadron."

"That means you were demoted!" Jonas said, amazed.

"Yes. I was demoted," Mikhail replied, bitter.

"Anyway. There's still the question. How did you get to be a Colonel, commander of a whole squadron, if you've never been a Party member?" Pavel asked.

Without uttering a word, Mikhail unbuttoned his shirt and showed his bare chest, marked by scars, scratches, and marks all over: "Like this! Risking my life day after day, thousands of times during the war years, so we could get the Fascist invaders out of Russia. And what reward did the Party give me for that? Being mistreated, watched, ignored, and then demoted. Transferred to the north, to fly a reconnaissance airplane. I don't need the Party for that! That's why I want to get out of this hell!"

Having listened to the Captain's reasons, the crew remained silent, thinking about their own situation.

"I think that in your case … in a sense … you're right. I don't blame you if you want to leave …" Pavel said, haltingly. "But even then, I think we should not betray our Motherland that way."

"Betrayal? Why do you call it betrayal?" Vasily asked. "We won't do something that will put the country in grave danger."

"As a matter of fact, we'd be the ones in grave danger," added Anatoly. "If we risk it and escape, we win. If we're discovered, they arrest us and we lose. I see no betrayal in that. Besides, I think the country will survive without us."

"I think I understand his feelings," Mikhail said. "While fighting the Nazis, many times I harbored the same thoughts. I thought that it was useless to continue fighting that stupid war. To me it was nothing more than one dictatorship fighting another. But when I saw those damn planes with their swastikas and those damn black crosses strafing our soldiers, mowing them like grass, I changed my mind. I decided to fight them until those monsters were exterminated from the face of the Earth."

Looking around, Mikhail noticed that he had captured the group's attention. "Had I stopped fighting then, I'd have made a big mistake. I'd have left my own people at the mercy of the Nazi hordes. That would have been a real betrayal. But this is a different situation! This time I'm not leaving my people at the mercy of someone worse than themselves! This time the fight is between them and us! This is a fight between the Party and our personal freedoms, for our own survival!"

Knowing that the success or failure of the plan depended on the technicians' decision, Mikhail approached them, trying to tip the balance in his favor.

"Comrades! I'm old. I've lived the best part of my life already. All I want to do is to die a free man. But you! You're still young! You have a lot of life to live! Are you planning to spend the rest of your lives here, doing whatever the Party says you have to do? Or do you prefer to go somewhere you could be, do, and say whatever you want, without anyone imposing on you rules about what you could be, do, and say, except the dictates of your own conscience? Ask yourselves what you really want to do with your own lives. You are the only ones who can give yourselves an honest, sincere, and direct answer. No one can do that for you."

The technicians looked at each other, their eyes asking what they should do. Anatoly stood up from the chair and approached the group: "Pavlik, Vanya, Yonka … when I was your age I thought the same way you're thinking now. I know what you feel. I was an idealist too. I thought Communism was the solution. By my own personal experience I saw that all this is nothing more than a deception. That's why I can tell you that what is being talked about here is not betrayal but survival."

"Agreed," Ivan was the first to talk openly. "I don't want to spend the rest of my life here as a simple cog in the machine. I have wishes and ambitions. I want to see more of this wide world. I've always thought it is ridiculous that a Soviet citizen has to have a passport in order to travel *inside* his own country. And more ridiculous still that he has to get a *visa* in order to *leave*. Now, I ask, How are we going to get out of here? We certainly can not ask for visas. Getting out of here is not an easy task!"

"Yes! It is easy!" Mikhail exclaimed. "It's easy if we all get together."

"I have to confess that in our routine flights, every time I see the Norwegian coastline afar, I always ask myself what it would be to live there," Ivan said.

"Not me. Whenever we fly over a British or an American vessel, I want to be onboard with them. Despite what they say here, that most of them are pirates, mercenaries, hooligans, and delinquents, I know that even then, they live better than we do," Pavel expressed his most intimate feelings.

"Why, then, don't you come with us?" Vasily asked. "I'm telling you. If we get together, we'll be able to reach the other side easier than if each one of us tries on his own."

"Well. If each one pulls alone on his side, I sincerely doubt that we could get to the other side. There is only one way to get out of here, and that's working as one group," said Anatoly.

"And that's why I want you to come with me," Mikhail ended the explanations of his two crewmen.

Suddenly, everyone turned to Jonas, the only crewmember who still had not made a decision. The technician in turn looked at the group with a confused look. "I don't … know what to say … Aaah … I really don't have a reason to leave with you."

"A reason? Is it not more than enough reason to know that your own country, Lithuania, is in the Soviet Union against its own will? Permanently occupied by the Red Army?" Mikhail shot word after word on the technician's face.

Indecision emerged on the face of the young Lithuanian. His frown showed the dilemma the youth was in. Remembering his native Lithuania, Jonas felt a knot in his throat. He also remembered his father's words about a 'Free Lithuania.' "Jonas, Communism is the common enemy of all the countries of the world. The Soviets, its representatives, are the hated occupants of our beloved *Lietuva*, and it's them we should fight. To death if necessary."

And to fight Simonas Tulauskas went. First he fought against the Soviets in their first invasion of the country. Then against the Nazis. Once these were replaced by the Red Army, Simonas joined the Lithuanian Liberation Army, to continue fighting against the Soviets.

While Simonas was a warrior, Jonas could see him frequently. Because of that, he had for the Soviet occupants the same feelings his father had. Once he was arrested, though, Jonas was taken under state custody. Being only a child, he was easy prey for the Soviet reeducational programs. Those programs taught him to see Lenin as the maximum figure and the Soviet Union as his own country, of which he should always be a loyal citizen.

When his friends confronted him with the situation of his people, once again he had an opportunity to think about it. His Soviet-educated brain told him to stay, to denounce the whole plot to the *Komendatura*. His Lithuanian heart, however, cried exactly the opposite. While in the crossroads of thoughts and counter-thoughts, Jonas looked at his friends, who waited for his decision.

Suddenly, his father's calmed voice resounded in his mind: "Jonas, escape! The USSR is not your country. *Lietuva,* Lithuania is your country. Jonukas, Jonukas, Jonukas, leave! Be free! Fight the Soviets! Help Lithuania be free again! Remember what you always heard me say, *'Lai gyvuoja nepriklausomą Lietuvą!'* Long live free Lithuania!"

Jonas stood up from the bed and with firm resolution announced: "Agreed. I'm leaving with you. What the hell! If you guys leave, I'll remain here, alone for the rest of my life. Besides, I think that from the West I can do much more for Lithuania than from here, serving its occupants."

On hearing the man's decision, the group burst in a loud cheer, shaking hands, exchanging kisses and pats on the shoulders. The noise lasted until Mikhail intervened: "Comrades! let's keep it quiet. I don't want to attract too much attention to us, or worse: a *Komendatura* guard telling us to quiet it down or spend the rest of the night sitting in a cell."

Notes in hand, Mikhail detailed the escape routes available. "I have only three possible escape routes. The first is a flight from Murmansk to Scotland. I already discarded the possibilities of using Finland as an arriving base. Finland and the Soviet Union have extradition agreements for such cases. I also discarded Sweden because there we'd be interned, jailed for some time, and then, most probable, kicked out. West Germany and France, there's no way we can reach those countries from here without being discovered before we get there. So, on that side we have only one possibility: Scotland."

"Captain," Anatoly intervened. "How will we evade the intense radar scanning in Murmansk, get across the Barents Sea, the Atlantic Ocean, and arrive in Scotland without meeting strong resistance? In Murmansk you have the General Headquarters for the Red Banner Northern Fleet. Right next door, in Severomorsk, you have a nuclear submarine base, and an airbase for TU-16 bombers. Besides that, the ships of the Northern Fleet are always patrolling and watching the whole of Great Britain. If we decide to go to Scotland, the second we head there, we'll have interceptors in our tail."

"Well, there are still two more possibilities. We could go to Alaska via Chukchi …"

"Yes. But for that to happen, first we have to reach Chukchi. How will we do that?" Alexey cut him off.

"Calm down, Alyosha! There are ways to get there. The only problem is finding them. If we put our heads to think together, we will surely find them," replied Mikhail.

"What's the other alternative?" asked Anatoly.

"Flying over the North Pole."

"As far as I'm concerned, you may discard that flight to Scotland. It's suicidal," Anatoly said. "I see more possibilities of success in the other two."

"I agree," added Yuri.

"What do you think about Alaska?" Mikhail asked.

"Personally, I don't like it," said Alexey. "We'd have to fly across all of Siberia and the Far East. Too many radar bases there. Also the Air Force's Early Warning Alarm System is there."

"I agree with Alexey," added Vasily. "The radar scanning in that area is very strong. As strong as in Murmansk, perhaps stronger. Besides, there have been several escape attempts in the Far East area. Since then, they have reinforced both the scanning and the security there."

"Not only that, the ships and submarines of the Navy bases in Vladivostok and Petropavlovsk-Kamchatskiy are always patrolling there," added Anatoly.

"Captain, suppose that we get there, somehow," Alexey said, "When they ask us who we are, how we got there, where we're coming from, and where we are going, what are we going to say? That we are flying in a stolen plane headed to Alaska because we are defecting?"

"I don't know … That Alaskan route would be splendid if it weren't patrolled so strongly," Mikhail replied.

"What do we do then? Bomb the airbases and shoot down all the interceptors they send after us? We'd be blown out of the sky before we even say the word 'Alaska'!" noted Anatoly. "Besides, we carry no bombs in our plane."

Mikhail produced a map of the Arctic and unfolded it on the table. "On first sight, we may choose several routes, depending on where we are heading."

"Well. At least in the Arctic we wouldn't have to fly over our own bases," added Alexey.

"But we'd be flying in international air space, which is the same thing for this matter. There they'd shoot us down the same as if we were flying in Soviet air space," stated Vasily.

"True, but this route offers more chances of success than Alaska. In the Chukchi area we'd be too close to the airbases. By the Arctic they'd be further away," replied Mikhail.

"Now, the main question is: How are we going to get across, or at least near the North Pole, without a radar seeing us and an escort following us?" Alexey asked. "That's the only way they'd let us fly around there!"

"What about during a routine flight? We have no escort in those flights," suggested Mikhail.

"But we have radar scanning," replied Anatoly. "Besides, by the time we get to the North Pole, we'd have fighters waiting for us there. You know they fly much faster than our plane."

"Anyway. In that route I see a possibility absent in the others," said Mikhail.

"What's that?" Yuri asked.

"The time factor."

"The time factor?" the whole group asked in unison.

"Yes. The time factor. If we reach the North Pole before they realize we're there, by the time they dispatch fighters to reach and intercept us, we'd be in Canadian air space."

"A very remote possibility, but still a possibility," said Vasily.

"Captain, what makes you think that even if we reach Canadian air space, and the fighters remain outside, that from there they will not shoot us down? They still can fire an air-to-air missile that would blow us up in a thousand pieces," Alexey commented. "Don't forget that in such a case, they will not care if we are in Canadian air space or not. They'll do anything to avoid our plane falling in foreign hands."

Before Mikhail had a chance to answer the question, Pavel protested: "Listen! You're making plans to go somewhere, but you'll go nowhere if Serghey finds out about this. What are you going to do with him?"

"Yes, Pavlik, it's true. What would *you* do about it?" Mikhail counteranswered the technician's question.

"Me? … well … Aaah … I don't know! We could whack him in the head or something like that!"

"Pavlik, don't worry about that now. First we have to find a way of getting out of here. Once we find it, then we worry about Serghey," Mikhail said.

"If what you want to do is to find a way to escape, what do you think about the *Okean* naval maneuvers? They'll be here soon," Ivan said.

"How do you know that?" asked Vasily.

"This morning I read it in the regiment bulletin board," replied the technician.

"*Tyshto!* The *Okean* naval maneuvers! I almost forgot about them! That's our chance to escape!" Mikhail exclaimed, excited. "*Posmotrim.* Who read that?"

"I read it," answered Alexey.

"Me too," Yuri added.

"Not me," said Anatoly. "I don't read that anymore."

"I got one of the flyers announcing the maneuvers. Here it is," said Ivan.

"Anything new there?" asked Anatoly.

Ivan read the announcement for the benefit of all:

NAVY OF THE SOVIET UNION
RED BANNER NORTHERN FLEET
NAVAL AVIATION

-ATTENTION ALL CREWS-

THE *OKEAN* NAVAL MANEUVERS WILL BE HERE IN FOUR WEEKS. PRIZES WILL BE AWARDED TO THE BEST PERFORMING INDIVIDUALS AND CREWS PRESENTING THE HIGHEST QUALIFICATIONS. PARTICIPATE KEEPING PROUDLY IN MIND THE SPIRITS OF V.I. LENIN AND ADMIRAL N.G. KUZNYETSOV. THE WISDOM OF THE FORMER, AND THE HEROIC DEEDS OF THE LATTER, GAVE BIRTH TO OUR GLORIOUS SOVIET MOTHERLAND IN THE GREAT RED OCTOBER, AND A COMMUNIST VICTORY TO THE INDOMITABLE SOVIET NAVY IN THE GREAT PATRIOTIC WAR.

THESE PROCEEDINGS WE DEDICATE TO THE IMMORTAL MEM-
ORY OF OUR DEPARTED MINISTER OF DEFENSE, MARSHALL OF
THE SOVIET UNION AND ADMIRAL OF THE SOVIET FLEET
ANDREY A. GRECHKO, WHOSE TEACHINGS AND DIRECTION ELE-
VATED OUR INVINCIBLE NAVY TO FIRST CLASS WORLD POWER
STATUS.

MAKE OUR GREAT SOVIET NAVY FEEL PROUD OF YOU!

Issued in The Kremlin, Moscow, on the 5th of July, year 1976

MARSHALL OF THE SOVIET UNION DMITRIY USTINOV
MINISTER OF DEFENSE

ADMIRAL SERGHEY GORSHKOV
COMMANDER IN CHIEF
NAVY OF THE SOVIET UNION

"I knew it. The same shit of always," said Anatoly, contemptuously.

"No, Tolya. The *Okean* maneuvers! The *Okean* maneuvers! They'll be here next month!" Mikhail exclaimed, more excited still.

"So what?" replied the technician, still not too interested.

"That means other routes to fly, other alternatives for escape," said Mikhail.

"Mmmm ... It's true. But how are we going to know if there is a way to escape if we don't even know we are going to participate?" the technician asked again.

"Tolya, think about it. At least it's a change in our flight routines," replied Vasily.

"At any rate. We can find out and do something. Improvise, at least," said Mikhail.

"And what can we do? They'll begin in three weeks!" noted Alexey.

"We could improvise a flight plan after the pre-flight briefing," suggested Vasily.

"No. Not that. I don't like it. It's too risky," Alexey said. "How are we going to know where the other planes will be at any given time? To arrive wherever we plan to go will take time. Besides, if we have a group of fighters in our tail, there's no way we'd be able to escape."

"I'm afraid it's so," Mikhail agreed. "We also have to think about our personal safety. Either we all make it to the other side, or we all stay … That leaves us only one other possibility: Get our hands on the maneuvers plans."

"I don't see how we'll do that. They're safely stashed in the Commander's office," Alexey said.

"If only we could get in …" mumbled Anatoly.

"Are you crazy? You'd be shot on the spot!" Alexey exclaimed, alarmed.

"Don't worry, Tolya. We'll find a way to have those plans in our hands," Mikhail comforted the crewman.

"Captain, the Commander has those plans in his safe, in his office. I don't see how we'll get them out of there unless we ask him for them. I think we're just wasting our time," said Vasily.

"Vasya, don't talk nonsense. Use your head! Think about someone, besides the Commander, who may have access to those papers," said Mikhail.

"Someone with access to the papers? The Commander's Secretary! That's it! He doesn't have direct access to the papers, but he has access to his office," Vasily said.

"Right! That means we could try him to get our hands on the plans … Let's see … What about getting him drunk?" suggested Mikhail.

"It won't work," replied Vasily. "First, drunk there's nothing he could tell us. The information contained in the plans is not something he knows by heart. Most probably he hasn't even seen those papers. Secondly and most important: He doesn't drink alcohol. The doctor prohibited him all drinks."

"How do you know that?" asked Anatoly.

"The doctor himself told me. He had to tell him to keep away from alcohol or he was going to be a dead man very soon. His liver was fried."

Anatoly looked at the bottle of *samogon* before him, then at the cup in his hand. Grimacing, he placed the cup on the table, next to the bottle, and pushed both away from him.

"Bribery. What do you think about bribing him?" Mikhail suggested once again.

"That would work better," replied Anatoly.

"Yes. Only that we would have to offer him a few thousands. He's no man to be convinced with only hundreds," said Vasily.

"*Khorosho*. Now. What will we tell him we need those plans for? We can't tell him we need them to get out of here!" said Alexey.

The group remained silent for a while, thinking. Then Anatoly exclaimed: "I got it! The maneuvers themselves! We want those plans, as a matter of fact, to escape, not to participate in them, but he doesn't know that. So, all we have to tell him is that we want the plans precisely for that, to participate. He'll never suspect we want them to defect."

"Mmm … I think I get your idea," Mikhail agreed. "We could tell him we want those papers to study them before anyone else, to have an idea of what those flights will entail, so we could win all the prizes."

"Do you mean to say we'll use the excuse of winning the prizes to obtain the plans for the maneuvers?" Alexey asked.

"Tochno! That way we can study them and see if there's any possibility of escaping. At any rate. If there's none, we still would win the maneuvers' prizes," Vasily answered the navigator's question.

"That's if we get to participate, which we still don't know," said Pavel

"Agreed," said Mikhail. Turning to Vasily, he asked: "Vasya, how much do you think we should offer him?"

"I'd recommend one to two thousand rubles."

"Two thousand rubles!" Alexey exclaimed. "That's too much. For that much I'd get the plans myself!"

"Yes, Alyosha. It's a lot of money. But our freedom is worth that and much more," replied Mikhail. *"Posmotrim.* How much money do we have?"

"Well, all my savings make seventy rubles," said Vasily.

"I can't say I have much: Thirty five rubles," said Jonas.

"All I have is fifty rubles," added Anatoly.

"Barely forty rubles. Put together with a lot of effort," said Ivan.

"Thirty," said Yuri, laconically.

"Twenty five," adds Pavel

After writing and adding the amounts, Mikhail announced the total: "Mmm … two hundred fifty rubles. That's not enough even to start. My life savings make five hundred rubles …"

"Five hundred rubles! That's a lot of money!" exclaimed Ivan.

"Yes, five hundred rubles put together over more than thirty years of scrimping and saving, denying myself everything, in order to use them for this moment. I knew one day it'd arrive," replied Mikhail, ten added: "But even then, all we have is seven hundred twenty five rubles, and that's not even half of what we have in mind. We'll have to do some tricks. Anyway, leave that to me."

"What will we do to get all that money together?" asked Jonas.

"Every day one of us will go to the base Savings Teller and ask him to withdraw all the money saved in the personal account. I suggest one every day in order to avoid suspicions. If we all go together the same day, they'll ask us why we, members of the same crew, are withdrawing all that money, and what we are going to do with it. Understood?" Mikhail explained.

"Understood," replied the group.

"Now, not one word about this outside this room. Don't talk with anyone, not even among yourselves, out of here. This is heard out there and that will be the end. Remember, walls have ears. That's why this escape plan was baptized 'Icarus.' If there's any need whatsoever of ever mentioning it as a plan, talk about Icarus, the mythological character, not about the plan," Mikhail finished his explanation.

"Agreed, Captain," replied the crew. Standing up, the group headed to the door.

Looking at his watch, Mikhail commented to himself: *Twenty two thirty. In an hour and a half the plan was summarized and started. Now it's just a matter of waiting for its development ... Vasya was right after all. By twenty three hundred there will be nobody here.*

CHAPTER 3

▼

A few days later, having collected the seven hundred and odd rubles from the group's savings, Mikhail, Vasily, and Anatoly headed to the Lenin Hall, to meet the Commander's Secretary.

The spacious hall was almost empty, ideal conditions for the trio to expose their shady deal. Standing at the door, they explored the room. It was common knowledge that the secretary frequented the hall at dusk.

Sitting on a sofa, his feet on a small table before him and a *papirosa* hanging from his mouth, the Secretary rested while reading the current edition of *Pravda*.

Approaching casually, the group asked him: "Lieutenant Dubov, we have a proposition for you," Mikhail started, going straight to the point. "We want to know if you could help us."

Detouring his attention from his reading, his eyes showing above the newspaper, the Lieutenant answered: "It depends on the matter."

Mikhail sat on the small table before Dubov. "The *Okean* maneuvers are almost here, and we want to get those prizes for our crew."

"And how do you plan to get them?"

"Well, we will if you give us a hand."

"How could that be?" asked the Secretary, putting the newspaper aside.

"Simple. The plans for the maneuvers are in the Commander's office. If you let us see them before the preflight briefing, we could have an idea of what we're going to find. Then we could prepare ourselves to make a perfect flight."

"What? Never! Are you crazy or drunk? Do you know that you just told me could cost you guys your heads? All three of you! Besides, those papers are very well kept in a safe. I don't know its combination, and it has two locks. The Commander has one key and I have the other. So how do you expect me to open it? Saying 'open Sesame'? If the Commander or one of the guards catches me opening that safe, that's the end of yours truly! Only the Commander has authority to open it. If I open it and I'm caught, I'll be sent to prison for the rest of my life, or worse: I'd be shot!" exclaimed the Secretary, indignant.

"We know that, Lieutenant, we know that," replied Mikhail, his voice calm in order to appease the character. "That's why we thought that if you take that risk to allow us to take a look at those plans, you'll also win in the matter."

"Me? And what can I possibly win in a contest for pilots? I don't even know how to fly. I get sick up there!"

"Of course. Directly you will not win, but if you help us, indirectly you could win something … *from us.*"

"Oh! You mean to say that if I help you get those plans, you'll reward me?"

"That's the idea! If you help us get those plans, we could win the prizes offered. We'd be recognized as the best crew in the whole region and the whole district. For that, Comrade Lieutenant, you can be sure we'd reward you."

"Yes? And how can I help you?" the Secretary asked again, half convinced, once he was aware that there was something to be gained by him.

"As I said, let us see the plans before the maneuvers take place. Then we'd be able to plan before the other crews."

"I don't know. I feel it's a bit dishonest to win that way."

"Perhaps. But it's a lot easier."

"But why are you so interested in winning now, Captain Makarov? As far as I know, you never gave a kopek about maneuvers and similar activities."

"Pride, I'd say. I have to maintain the prestige. Besides, that also represents an opportunity for a promotion. You know that."

"*Khorosho.* The size of my help depends on the size of your generosity."

"How generous do you want us to be?"

"One thousand rubles cash," replied the Secretary, greed shining in his eyes.

On hearing the Lieutenant's price, Mikhail opened his eyes in amazement, but immediately looked at him straight in the eye. "You have a high price, Comrade, but we also think your help is worth it. Agreed, we'll pay. And in order to guarantee your help and our generosity, I double the offer."

Surprised, the Secretary drew a wide grin. He didn't think he'd get so much money. As a matter of fact, he chose that particular amount in order to bargain it to a lower number and still obtain high profits.

I wonder if the Captain's escape wish isn't taking him too far, Vasily thought. *Where will we get the other thirteen hundred rubles to complete the offer? We put all our savings together and barely made a bit more than half what this man demanded, and much less than what the Captain offered. Perhaps he knows something I don't know.* Despite his thoughts, the copilot remained silent, waiting for Mikhail to finish his proposition.

Is the Captain going nuts? Anatoly thought. Looking at Vasily, the technician questioned him silently with his eyes. Seeing the copilot calm, Anatoly decided not to intervene.

"Yes, Lieutenant. Two thousand rubles cash. Five hundred in advance right now, two hundred fifty on delivery, and one thousand two hundred fifty more when we get the prizes, after the maneuvers. That way I can guarantee your help, and you can guarantee my generosity towards you."

In his greed to obtain money, the Secretary didn't think about the unusual offer. The sight of the five hundred rubles Mikhail discreetly showed him, and the idea of knowing that in the near future he'd receive fifteen hundred more, were more than enough to embark him in the adventure.

On hearing that, Vasily and Anatoly laughed in their minds. Both knew that if those plans offered an escape opportunity, Lieutenant Dubov would not receive the third payment.

"You are really interested in getting those prizes!" exclaimed the Secretary, amazed. "*Khorosho.* The operation is risky, but for that sum I think I can afford to be bold. Now, I have two problems. The combination of the safe, and the other key, the Commander's."

"Don't worry about the other key," Anatoly intervened. "My father was a locksmith. I used to help him when I was a kid. I learned to make keys. I'll give you clay which you'll use to make a die. I'll take care of the rest."

"And the combination?" asked the Secretary.

"That's your part, Lieutenant. You'll have to get it," Vasily answered.

"Done deal! Comrades, give me a week, and you'll have those plans in your hands for a whole night."

"Impossible. We don't have so much time. We give you three days, at the most," said Mikhail.

"Three days! I don't think I can do it in such a short time," Dubov exclaimed. Seeing the bag full of money Mikhail dangled before him, however, made him change his mind. "Agreed," he said, taking the bag.

*   *   *   *

Standing a few meters from *Red 67*, Vasily waited for Mikhail to be closer. An important matter was bothering him, and he wanted to clarify it once and for all. *"Dobroe utro*, Captain!" he said.

"Dobroe, Vasya! How's everything?"

"Normal, nothing new. Who do we fly with today?" asked the copilot.

"Major Prokopov," replied Mikhail.

"The new pilot? What's his plane, *Red 23?*"

"Aha, the same. As usual, we'll be the leader, and he'll be the led."

Lowering his voice, Vasily changed the subject: "Captain, something's bothering me. It's about Icarus. How will we meet again? That is, the first time we could get together without Serghey because we got him sick. If Lieutenant Dubov is able to obtain those plans, where and how will we meet to study and discuss them? We can't get Serghey sick again!"

"I see. I think we'll have to use some other tricks."

"Such as?"

"We'll have to meet at night, in our room. As usual."

"And how will we get there? If Serghey finds out that we go to your room too often, he'll become suspicious and start asking questions!"

"My dear Vasya, as I said before, he doesn't have to find out. Out of sight, out of mind."

"What do you mean?"

"We can meet in the hours before dawn, when everyone one, even Serghey, is asleep. All should be able to sneak from their rooms and into ours."

Fortunately for Mikhail and his crew, the base personnel was lodged in one huge building. Mikhail, Vasily and other officers slept in the second floor. Noncoms and soldiers slept in the first floor.

"Understood. However, that will be around 2400 and 100 tonight."

"I'm afraid so, but that's good because, on the one hand, we won't have to worry about Serghey. On the other hand, however, we'll have less hours to sleep."

The crew chief of the *Red 67* maintenance team approached the pilots. His olive green jumpsuit was a sea of oil, grease, and gasoline spots. Cleaning his hands on a rag as dirty as his hands, he greeted them: "Captain Makarov, your plane is ready for take off."

"Spasibo bol'shoye, Sergeant. Very kind of you. I'm glad to have a crew chief as good as you taking care of my plane."

"Pozhaluysta, Captain. It's in perfect order, as it has always been and will be my norm," the crew chief replied, giving Mikhail the acceptance pad. Mikhail signed and returned the greasy pad.

"Sergeant! Listen! I want to ask you something," Yuri's voice came from behind them.

"Me?" asked the Sergeant.

"Yes, you. Did you check the fuel gauges as I asked you?" the Flight Engineer asked, near the nosewheels bogie.

"Yes, Lieutenant. We checked it all and found everything in order. Nothing to repair or replace."

"Good! I don't like not knowing exactly how much fuel I have available. I hope this time I'm not going to have any problems."

"Don't worry, Lieutenant. My work is guaranteed."

"Spasibo. Have a nice day, Sergeant."

Yuri joined his companions. Vasily still tried to clarify the problem. "Very well. We'll meet in your room. But, how will we tell the others about the change?"

"Leave that to me," Mikhail said, heading towards the cockpit ladder. The two Lieutenants followed him.

The maintenance team finished picking up their tools and equipment and placed everything in a truck. The technical crew ascended the ladder in the nose-wheels well, then headed to their respective stations. Anatoly waved his hand to the three maintenance men below. They unhooked the ladder from the nose-wheels assembly and placed it on their truck. Anatoly then closed and locked the access hatch.

*   *   *   *

Having reached the cruise speed and altitude specified in the preflight briefing, Mikhail asked for a status report.

"Altitude: ten thousand meters; speed: four hundred twenty five kilometers an hour. Stabilizing at cruise altitude and speed," Vasily informed.

"Heading: three-six-zero; time in flight: fifty seven minutes, fifteen seconds; three hundred eight kilometers from Kuzomen, entering Murmansk's flight zone," Alexey responded from his station, in the airplane's nose.

"Flight Red Sixty seven, from Kuzomen, calling Murmansk Control Center. *Priyom*," Mikhail called his call sign.

"Murmansk Control Center. We hear you, Sixty seven. *Priyom*."

"We're entering your flight zone. We're going in routine flight to inspect a friend's toys. *Priyom.*"

"Understood, Sixty seven. Entry authorized. *Priyom.*"

"Understood, Murmansk. *Priyom,*" Switching to the intercom, Mikhail asked his navigator: "Alexey, is there something you'd like to ask Murmansk? If that's the case, go on."

"Yes, Captain," replied the navigator. Switching to external frequency, the navigator asked: "Murmansk, Sixty seven navigator here. Has there been any change of significance in the meteo report for the North and Central Atlantic in the last thirty minutes?"

"Negative, Sixty seven. Weather in that area still the same. No changes expected for the next 24 hours. *Priyom.*"

"Understood, Murmansk. *Priyom.*"

"*Spasibo*, Murmansk. Red Sixty seven ends transmission." Mikhail closed the com link.

Following the leading-led system then in effect in the Soviet Naval Aviation, *Red 23,* the TU-95 piloted by Major Prokopov, flew two kilometers behind *Red* 67 in this crew's first flight out to meet a foreign vessel.

After several minutes the Rybachi Peninsula slowly disappeared behind them and to their left. With it disappeared the last bit of *terra firma.* Then they entered the air space over the ice-cold waters of the Barents Sea.

Feeling a bit hungry, Mikhail called the Flight Engineer: "Yura, did you bring the cookies and the tea?"

"Yes. I have them here with me."

"Could you please bring me some?"

"Of course!" said the Engineer.

Then through the intercom came Alexey's voice: "Yura, could you please bring me some tea also, if it's not much bother? I think I'm going to fall asleep here."

"No bother at all. Do you also want something to eat? There are cookies, cakes, and *pirozhki.*"

"No, Thank you. Only tea."

Yuri pulled his trusty canvas bag from under his seat. From there he took a stainless steel bottle, and poured tea in three cups.

Cups of tea and a box of cookies in hand, the Engineer entered the cockpit. Perhaps if the radioman hadn't been so antagonistic he could have participated in the crew's conversations and treats. But that was never the case. In one of the first flights they had together as a crew, Lieutenant Molotko set the pace for his relations with the rest of the crew. Yuri remembers Lt. Molotko's reply when he asked him if he wanted tea:

"No. I am not going to drink from your piss bottle!"

"Come on. You know nobody uses it for that here. I certainly don't. Do you?" Asked the Flight Engineer.

"No, I don't. But I don't know if you do. And I'm certainly not going to drink from it. You don't piss where you drink from."

Since then, Serghey, fearful of being mocked before the others, as well as to maintain his distance from them, just listened to what they said and asked questions related to his job as both radioman and political informer. Usually only Mikhail answered his questions. Physically he was present in the airplane, but a wall of ill feelings of all sizes and calibers separated him from the rest of the crew. Serghey, seated before his radio console, cigarette in hand, to the right of Yuri, usually spent his time in flight thinking about his own matters.

"Here you are, Captain. Piping hot tea and some cookies."

"Spasibo, Yura."

"Vasya, some tea?" the Engineer asked.

"No, thank you. Not now. Perhaps later. Thanks anyway."

Leaving the pilots behind, Yuri entered the tunnel that joined the cockpit to the navigator's console, in the nose of the plane, where Alexey sat. "Alyosha, here's your cup of tea. By the way, next time you come to the cockpit to get it. I don't like entering that tunnel. It's too narrow!" said the Engineer, half-jokingly.

"I'm so sorry! Yura, you shouldn't have bothered! You should have told me you were on your way. I'd have waited for you in the cockpit."

"Don't worry about it. No big deal," said Yuri, smiling.

"Spasibo, Yura."

"Nye za chto," replied the Engineer, turning around and entering the tunnel once again. Leaving the tunnel, he was stopped by Mikhail: "Yura, have you ever heard about Icarus?"

The Engineer was taken off guard by the question: "About *what?"*

Vasily immediately intervened: "Captain, are you talking about the character in Greek mythology?"

"Aha. That one. Do you know that, according to the legend, he and his father were prisoners in a maze in the island of Crete, and in order to escape they made wax wings?"

"Yes. I read about that, somewhere," answered the Engineer, now that he understood the Captain's question. In his mind, however, he asked himself what that had to do with the other Icarus, the escape plan.

"What you don't know is *how* they made those wax wings to be able to escape." Mikhail repositioned his microphone so the crew could listen more clearly. As soon as the cue word 'Icarus' was mentioned, Mikhail knew the whole crew, except the radioman, would be all ears.

Serghey also listened to the conversation. The words, however, had no meaning whatsoever for him, so he remained silent and let the Captain continue: "Every night, when the guards thought they were sleeping, Icarus and his father quietly went to a beehive farm they had there. They took some wax from the combs and used it to make part of the wings." Mikhail paused and markedly separated each one of the words he said: "And that happened every night, night after night, after night, when the guards thought they were sleeping. So, after several nights in the task, they could finish making the wings molds. Then they put bird feathers in them and, strapping them on, flew out of the maze."

In the technicians compartment, Ivan and Anatoly looked at each other, confused. Ivan pulled a pencil and scribbled a note, signaled Anatoly to attract his attention, and gave him the paper. Anatoly quickly read it: *'What did the Captain mean to say with that about Icarus?'*

'I think it has to do with us meeting at night, when everybody else is asleep,' Anatoly scribbled back.

'Are you sure?' Ivan asked again.

'Well, one could ask him, right?' Anatoly asked back.

'Ask him? How? If Serghey hears the question, he'll keep on asking,' Ivan replied.

'No. I'll ask him if that's what he meant. I think I know how to ask him,' Anatoly wrote back.

Placing his hand on his neck microphone, he called the cockpit: "Captain, Anatoly speaking. That story reminds me of the one about Penelope, the wife of Ulysses of Ithaca. She wove during the day. At night, she undid what she wove."

"Yes, that legend went like that, if I'm not mistaken."

"What I'm not sure is why she did that," said the technician. Emphasizing his words, he highlighted the question: "Was it to keep certain people away from her, until Ulysses came back home to liberate her from the siege?"

"Exactly! That's why she did that. Penelope, just like Icarus and his father, worked at night, when everybody was asleep, undoing what she wove during the day. That way she kept away from her all indiscreet eyes and ears."

Anatoly, hearing the confirmation to his assumptions, scribbled a note to Ivan: *'It looks like we'll have to meet in the Captain's room, late at night, if we want to continue refining the plans.'*

'Ask the Captain when and at what time,' Ivan asked.

'I don't think it would be prudent to ask him now. I can always find out later. Then I'll let you know,' replied Anatoly.

'Agreed.'

Their scribbling was suddenly interrupted by the harsh and coarse voice of Serghey, the radioman, cracking in their headphones: "Captain, I didn't know the crew was interested in Greek mythology."

"Oh! … Well … Aaah … Yes! Those legends of the Greek mythology have always been interesting. Besides, they make you smarter. The crew has always shown a great interest in them. I also share in that interest."

"I see … That's strange. I never noticed that interest before."

"Perhaps you weren't around whenever we discussed the subject. Don't you like Greek mythology, Lieutenant?"

"I read about it, but that was a long time ago. It's not that I don't like it, but I don't have time to waste reading about myths and legends."

Yes! You don't have time to read them because you're too busy spying on us, so later you can spit it all to your taskmasters, mudak! Mikhail thought. Then commented: "What a pity! You don't know what you're missing!"

Vasily let escape a hearty laugh on hearing the Captain's comment.

The sea below could be clearly seen by kilometers and kilometers around. Mikhail called his navigator: "Alyosha, give me a status report, please."

"Understood, Captain. Heading three-six-zero due north of Vadsø, Norway. Three hundred kilometers northwest of Murmansk. Time in flight: eighty six minutes. Entering grid Pavel-zero-four-one. Following this same heading we'll be entering the second stage in seven minutes, eighteen seconds, local time."

"Seven minutes! I knew we didn't have to wait too long to enter the second stage," exclaimed Mikhail.

"Of course, Captain. You've been flying this route for I don't know how many years. You know it by heart!" Vasily commented.

"Yes, it's true," Mikhail replied in a tone of voice that left no doubts about his feelings. His mind left his body, just like it had been doing in the last few days. *So many years in that northern prison … But if our plan works, I won't have to spend another year there. I'll be in the West … or I'll be dead!*

Then he heard Alexey's voice in the intercom: "Captain, are you there? Three minutes for the second stage. Are you listening?"

"Ah? … Eh! … Yes! Understood! Three minutes for the second stage. *Spasibo,* Alyosha."

"*Pozhaluysta,* Captain," the navigator replied, asking himself if it was Icarus what was keeping the Captain so distracted.

Serghey almost stood up from his seat to bring Mikhail back from his mind's depths. Having heard him answer the navigator, however, he remained put on his seat. Calling the Captain on the intercom, he warned him: "Captain Makarov, what's wrong with you? Lately you don't seem to have your head in this plane but somewhere else. As crewmember of this airplane it's my duty to warn you about the consequences of that irresponsible attitude! It doesn't benefit you nor us. I suggest you stop the practice immediately!"

"Yes, Lieutenant. It's true. I'll see what I can do about that. *Spasibo bol'shoye,*" replied Mikhail while commenting to himself: *Damn stoolie! You were right. I don't have my head here but in the West.*

"Forty seven seconds for the second stage!" Alexey informed.

"Understood. Vasya, start the countdown and turn to the indicated heading."

"Understood, Captain. Starting countdown now," replied the copilot.

"Yura, how's it going so far?"

"As good as always. Enough fuel for about ten more hours flight time. Oil: Normal. Hydraulic pressure: Normal. Compressors internal temperature: Normal. Electric system units: Normal. No problems to report in the logbook. It looks like this time they did fix those fuel gages."

"Splendid! It's good to know that the maintenance crew knows what they are doing when they fix these machines," Mikhail commented.

"It's true. I've seen them working on the plane, and I can attest to their expertise. Although sometimes they screw up," replied Yuri.

"Turning to heading three-one-zero now," Vasily said. The giant airplane initiated a slight dip to port while the needle of the magnetic compass slowly descended to the indicated heading.

"Heading: three-one-zero; speed: four hundred seven kilometers per hour; height: eleven thousand two hundred meters," Vasily informed once again, at the end of the turning maneuver.

*   *   *   *

That morning, the Commander's Secretary entered his superior's office without saying a word or making a sound. He knew that was more or less the time the Colonel opened the safe.

As he expected, the Colonel was turning the safe's combination lock. The lieutenant took advantage of the situation and carefully followed the Colonel's hand movements. He concentrated his attention in recording in his mind all the numbers the dial stopped at, and the direction changes necessary to open the small steel door. Finishing the operation, the Commander called:

"Lieutenant Dubov, please, bring your key."

"Here I am, Colonel."

The Commander was surprised to hear the voice behind him. Turning around, he asked: "How long have you been standing there, Lieutenant?"

"I just got in here, Colonel."

"Where's your sense of ethics, Lieutenant? Since when do you enter my office without first knocking at the door? Besides, I was in the middle of a very important operation!" screamed the Colonel, visibly angry.

"I'm sorry, Commander. Please, forgive me!"

"I hope this situation is not repeated ever again!" the incensed officer screamed once again.

*   *   *   *

Leaving behind the Barents Sea around the Norwegian port of Tromsø, the third stage of the flight had just started. Both airplanes still had before them more than five thousand kilometers to fly, before they reached the coordinates for the meeting with the American aircraft carrier. Aboard *Red 67*, Mikhail turned on the automatic pilot, and let the machine fly the plane.

"Hey, Vasya! Long flight before us, right?"

"Yes, as usual. But I think I'm getting used to it."

"By the way, Captain," Pavel asked, "how come we're heading so deep over the Atlantic? I mean, we're heading practically to the middle of it."

"The American Navy is sending its newest aircraft carrier out on its first deployment."

"A new aircraft carrier?" Asked Jonas.

"Yes, it's called *'Nimitz'*, I was told. *Bort* Number 68. It's their largest aircraft carrier, so far."

"Bigger than the ones we've seen so far?" ask Jonas, again.

"Yes, bigger still," Mikhail answered.

"And nuclear-powered, I suppose," said Anatoly.

"Yes, that too ..."

Suddenly, they heard strange noises in their headphones. Mikhail craned his neck and looked behind him in order to investigate the source of the unusual noises. To his right, behind Vasily, Yuri put aside for a moment his duties as Flight Engineer, and happily blew in a harmonica held in his hands.

Vasily, on his part, didn't recognize the noise immediately, partly due to the constant high level drone of the four Kuznyetsov NK-12MV turboprops outside. However, after identifying the rhythm of the music, turned his face towards the Engineer and commented: "Yura, that's really gracious of you! To play precisely that song!"

The Engineer stopped playing and said: "Yes, *'Vasya, Vasilyok,'* played especially for our copilot, with my compliments."

"Spasibo. Spasibo bol'shoye. Ochen' tebye blagodaren!" the copilot thanked his friend.

"Hey! what's going on back there?" said Alexey.

"Yes! What's that noise we heard?" said Anatoly.

"Yes, what's that noise? What's happening to you guys up front?" asked Jonas.

"Calm down. Nothing's happening. Everything's alright. It's just Yura playing a song with his harmonica," Mikhail answered his crewmen's questions.

"Yura? I didn't know we had a musician aboard," commented Alexey.

"Neither did I," said Anatoly.

"Then we're three, because I didn't know that either," said Jonas.

"That means to say all of us, because it looks like no one knew that," said Pavel.

"I think so!" said Mikhail. "Yura, where did you get that harmonica from? How come we never saw you playing it before?"

"It just came last night from Murmansk. My family sent it to me. I always wanted to play the harmonica, but around here I could never find one I liked, so I wrote to my sister, there in Slaviansk, telling her to send me one and, well … Here it is!"

"I see. May I?" Mikhail asked, then stood up and approached the Flight Engineer's station.

"Konyechno!" said Yuri.

Mikhail took the instrument in his hands and looked at it attentively, passing his fingers by the colorful and intricate hand-carved decorations, handiwork particular to the Kuban, in Southern Russia, by the Black Sea, the native region of the Engineer.

"It's beautiful! They do know how to do artwork in your region," commented Mikhail.

"That's not difficult for us Kubanis!" said the Engineer, full of pride.

"Could you, please, play *'Kalinka'*? That's an old song I'd like to hear," said Vasily.

Before the Engineer had a chance to even get the instrument close to his mouth, in his earphones burst the coarse voice of the radioman:

"Lieutenant Kazakov! That music bothers me, so I demand you put away that … thing. This is no flying concert. Besides, you know that it's against regulations to bring aboard instruments foreign to your job, and use them while on duty. So, return to your job."

"*S udovol'stviem*, Lieutenant." Yuri returned the harmonica to its padded case. In his insides the Engineer was boiling mad, feeling like smashing the man's face with one single blow. Mikhail knew that, despite having a higher rank than Serghey's, he couldn't interfere with some of his observations, especially those that had to do with rules and regulations.

The Captain looked at his copilot and, pointing his head to the radioman, placed his right thumb between his index and middle fingers, in the *v karmanye* sign, the Russian version of the western erect middle finger in a closed fist. Despite the thick air in the cockpit, Vasily could not help let escape a hearty laugh. For the rest of the trip, however, the crew remained silent.

*   *   *   *

Arriving to the zone where according to the latest reports from Severomorsk the American aircraft carrier was sailing, the sun was shining in an almost cloudless sky, acquiring golden tones as its rays reflected in the few scattered cumuli around. Local Time: 08:00. Visibility: 10 to 15 kilometers. Sea waves: 1 to 2 points. From cruising altitude, the sea below seemed like a gigantic green-gray carpet.

"Vasya, descend to nine thousand meters, same speed, same heading. Be on the alert. The American airplanes may appear at any moment. Let *Red 23* know," said Mikhail.

"Understood, Captain," replied the copilot.

Suddenly, the panels before Ivan came to life as lights blinked and sirens sounded intermittently, when the SPO-3 *'Sirena-3'* Radar Detection and Warning System received high frequency signals directed at the Soviet airplane.

"Captain, Ivan here. They're illuminating us. A signal from starboard, before us. Probably it's from one of the American radar airplanes."

"Understood. Let's see what happens."

Pavel turned on the onboard *Lira* tape recorder in order to intercept and record all communications between the airplanes around them and the carrier, or between the carrier and its escort, in all available frequencies.

Aboard an E-2C 'Hawkeye' Early Warning and Detection airplane, one of those then based aboard the USS Nimitz (CVN 68), the discovery of the intruders set the whole Carrier Group defense system in motion. "Commander, 'zombies' approaching by port. Heading: one-niner-five. Angels niner. Seven hundred twenty clicks. Radar signature indicates large size. IFF identifies them both as 'foes,'" informs the radar controller in the Combat Information Center.

"Most probable they're Russian 'shadows.' Retransmit the data to the carrier," replied the Commander.

"Roger," agreed the controller.

Aboard the USS Nimitz, alarms howled, sirens wailed, and loudspeakers blared. "General Quarters, General Quarters. All hands to battle stations. All hands to battle stations. This is not a drill. Repeat, this is not a drill." A yellow alert was initiated, requiring the immediate interception of the approaching adversary.

Sailors, pilots, mechanics, and technicians ran in all directions in the insides and on the deck of the huge ship. On the deck, the Sikorsky S-61 'Sea King' rescue choppers shot up. Maintenance technicians readied the F-4J 'Phantom II' interceptors for catapulting, while their pilots ran to their cockpits as fast as their legs allowed them. The old pirate symbol of the skull and crossbones over a black background, plus the letters 'A—J' on the rudder, identified the fighters' squadron as VF 74 of Carrier Air Wing 8 (CVW 8), the 'Be devilers.' The words 'USS Nimitz' on the fuselage indicated the airplanes' mother ship.

By the time the pilots reached their seats, the engines were already on and revved up. Seat belts locked and tightened, oxygen masks on and connected, canopies were closed. His right thumb up, the pilot gave the 'all ready' signal. The Deck Officer gave the signal for launch. The pilot pushed the twin throttles to maximum afterburner, the aircraft's brakes were immediately released, and the powerful steam catapult pulled all nine tons of the heavy twin-engined F-4 'Phantom II' jet fighter. The pilot and his Radar Intercept Officer sank in their seats due to the sudden acceleration caused by the combination of the mighty turbojet engines at full thrust plus the pull of the catapult. The interceptor zoomed up from zero to one hundred ninety kilometers an hour in only five seconds.

The first aircraft already in the air, the second was ready to join it, running on the angled deck runway. When the second airplane took to the air, the third fighter was ready to follow it. In scarce minutes, three interceptors were on their way to meet the 'zombies' detected by the 'Hawkeye.' Meanwhile, the RIOs received from the E-2C CIC the necessary interception coordinates.

Aboard *Red 67*, its crew was also on the alert. "Captain, Anatoly here. I have the radar airplane on my screen. Heading two-eight-zero; altitude: nine thousand meters. Behind it there are three more crafts; same heading, high speed. Probably they're interceptors, since they're advancing at our same height in this direction."

"IFF identifies them all as 'Adversaries,'" said Ivan.

"Well, here we have the 'reception committee.' Anyway, even if they don't like it, we'll take a peek at their little boat," commented Mikhail. "Vasya, start descending to intermediate level. Stabilize at three thousand meters."

"Alexey here. Interceptors approaching. Meeting in fifteen minutes, by starboard," informed the navigator. In his radar screen the three dots continued their advance at more than one thousand kilometers an hour. As the Soviet airplanes approached the area where the vessel of their interest was sailing, the flow of data from the former to the latter increased, as well as the aerial and the electronic activity around them.

"Captain, Ivan here. All the radars out there have us illuminated, in sight, and measured. I'm receiving signals from at least four in the air and six on the water."

"That's exactly what is there: an aircraft carrier and five more escort ships," added Anatoly. On his radar screen, the enormous size of the floating airport made it easy to distinguish among the other vessels.

"Tolya, how long until we reach the carrier?" Mikhail asked.

"Ten minutes, more or less."

"Alexey here. The three fighters are approaching. Vector zero-three-zero."

To the right and above appeared three small dots leaving a wake behind them. As the distance between them and *Red 67* decreased, the small dots increased in size until they became the large turbojets, zooming above and to the right, to the left, and directly over the TU-95 RTs, like swift eagles.

Shortly after, the three fighters sent by the American Commander turned around and positioned themselves behind and on both sides of the Soviet airplanes. The latter, due to their huge size, made them look small. The white stars over the blue circles with red and white side stripes by the engines air intake, and the word '**NAVY**' in bold black letters painted over their off-white fuselages, positively identified them as American to the Soviet crewmen.

Peeking out his side window, Serghey made one of his usual comments for the consumption of the crew: "Look at their tails: Pictures of devils and their flag! Mercenaries! Pirates! Bandits! They're not even supposed to be this close to us! Nothing but provocations!"

Serghey's comments, as usual, were received in silence by the rest of the crew.

"Alexey here. Carrier by starboard. Has company: two cruisers, two destroyers, and one that looks like a tanker," informed the navigator from his observation post in the plane's nose. His binoculars confirmed what he had seen previously on the radar screen. Through the transparent panels of the airplane's glazed nose, Alexey distinguished the ships below and before him. The enormous white '68' over the bow deck identified the ship as the intended vessel. On the carrier's deck, its fighters neatly aligned.

The pair of TU-95 RTs approached the carrier group. Aboard *Red 67,* Pavel in the tail and Alexey in the nose, grabbed their high resolution long-range cameras and snapped photographs of the ships, especially the aircraft carrier. This was the main purpose of their long flight from Kola Peninsula to the North Atlantic Ocean. Later the photographs were sent to Severomorsk for their study by the Navy Intelligence Service crews there.

Serghey and Ivan speak English, product of their training as radiomen, so they eavesdropped on all the transmissions in the open. Despite the electronic equipment available to them, besides a lot of static, caused by the carrier's electronic jamming system, they just captured a few messages here and there, which for their purposes had no strategic importance whatsoever. Since most of the captured material is inconsequential, they soon tired and stopped the eavesdropping. The important ones, the real objects of their attentions, were already being recorded, for the benefit of the cryptanalysts in the USSR.

The radar and ECM operators, Anatoly and Ivan, tested their equipment with that of the ships. Having strict orders of not interfering with the American vessels' communications, Ivan only tried different wavelengths and interception frequencies in case of possible electronic jamming.

Before his screen, Anatoly followed the same routine and, after detecting the carrier and its escort in the guided missile control radar, he followed the normal procedures in such cases. In his mind he aimed and guided an imaginary missile towards the carrier, which he later detonated. In his ideal scenario, a small cloud appeared and then disappeared in the spot on his screen where the real position of the ship was indicated.

"Straight on target! The carrier has been obliterated by a nuclear missile from one of our submarines!" the technician exclaimed, aloud. In his fantasy Anatoly got to divulge the results of the drill he was conducting in his imagination.

"What!" exclaimed Mikhail.

"He said the aircraft carrier was destroyed!" said Vasily.

"What did you say, Lieutenant Kiprenko?" asked Serghey.

"Nothing, nothing! It was just a practice! I guided a missile from one of our submarines to the aircraft carrier, where it blew up. But it was just an exercise!"

"*Khorosho*, Lieutenant. In the future abstain from that kind of actions," retorted Serghey. "Practice your abilities without exclamations. They interfere with the smooth functioning of the crew, worrying them unnecessarily." The radioman finished his reprimand with a noisy click as he turned his intercom switch off.

"Vasya, tell *Red 23* that we'll sink further." Mikhail decided to descend even further in order to obtain clearer photographs, as per the requirements given to him that morning in the pre-flight briefing. The copilot acknowledged the order. Mikhail gently pushed the control wheel and the airplane descended, stabilizing at four hundred meters high.

In order to obtain better images, Mikhail flew alongside the ship, by starboard. Turning around, the plane once again flew alongside the ship, now by port. Each time, Alexey and Pavel continued their task of taking photographs of the aircraft carrier and its escort, always followed by the interceptors of the former trying to push it away from their mothership.

Pavel classified the ships they were reconnoitering, as well as their characteristics. Among them, the nuclear powered cruisers *USS South Carolina* and *USS California*. This report was also sent to Severomorsk, as a complement to the photographs, for the benefit of the Intelligence Service crews there.

From this low height Mikhail and Vasily saw even clearer below them the rows of airplanes parked on the deck, ready to take off in seconds, giving them an idea of the power assembled in only one ship. They could also distinctly make out the faces of the American sailors walking among the airplanes, looking up at the airplane that came 'from the other side.'

"Well, I think we've gathered enough information about that carrier to keep the people in Intelligence busy for a few days," Mikhail commented as he over-flew the vessels for the umpteenth time.

"I agree. In my own and humble opinion, I think we can head home," said Vasily.

"*Ladno*. Attention, this is the Captain. Cease all activity. We're going home."

"Splendid!" was the single expression heard in the intercom.

Their job finished at last, to Severomorsk flew via telex the radio report prepared by Serghey: 'Beginning transmission: Found and visually inspected American aircraft carrier 'Nimitz'—BN 68. Latitude: 40° 30' North, Longitude: 23° 31' West. Speed: 5 knots, heading: 100°. Weather in the target zone: clear. End transmission.'

Increasing the turboprops power, both pilots pulled their control wheels. The flying Goliath started its ascent, leaving behind the carrier object of its scrutiny, joined its flying companion, and both continued ascending to cruise altitude.

In the tail, Jonas kept his eyes over the ships while the plane continued its ascent, getting further away from the area. Soon the fleet was nothing more than small spots leaving a white wake on the gray ocean surface below.

"Home, here we go!" commented Vasily.

"Well, it looks like the American planes also want to go home with us," said Jonas.

"I wish they did. Do you imagine the amazed faces of the people back in the Union if they see us arriving there with three American fighters in the tail?" Ivan asked, in jest.

"But they won't do it," said Anatoly. "First of all, I doubt our interceptors will allow them to enter our air space. Second of all, I don't think the Americans want to get into such a huge mess. Third and last, even if they wanted to, they can't. Those airplanes do not have the range to get there."

Then Serghey's voice burst in the intercom: "Lieutenant Kiprenko, you should concentrate more in your duties, and stop talking about subjects foreign to them!"

"But, Lieutenant Molotko, I already finished my duties! The Captain said we're going back home!" replied Anatoly.

"That's no excuse. There must be some checking you could be doing in your equipment, instead of talking about Greek mythology or about enemy airplanes invading Soviet air space!"

Anatoly, knowing that entering into an argument with the detested character was a waste of time, since in his report he could have written whatever he felt like writing against his victim, and his superiors in the Political Department would believe him and not the latter, he decided to leave the situation as it was. "Yes, Lieutenant. I'll try to do something more important."

His tone of voice nevertheless betrayed his inner anger. It was just their bad luck that tied them to the individual who had the fame of being the most fanatic and strict of all the KGB agents in the base, making life impossible for the crew of the airplane where he served.

The irritation the incident caused in Ivan led the technician to take revenge in his own hands. *This damn sonofabitch thinks he's a General just because he's this plane's stoolie. He needs a lesson badly, and I think I'm the one to teach him some respect.*

From thought to action there was only one step. The technician moved the controls in his panels and placed his dials in the same frequency of the radioman's. Then moved other dials to echo multiplication, capable of producing an annoying loud squeak in the headphones of whoever was listening in that same frequency. Increasing the jamming volume to the maximum, Ivan then turned on his transmitters.

Serghey, sitting before his radio console, suddenly stood up in one single jump, took off his leather helmet and threw it to the floor, all the while looking around with a killer look and barking curses of all sizes.

Hearing the sudden commotion behind him, Mikhail turned around: "Lieutenant Molotko! What's happening?"

"*Blyad!* Someone was trying to jam my radio and left me almost deaf! My ears still hurt!" yelled the angry radioman.

"Perhaps the Americans out there are still jamming our communications!" suggested Vasily.

"That would happen only if those airplanes out there knew our frequency. And I'm very sure they don't. Plus, they don't have that kind of jamming equipment. Here there's only one way for that to happen …" Cutting his explanation short, and without uttering another word, Serghey picked up his helmet, neared his radio console, lowered its volume to the minimum, and slowly raised the volume.

"… The damn jamming stopped. But here there's only one person that can do that."

At his station by the cupola, Ivan was still laughing in his insides when he heard the radioman's harsh voice explode in his ears: "Lieutenant Krylov! What's wrong with you? Why did I register intense jamming in my radio and in my frequency?"

Even though the radioman's accusation took him by surprise—he was not expecting Serghey to find the origin of the jamming—he didn't show it. "What the devil I know! Don't ask me! It's not my fault the Americans want to jam your damn radio!"

Screaming in the intercom, the radioman hysterically reprimanded the technician. "Lieutenant, you know as well as I do that those planes out there can not jam my radio just like that. For that they need to know my frequency and they also need to have the equipment to be able to do it. You are the only one here that can do that! And you did it on purpose! You know it's forbidden to interfere with the functions of the crew of a Soviet aircraft, and more forbidden yet: to jam its communications! This is rebellion and mutiny, Lieutenant! I'm going to report this incident in the flight log! You will not fly in this airplane anymore!"

Mikhail knew that if Serghey reported the happenings, he and his crewmen, especially Ivan, would have had the next few days full of questionings, hellish interrogations answering the same questions time and again, and mountains of papers and reports to be filled. All followed by interviews with everyone in the base, from the Base Commander and his deputy, the Regiment Commander and his deputy, the doctor, and the psychiatrist, to the KGB men responsible for the political health of the crews, the Political Commander and his Deputy, the Regiment Political Commander and his deputy, and so on, and on, and on.

Mikhail himself, as Captain of the ship, was politically responsible for his men before the Regiment Political Commander, so the radioman's report could have presented him as a failure in the eyes of the Colonel. All this went without mentioning that if the matter became serious enough to reach beyond the base limits, then the *nachal'stvo* from Murmansk or Leningrad, and even Moscow, would have been involved in the case.

Of course, if it reached that stage, transfers to other bases would have taken place, the crew would have been disbanded, and with them Mikhail's ambitions and wishes of escape.

Since that report would have placed Icarus in mortal danger, Mikhail, for Ivan's own good specifically, as well as for that of the whole crew in general, intervened on behalf of them all. "Lieutenant Molotko, I don't think it's necessary for you to report this incident. You already correctly reprimanded him. I give you my personal assurance that this will not happen again. I'm the officer in command of this crew, and as such, I'm responsible for my men's actions. I take full responsibility in this case."

On hearing Mikhail take on himself the blame for his crewman, but also feeling a greater conflict boiling, Serghey decided to leave the matter there, in order to avoid a major incident.

"Agreed, Captain Makarov. I'll leave this whole matter under your whole responsibility. After all, it's you who's supposed to impose a Communist and military discipline in this aircraft, not me. However, make sure your men do not repeat this kind of incidents. You know very well the results of the same."

Serghey decided to yield because, in the long run, he could also have been a loser if he informed about the happenings. It could have been seen as a negative spot in his KGB service sheet, which could have placed in danger his chances for future promotions. Besides, he was not exempt from all the questioning the others had to go through. If the incident became serious enough, he would have gone through the same interrogations, just like the rest.

"*Spasibo,* Lieutenant. I'm glad we could reach an agreement." Having obtained a happy ending to the small conflagration, Mikhail focused his attention in other matters.

"Yura, how is it going with you?"

"Up until a while ago everything was going smooth. Now the damn gages are indicating incredible numbers. Fortunately, I'm keeping good control of fuel flow and consumption, so I know how much we have left."

"I thought they repaired those gages," said Vasily.

"That's what I thought too. When we left they were working alright. I think they'll have to replace them," replied the Flight Engineer.

"Vasya, report," said Mikhail.

"Stabilizing at eleven thousand five hundred meters. Speed: four hundred thirty kilometers an hour, stabilizing at cruise speed."

"Correct. As far as piloting this airplane is concerned, I think very soon I'll be able to retire. You know how to fly it as well as I do."

"Come on, Captain! I don't have your experience. Plus all those thousands of flying hours you have, I don't think I'll have them until twenty more years, at least."

"And by then you'll have my age, you'll be training your copilot, and you'll be telling him the same things I'm telling you now. As you can see, the cycle repeats itself time and again."

"So I see. One leaves, others come. New airplanes, new pilots, new techniques, but the cycle is the same."

"Right," said Mikhail. Then Jonas said in the intercom: "They're leaving us! The American fighters are returning to their ship!"

"Well, drink *borzhomi* and have a nice trip! We're also going back home!" Mikhail commented.

After having flown over the North Atlantic for six hours, in five more hours they reached Kuzomen. During the flight the crew only thought about the deserved rest that awaited them after a long day. Meanwhile, Mikhail thought about the escape, testing in his mind all the routes, coordinations, probabilities of discovery and interception, searching to find, if there were any, a route better than the one they already had.

With its human drama of anxiety, desperation, respect, and hatred, the giant aircraft and its companion continued their long and boring flight back to Kuzomen.

CHAPTER 4

▼

That night, Anatoly met the base Commander's Secretary in the officer's quarters.

"Could you get the combination?"

"Yes. It cost me a reprimand from the Colonel, but I got it."

"Good. At any rate, you already have it, and that's what's important," said the technician. Taking a small pack out of his pocket, Anatoly gave it to the Lieutenant. "Here. This is the clay you'll use to make the mold for the second key."

"How should I do it?"

"Simple. Just take the Commander's key and press it against the clay. It'll make an impression on the clay which I'll use as a model to make another key."

"I don't see how I'm going to get that other key from the Commander."

"Well, you'll have to come up with something."

"*Ladno.* I'll see how I'll do it."

"But do it soon. Remember that tomorrow night you should give me back the clay mold."

"Agreed. *Do svidaniya,* Lieutenant."

"*Do svidaniya,* Lieutenant Dubov."

Anatoly left the Secretary alone in his room.

*   *   *   *

At the end of the day, Colonel Boris Rodyonovich Degtyaryov, Commander of the Kuzomen Naval Air Base, ready to retire to his quarters, closed the safe and applied wax to its door. Then his Secretary asked in a very casual way:

"Commander, sometimes I ask myself, what would happen if one of these keys gets lost?"

"I know what would happen," answered the Colonel. "If any one of these keys gets lost, everyone in the base, from myself down to the gate guards, is placed on a strict search team. Everything in the base will be stripped and searched. Nothing will be left unmoved. From drawers and boxes to garbage dumps and even the grass outside. If three hours after the safe's closing time it still has not been found, then a duplicate is requested by special airplane to Region Headquarters in Murmansk. Now, if the key is really lost, that is, if it's not found after twenty four hours of intense search, well, you better get lost together with it, because then the lock is changed ... together with its former owner."

"Talk about tight security they have!" exclaimed the Secretary.

"Too many important papers inside that safe to risk them unnecessarily."

"I think what they should do is to make both locks open with the same key."

"That's absurd! What's the use of having a safe with two locks that open with the same key?"

"If one key gets lost, one still could use the same key to open the second lock."

"But there's no security like that! It would never be as safe as when it has two different locks. Whoever has one key could open both of them!"

"Can I see your key, Commander? I'd like to compare them and see if they're really different."

"Yes, they're different. Look," said the Colonel, then he gives his key to the Secretary.

The Lieutenant, taking the key, let it fall from his fingers. As it fell, in a fake attempt at trapping it in mid air, Dubov batted it with his open hand. The key flew the length of the room, falling behind the Commander's desk.

"Oh! I'm so sorry! How clumsy I am!" Dubov exclaimed, running to the location where the key fell. Once behind the furniture, and while hidden by the same, in a quick movement he uncovered his left forearm, where he had previously attached the clay with adhesive tape and covered with his shirt sleeve. Pressing the key against the clay as hard as he could, he made a mold, then covered it again with his sleeve.

"What's happening? You can't find it?"

"Yes. I found it. It's here, under your chair."

"Ah! I'd really hate to lose that key!" said Degtyaryov.

"I don't blame you," said the Secretary.

Standing up and extending his arm, Dubov gave the key to the Colonel. "Here you are, Commander."

"*Khorosho*. Lieutenant, let's get out of here. It's already late."

*   *   *   *

On his way to his own quarters, Dubov stopped by Anatoly's room once again. *"Dobryy vyecher!"*

"Oh! It's you, Lieutenant Dubov," replied the technician. "Come in. I thought you were one of the guys of my crew."

"I finally got the mold. I had to do some tricks, but here it is," said Dubov, folding his shirt sleeve and showing the clay still stuck to his forearm.

"Very ingenious. Let me see it."

Dubov removed the clay from his arm and gave it to Anatoly, now the crew's locksmith. "Mmm ... it didn't come out as good as I'd have liked."

"When I made it I didn't have much time. Let's say that it was right under the Commander's nose."

"Don't worry about it. I still can make a duplicate using this mold."

"*Khorosho*. I'd hate to have to go through all that again. I don't know what excuse I'd use with the Commander."

"*Ladno*. Come back tomorrow afternoon. By then I should have the duplicate ready."

Armed with only a key of similar shape, the mold, and a file, Anatoly spent the rest of the night working on the key duplicate for the safe. Since the technician didn't have to fly that day, he filed the small piece of metal with the tool until well after sunrise. In the morning he kept working on the key until he had one that matched the mold as much as it was possible for him. In the afternoon he gave it the final touches.

While engaged in the task, a voice called his attention.

"Lieutenant Kiprenko!"

"At your service!" Anatoly said as he stood up and placed both the tool and the duplicate aside, away from prying eyes. Realizing who it was, he relaxed: "Lieutenant Dubov! *Zdrastvuyte!* I thought it was someone else."

Dubov did not return the greeting, going instead straight to the point: "The duplicate, is it ready?"

Anatoly sat down, took a piece of paper, retrieved the key, and wrapped it. "Here you are. Use it when most convenient. I tried to make it as close as possible to the mold you gave me. Even then, it may not be a perfect duplicate. Anyway. I hope you have no problems with it."

"I hope that too. What should I do with the key once I return the papers?"

"Dispose of it in an appropriate place. To avoid problems. You know."

"Very well. That's what I'll do."

"Lieutenant, don't forget we need those papers for tomorrow night, the latest. Otherwise, we won't be able to pay you."

"Don't worry about it. Tomorrow night you'll have them."

"I hope so. *Spokoynoy nochi,* Lieutenant."

✻   ✻   ✻   ✻

At the end of his work day, Commander Degtyaryov placed several documents in his desk's drawers and some in his briefcase. Then he called his secretary. "Lieutenant Dubov, time to lock the safe."

"Yes, Commander. I'm on my way."

Degtyaryov placed document after document in the safe while the Secretary recorded each instrument as it was placed there.

"Intelligence Report №8."

"Recorded."

"Order of the Day from Region Headquarters."

"Recorded."

"Maps and flight plans, *Okean* Maneuvers."

"Recorded," the Secretary repeated. His eyes followed the Colonel's hand, noticing where he placed the envelope containing the documents.

After placing all the documents in the safe, Degtyaryov closed its small door, turned its dial and inserted his key in lock number one. "That's it. Now's your turn, Lieutenant."

The Secretary, key in hand, inserted it in lock number two. The operation finished, the Commander took a matchbox, struck one of the matches and placed a wax bar on its flame. Then pressed the soft wax bar against the safe's door, leaving two seals on it. They should be in exactly the same shape tomorrow. Dubov followed with his eyes the location where the officer placed the wax bar: on the file cabinet, behind a photograph of the Colonel shaking Premier Leonid Brezhnev's hand. *It'll be easy to find.* He thought.

The Colonel turned a portrait of V.I. Lenin on its hinges, thus covering the safe and disguising it as a national hero. Both officers then signed the registry of documents kept in the safe.

Back in his office, Dubov sat at his desk. Degtyaryov, on his way out, briefcase in hand, asked. "Lieutenant, are you staying? It's late!"

"Yes. I still have work to do."

"Very well. *Spokoynoy nochi.*"

Several minutes later, after having finished next day's paperwork, Dubov took some documents and placed them in his briefcase. Taking the case, he entered the Commander's office. Fortunately, the Colonel never bothered to lock its door.

Closing the door behind him, the semi dark room acquired a phantasmagorical aspect. Lenin, his portrait on the wall right next to that of the Premier, seemed to look straight at him, as if recriminating him for what he was about to do. Disregarding the national hero before him, Dubov turned the portrait on its hinges, pulled out of his wallet the paper where a few days before he recorded the safe's combination, and turned the safe's dial according to the instructions he wrote on the same paper.

Digging in his pockets, he pulled his key and his duplicate of the Commander's key. Inserting his own key in lock №2, he turned it and the lock opened. After inserting the key duplicate in lock №1, he tried to turn it, but it didn't move.

After a few trials the key still didn't budge. "*Blyad!* It looks like this piece of shit wasn't well made!" He exclaimed under his teeth while still jiggling the key, attempting to turn the lock. His efforts and the tension made sweat drops appear on his forehead.

Suddenly, the lock yielded and turned. Grabbing the door handle, he turned it, breaking the wax seals and opening the steel door. The wide open safe showed him all its secrets. However, something took him out of his momentary exaltation. Afar he could hear the clicks of the sentry's boots. Quickly he closed the door and returned the portrait to its place.

In a few long steps he reached the other side of the room and flattened himself against the wall, next to the window, hoping not to be seen. Otherwise, he could have kissed this life goodbye. The sentry was getting closer, his boots' clicks sounding ever nearer. Dubov, however, could hardly hear them. They were drowned by his own heartbeats exploding in his eardrums like cannon thunders.

Suddenly the clicks stopped. Through the window, the sentry glanced inside the office. From his position next to the window, Dubov could see the sentry's long shadow projected against the wall on other side. He felt the guard's eyes searching for possible intruders in the Commander's office. Unexpectedly, a light shone in, its beam going from one side of the room to the other, stopping momentarily on Lenin's portrait. As quickly as the flashlight was turned on, so it was turned off.

Having satisfied his search duties, the sentry continued his routine watch. Although the guard left, Dubov didn't move, not because he didn't want to but because he couldn't. His body remained rigid due to the fear bordering on terror he still felt. He waited until he calmed down.

After a few short seconds—which felt more like long minutes—Dubov felt his heart return to its normal rhythm. His body rigidity had almost disappeared. His legs could move once again. Sliding quickly but silently, he approached the portrait once again. With one hand he turned it on its hinges. With the other hand he grabbed and turned the safe's door handle, pulling and opening at the same time. In scarce seconds he dug among the papers and documents until he finds, at the exact location he saw the Commander place it, the yellow envelope with large red letters stating the highly classified nature of its contents:

СОВЕРШЕННО СЕКРЕТНО

A glint coming from the rear of the safe caught his eye. He stretched his arm to grab whatever was there, pulling it to the semidarkness of the room: A bottle of vodka. Reading its brand, *'Finlandia,'* he knew it was not Soviet, most probably smuggled into this country from that other country. Quickly turning its cap, he took a trial sip. Tasting its flavor for a few seconds, he then took a longer drink. *"Good vodka the Colonel gets!"* he thought, then recapped and returned the bottle to its place.

Taking the yellow envelope, he placed it in his briefcase, closed the safe, and returned Lenin's portrait back to its place. Suddenly, his eyes met Lenin's, his accusing sight penetrating him to the bones. Knowing that portraits don't talk, Dubov turned around, returned to his office, and sat at his desk.

Once the agitation caused by his incursion in the office next door had subsided, he dried the copious sweat from his forehead. Looking at his watch, he was amazed to see that he spent only seven minutes there. It felt more like seven hours.

Standing up, he took his briefcase and headed to the door. He was in a hurry to reach the officers quarters and deliver the compromising papers to those involved in the plot. Outside, perhaps because of his rush, he stumbled and fell. Attempting to stop his fall, he let go of the briefcase, which flew some meters, landing near one of the guards. Due to the impact it opened up. Some papers and a yellow envelope fell by the guard's boots.

One of the guards ran to help him stand up. Dubov, seeing the briefcase open and its contents picked up by the other soldier, stood up in one single jump. The first soldier didn't have time to even get close to him. The second soldier finished picking up the papers and the yellow envelope. He placed them in the briefcase, closed it, and returned it to the Lieutenant. Dubov almost snatched the case from the guard's hand. His face showed a grimace more of fear than hostility. The briefcase once firmly held in his hand, Dubov smiled and thanked the soldier. He left the scene at an accelerated pace, heading to the officers quarters.

∗   ∗   ∗   ∗

Next morning Lieutenant Dubov arrived at the office earlier than usual and in a hurry. He zoomed through his office and entered the Colonel's. Repeating the maneuver of the night before, he opened the safe and placed the yellow envelope in the exact location he found it.

Closing the steel door, he jumped to the file cabinet, took the wax bar, pulled out his lighter and actioned its wheel. Some sparks flew from it but nothing else happened. Repeating the maneuver several times, he obtained the same results.

Looking at his watch, he cursed. Blyad! *This shit doesn't work, and the Colonel is almost here!* Vigorously shaking the lighter he tried once again to light its wick. This time a weak blue flame appeared. *I forgot to refill its fluid, but it still has some!* he said. His trembling hand passed the wax bar over the feeble flame. Pressing the bar over the broken seals, he repaired them, leaving them as they were originally. After returning Lenin's portrait to its place he took his briefcase, turning around on time to see the office door opening and Col. Degtyaryov entering.

"*Dobroe utro*, Lieutenant. Here so early? What are you doing in my office?"

"*Dobroe utro*, Commander. I was just admiring your collection of diplomas and certificates. I wish I could have them myself, but I don't know how. I admire you, Commander! You must be very smart and able to have so many diplomas!" replied the Secretary, waving his hand in front of the several diplomas on the wall surrounding Lenin's and Brezhnev's portraits. Quickly changing the subject, he continued. "I had to come early this morning because I still have too much paperwork to finish. Last night I left late and still could not finish because I was dead tired. I'll see if by noon I can finish it all. I don't want to stay another evening trapped behind that mountain of papers!"

"*Ochen' khorosho*. That's the way I like my people working! That's the way a true Communist should work, sacrificing his own rest hours, if necessary, to finish his work. Lieutenant, sometimes I ask myself if we really need all that paperwork for the good functioning of the base. At least you're done with the Order of the Day, aren't you?"

"Yes. It's on my desk."

"Very well. Bring it so I can sign it. By the way, about those diplomas, son, all you have to do is to keep on working hard, study a lot on military tactics and command, Marxist-Leninist politics, history and ideology of the Party, and above all, always be a good Communist, loyal to the Party. Don't forget to put the Party above everything else and, who knows, perhaps someday you too may become a base Commander like me. You're still young and have a long and bright future before you."

"*Spasibo bol'shoye,* Commander. So I hope. I'll study more and harder to become a better Communist," Dubov replied, thinking: *If the Colonel entered his office two minutes earlier, by now I'd be under arrest.*

✳   ✳   ✳   ✳

"Let's see, Alyosha. What did you get out of those plans?" Mikhail asked.

Stretching his legs and arms as long as they were, and yawning as wide as he could, Alexey took his briefcase and pulled out several papers and navigation charts. Spreading the documents on the table before him, he looked at his watch, yawned once again, and complained. "I didn't sleep the whole night just copying those damn plans. We had to fly this morning. Tonight it's already forty past midnight, and I'm still up. I haven't slept in almost two days! I think I'm going to fall asleep right here, right now. That's what I got out of those plans."

"Stop complaining and tell us what will happen in the maneuvers," Mikhail insisted.

"Well, here I have the list of participating regiments," said Alexey, then read:

NAVY OF THE SOVIET UNION
RED BANNER NORTHERN FLEET
NAVAL AVIATION

"Cut the shit and get to the point!" Anatoly complained.

"*Ladno,*" said Alexey, then he read the list:

OKEAN MANEUVERS
LIST OF PARTICIPANTS

392nd ODRAP (Kipelovo)

Commander:
Major Arkadiy Ivanovich Krasnosyel'skih (Leading Aircraft)
Major Vitaly Sergheyevich Goncharov (Led Aircraft)

967th ODRAP (Olenyegorsk)

Commander:
  Major Viktor Pavlovich Kazantsev (Leading Aircraft)
  Major Vadim Gheorghievich Galenko (Led Aircraft)

364th ODRAP (Kuzomen)

Commander:
  Lt. Col. Leonid Ivanovich Rudenko (Testing Aircraft)

"As you heard, it's two crews from each regiment in Kipelovo and Olenye-gorsk in one leading and one led aircraft, respectively. Our regiment will send only one crew, and it's dead last," Alexey finished reading.

"And as you heard, that one crew is not us. We will not participate," Yuri said.

"Right. Only the Regiment Commanders crews, precisely. But depending on what possibilities the maneuvers offer us, we could try to get in them or not," Mikhail said.

"Get in them? How!" Jonas asked.

"As I said, it depends on what they have to offer us, Yonka," Mikhail answered. Turning to Alexey, he asked: "Alyosha, how will they be conducted?"

"They'll take a whole day, from dawn till dusk."

"What's their purpose?" Vasily asked.

"The same thing of always. Test new equipment, new defense and attack techniques to see how the Navy and Navy Aviation would react in such cases. In brief, measure the state of alert and readiness of the naval forces."

"Where will they take place?" Yuri asked.

"They'll cover from the Norwegian Sea to the Mediterranean, although most of the action will be in the Central Atlantic Ocean."

Pointing on the maps at the locations he mentioned, Alexey continued: "Most of the forces will be in this area, from Iceland to a point northeast of the Azores."

"How nice! Back to the Azores!" commented Anatoly.

"Right. Three major groups will participate. On the Atlantic side there will be two groups. Group One will be made by the Northern Fleet. Group two, by the Baltic Fleet. Those two groups will represent, on the one hand, an attacker coming from the Azores; on the other hand, a defender in the area around Iceland which will protect the northern ports."

"Which group will our Regiment be in?" asked Mikhail.

"It will be in Group One, the defenders. Group Three will be made by the Black Sea Fleet. This group will be covering from the Bosphorus to Gibraltar. It will guarantee the free access of the Navy ships to the area ports, and also eliminate any interference by enemy ships trying to enter, or already in, the Mediterranean."

Smoothing his hair, Alexey yawned once again and continued his detailing of the maneuvers. "The Pacific Fleet will watch Asia from Japan to Yemen, reporting to Vladivostok and Kalinin any maritime movement there, neutralizing it if necessary."

"Some maneuvers they've planned!" said Pavel

"Yes. They're the biggest maneuvers planned by the Navy so far."

"What part will our Regiment have in them, and where does it fly to?" Vasily asked.

"In cooperation with the TU-22 from Arkhanghelsk, the TU-16 from Severomorsk, the TU-26 from Olenyegorsk, the Ilyushin 38 from Ponoy, and the Beryev 12 from Pechenga, they'll open the initial phase making reconnaissance flights, localizing any ship or submarine in the attackers area, then retransmitting that information to Group One, which will meet them."

"Mmm ... interesting ..." Mikhail mumbled.

"Our Long-range airplanes will overfly the Central Atlantic Ocean. Short range planes will overfly the northern European coast. Southern Europe and the Mediterranean will be overflown by the planes in Group Three."

"That means they will fly to the Azores," Mikhail said.

"Yes. Taking off from Kipelovo, Olenyegorsk, and Kuzomen they'll fly down Norway, Iceland ..."

"It's almost like our normal flight routes!" Vasily exclaimed.

"Right. Except that from Iceland the crews from Kipelovo will continue flying past Greenland, down the eastern coast of North America, then land in Cuba."

"Cuba?" Vasily asked, grimacing.

"Yes, to our Cienfuegos base there," answered Alexey. "The aircraft from Olenyegorsk will fly to the Azores, then down to Angola, Africa."

"What about Rudenko's plane?" asked Vasily.

"Col. Rudenko's plane returns to base."

"By the way, how come his is the only plane flying from here, and alone at that?" Asked Pavel.

"Yes, and why only his plane returns to base?" asked Anatoly.

"Because the planes from Kipelovo will join him on the way to the Atlantic. Once over the maneuvers area they'll test a new acquisition, targeting and control radar."

"A new radar?" Anatoly and Pavel asked at the same time.

"Yes, the *'Korshun.'* They say it's an improved version which will solve most of the guidance and control problems of our current *'Uspekh'* radars."

"I suppose we'll test it against the NATO ships in the area, right?" asked Pavel.

"Wrong. They'll test it against our own ships. Then, depending on the results, they would be installed in all our new long-range reconnaissance planes, as standard equipment."

"That means it will be installed in our plane too," Anatoly added.

"No, only in the new Tu-142M's at Kipelovo."

"So, how are they going to test that radar?" asked Pavel

"Yes, especially if they're going to install it only on TU-142s," added Anatoly

"We're not going to have it. In our regiment only Col. Rudenko's plane will have it installed. They'll test it."

"Only *Red 57*?" asked Pavel.

"Yes. Not only that. As I said before, his is the only airplane returning to the Union. The others will continue flying down to Cuba and Angola."

"Hold on a second! That's more than eight thousand kilometers already! If he's not flying to Cuba, will he have enough fuel for the return flight? If they don't do something there to fix that, he won't have enough fuel to reach Murmansk, much less Kuzomen," Yuri noted.

"Yes. Here, by Scotland, they will have an in-flight refueling. Then they'll return to base."

"Tyshto! Some flight!" exclaimed Pavel.

"Da. It'll be long. Almost eleven thousand kilometers," said the navigator.

"Eleven thousand kilometers! They'll be flying the whole damn day!" exclaimed Anatoly.

"Unfortunately, yes. Seventeen hours in flight," replied Alexey.

Hearing that, Anatoly grimaced.

"That route looks very attractive to reach Scotland," said Mikhail.

"Well, it's just a matter of knowing which route is the best, when the possibilities of coordination, discovery, and interception are taken into account, and compared one with the others," said Alexey.

"Right," added Jonas. "For example, knowing where each plane or ship will be at any given moment, we could calculate the best moment to initiate the escape."

"Let's see the possibilities of reaching Scotland," suggested Pavel.

"In my own opinion, almost nil. As a matter of fact, during the maneuvers we'll have less opportunities to arrive there than during our regular flights in that same zone. During our routine flights we're under the control of the base, at the most, and usually all we have flying around us is the led TU-95. During the maneuvers we'll have all the ships of the Northern and Baltic Fleets floating around us! Not to mention the control from Murmansk and Leningrad," explained Alexey.

"Not only that," added Vasily. "You said there will be Ilyushin 38, TU-16, 22, and 26 flying together with us. That means the air around us will be boiling with all that aerial activity. How will we make a wrong movement without being noticed? And worse yet: to escape!"

"Tell me something, Pavel," Mikhail asked the technician. "Those will be military maneuvers, right?"

"Right."

"What do you think the British, the Americans, the Norwegians, the Swedish, the French, and practically everybody else that has even a rowboat there, will be doing?"

"Watching everything, I suppose."

"Right. And what else?"

"Well, they'll be ready to confront any unusual circumstance."

"Right. So, the second they see something strange happening, their planes will come to see what's going on. If they're watching everything, and suddenly one of our airplanes enters their air space, do you know what would happen to that plane?"

"It would be erased from the sky in the blink of an eye," was the concise answer of the technician.

"That's if it gets to reach British air space, for example. Remember that a lot of our own airplanes will be flying around us there. If they see you doing crazy things, they'll blow you up with no questions asked," added Mikhail. "In this phase of the maneuvers we can discard Scotland."

"Listen! Even if we get around there flying by ourselves," said Anatoly, "we'll be in the same situation. Remember that the last time we discussed this subject, we had to discard Scotland because of the radar scanning. It's too watched down there! Scotland offers no possibility at all!"

"Anatoly's right," added Mikhail. "Even if we get close, there's no human way we'll reach that place in one piece."

"Well? What do we do then? From there they go to the Azores, then back to Iceland for the refueling," said Alexey.

"Anyway. What's the purpose of the flight to the Azores?" asked Vasily.

"All three planes will locate and classify all the ships in the area. That information will be retransmitted to our submarines near Iceland."

"After that, what else?" Mikhail asked.

"The defenders will enter the scene. If the new equipment works as it should, they will be able to destroy the attackers using surface-to-surface missiles using the information gathered and transmitted by the TU-95s by the Azores. Then the four planes from Kipelovo and Olenyegorsk will proceed to Cuba and Angola, respectively, and Col. Rudenko's plane will return here," Alexey answered.

"I don't like that continuation flight to Cuba," said Vasily.

"Neither do I ... But, returning to the subject of our interest. For Rudenko the maneuvers will conclude by Scotland, where he'll have an in-flight refueling, then he flies back here, right?" Mikhail asked.

"Right. If we can't go to Scotland when we're around there, then I see only one last possibility. Either we use it and escape, or let it go, return, and remain here forever," said the navigator.

"What possibility is that?" Anatoly asked.

"Speed up to Scotland after the refueling."

"Speed up to Scotland? Do you mean at maximum speed?" asked Vasily.

"Aha," Alexey answered, matter-of-factly.

"Very well, but, what about the radars in the ships there? I'm very sure there will be all kinds of ships there, including INTEL. They'll see us right away!" exclaimed Jonas, alarmed.

After a short, silent pause, Mikhail intervened. "Thinking about it, I came to the same conclusion. The radars in all of our ships will be scanning us all the time. They'd know our exact position at any time."

"Correct. That means they could take care of us anyway. One missile and that's it," said Vasily.

"Mmm ... What about if we not only fly at maximum speed but also at low altitude? That's a sure way to evade a radar!" suggested Ivan.

"That makes sense. At what altitude should we fly?" asked Mikhail.

"I would say twenty or thirty meters high," answered the technician. "That's a very good altitude for radar evasion."

"And very low too. Flying a TU-95 at twenty meters high and at combat speed is not as easy as it seems," Vasily said, not too sure of the validity of Ivan's suggestion.

"I agree with Ivan," said Mikhail. "If we make a low flight once we start to speed up, we'll be too low for the ships radars to see us. If they do, we'll be in their horizon. The radar signals would bounce off the ocean surface, so we'd appear too confused in their screens for them to have an exact reference point. They could detect us only with infrared, and even then still not too clear, since in that equipment we'd be in its horizon too."

"When would it be the best moment to descend?" Vasily asked, partially convinced.

"I'd say some ten to fifteen minutes after the refueling. That's when they think we'd be heading back to base, which we won't do, disappearing from their radars instead," suggested Alexey.

"Agreed. It's a bit risky but it's the only way, for the time being. Perhaps we could improve it later. Will there be fighters around?" Mikhail asked the navigator.

"Don't worry about them. All we'll have will be the Yak-36s from the *'Kiev,'* and they don't have much of a range. If we fly a bit further, we'll be completely out of their range. Don't even worry about the Kamov-25 helicopters on the *'Moskva,'*" said Alexey.

"We'll have to tell them something until we get out of their range. Otherwise they'll ask us where we are and why we're flying so low. If we don't give them a good excuse, they'll start to get nervous and perhaps alert all the ships in the area. They could even send fighters to search for us and make us return!" Vasily said.

"That's true," added Anatoly. "Besides, we'd have all the other planes flying around us."

"I don't know, but I have the feeling that this is our escape window," Anatoly said.

"I agree," added Vasily.

"I agree with you all, comrades. But we have to fly this morning. It's already 0300 and we should be up by 0530. So let's go to bed and rest for a while. We can continue the planning another time," suggested Mikhail.

The men stood up, some of them picking up papers and notes. All of them except one. There was no need to tell Alexey to go to rest. He was already in seventh heaven, fast asleep.

*   *   *   *

A few nights later, the group met again to continue the detailing of the escape plans.

"Captain, I can't continue sneaking in here to discuss these things," Ivan complained. "I'm afraid I'll get caught."

"In that case they'll catch us all, because the other guys also have to sneak in here," said Vasily.

"Don't worry about that, Vanya. That will be for just a few days, until we get everything ready to escape," Mikhail consoled the crewman, then commented, "By the way. What happened last night, downstairs? I heard a horrendous hullabaloo, screaming, curses, people hitting each other. When I woke up to look out the window a group of men from the *Komendatura* was getting off a truck, then took a bunch of people to the brig."

"I'm not too sure about what happened," said Pavel. "When the screaming woke me up it had started already. But I wouldn't be surprised if it was another fight."

"I heard that one of the corporals caught another guy stealing his fur boots," said Ivan.

"And what the devil does that guy want someone else's fur boots for? It's not winter yet," asked Alexey.

"That's precisely why. Since it's not winter yet, the other guy wouldn't have realized his fur boots had disappeared. Then the thief keeps them since he probably already sold his. It's that, or he'd sell them in the black market. You know they pay good money for fur boots in good shape," Anatoly explained.

"Most probably that's what happened," said Pavel.

"That of the fights, the thefts, and the mutinies will never end. I don't think it's the men's fault that those things happen here. It's this rotten system," Mikhail said. Looking at his watch, he noted the time: 0030. *"Posmotrim.* Last discussion we had was about the flight plan with refueling."

"Right. Here I have it," Alexey said, opening his briefcase and pulling out the flight plans he had already drawn. "We could have an opportunity to escape after the in-flight refueling. We could speed up to Scotland at some twenty meters high."

"Right," Vasily said. "However, I see two big problems there. First of all, for that to happen we have to participate in the maneuvers, which we will not do. Plus, to come back to base we have to physically *be* in Col. Rudenko's plane. How are we going to do all that?"

"That's impossible!" exclaimed Jonas. "There's no way he'll let us fly *Red 57*. You know how picky he is with his plane."

"And much less with the new radar already installed," added Pavel.

"Right," Ivan agreed.

"Wrong!" Anatoly disagreed. "Difficult, perhaps, but not impossible."

"He's right. Nothing is impossible," Alexey said. "We thought that getting the *Okean* plans was practically impossible, and see, we got them," said the navigator, smiling.

"*Ladno,*" said Ivan. "How are we going to get in that plane?"

"We don't have to," said Anatoly.

"What do you mean?" asked Jonas.

"Think about it. We want to be in that plane because it's the only one returning to base. Right?" Anatoly asked.

"Right" voices said in unison.

"Now: *Why* is it coming back to base?" Anatoly asked again. "Because it's the only one having the '*Korshun*' radar," he answered his own question, paused, then continued: "Now, if we somehow get the radar installed on *Red 67* instead of *Red 57*, then *we* participate in the maneuvers *and* we have to come back to base."

"Killing two birds with one stone," Mikhail agreed.

"HA!" burst Jonas. "Now you've gone from practically impossible to definitely impossible!"

"Yes, I want to see how we're going to pull that one!" agreed Pavel.

"You of all people should know that, Pavlik," said Anatoly.

"ME?" asked the technician, surprised.

"Yes, you. Let's see: What do we need to participate in the maneuvers?" asked Anatoly.

"I don't know. The radar, I suppose," replied Pavel.

"Right, and if we have it installed in our plane, that guarantees our participation, right?" Anatoly continued asking.

"Yes, but that's precisely the point. How are we going to have the electronic maintenance guys install a brand-new radar, no less, in our plane?" Pavel asked again.

"Pavlik, Pavlik, don't we go there all the time to tell them our problems with the equipment and fill up those lengthy reports detailing the smallest quirk we noticed in them?"

"Yes, but that doesn't mean that we can go there and tell them: 'hey guys, the new radar, the one Col. Rudenko's plane is supposed to have, we want you to install it in our plane.'"

"True, but we can go there and in the same way that we got them to do some 'special work' for us before, well, we could get them to install it in our plane," Anatoly said.

"As I said before: I want to see how you'll pull that one out," said Pavel.

Turning to Mikhail, Anatoly reassured the group. "Don't worry, Captain. Leave that to me. I have ways to make them do that," he said, winking.

"And what if once they have it installed in *Red 67*, Col. Rudenko blows his top and orders them to uninstall it from our plane and reinstall it in his?" asked Alexey.

"Yes, you know what kind of *mudak* he is," added Ivan.

"No, it takes several days to install and test it. Once it's installed, I doubt he'd want it uninstalled and reinstalled in his plane," Pavel explained.

"Yes, especially if the installation and testing is finished one or two days before the maneuvers," Anatoly added. "There's no way that Commander Degtyaryov is going to let him do that so close to the date of the maneuvers. That would mean no plane from the 364th ODRAP is going to participate in them. And you know how much those things mean to the *nachal'stvo*."

"Understood," Alexey agreed, thinking about the many chances for promotions, prizes, and awards that excellent participation in naval maneuvers represented to those involved.

"By the way, how are you going to avoid Rudenko noticing that they're not working in his plane, installing the new radar?" asked Jonas.

"Very simple, Yonka. Since his plane is going to be out of commission for several days while they install it, they can't fly. Plus, his radar operator, Lt. Rybakov, will be in Leningrad, training on the new radar. So, he gave his crew all that time off. He himself is leaving to visit his family," Anatoly responded Jonas' question.

"Well, assuming that you're able to make the switch, which I honestly doubt," Vasily intervened, "That would solve our two most immediate problems: participating in the maneuvers in the plane that returns to Kuzomen. However, I see another situation here."

"What's that?" asked Anatoly.

"If they replace the *'Uspekh'* radar with the new *'Korshun'*, who's going to test it in flight? *You?*" Vasily asked. "You and your radar would be replaced together, which means we'd have to leave you behind. And there's no way we can escape without you, and especially with a second danger aboard."

"A second danger?" asked Jonas.

"Yes, a second danger. Lieutenant Molotko is our first danger aboard. The second danger would be the radar operator, Lieutenant Rybakov, since he's Col. Rudenko's controller for the *'Uspekh.'* And he's going to be trained in its use, so they'd have to assign him to fly with us. We already have enough problems with the first *mudak* aboard to add another one."

Vasily's concern made everyone in the small room look at each other's worried faces, searching for a solution.

"Still, I have ways to get around that. Just give me some time to see how I can tie up all this together. Trust me," said Anatoly. His words seemed to relax those present. Then he continued: "Comrades, we've planned an escape to Scotland. I suppose that's because Britain is the nearest NATO country we can go to."

"Right," confirmed Mikhail.

"We'll be flying a few hundreds kilometers from Iceland. So, why not just land there instead?"

"Because of the same reasons we don't go to Sweden or Finland. In Iceland they have the same laws as in those two countries," replied Vasily.

"I understand the Americans have an air base there," Anatoly said again.

"Yes, Keflavík. But that doesn't mean that air base is America. In our case, Iceland's laws would still apply, even if we eventually land at that base. Do you know what would happen if we land there?" Vasily asked Anatoly.

"No. What would happen?"

"We'd be interned, jailed, and then, after some time, freed to be kicked out of the country," Vasily answered his own question.

"I understand your reasons. However, in that flight to Scotland I'm seeing something I don't like," Anatoly said, frowning.

"What's that?" asked Mikhail.

"Look. Once they realize we've disappeared from their radars, and taking into account that they know that in our case Iceland is useless for us to request political asylum, the most logical place for them to start searching is Scotland. That's NATO's closest ally."

"*Tak,* what do you suggest?" asked Alexey.

"That before we streak to Scotland at low height, we *visibly and directly* turn towards Scotland. Then, after a time long enough to make sure they have seen us heading there, we descend, make a hundred eighty degrees turn, and speed up towards America," concluded Anatoly.

"America!" exclaimed Vasily. "You're crazy! America's too far! By the time we get half way there, we'd be discovered!"

"How will they see us?" replied Anatoly. "We'd be flying too low for them to see us in their radars."

"I don't know! Anyway. I don't like the idea of running to America. As if escaping to Scotland weren't risky enough!"

"No, Vasya. I think I understand what Tolya has in mind," Mikhail intervened. "If we fly to Scotland, they'd have enough time to alert the ships patrolling the area. By the time we reach that country, they could have missiles ready to shoot us down. That's if they don't send supersonic fighters instead."

"Exactly!" said Anatoly. "But if we turn to Scotland when they still see us, we'll give them the false impression that we're heading there, when in reality we're heading to America. Of course, everything should be done following the original plan."

"What do you mean? I don't understand," said Alexey.

"Listen. In the original plan we head back to the Union for a few minutes, then we turn towards Scotland. Now, we let them see us for a time long enough, then we descend, get lost from their radars, and turn towards America at maximum speed. It's important that they see us heading towards Scotland. Once en route to America, we should avoid detection by all means," Anatoly explained his suggestion again.

"It could be like that," said Mikhail. "If we head to America instead of Scotland, they'll never suspect we're heading in the opposite direction."

"I think that could be our definite escape plan," said Alexey. "With this fake escape to Scotland we'll have enough time to reach America at combat speed."

"Hold on one second!" exclaimed Yuri, calling the group's attention.

"Yes, Yura," Mikhail said. The group gave Yuri their undivided attention.

"Tolya, you know your radars and your electronic equipment very well. My congratulations. But when the matter is flying the plane, that's something else. Every time we descend from cruise altitude to lower heights, fuel consumption increases tremendously. The lower we are, the more fuel will be consumed. If we put those engines to push us at maximum speed and minimum height, they'll swallow almost triple the fuel they'd use flying the same distance at cruise altitude."

Everyone paid listened attentively to the technical details provided by the Flight Engineer. "In the flight to Scotland I didn't mention that fact because, since it's a short flight, fuel consumption wouldn't be critical, especially flying with full tanks after the refueling. By the time we'd reach Scotland, we'd still have enough fuel for a few more hours in flight. Now, America is a totally different matter. America would be at some two thousand kilometers from the refueling point. If we follow the plan as it has been laid out, there's a possibility that we could reach even the United States themselves, with fuel remaining for a few more hours of flight. That is counting in the detour to Scotland and flying at maximum speed. Even then, if that detour is for only one thousand kilometers, we'd have spent enough fuel to fly three thousand kilometers, and we'd still have enough fuel to reach America … *as long as nothing happens in the way*," emphasized the Engineer. "In other words, if for any reason we have to deviate from the planned route, or if we have to accelerate to that speed and descend to that height again, it's very probable we'd have to ditch the plane."

The group grew silent. Up to that moment no one had taken into account the problem of fuel consumption.

"In my opinion, I'm still for the flight to America," Anatoly debated his point of view. "The probabilities of reaching America in one piece are more than those of reaching Scotland in the same condition. In the area around Scotland it would be easier for them to find us and blow us up. And that would never be under our control. In the case of America, finding us would be harder, so we could reach it, albeit with fuel tanks almost empty. Besides, in that case we'd have more control of the situation, since to get there we'd only have to be thrifty with the fuel."

"It's a matter of heading to Scotland with the possibility of being discovered, or heading to America with the possibility of not reaching it," said Vasily.

"That's as if they were asking me: 'How do you want to die, in the wolf's mouth, or in the bear's hug?" said Alexey.

"Despite the risk, I'd still go to America," said Pavel. "If we're discovered on the way to Scotland, we'd be blown up for sure. If we ditch the plane in the Atlantic, we'd still survive. A passing ship might pick us up."

"I agree with Pavel," added Mikhail. "I prefer to ditch in the sea than be ripped apart by a missile. Besides, that of ditching the plane is if we get to deviate somewhere else in the way to America, otherwise we'd get there, wouldn't we?"

"Yes, that's so. I think Anatoly's right. I think it's preferable to reach America, after all," said Ivan.

"Well, Yuri. What do you think?" Mikhail asked.

"Well, if all agree to head to America under those circumstances, I have no objections."

"I share that opinion," said Vasily.

The group turned to Jonas who, as usual, was the last one to decide. "Yonka, what do you decide? Do you agree?" asked Mikhail.

"Whatever the experts say, that's what I'll do."

"Agreed," concluded Mikhail. Turning to the navigator, he ordered, "Alyosha, draw a flight plan based on the refueling, the dash to Scotland, and the flight to America."

"Understood, Captain."

"By the way, aren't we forgetting something?" asked Vasily.

"What?" asked the group in unison.

"The autodestruct system. If after a prudent time we're not clear with the base, they'll simply blow us up. And there's nothing we could do to avoid that!"

"Yes, there must be something we could do!" Mikhail interrupted his copilot. Turning to Anatoly, he asked. "Tolya, those systems are detonated by remote control, based on a radio signal, right?"

"Yes. A high frequency signal detonates them," Anatoly responded.

"Therefore, if it's a radio signal, it can be jammed, right?"

"Right."

"So we could use the plane's electronic jamming equipment and jam the signal, so it never reaches the receiver."

"Well. In theory that would be possible. But that's in theory. In reality they already thought about that same scenario and designed the damn system in such a way that it receives signals in only one frequency, which I don't know. All I know about it is that it's very high, beyond the limits of most jamming equipment."

"You don't know it?" asked Ivan. "Because if you knew it perhaps we could jam it."

"That's exactly what I just said. I don't know it. Only the technician in charge of that system, the Base Commander, and the Base Political Commander know it. Besides, if I knew it, I'd have already suggested something about it."

"Captain, do you have anything to do with that system?" asked Alexey.

"With the system itself, yes; but not with its frequency. That I don't know. All I have is the responsibility of initiating the countdown to detonate the explosive charge when the system is activated manually. I have a key that I insert in a special panel. Then I push a red button that starts a countdown long enough to allow the crew enough time to abandon the airplane."

"Jumping out in flight?" Alexey asked again, surprised.

"Yes. Supposedly," Vasily responded his friend's question, referring to how difficult it is to jump out of a TU-95 in flight.

"So if that countdown starts, we jump out of the plane, and get killed outside, or we stay inside and get killed when it blows up," said Alexey.

"Correct," said Vasily.

"Killed by the wolf, or killed by the bear, again!" said Alexey, dispirited.

"Exactly, Alyosha. Hey, you're getting good at this!" Vasily said again.

"Enough of this talk, Alyosha," said Mikhail, bringing the youngest member of the crew back to the problem at hand. "I wonder if there's a way to find out that frequency."

"I don't know if there's a way, but at least we could try to find out," said Anatoly.

Mikhail remained silent for a few seconds, thinking. Then asked: "And once we have the frequency?"

"Then it's just a matter of seeing how we could jam it," answered the technician.

"How?" asked Alexey.

"Well, that's another story altogether. We can not jam it ourselves. That I know as a fact," said Anatoly.

"And how are we going to avoid that signal? If they push the transmitter's button, *do svidanya!*" exclaimed Vasily.

"In my opinion, I think we should worry about jamming the signal after we find out its frequency. If we don't know that, we will not be able to jam it," Jonas said with an air of expertise.

"I agree," said Pavel. "We should find a way of getting that frequency."

"Besides the Commanders, who else knows that frequency?" Mikhail asked.

"As far as I know, here in the base only the Commanders and the technician," Anatoly answered.

"And of course, we can't ask the Commanders," noted Alexey.

"That leaves only the technician," Mikhail said again. "Do you think he'll be easy to tackle?" Mikhail inquired.

"I think so. He's always in the hangars, checking the equipment. The only problem is that where he works is restricted area. Only he and the Commanders have access there," answered Anatoly.

"And how are we going to talk to him?" asked Alexey.

"I think I know how," said Anatoly. "I know him. I met him once in the town's bar. We were drinking together. He drinks like a sponge! Best of all, when he's drunk he talks like a parrot!" said the Engineer, smiling.

"That gives me an idea! What about this: You 'invite' him to drink, get him drunk, and while he's drunk, you 'ask' him some questions," suggested Mikhail.

"That sounds good. I'm pretty sure he'd appreciate one or two bottles of *samogon*. That's his 'water of life.' He'd never refuse an invitation to drink. However, we'd have to wait for an occasion to do that," replied Anatoly.

"When do you think we could do that? Remember that we're short of time. We have less than two weeks already," Mikhail said.

"I don't know. It has to be on his day off. Otherwise I won't be able to see him."

"When is his next day off?" asked Vasily.

"I don't know that either. I'll have to find out."

"Khorosho. Find that out as soon as possible," said the Captain. Looking at his watch, he noted the time: 0250. "Comrades, it's almost 0300. Let's rest a bit. We fly today."

CHAPTER 5

▼

Yuri, Anatoly, and Pavel arrived at the repair hangars.

"*Leytenanty, dobryy dyen,'* what a nice surprise! Why do we have the honor of your visit?" Senior Sergeant of the Technical Service Vyacheslav Sudaryev greeted the men.

"*Serzhant Sudaryev, dobryy dyen'!*" greeted Yuri. "I just came to thank you personally for the way you repaired those fuel gauges. Finally I am able to calculate *exactly* how much fuel I'm dealing with in the tanks."

"*Pozhaluysta, Leytenant.* It's an honor to work for you guys. Actually, you the crewmen of *Red 67* are the only ones that usually thank us for a job well done on your plane. The others simply grumble an acknowledgment and leave it at that."

"Well, It's the fair thing to do," said Yuri. While the Engineer was making his comments Anatoly's eyes were searching around the area, looking for the enormous crate containing the new *'Korshun'* radar equipment. Wanting to expand his search area, he gave Pavel a sign with his head.

"Sergeant, where's the toilet?" asked Anatoly.

"All the way to the back," answered the sergeant, indicating the general direction to the rear of the hangar.

While Yuri continued engaging Sergeant Sudaryev in conversation, Anatoly and Pavel walked towards the rear of the hangar, then furtively sneaked out to find the radar.

Finally, in a large crate, by a wall, the technicians found the object of their search. The wooden box, sporting the name and city of its designing office, was verified by the technicians:

Ministry of the Radio Industry
Aviation Electronic Equipment Production
196066 City of Leningrad
Moskovskiy Prospekt, 212
OKB № 283 named 'Leninets'
Equipment RLS 'Korshun'
Equipment EVM 'Orbita-260'
Art. AEO-ChKh9234538

"Well, I suppose this is the real thing," Anatoly said.

"Yes. Now, how are we going to get the sergeant to install it in our plane? After all, you were the one who said you could do it," Pavel said.

"Posmotrim ... First, we must find the working files for the planes," Anatoly said, looking around for possible locations for the files in question.

"They have to be in files cabinets somewhere around here," Pavel said, also stretching his neck in the search.

Seeing a row of file cabinets by a wall on the far side of the hangar, a few meters away from them, the two technicians calmly walked to the rear. The other mechanics in the hangar, busy as they were working in a TU-95 RTs under repair, simply ignored them as they walked under the enormous fuselage.

"This is it? Just *five* file cabinets?" Pavel asked, surprised.

"Well, here there are only twelve TU-95s and two AN-2 for liaison," said Anatoly.

"*One* AN-2. Remember that one was demolished day before yesterday," corrects Pavel.

"Yes, one. So there are not that many airplanes to keep track of. Now, what it says on these drawers ..." Anatoly said as he approached the file cabinets. On each drawer, a label identified its contents. Then he read the labels:

"*Red 17 ... Red 23 ... Red 42 ... Red 42*, mmm...." Anatoly repeated as he tapped the label, then continued reading. "... *Red 57*, Col. Rudenko's plane ... *Red 67*, that's us ... *Red 69 ... Red 75 ... Red 88 ... Red 95* ... Perfect! Now all we have to do is find the '*Korshun*' install order and switch it from Rudenko's plane to ours!"

"And how are we going to do that, opening all the drawers and pulling their contents out? We can't do that!" Pavel complained. "They see us doing that and we could be jailed for espionage!"

Pavel alluded to a white sign with red letters stuck on the wall, above the file cabinets:

ATTENTION

ANYONE FOUND OPENING THESE DRAWERS
AND RETIRING THE DOCUMENTATION CONTAINED HEREIN
WITHOUT THE AUTHORIZATION OF THE OFFICER IN CHARGE
MAY BE ARRESTED AND COURT MARTIALED
UNDER THE CURRENT PENAL CODES
FOR THE CRIME OF ESPIONAGE AGAINST THE SOVIET STATE.

"Pavel, stop being a hen," Anatoly pooh-poohed his friend's fears. "Do you think these guys here care that we're opening them? They're too busy doing their job!" Anatoly said as he knelt, opened *Red 57's* drawer, and walked his fingers among all the folders and documents.

"Engines, Hydraulics, Communications, Electrical … You can't deny that Sergeant Sudaryev runs a tight ship here. It's a joy how neat and ordered he keeps these files!" the technician commented as he searched for the needed documentation, then continued. "… Maintenance logs … Electronics! The order should be in this folder," he said as he pulled the folder out of the drawer.

Carefully reading the documents, Anatoly searched for the 'passport,' the radar's technical documentation. After a few moments at it, he exclaimed, "Found! The passport for the *'Korshun,'* sent from the OKB Leninets, and all its attached papers."

He pulled the document out of the folder for *Red 57,* closed its drawer, opened the drawer for *Red 67* and placed it in the same folder location for the latter.

"Now, for the installation order …" On top of the file cabinet, duly kept, rested a clipboard with the many work orders for the different technical departments in the hangar. Leafing through the papers, Anatoly found the installation order for the *'Korshun.'* The technician verified that the order had Cdr. Degtyaryov's signature, then pulled his pen from his breast pocket, and in one single stroke changed the receiving plane's number from *Red 57* to *Red 67.*

"There we are. That will make sure that radar will be installed in our plane."

"Tolya! We can't do that! They're seeing us!" exclaimed a visibly agitated Pavel.

"We can't? We just did!" Anatoly said as he returned the clipboard to its place on the file cabinet.

With the same *sang froid* that he approached the file cabinets, opened their drawers, and changed the document, Anatoly turned around and left.

Pavel felt his legs become rubber. Thick sweat beads dropped from his forehead. "Tolya, I think this time we went too far. We still have a lot to prepare to get out of here, and when they find out that we changed the install order, we'll be arrested for sure!"

Anatoly looked at Pavel, placed his hand on his shoulder, smiled, and reassured him: "Then we'll be arrested together!"

As they walked towards the hangar gate, Pavel tried to regain his composure before he approached Yuri and Sergeant Sudaryev, who were still conversing.

Yuri, seeing the two men coming back, placed his sight squarely on Anatoly's eyes, silently questioning him about the success of the mission. The technician responded the question with a slight positive nod of his head.

"Well, Sergeant, as I said before, it's a pleasure to have you in charge of the maintenance of our plane. Even though they say that the team handling Col. Rudenko's plane is the best here, I still feel yours is the best."

"Spasibo bol'shoye, tovarishch leytenant! It's good to hear those encouraging words once in a while. They mean a lot to me and my team!" said the Senior Technical Sergeant, his wide smile going from ear to ear.

"Do svidaniya, Serzhant Sudaryev!" All three men shook Sudaryev's hand. Sudaryev couldn't help but noticing how cold Pavel's hand was, and the ashen look in his face: *"Leytenant* Krylov, are you alright? You look like you're about to die!"

"No. Lately I've been feeling indisposed. It must have been something I ate," said the nervous man. Immediately the other two men turned and left the hangar, followed by Pavel.

Outside the hangars, Yuri asked: "Pavlik, are you alright? You look like a ghost! What happened back there?"

"I suppose I am alright," Pavel replied, holding his belly ... then ran towards the hangar outside wall, where in one single and violent eruption he emptied the contents of his stomach.

As they walked to the Lenin Hall for that week's 'Political Hour,' amid laughs, Anatoly let the Flight Engineer know the reasons for Pavel's sudden illness.

*   *   *   *

Lenin Hall. During the political session conducted by the Regiment Deputy Political Commander, Lt. Col. Nikitin, Mikhail made some comments: "I think it's ridiculous that they allow the free entrance of liquors in the base. It's a business that is not only illegal, but also dangerous."

"I understand very well the dangers of the liquor smuggling," replied Nikitin. "There are, however, other priorities we should take into account, other problems more acute and more important to tackle before we solve small problems like that one, Comrade Captain Makarov. The Party can not worry about solving the problems in this base when it still has the problems of the whole Union to solve!"

"But that's precisely where you're mistaken! The way to solve the big problems is solving the small problems first. They are the same all over! You know as well as I do that liquor smuggling is the biggest business in the whole country. Even the officers take part in it!" Mikhail answered back. His amazed crew only listened, worried. It was that defiant attitude that took Mikhail to those encounters and clashes with the Party that practically destroyed his career.

"Captain Makarov! Are you suggesting the Party is ruling the country wrongly?" Nikitin asked, scandalized.

"Not precisely wrong as a whole, but it's mistaken. The Party must acknowledge the individuality of man. That a single man is as valuable as a million men. If they eliminate the causes for which one single soldier gets drunk, they'd eliminate the causes for which a whole military base gets drunk, which is against regulations, anyway," Mikhail replied.

"Captain, I know the regulations by heart, it's not necessary for you to remind me. Besides, What's the big deal if a soldier gets drunk? Doesn't he have the right?"

"*One* soldier, that's nothing. But a whole base? Besides, drunk while on duty? That way he endangers his life and the lives of those around him. Too many accidents have happened here already because of drunk soldiers. Don't forget what happened on runway 14 just two days ago, or more recently yet: what happened this morning in the hangars."

Hearing this, everyone recalled both incidents. Two days before, an Antonov AN-2 at the head of runway 14B, waiting for its turn to take off, started the take off run without tower authorization, running right in front of a TU-95 that had already landed and was crossing runway 14B, on its way to the dispersion area.

Fortunately, neither one of the planes was aloft. The smaller AN-2 got in front of the larger plane, before the amazed and astonished eyes of its pilots. However, the 5.5-meters-long propellers of the TU-95's engine number one cleanly sliced the tail of the AN-2, turning it into aluminum scrap. The small airplane's cockpit came to rest on the runway side, a mess of aluminum, wires, and cables.

The immediate investigation revealed that both pilots of the AN-2 had spent the night before drinking. By morning they were so drunk that they couldn't stand on their feet, much less fly an airplane.

In the second incident, that morning, in the repair hangars, one of the sergeants of the technical services, drunk to a stupor, worked in the console of the main ventral radar of one the huge Tupolevs. In his torpor, the man turned the radar on and increased its power to the maximum. The intense microwave radiation emanating from the powerful control radar enveloped a corporal, also from the technical services, who was working under the antenna. His dark-green uniform spontaneously burst into flames.

Fortunately for all, the fire could be contained before it killed the technician or reached the fuel tanks in the airplane's wings or the oil and alcohol barrels stored just a few meters from the burning man.

Results: In the first incident, two propeller sets completely destroyed in the TU-95, an AN-2 demolished and ready for the scrap heap, and two drunk pilots in the brig and ready for court martial. In the second incident, a man almost dead, horribly burned, and a drunk sergeant jailed and waiting for trial.

Reviewing both incidents, even though everyone knew that those guilty were to be severely punished, they couldn't help but support Captain Makarov's criticisms a hundred percent. But they also knew that here in the base they would not only not pay any attention to him, as usual, but also that no one would stop the drunkenness, the thefts, the muggings, the fights, or the brawls, for several reasons.

The very first reason was that the main person responsible for the smuggling of liquors into the base was the Political Commander himself, Col. Yakovlev. He shared his profits with all the other officers, starting with his own superior, the base Commander, Colonel Degtyaryov. His helper, the Deputy Political Commander assigned to the 364th ODRAP, Lt. Col. Nikitin, present here in this political indoctrination session, as well as the Military Commander of the regiment, Col. Rudenko, also profited from the enterprise.

Everyone knew that, as long as those officers were making money out of the situation, it would not stop, that everything would continue unchanged until they felt like stopping it, or until the *nachal'stvo* in Murmansk intervened and ordered them to stop. However, both possibilities presented very remote chances of happening.

"I haven't forgotten what happened with the mechanics or on the runway," said Nikitin. "If you notice, Captain, those responsible for both incidents are already in jail. They are the only ones guilty and now they'll pay for their crimes."

"You don't understand or you make us believe you don't understand," said Mikhail. "This shame will not stop because you arrest a poor drunk soldier. You should arrest those who bring in the liquor, not only here, but in each and every military base in the whole Union, starting with the main bosses of the contraband."

Hearing that, Nikitin lost his patience. "Captain Makarov, I think I've heard enough of your complaints! I've told you time and again that my work is to train our men in political matters. Your complaints about arrested drunkards take them to your Commander, not to me. Besides, I consider your constant interruptions very bothersome. I'll have to write a report about that!" Nikitin yells, standing up.

Springing up, Mikhail yelled back. "Do whatever you feel like doing! About my complaints on what is happening here, write a whole book if you wish! So many things happen here every day that you'll have enough material to fill two hundred pages!"

Everyone listened in silence how the only one of them with enough courage to speak up, demanded better living conditions in the base.

As he sat down, Mikhail saw his crewmen sitting behind him. With one single nod of his head he asked them about their mission in the repair hangars.

Yuri replied with a positive nod.

*   *   *   *

Next afternoon, on his way to Headquarters, Mikhail asked himself why the Political Commander asked to talk to him. Once in his office, Col. Yakovlev filled him in.

"Captain Makarov, the sentries on the night shift have noticed that lately the lights in your room go off very late."

Mikhail felt cold chills run along his back. However, he remained rigid and firm, standing in attention before the officer.

"On the other hand, the report Lt. Col. Nikitin has sent me about your men is horrendous. The political morale of your men is the lowest in the whole base, and yours in particular is the lowest of the whole crew. And you're the Commander of that airplane! He also notes that during the 'Political Hour' you're constantly attacking Party discipline, making comments and criticisms about what happens here at the base, contradicting and rebutting what he affirms, and when he tries to impose a Communist discipline on your crew, you make all his effort seem in vain."

Mikhail asked himself what else the Colonel knows, and what other things Serghey had spit to Nikitin.

"Captain Makarov, I'd like you to stop whatever it is you're doing so late at night. That's very harmful to your health. You need to rest after those long flights. Besides, I'd like you to improve your political morale and that of your crew. As Captain of *Red 67* it's your duty to the Party, the Navy, and the Motherland, to be responsible for the political training of your men, together with the Deputy Political Commander assigned to your regiment. The military discipline of your crew is your business, and about that we have no complaint whatsoever. That's why we leave it all to you. Communist discipline, however, is as much your business as it is the Deputy's too. That's a matter both of you should work together. However, what happens here at the base is totally unrelated to you. There are officers specifically in charge of that, so leave those matters to them. You are not their superior and only their superior can say if they're doing their job or not. Besides, I don't feel it is fair neither to those officers, nor to their superiors, nor even to your own crew, that you make those inconsiderate criticisms during the 'Political Hour' with everyone present."

Mikhail relaxed a bit even though he still felt slightly tense. He was expecting to hear something more serious, such as about 'Icarus' or about the plans Lieutenant Dubov delivered to Alexey.

"I appeal to you, Comrade. Cooperate with your Deputy Political Commander. For your own good and that of your crew."

"I'll do my best to improve the situation," Mikhail said.

"I hope so. Perhaps *Red 67's* next report will be more satisfactory and show a definite change towards a more patriotic attitude and a more Communist political morale. Otherwise, I'll have to take measures accordingly. That's all, Captain. Dismissed."

On his way to the door, Mikhail thought about the measures the Colonel would have taken if he didn't do something: Political retraining, or worse: disbanding of his crew and his men sent to other planes in the base or to other bases in the Union. He himself could have been shipped anywhere.

Knowing this could have placed Icarus in mortal danger, becoming a hard blow to his escape plans, Mikhail started thinking about the minor changes he'd have to do in the plans, and let the crew know about them.

On the other hand, since it was to his advantage to have the Political Commander, Col. Yakovlev, as well as the Regiment Deputy Political Commander, Lt. Col. Nikitin, quiet and unworried about him, Mikhail decided to stop his attacks on their activities in the black market.

As a matter of fact, it was even more advantageous if he joined their liquor distribution network. As much as he detested to become part of the corruption, if he joined the traffickers for the time it would take him to complete the escape plans, he could make them believe that he didn't care about their business anymore, that he became as corrupt as they were, that he wanted to share in the profits, and so dispel any suspicions they might have had about him.

*   *   *   *

The much awaited opportunity for Anatoly to interview the technician of the auto-destruct system receiver came on the following night, when the man enjoyed his day off. Conveniently armed with eight bottles of *samogon*, obtained on credit from the local black market, Anatoly arrived at the warehouse where the technician, *papirosa* in hand, was resting over some boxes.

"*Zdrastvuy*, Pyotr Davidovich! How's it going with you?"

"Hey! *Zdrastvuy*, Anatoly Filippovich! What are you doing here? I thought you'd be in the Lenin Hall, together with the others."

"Well, I just stopped by to see how you're doing. Anyway, here I have some bottles to spend a cheerful night."

"What is it?"

"*Samogon*. I know it's better than the *alghidras* you usually drink."

"*Samogon!* I haven't had that in such a long time, that I don't even remember its taste. So much drinking of that damn alcohol has dulled my taste buds for the finer things in life."

With Pyotr happened the same thing that happened to those on the lower end of the scale. Because he spent his monthly salary of five rubles as soon as he got it, buying *samogon*, he was always broke. In the towns around the base the black market prices for real liquor reached relatively exorbitant levels, especially if the drink happened to be vodka or wine. *Samogon* was just the cheapest of all, so the technician had no choice but to buy the 'bottled fire.'

Once he ran out of cash the technician resorted to drink *alghidras*. The chemical was easily obtained from any parked airplane. Since he worked by himself in the hangars, he had no difficulty whatsoever in milking a few liters of the liquid from the storage tanks of the plane he was working on.

Of course, since methanol is not fit for human consumption, its effects on them were predictable. The base had countless cases of blindness, dementia and even death by poisoning, caused by the excessive consumption of the alcohol. Those cases, of course, always went unreported. They'd have looked tremendously bad on the safety record of the base.

"*Nu*, make yourself comfortable and bring those bottles here," demanded the rude *sibiriak*.

Anatoly pulled two boxes, placed one on its side, to use it as a makeshift table, then sat on the other. Taking a bottle each, they pulled the corks with their teeth.

"*Za tvoyo zdorov'ye!*" toasted both men in unison, clicking their bottles. The Siberian downed the first round in one single and long gulp.

"So. What do you say, Anatoly Filippovich?"

"There's not much to say. Waiting for my vacation time to start."

"Yeah, me too. I'll have mine by the end of next month."

"Aha. Mine will be at the beginning. It'll be a change from our routine flights over the Atlantic. They're so long and boring."

"I imagine. Life here isn't precisely the latest in fun," Pyotr said.

"I know. Except when the people in Murmansk remember that here in Kuzomen there's an airbase, and send a music group, a new movie, or something like that. Otherwise here feels like a cemetery."

"Then in the movie hall they make you sick showing the same movies day after day, week after week, until even the badgers and the beavers have seen it three and four times, get bored and never come back. I tell you, if it weren't for the *alghidras*, the *samogon*, and the occasional vodka that falls around here once in a while, one would end in a sanitarium," commented Pyotr.

"Whenever I get a pass, even if it's for only one day, I go to Murmansk. There is more to see there than in this swamp."

"Me too. I go to Murmansk, Arkhanghelsk, Kirovsk, or wherever. Anything is better than being here!"

"Changing subjects. I heard we're getting a new radar system, more powerful, to be installed in our airplanes. Have you heard anything about that?" Anatoly asked, trying to steer Pyotr to the subject of his interest.

"A new radar system? No, I haven't heard anything about it. Who told you that?"

Anatoly remembered that he obtained the information from the plans provided by Lieutenant Dubov and therefore it was restricted information, to which he was not supposed to have access. Trying to momentarily detour the technician's attention to other subjects, Anatoly answered his own question and immediately started a ruse. "No one in particular. That's just a rumor I heard through the grapevine. By the way, I bet you one ruble you can't empty a bottle faster than me!"

"HA! Forget it! You'll never catch me! I can drink not one but three bottles of this without even getting dizzy!" The Siberian praised his own drinking ability.

Although among *sibiriaki* this feat of the bottles is nothing out of this world, however, as a result of the heavy drinking a high-caliber bombing usually showed up as the final result.

Anatoly, seeing that his fish took hook, line, and sinker, continued inciting: "Do you think so? You're on!" Of the six remaining bottles he took two and opened them, gave one to the Siberian and kept one for himself. Once both men were ready, he started the countdown. "Ready? *Raz, dva, tri!*"

Both technicians started to drink straight from the bottles. Anatoly intentionally drank as slowly as he could. Sometimes he only filled his mouth but didn't swallow. Pyotr, on the other hand, swallowed *samogon* like a funnel. The liquid he couldn't swallow just poured out of his mouth, flowed over his thick beard and fell on his chest.

After several seconds in the mad race, Pyotr had already emptied his bottle. Anatoly was only halfway through his, not counting the alcohol he spat from his mouth, plus what he poured behind him.

Laughing, Pyotr placed his empty bottle over the table. "I told you! You can't win a contest of that kind against me! Here's my empty bottle, and yours is still halfway. Give me my ruble!"

"*Pozdravlyayu!* You're a fast drinker. Here you are." Anatoly pulled several coins from his pocket, and made a ruble with them. In his mind, however, he congratulated himself. *Great, Anatoly! Now all you've got to do is wait for the samogon to do its job.*

The men continued drinking from the remaining bottles, albeit more slowly. After several minutes of heavy swallowing, the effects of the contest became noticeable in the radar technician. Anatoly, noting that Pyotr was already talking incoherently and in a muddled voice, brought once again the subject of the radar system.

"Pyotr, that radar system I mentioned before, they told me it could practically beat any radar in service now."

Pyotr couldn't hear him. He was beyond all hopes. Taking advantage of the situation, Anatoly took the initiative and asked: "Pyotr, exactly what kind of work do you do?"

In the foggy brain of the technician, Anatoly's words came as if from another, distant planet. He registered them confused, making no sense. One side of his brain told him, between reason and madness, that it was forbidden for him to talk about his technical duties since they were a military secret. The liquor, however, loosened up all his senses, among them his inhibitions. Feeling like he could stop the whole world with just one finger, Pyotr loosened up his tongue, already made heavy by the fiery drink, and spat all his secrets. "I repair and maintain … ze resheiversh of ze … autodeshtruct shyshtem … I playshe ze exploshive chargesh …" replies the technician in a hardly intelligible voice.

"Those charges I suppose they can be detonated by remote control, right?"

"Yesh … a transhmitter … activates the whole thing."

"Fascinating!" Anatoly feigned fake interest. "Explain to me how exactly the whole system works."

"Very shimple … If you shend a shignal … in the frequenshiesh between … let's shay … ten gigahertz … and …"

Anatoly pulled from his breast pocket paper and pencil, and wrote down all the information supplied so 'willingly' by the technician, with all the details.

Next morning, well after sunrise, Senior Lieutenant Kiprenko, Anatoly Filippovich fell on his bed with the biggest hangover he had ever had. His head hurt as if one hundred hammers were all banging his brain at the same time. He hardly noticed the pain his whole body felt after having spent the whole night sleeping over two boxes in the hangar. All of this, however, did not matter to him. He also had with him the most important information he ever learned in his whole life, information that perhaps could get him and his friends out of the Soviet Union and in the end, perhaps, could also save their lives.

That day he slept like a baby until very late in the afternoon.

✳   ✳   ✳   ✳

When Anatoly entered the Captain's quarters, the whole room was dark. "Hey! What's happening here! Turn that light on!"

"We can't. The night guards reported that the lights here are being turned off late. It has been decided that from now on we'll meet in darkness," said Vasily.

"That's nice! Like owls!" commented Anatoly.

"At least they're wise, as the story says," Vasily replied.

Mikhail asked: "Tolya, could you get anything out of the receiver's technician?"

"Yes. I got all the necessary technical information about the autodestruct system. How it works, frequencies, components, and, very important: its approximate location inside the airplane. Of course, the data is not too specific due to the circumstances in which I obtained it. Even then, I think it's still good enough for our purposes."

"Very well. What can we do with it?" asked Mikhail.

"Just as I thought, the transmitter's frequency is way over the maximum limits of most jamming equipment."

"Then we won't have any possibility of jamming that signal!" Vasily said, worried.

"I didn't say there's no possibility of jamming the signal, only that we can't do it using most jamming equipment," retorted the technician.

"How, then, are we going to jam it?" asked Mikhail.

"That's another story. Since that frequency is so high, we'll have to find a way of getting a transmitter that works in that same frequency."

"And where can we get a transmitter like that?" Mikhail asked once again.

"I don't know," was the technician's terse answer.

"Then how the devil do you expect us to jam the damn signal! Cursing it?" Alexey yelled, displaying his characteristic impatience.

"Take it easy, Alyosha. Don't be so defeatist! There must be a way of jamming that device, one way or another," Mikhail said.

"Tolya, what do you think about getting a transmitter and increasing its power enough to jam the signal?" Pavel suggested.

"Increasing? … Mmm … Perhaps then we could jam it. But, how are we going to do it? For that, first we need a transmitter, then we'd need a power booster, and to build a booster we need parts. Parts that we don't have. Where are we going to get them?"

"What kind of parts do you need?" Mikhail asked.

"All kinds of electronic parts. From simple resistors, diodes, capacitors, tubes, and transistors, to complete oscillating and frequency generating circuits," Anatoly answered.

"If you get similar equipment, would you be able to build the booster using their parts?" Vasily asked.

"To build a booster, we'd need parts from a high frequency equipment, preferably of the same kind as the transmitter itself."

"Of the same kind!? And how do you expect us to get it? Stealing it?" Alexey asked, sarcastically.

"That's a good question, and an equally good answer," said Yuri.

"Come on! Perhaps we could steal it. Let's see. Where are they stored?" Mikhail asked.

"Central Depot, Electronics Section," answered Jonas immediately. "A very well secured and watched section. To get anything from there one must have the report of the technical inspection of the equipment to be replaced signed by at least two technicians, as well as authorization in triplicate signed by the officer in charge. That's assuming we are the technicians in charge of the repair and maintenance of that equipment! In other words, since we are not repair technicians, only the users, we can not even get around there. Only the maintenance technicians have access to that section."

"How do you know all that?" Vasily asked.

"Once I saw the maintenance crews troubleshooting my radar. I saw all the paperwork they had to swim through in order to get just one Direct Current power supply. That made me sick!"

"Then we'll have to discard the possibilities of requesting or stealing anything from there. Does anyone have another idea or suggestion?" Mikhail asked.

"What about bribing one of the maintenance technicians?" suggested Alexey.

"Excellent idea, but we can't. We're broke. We used our last kopek bribing Lieutenant Dubov. We still owe him one thousand two hundred fifty rubles. If we're lucky we'll be able to get out of here before we have to pay him that amount," answered Mikhail.

"Not only that, comrades. You're forgetting that here at the base we don't even have such transmitters as those used for jamming signals. Our planes don't use them," added Vasily. "However, Tolya, you said we need equipment used in signal jamming. Right?"

"Yes, that's right," said Anatoly.

"Now, does it matter what kind it is? I mean, could it be an old one taken from an old plane?"

"I suggested such equipment because it would be the most powerful we could get, in a size comfortable and manageable enough to be able to hide it and later smuggle it in the plane. But any similar equipment could do it. The only thing is that perhaps it wouldn't be powerful enough to jam the autodestruct system's signal. Anyway. We could try using any equipment. What? Do you have one?"

"No, I don't have one. But I know where we could get one," Vasily answered.

"Where?" Mikhail asked, his interest piqued.

"They told me that about two and a half years ago they were ferrying some TU-16s from Severomorsk to some airbase down south, when one of them had troubles and had to land. Suddenly it fell down, almost at the head of Runway 14A. It crashed in the marshes by the river."

"I think that if the equipment in that plane survived the crash, by now it's swimming in a meter and a half of swamp water," said Alexey.

"What makes you think the equipment inside that plane survived the impact? That's delicate equipment!" noted Anatoly.

"Not really. As far as I know, one of the members of the rescue team told me that it was in winter, so the Varzuga was frozen solid. The airplane tail broke on impact with the ice. The front half glided with the wings, falling on its belly on the fresh snow of the river."

"And it didn't blow up?" asked Alexey.

"Well, when it hit the riverbank, the fuselage broke again, the wings and engines became a ball of fire, but the forward fuselage broke away and went sliding until it came to rest among the trees beyond. The rescuer also told me that inside that portion, besides a few broken things here and there, everything was practically intact."

"Any survivors?" asked Mikhail.

"The forward fuselage breaking away from the wings and the engines, and then falling on the fresh snow, saved the lives of the crew inside. Had the plane crashed on dry land or hardened ice they'd have been crushed to death. The pilot died. They could save the copilot, very badly hurt, though. Actually, the pilot didn't die because of the fall itself, but because a tree branch pierced the left side of the cockpit, impaling and killing him on the spot."

"So, according to your story, as far as the crash is concerned the equipment might have survived. But perhaps the maintenance technicians already cannibalized whatever was left there, to use it as spares for other airplanes," said Pavel.

"I don't think so. The difficulty of access to that side of the runway makes it almost impossible for anyone to get there. The rescue team got there after almost two hours of marching through the swamps."

"Did he survive?" asked Alexey.

"I'm not sure. I think he died later, in the hospital. Anyway. Once everything was back in order, the remnants of the plane were left right where they fell. As far as I know, no one ever returned there. I suppose the remains and all its equipment should still be there," Vasily finished his narrative.

"*Khorosho.* Now, I have two questions: First, how do you know that plane had jamming equipment? Two, let's assume the equipment survived the fall and it's still there. How are we going to get there?" asked Alexey.

"It was a TU-16, P version, the electronic warfare type. That answers your first question, Alyosha," said Vasily.

"If the rescue team could get there, so can we," Mikhail emphatically answered the second question.

"Agreed. Now, tell me, how are we going to make sure that equipment still works after all the water, snow, cold, and sun it has taken for the last two and a half years?" Alexey asked again.

"I don't think the rain, the snow, the cold, or the sun could have done more damage than the crash itself. At any rate, if we try to get that equipment out of there, we won't lose much, perhaps a day off, the most. On the other hand, if that equipment is still in good functioning order, or if it's repairable, we'd have a way to jam the autodestruct system's signal," noted Anatoly.

"*Ladno*. Let's see how we can get that equipment out of there," said Mikhail.

"Let's assume we get the equipment and we make the booster. How are we going to smuggle it into the plane without Serghey, the maintenance crews, or anyone outside our group noticing it?" Alexey asked once again.

"Alyosha, we'll worry about that later. First, let's get the equipment," replied Mikhail. Noting the insisting questioning of the young navigator, he asked: "What's happening? Why are you asking so many negative questions? Are you afraid to escape?"

"No, it's not that but exactly the opposite. I'm afraid we won't be able to get the equipment, or that it doesn't work, or that the whole plan will fail and we'll have to remain here."

"Don't worry about that. We'll get out of here one way or another. Alive ... or we'll die trying," Mikhail said, smiling.

"Thank you, Captain. Very kind of you, those comforting words," said the navigator.

"By the way, you have noticed that when American pilots fly around us, some of them become rude and start showing us obscene gestures," Pavel commented.

"*Da*. And we do the same to them!" said Vasily.

"Right. I remember that one of them even mooned some of our crews!" said Alexey.

"Yes, and they mooned him back!" said Pavel, laughing. "But I don't think we should do that when they intercept us. Because they will intercept us when we're about to enter their air space, you know."

"True. We should show respect," said Mikhail.

"I think I have the solution," continued Pavel. "Let's make an American flag. I can show it through one of the observation blisters. That way we can prove to them that we're friendly."

"We don't have that many options, but that seems to be one of them," said Vasily.

"*Khorosho*. We could do other things besides that, like transmitting our intentions to them via the radio, that could help too," said Mikhail. "*Posmotrim*. How exactly is that flag?"

"It has, I think, fifteen stripes, eight red and seven white, or eight white and seven red, or something like that, I think. The upper left corner has a blue rectangle with many white stars," answered Alexey.

"I think it's fifty, fifty stars. One for each state, I heard," added Yuri.

"Very well. How are we going to get the material to make it?" asked Mikhail.

"The main body we could make it using a white bed sheet," suggested Pavel.

"The red stripes?" asked Mikhail.

"Red stripes? That's what we have the most of here. Captain, just take a Union flag, rip it in narrow stripes, and throw away the rest," said Vasily.

"You better do that wherever they don't see you. They catch you ripping a Union flag and they'll rip you apart in a thousand pieces," noted Jonas.

"They'll rip us all apart in a thousand pieces," said Alexey. "They'll rip you too. You're also part of this group. Besides, this is supposed to be done in secret. If they find us making an American flag, they'll bury us all together with it."

"Stop talking nonsense!" Mikhail ordered the two men. "Let's continue. The white stars?"

"The way I see it, if the main body is white, we could take a blue towel and cut several star-shaped holes in it. The bedsheet will be the white background we need for the stars, while the towel itself will be the blue rectangle," suggested Alexey.

"That flag will have only one side!" exclaimed Ivan.

"What else can we do? Write a letter to the damn American Embassy in Moscow and ask them to send us a gift flag?" replied Alexey, raising his voice.

"Right! And in the letter we'll tell them we'll use it to pay them a visit in our plane!" replied Ivan in an equally loud tone of voice.

"Silence! Comrades! This is too important, and we don't have time to waste in stupid arguments! So, shut up you two, once and for all!" Mikhail firmly ordered once again.

After several seconds of silence, normality returned to the group. The Captain continued: "We need a white bedsheet, a blue towel, and a Union flag."

"I'll get the towel," said Pavel.

"The bedsheet?"

"I'll bring one," said Jonas.

"Very well. The flag?"

"That's easy. Just go to the Central Depot, say you want a flag to hang in your room together with a portrait of Lenin you just got, and that's it!" suggested Anatoly.

"Well. Who volunteers to get the flag?" Mikhail asked.

"I'll get it," replied Ivan.

"Agreed. Pavlik, you get the towel; Yonka, you'll bring the bedsheet; Vanya, you'll get the flag."

"Understood, Captain," said all three.

Taking a quick look at his watch, the glow of its hands and numbers indicated to the Captain that it was time to retire: "Comrades, it's 0242, time to go. We'll meet again next day off, in the morning. Those in charge of getting the material for the flag, do what you have to do here at the base. The rest, we'll go to inspect the remains of the crashed plane, and see what we can salvage from it."

Little by little, Icarus forged his wax wings.

*   *   *   *

Some of *Red 67's* crewmembers sat in the back of one of the regiment's ZIL-131 trucks, requisitioned for a trip into town to bring produce and other provisions for the mess hall. At least that's what was written in the requisition form they got. In reality the form was quickly obtained, authorized, and signed by Commander Degtyaryov himself, as soon as Mikhail let him know of his intentions of becoming part of the trafficking in *samogon*. As a test of his words, the Colonel sent him to the *kolkhoz* 'Red Dawn' to pick up several boxes of the liquor. The farm was located in the outskirts of Olyenitsa, a small town some eighty kilometers from the base, and one of the many collective and Soviet farms that brewed and supplied the drink for the thriving black market.

Mikhail sat at the wheel with Vasily at his side, like in the plane they flew. Anatoly, Alexey, Yuri and Pavel sat behind, on the truck's bed. The vehicle was idling at the main gate while the sentry on duty checked their passes. Then the radioman aboard *Red 67*, Lieutenant Molotko, came running to Mikhail's side: "Are you going somewhere?" he asked.

"Yes, Lieutenant. We're going to Olyenitsa. We'll spend the rest of the day there," said Mikhail.

"Did you get passes from the Colonel?"

"Of course! You know that without them we can't leave the base!"

"Why wasn't I told about this earlier?"

"You weren't told? What a pity!" replied Mikhail, sarcastically. "What are you planning to do today?"

"Nothing specifically. I was planning to stay here the whole day."

"Do you have a valid pass?" Mikhail asked once again.

"No, I don't."

"Then you can't come with us. I'm sorry, Lieutenant, but rules are rules. You know: No pass, no leave. Be healthy!" Making a slight military salute, Mikhail pushed the clutch, engaged gear, and sped up. The truck departed leaving the open-mouthed Lieutenant returning the salute, still standing in attention.

After having covered a few kilometers westbound, the vehicle abandoned the main road and entered a side road, almost nonexistent due to lack of use.

Once they reached the end of the dirt road, the group descended from the vehicle and got deeper into the trees, thus starting the long and laborious journey into the swamps and marshes there.

Surrounded by pine, birch, spruce, and other trees typical of the pre-arctic vegetation of the Kola Peninsula, Anatoly brought memories from days long gone: "Aaaah! This reminds me of my childhood, when I was a Pioneer. The woods, the smell of damp grass!"

"This also reminds me of something else, but it's not that pleasant," said Mikhail.

"What's that?" asked Vasily.

"Not much. Just one of the many times I was downed behind German lines during the war."

"*Chyort!* And how could you get back to our lines?" asked Alexey.

"Sometimes I had to spend whole days hiding in the woods, starving, with no food and no water. Walking ceaselessly during the night, using the stars to guide me, and sleeping during the day. I had to hide deep in the bushes, very well covered, or climb high into a tree top. Sometimes I woke up startled because I thought I was falling down, or because I thought I heard German troops coming. In winter it was worse, since all I had was my flight jacket and my overalls. During the night I almost froze to death. Even though they were made of thick leather and fur, it was not much they could protect when the temperature descended to minus twenty or thirty degrees. If I was lucky I was found by Soviet partisans who hid me and helped me reach our lines. Unfortunately most of the time that didn't happen, so I had to find my way alone, any which way I could."

"It must have been a terrible experience," said Vasily.

"I must confess it was. Sometimes I was wounded, whether by the bullets of a Messerschmitt, or by the German FLAK. Or that time when I had to crash land the plane in a potato field, and hit the instruments panel here, on my right eyebrow," he said pointing to his head. "Almost blinded by the blood, I had to run as fast as I could! The damn Nazis saw me falling, so they ran after me in their trucks. When I reached the edge of the woods, I ran deep into them and hid there. I readied my trusty Tokarev, made sure its magazine had enough bullets and decided that if I could not escape, they either killed me or I'd shoot myself with my last bullet, but I wasn't going to be their prisoner."

"I don't blame you," said Anatoly.

Pausing for a few seconds to let the impact of his words sink in, Mikhail continued. "A few minutes later I could see the Germans getting closer, still searching for me with their dogs. When they were just a couple of meters from my hideout—and I was ready to spray them with bullets—for reasons known only to them, they turned around, climbed back on their trucks, and left."

"Perhaps they left because they were afraid of getting deeper into the woods," Vasily added. "There were so many partisans there, that if they entered the woods, they risked being ambushed and massacred by the fighters. That happened many times."

"Most probably," said Mikhail.

Thus, Mikhail reminiscing his adventures and misadventures during the Great Patriotic War, and his crew listening attentively, the group spent an hour and a half walking, crossing brooks, swamps, and marshes.

Finally, they reached the location of the wreck. "There it is!" exclaimed Vasily.

Among the trees, like crumpled and discarded paper, rested the remains of the airplane, covered by broken branches and leaves. Its once bright *bort* number almost gone, what little was left of it already faded by the many months of sun, snow, and rain, the same elements that also dulled its once shiny bare aluminum skin.

The surrounding trees still carried on their barks horrendous wounds and long scars, sad souvenirs of that day when death fell from the sky.

"The plane crashed in that spot and broke its tail right there. The tail sank in that same spot," Vasily explained pointing to the locations of his description. "The rest, as you can see, glided up to there, where it hit the ground once again. That's where the wings and the engines blew up, the forward fuselage broke, then slid on the snow hitting all those trees, until it came to rest among those trees over there."

"Did they ever find out why it fell?" Mikhail asked.

"They said it suffered a flameout in the right engine, then it fell like a brick," Vasily responded to the question.

"A flameout? Why would that happen in those engines? They have been around for longer than I care to think," said Alexey.

"Bad maintenance, most probably. Not surprising around here," said Anatoly.

"This reminds me when Major Ogorodnikov's plane fell," said Mikhail.

"That's right," said Vasily. "His plane, what was it, *Red 42?* went down right after take off."

"Right. About two or three months ago. I remember," Alexey agreed.

"Yes, who could forget that blast! It fell on the other side of the river, by Varzuga, and blew up practically all the window panes in a radius of five kilometers from the crash site!" said Pavel.

"Well, ninety tons of fuel hitting the ground at more than two hundred and fifty kilometers an hour make for a tremendous explosion. You can believe that," said Mikhail.

"Did they ever find out the reason for that crash?" Vasily asked.

"I was at the control tower when Ogorodnikov sent his last transmission. He screamed that all four engines failed one after the other in succession, then the plane fell," said Mikhail.

"Massive failure in all four engines?" asked a surprised Alexey.

"Yes. Just as you heard," said the Captain, "And, of course, they made all the necessary 'investigations' checking all the maintenance logbooks, medical records of the crew, etc., etc., etc."

"And in the end?" asked Anatoly.

"In the end the reason was bad maintenance caused by the maintenance crew being drunk beyond all reason almost all the time. But since that was a direct indictment on the *nachal'stvo*'s business, that report was duly 'filed' by Commander Degtyaryov," Mikhail explained. "The only losers in this case were the Soviet State losing a very expensive TU-95 RTs, the crew of *Red 42*, Major Ogorodnikov and all his men, dead because of the carelessness of a bunch of drunkards, and all the drunkards sent to prison for a long time. But the real culprits, Cdr. Degtyaryov and all his *apparatchiki*, are still there, free, and becoming fat, rich *kulaki*, right under the noses of the KGB. But they, like the rest, are also corrupt to the roots, profiting from all the money they suck from all the poor drunkards they are exploiting with their *samogon* business ..." Mikhail finished his explanation.

Then, in a sudden and unexpected move, the Captain dove head first into the nearest bushes. The rest of the group imitated his jump and dove into the bushes too.

*   *   *   *

The morning flight from Murmansk was slightly late. For this reason, one of its passengers felt tremendously uncomfortable.

KGB Colonel Konstantin Denisovich Yakovlev, Political Commander of the Navy Air Base at Kuzomen, still had to organize the squads that would reinforce security at the base. He was also still stuck inside the aircraft, an Antonov AN-24 cargo and passenger plane. At least he knew that it wouldn't take much longer to get there. More than twenty minutes before the plane had left behind the town of Revda, located between the lakes Umbozero and Lovozero. These two lakes, midway between Murmansk and Kuzomen, served as a reference point. To fly between them was a sure way to reach the base. To his left the Colonel had lake Sergozero, distant some seventy kilometers from the base.

In his briefcase Yakovlev carried, besides routine paperwork, the schematic diagram of his security plan. His trip to Murmansk had the double purpose of obtaining approval from his superiors, as well as obtaining from them the reinforcement agents, necessary for the effective application of the plan at the base.

The Colonel dedicated several months to prepare his plan. This was his third trip to Region Headquarters and, if everything went well, his last. The urgency of preparing the security reinforcement, plus the participation of the base in the *Okean* maneuvers, brought the officer a severe migraine. To this was added the responsibility of the visit by Headquarters Security Inspectors on the same day of the maneuvers. A delay in the Antonov's take off, due to a malfunction in one of its engines, only contributed to increase his suffering.

On the horizon, at last, emerged the coastline of the south shore of Kola Peninsula, where the base was located. To the left, the river Varzuga, on its right shore, the town of the same name. Soon he'd be in his office directing his men. As the aircraft approached the base he continued thinking about the reinforcements and his plan. He knew this was his masterpiece, the most important task he had ever accomplished in his military career.

Everything had to function like clockwork for the arrival of the Inspectors. His position, his career and his head all hung on it. Leaving his problems aside so he could get rid of his migraine, he got closer to the window and looked at the approaching base below.

Like toy houses, the service hangars contrasted their huge size against the living quarters and administration buildings. The giant four-engined TU-95 RTs planes, the brilliant morning sun reflecting on their naked aluminum fuselages, were neatly arranged in an orderly row, occupying the main portion of the dispersion area. In the west corner he could see the communication and liaison airplane of the base, the old and trusty Antonov AN-2 biplane. More to the south, by the air base main gate, mounted on a steel beam acting as pedestal, there was a copy of the Ilyushin-2 *'Shtormovik,'* the legendary 'Flying Tank' dive bomber of the Great Patriotic War, as perennial and silent sentry.

Beyond, at the end of the road—and also at the end of all civilization—by the river's mouth, the small, dead-dog town of Kuzomen—population 100 souls in winter, more in summer, when vacationers trekked down from Murmansk—some 15 kms southeast of the airbase, with its small harbor and related installations. From his seat Yakovlev distinguished several fishing boats entering and leaving the harbor, mostly fishermen coming from or going to their fishing chores in the White Sea. A few others, in bigger boats, were on their way to Karelia or to Onyega and Severodvinsk, on the other side of the White Sea.

When the plane started its descending glide to Runway 14B, for a split second the Colonel glimpsed a group of people walking in the swamps, among the trees below. By the time he got his face closer to the window to have a better look, it was too late: the group had disappeared, the place was empty.

Did I have a vision? He asked himself. *Who could have been walking in those swamps, infested as they are with wild animals and insects? And what for?* He still was not sure if in reality he saw people down there or not, so he tried to convince himself that it was nothing more than a vision caused by his pounding migraine.

The runway quickly came closer to meet the plane. The soft bump of the plane's landing gear hitting the concrete got him out of his thoughts. Having more important matters to worry about, soon he forgot the whole incident. On the tarmac his assistant, Deputy Political Commander Lieutenant Colonel Nikitin, was already waiting for him.

✳   ✳   ✳   ✳

"I didn't hear that plane coming!" said Mikhail leaving his hideout.

"I'm not surprised. So many years flying those damn noisy planes is making us go deaf," said Anatoly, bringing to mind one of the TU-95's least endearing qualities: the deafening roar caused by the thirty two blades of its eight contra-rotating propellers turning at supersonic speed.

"Is that the morning flight from Murmansk?" Vasily asked, confused.

"That's what it looks like, but it seems that today it's late," Alexey answered, looking at his watch. "It should have landed about an hour ago."

"If we hadn't sprinted out of the way quickly, we would have been seen here. Then the problems would start. In the blink of an eye this place would be full of *Komendatura* people, asking us what the devil we're doing here, and what we're looking for," said Pavel.

"Do you think we were seen?" Anatoly asked, nervously.

"I don't think so. We got out of sight as soon as we saw the plane coming. Besides, this is an uninhabited area. They wouldn't think there's anyone here. If they did see something down here, they'd confuse us with animals or trees," Mikhail answered in a comforting tone of voice.

"I saw a face peering through one of the windows ..." said Anatoly, still not too convinced.

"That means someone saw us. I don't want to be here. I'm going back to the base. Soon here will be crawling with *Komendatura* people," said Yuri.

"No, Yura. Don't leave. Either we all go, or we all stay. No one will go back and leave the rest of the group behind. If we have risked so much and already got here to get that equipment, it would be stupid to return empty handed. Especially now that we're so close to it. Besides, if we don't get it, everything we've done so far would be a waste of time," Mikhail said.

"That's true," said Anatoly. "Our only hope, our only opportunity to jam that damn system, and to get out of here once and for all, forever, is in that equipment. If we don't get it now, we'll have to stay here. And this place I can't take anymore. So let's see what's in there."

The group remained silent for a few seconds, looking at each other. Vasily then took the initiative and started to walk towards the battered remains of the plane. Soon, one by one, the rest followed him.

The wreck, a twisted mess of broken aluminum, lied among the trees, its broken cockpit window panes looking up to the sky, like empty orbits. On the left side of the cockpit, a big hole on the aluminum skin. Part of the branch that impaled and killed the pilot still could be seen.

"*Tyshto!* Look at that hole!" exclaimed Alexey.

"It was made by that sawed off branch you see there. It impaled the pilot, killing him immediately," Vasily explained.

"What a way to die, especially after surviving such a crash!" said Mikhail.

While the others examined the outside, Anatoly entered through the immense hole left in the forward fuselage when it broke off. Alexey followed him and headed towards the cockpit. The rest of the group followed them.

Anatoly approached the objects of his interest, the electronics racks, located to the left and to the right of the fuselage. Here were located the communications equipment, the jamming transmitters, and other electronic components. Despite it all, the rows of electronic equipment seemed to be intact. Perhaps the cold and dry weather of the area, with its minimal temperature changes between summer and winter, allowed this to happen.

In the cockpit there was broken glass here and there, instruments sticking out of their panels, their guts showing through their broken dials. From the cockpit Alexey moved forward to the navigator's seat, located beyond the pilots seats. Suddenly, a loud exclamation came from there. Startled, the group jumped to the side, just in time to let a gray shadow whoosh by their legs.

The surprised group didn't know what to do. The shadow stopped at the edge of the broken fuselage, took a fast look behind it, made sure the intruders were not following, and jumped to the humid ground outside. Running as fast as it could, the badger got lost among the trees.

"Damn animal! It scared me to the bones!" exclaimed Alexey.

"Don't be a hen, Alyosha! It was just a badger! It made its den here," said Mikhail.

"That's better! I thought it was a lynx, jumping up to attack me," replied the ashamed navigator, still a bit nervous.

"Don't be ridiculous! Have you ever seen a lynx around these latitudes? The cold would kill it!" Vasily scolded the young man. Disregarding the embarrassed Alexey, the copilot turned his attention to Anatoly, still inspecting the equipment gathered on the racks there.

"Everything seems to be alright. Dirty and soiled, but still in good order," said Anatoly.

"*Khorosho*. Let's take out what we need, and hope it works," said Mikhail.

The rest of the group joined them. Pavel got nearer, holding a canvas bag containing a tools case, necessary to remove the equipment.

"Pavel, please, give me a flat screwdriver," Anatoly asked the radar operator. The technician pulled the requested tool out of the bag.

"Wirecutters."

"Wirecutters," repeated the technician.

"Pliers."

"Pliers," repeated the technician once again.

With surgical precision, Anatoly and Pavel pulled equipment after equipment out of their location in the racks. The rest of the group, meanwhile, observed the two technicians. Once the racks had been cleaned of any and all electronic components useful to their purposes, Anatoly examined them.

"Well. Perhaps these devices might work."

"So I hope," said Mikhail. "Let's take it all back to the truck. Later we'll test them, back at the base."

Carrying the instrumentation on their arms, and their hopes in their hearts, Mikhail and his companions left the crash site. Once again they set forth on the long trek through the swamp, leaving behind what remained of the once beautiful metal bird: a jumble of twisted aluminum and useless debris.

After another odyssey across the swamps, during which they hardly talked, the group reached the truck. The black boxes were placed on the ZIL's bed, and covered with canvas. Anatoly and Pavel sat on them.

"First thing I'll do when I get to Olyenitsa will be to down a glass of vodka. I'm wet to the bone will all that swamp water!" complained Alexey.

The truck started and left, the group still laughing about the navigator's comment, all agreeing with him. Returning to the main road, Mikhail turned west, towards the neighboring town.

*   *   *   *

Back in his office, having relayed the necessary instructions to his subordinates, Col. Yakovlev hung up the phone. He hoped not to use it again for the rest of the day, so he could concentrate on the other pending matters.

Relaxing a bit, he closed his eyes. This brought to his mind his long gone days as a student at the Military Academy, where he was exemplified as one of its best students. This got him several trophies, and these, in turn, got him the coveted Lenin Prize for Military Achievement, which in the long run got him to occupy the position he had as Political Commander of a whole naval air base.

In a few more days he'd have the most difficult test he'd ever had. He wanted to increase the base security according to his own plans. That was the first time something like that was done not following the instructions from the *nachal'stvo* in Murmansk. Instead, his superiors would allow him to do it independently. Another positive mark in his military service record.

The officers under his command had already received his instructions. To complete the picture, only a few minor details here and there needed to be taken care of. Among them the arrival of the new agents sent from Murmansk, for the tight security net around the base to be complete.

Region Headquarters would send inspectors to personally verify the actions of the Colonel as he swam in his own waters. Once the inspection was finished, Yakovlev was sure that he'd be not only congratulated by his distinguished visitors, but also, following their recommendation, promoted in rank by his superiors, perhaps to Major General. Nothing then could obstruct the road to the successful completion of this operation. It was going to be the climax of his career. Then he'd step down with honors from his position to retire peacefully.

Suddenly he was assaulted by the vision he had earlier that morning, while the plane that brought him from Murmansk was landing. *Were there people down there, for real?* he asked himself. Even though he didn't pay too much attention to the matter then, for the first time since his arrival he could relax and think about matters unrelated to the base security net or to the inspection, so he could think about it. Only then he was able to set aside time to think about trivial matters such as the happenings near Runway 14A, before his plane landed.

Who could have been down there, and what for? He was not too sure of how many he saw: three, four, five men. He only saw them hiding under the trees. No one lived around that area of the base. The nearest town was Kuzomen, some 15 kms. down the road and from where the air base got its name. Besides that, the only other town around there was Varzuga, some 18 kms up river, so he couldn't say it was a group of local residents. *Almost all are fishermen, and at that hour of the morning they're engaged in their fishing in the gulf. Besides, they all know that the immediate area around the base is restricted and that if they're seen snooping around there, they'll be fired upon. Finally, that side of the base, by Runway 14A, is practically inaccessible … Could it have been a group of spies?* he asked himself, then doubted it: *The way security is handled in this base would make that option not only improbable but impossible. In my files I have classified each and everyone of the residents of both Kuzomen and Varzuga, from the youngest to the oldest. I know they're all good citizens, most of them good Communists and loyal members of the Party.*

That means that if whatever I saw were spies, then they're not from around here. A group of people with strange faces would have been detected long ago. That possibility, however, even though remote, may still exist.

Could they have come because of the new radar system? No. They'd gain nothing from it. That equipment is a technical matter. It's not something like a new airplane that you can photograph and obtain a lot of information by only seeing the picture. That new radar is inside the plane, and the only way anyone can obtain information about it, is by asking the technicians directly. So that possibility may be discarded already.

To take photographs of the airplanes here? What for? In this base the only planes we have are Tupolev TU-95 RTs and Antonov AN-2. Why would a foreign power want to come here to take pictures of airplanes that have been flying for more than twenty years, almost daily, over their own ships, when they could do that from the ships themselves? Without the complications of having to send men for that purpose! And a whole group at that!

About the strategic implications of the Antonov AN-2, Yakovlev didn't even bother to think. That biplane flew for the first time during the forties.

The base has only two runways: 14A and 14B. The TU-95 RTs use only Runway 14A, the widest and longest of the two. Runway 14B is used only by the small liaison planes and other transport and cargo planes that make regular stops here. Runway 14A is not the best place to take pictures of the base or the planes, even though it is the main runway. If that was a group of spies, and they had intentions of taking photographs, then they made a bad choice. Any smart spy, wanting to take good pictures, would have stood anywhere else but by Runway 14A because, what can he see from there?

As his mind worked on the puzzle, his hand drew a big question mark on the pad before him, symbolizing the great enigma boiling inside his head. *Was it vision, or reality? If reality, who were they and why were they there? I've got to find the answer to those questions, both because of the base security as well as for my own sanity.*

Suddenly, the phone rang, echoing in his head like church bell. His Deputy informed him that Lieutenant General Griboyedov himself was calling from Murmansk. Back to the inspection. *Will they ever let me take a break?* he asked. Soon Yakovlev got deeply involved in the conversation. The vision was once again filed in a corner of his mind.

✳   ✳   ✳   ✳

Driving the ZIL on the two-way coastal road going from Kuzomen to Kandalaksha—barely wide enough to hold two trucks side by side—Mikhail entered Olyenitsa through its main street, which was the same road he was driving on, anyway. Many years of disrepair left wide, deep ruts in the sandy ground. As it ran the truck raised dense dust clouds. Throughout the years this grayish dust fell in layer after layer over the wooden huts and houses that bordered the main street. By then all of them looked as if gray had been the original color the State Planners assigned them when they were built, their original colors long gone.

"Captain, the guys want you to stop at the store. They want to buy some vodka," said Vasily.

"I bet you that was Alyosha's suggestion," said Mikhail.

"Aha. Although you've got to admit that having a drink now would be fitting. Don't you think so?" Vasily asked.

"Khorosho. We'll stop, but just for a short while. Don't forget we still have to get to the collective farm and pick up those boxes of *samogon.* We were delayed enough in the swamps."

Asking a fat *baba* who, basket in hand, carried some produce home, they obtained from her the address of the only store in town. It was located several streets further west.

The truck stopped before a dilapidated wooden building in sore need of repairs, like all the other buildings in town. On its façade, a long sign with the words **FOOD STORE**. A couple of drunkards, dreaming about who knew what, were sound asleep on the wooden sidewalk, one on each side of the door.

The group got off the truck. Looking at the sleeping drinkers, first with pity, then with dislike, the group entered the shop.

The shelves and glass counters inside, mostly bare and devoid of merchandise, displayed only a few loaves of rancid bread; several rows of canned products, most of them already expired; some cheap trinkets, and row after row of vodka bottles. The latter was the hottest product in town, and the only one the State provided in quantity enough to cover the huge demand. In a corner there was still in exhibition a 1960 vintage washing machine, placed there by the State Planners. The objective then was to provide the customers some of the comforts of modern life. But its extremely high price, beyond the means of the townfolks, coupled with the lack of electricity, converted it into a useless luxury in a place where most of the people wore their clothing until it literally fell apart on them.

On the other side of the counter, seeing the soldiers arrive, a slim, tall individual sprang up like a jack-in-the-box. His face showed one thousand and one wrinkles and pockmarks, sunk eyes, a truncated smile, formed by yellowish teeth—already blackened by the constant, excessive smoking of *papirosy*—and the gaping holes left by those teeth destroyed by the lack of dental hygiene, made his features appear ten years older than his real age.

With a raspy and sibilant voice, perhaps another by-product of the strong tobacco of the *papirosy*, the clerk inquired: *"Dobryy dyen'* comrades. What can I do for you?"

"How much is the vodka?" Vasily asked.

"Small bottle, seventy five kopeks. Large bottle, ruble and a half," answered the lanky character, placing samples on the counter.

"Well, let's make a collection for a large bottle," said Alexey. "I have twenty kopeks."

After completing the liquor's purchase price, the group immediately attacked the bottle.

"Comrade, we're coming from Kuzomen. We're going to the Collective Farm 'Red Dawn' to pick up some produce. Do you know where it's located?" Mikhail asked.

"Aaah ... Follow the main road, as if you were going to Umba ... Some twenty kilometers from here you'll find a checkpoint ... I think the farm should be some two kilometers after that, on the right side of the road," said the clerk. His words came out hissing, like a broken teapot.

The group climbed on the truck and continued on its trip, leaving behind the sleepy town with its problems of alcoholism, dullness, apathy, monotony, tedium, indifference, and boredom, boredom, boredom, and more boredom.

Arriving at the checkpoint the sentries posted there, obviously fed up with the tranquility of the place and vehemently desiring to finish their service time and get out of there forever, stopped the truck and asked its passengers to show papers.

After the routine visual inspection, the soldiers made hand signals for Mikhail to continue on his way. One of the conscripts wrote in the sentry log the passing of another truck. The third of the day.

A large sign spanned high over the entrance gate. A red rising sun with a yellow Soviet hammer and sickle in its center—already faded by the passing of time—announced to all the location of the Collective Farm. The group headed to the collection of huts and houses that sheltered the *muzhiki* and their families. They were neatly located on the edge of a square surrounding a huge potato field, main harvest of the farm and from where the *samogon* was brewed and distilled.

Every year, at the end of the harvest, the director of the farm falsified the harvest records. This allowed him to dedicate about half of the crop to the production of *samogon*. In only one month the sale of the liquor produced more profits than the sale of all the tons of potatoes the farm produced in a whole year.

'Red Dawn' was the biggest and most active of all the Collective and Soviet Farms brewing *samogon* in the area. It had the protection of all the military base commanders around—its best customers—who also took charge of the liquor distribution to each and every one of them in the whole region, from Kuzomen to Kandalaksha. The liquor black market was a strong and thriving business, where all the participants received some kind of benefit, whether in the form of money, gifts, or boxes of the liquor. These, in turn, were sold or exchanged for articles stolen or smuggled from Finland, to the west.

Mikhail headed to the house with the best façade, where the Farm Director obviously lived. On the way, the *muzhiki,* many of them patently drunk, greeted the new arrivals. Barefoot blond children and *babushki* sitting before the huts looked at the men with a mixture of curiosity and indifference at the same time. The only ones showing some excitement were the marrying-age girls of the farm, waving their hands to the technicians sitting on the truck bed on the vain hope of trapping one of them, so they could get out of the monotonous farm life. Most of the farm population, men, women, and children, worked in the production of *samogon*. On the potato fields remained working only a few women, directed by some men.

Stopping before the Director's house, Mikhail entered the building. A few minutes later he appeared at the door, following an individual of medium height, perhaps thirty five to forty years old, face hard and rude, sporting a dirty and disheveled beard. His clothing, unable to carry one more dirt spot, and old military boots, completed his impression on Mikhail.

After a few minutes in conversation, Mikhail made signals for his men to follow him. Passing a fence near the man's house, the group entered a barn. The strong smell produced by the horses, pigs and cows sheltered there made the technicians' stomachs jump up and down. Even though for them this stench was nothing new, smelling it was not their custom either.

The distilling boiler, enormous, occupied almost half of the place. Its copper coils poured the liquid, drop by drop, on large containers. From them the liquor was transferred to countless bottles, which were then placed in boxes. The farm's production of the liquor was stored in a warehouse to the rear, behind the barn, between two rusted tractors.

The Farm Director made signals for Mikhail to get closer. *"Posmotrim.* For my friend, Colonel Degtyaryov … he gets today … twenty five boxes," said the man, verifying his notebook.

Mikhail looked at the book over the man's shoulder, reading in it similar numbers for all the military bases in the area:

Colonel Makeyev, Umba	30 boxes
Lt. Col. Simonov, Kolvitsa	35 boxes
Colonel Degtyaryov, Kuzomen	25 boxes
Colonel Lazaryev, Nivskiy	30 boxes
Colonel Fyodorov, Kandalaksha	50 boxes
Colonel Daryenskiy, Apatity	45 boxes
Lt. Col. Bykov, Polyarniye Zori	40 boxes
Colonel Boyko, Byeloe Morye	20 boxes
Colonel Eryomenko, Kirovsk	50 boxes
Total boxes for today:	325

Seeing the numbers, Mikhail couldn't help but to be amazed at the size of the operation. *More than three hundred boxes a day, distributed to all the military bases in a radius of three hundred kilometers! These people must be rotting in money. Yes, they're as rotten as the system.*

"*Khorosho.* Captain, serve yourself," said the Director.

Once all the boxes were placed on the truck, the group departed. At the farm's gate they met another military truck entering. More bottles for the market.

After an uneventful return trip, they reached the base. At the main gate a corporal approached the truck's cabin. Another soldier approached its bed.

"*Dobryy vyecher, tovarishchi, bumaghy, pozhaluysta.*" After the perfunctory military salutes, the corporal requested from his comrades the necessary documentation for entering the base. The scene was repeated in the truck's rear.

All gave their documents to the sentries, who verified that the faces on the cards belonged to the men before them. Once satisfied, the papers were returned.

"I see you were in Olyenitsa. How's that over there?" asked the corporal.

"Normal," answered Mikhail.

While Mikhail and the corporal by the truck's cabin made small talk, the soldier by the truck's rear also asked questions. "Your boots are muddy! Where were you, guys?"

"We went to the farm 'Red Dawn' and … well … you know how muddy it is in those farms," Anatoly replied. While he answered the soldier's question, the sentry examined the technicians' footwear. Something was amiss with them, but he couldn't put his finger on it.

"And those boxes? What are you carrying there?"

"Vegetables. For the kitchen," said Anatoly.

"Please, show the requisition and transportation papers," asked the sentry. Anatoly gave the man the requested documentation. Suspecting what was inside the boxes, however, the soldier demanded: "Open one of those boxes. I must inspect it."

"Private, I don't think there is any need to do that. These boxes are coming with Commander Degtyaryov's authorization," said Anatoly.

"I know. I saw his signature, and I know how to read. But orders are orders, and my orders are to inspect anything coming in or out through this gate." Nearing the boxes, the soldier took one and ripped open its flaps.

"What's this? This doesn't look like vegetables to me!" he said aloud. Taking one of the bottles, he opened it with his teeth and drank from it. "Liquor. You know that is strictly forbidden here at the base. I'll have to place you all under arrest."

Anatoly remained speechless. *I wonder if this simple private knows what he's getting into. If he makes a scandal with Degtyaryov's bottles, most probable he'll end his service time somewhere in Siberia. And he'll never go beyond the rank of private.*

Hearing the man's loud voice coming from the back, Mikhail got off the truck. The corporal followed him. Both approached the scene. "What's happening?" the Captain asked.

"Captain, here you have bottles of liquor and these papers here talk about vegetables. The regulations have not been followed," explained the private.

On hearing his companion's explanation the corporal, once aware of the reason for his excitement, turned to Mikhail: "Captain, he's right. The regulations have not been followed. Do you understand what I mean?"

For a moment, Mikhail didn't understand what the corporal meant by the 'following of regulations.'

"Listen, Captain. These papers say one thing, and here you're bringing something else. You cannot expect us to allow you to enter with these boxes just like that. Do you understand? There are *regulations to be followed.*" The corporal distinctively enunciated the last words.

"And what do those regulations say?" Anatoly asked.

The guards couldn't believe that for these individuals the regulations were so difficult to understand. The corporal, however, seeing that they were new faces in the business, decided to clarify matters a bit. "The regulations say that if you're carrying forbidden articles into the base, you should pay a fine. Do you understand now? Otherwise these boxes will go nowhere and we'll have to place you all under arrest."

"And why arrest us? These boxes, after all, do not belong to us. They belong to Commander Degtyaryov!" Mikhail defended his position.

"We know that. But you're bringing them in. We can't arrest Degtyaryov, but we can arrest you," replied the private.

"You can't arrest me! I am a captain!" Mikhail responded, pulling rank.

"True, but the *komendant* can. He's a colonel!" retorted the corporal.

"Anyway. How much is the fine?" Mikhail asked, anxious to end the delay once and for all, and continue his way in peace.

On hearing this, the corporal displayed caution. Even though this was not the first nor the last time he'd see a shipment of *samogon* coming through that gate, this was the first time he saw new faces. If he had them all arrested, he knew that those in control of the liquor black market in the base would find out very soon about the incident, and he would lose his head, literally. But on the other hand, he didn't want to miss the opportunity of laying hands on the 'fine.' Despite it all, he still beat around the bushes: "Captain, let's make an arrangement, you do something for us, and we forget the whole deal. Agreed?"

"Agreed. What do you want me to do for you?"

The Corporal looked at the bottles of *samogon* and pointed to them. Then he raised the five fingers of his right hand. Five bottles of *samogon* would be more than enough for him and his companions to spend a happy evening thanks to the traffickers.

"Oh, I see!" exclaimed Mikhail.

The guard smiled, seeing that Mikhail finally realized it all.

Mikhail pulled five bottles of liquor out of the box. The soldier looked around to make sure they were not being seen, then made gestures for the Captain to get closer. Mikhail surreptitiously passed him the bottles, which the soldier hid under his jacket. While this was happening, no one noticed the private moving the boxes of *samogon*, discovering another cargo. This last one was covered by a canvas. Calling the corporal, the private showed him his discovery.

"And this? What is it?" The corporal asked once again. In reality, the question was asked more out of greed than out of curiosity. Perhaps it was another contraband of some forbidden item, of which he and his companion could receive a sample or two.

Uncovering the cargo, the private saw only several black boxes with buttons, dials, and wires protruding out of them.

"What are those black boxes?"

Running to the private's side, Anatoly took the canvas from his hands and covered the cargo again. "Those are old vacuum tube radios I got back in town. I'm a technician, you know? I collect old radios. Just like others collect stamps and coins, I collect old radios. These models are of the first radios made in the Union. That's why they're so big. They must be at least twice my age."

The explanation seemed to satisfy the guards. Seeing that it was nothing of their interest, they decided to let the truck enter after paying only the 'fine.' Besides, there was not much to do with 'old vacuum tube radios' around there. Both soldiers returned to their booth.

Once in the truck, Mikhail thought about the event. Blyad! *We were almost discovered! They could have really arrested us all! If the sentries had not swallowed that story of the old radios, they would have asked us for papers for them, which we don't have. Then they'd have asked why we had all that equipment hiding under canvas, and why we tried to fool them making believe they were old radios. From there other questions would follow, until the whole mess blows up in our faces. They wouldn't need more proof to send us to prison for the rest of our lives.*

Pressing the pedal of the ZIL, the Captain returned the salute from the corporal in the booth and headed to the garages. Later they'd take the equipment out of the truck to take them to his quarters.

On the North side of the base, a TU-95 RTs with its landing gear down descended for a touchdown on Runway 14A. The reconnaissance patrol of the day returned home after having spent the whole day flying over some NATO vessel in the North Atlantic Ocean. As its pilot applied maximum power to the four powerful Kuznyetsov turboprop engines of the flying giant, their loud drone sounded like music to Mikhail's ears.

CHAPTER 6

▼

That night, even before Mikhail got up from his bed to continue the development of the escape plans, muffled knocks came from his bedroom door. Looking at his watch, he noted the time: 2320. Asking himself who could be coming at this hour and what could be the matter, he headed to the door.

"Yura! What brings you here so early? I'm not expecting anyone until an hour later, at least!" Mikhail whispered.

"Captain! Excuse me for coming this early, but I received this telegram from Region Headquarters that's got me very worried. Look!" Taking the official envelope with the emblem of the Red Banner Northern Fleet, Mikhail pulled out the telegram:

First Military District Leningrad
Murmansk Military Region
Kuzomen Naval Air Base,
To Senior Lieutenant
Kazakov, Yuri Yevdokimovich—24356326263

By this means you are notified of the approval of your transfer to the 943rd Reconnaissance Air Regiment at Oktyabrskoye Naval Airbase, Crimean Military Region, Odessa Military District, effective August 3rd, 1976.

With respects
Lt. Col. Pastukhov, Ivan Nikolayevich
Director

Directorate of Coordination and Transfers
Red Banner Northern Fleet
Murmansk Military Region
First Military District Leningrad

"Did you ask for a transfer to the south?"

"Yes. I wanted to be nearer to my family in Slaviansk. But I made that request more than a year and a half ago, before I was assigned to *Red 67!* I thought they forgot about it and just filed it away, so I completely forgot about the whole matter!"

"Well, it looks like they remembered it now. Don't forget that these matters are handled at bureaucratic speed at best: snail pace when they're going the fastest. Do you still want to go to Crimea?"

"No. I prefer to get out of here, to get out of the Union. I want to leave together with you."

"Good choice. Now, this telegram only brings problems. According to the date, you're transferred the day before the maneuvers!"

"And that's why I'm worried."

"Don't worry, I'll tell the others. Perhaps they could suggest something to do. We have ten days to solve this. By then we should have thought of something to make you stay."

"I hope so. I'd hate to stay behind."

Several minutes later Pavel and Anatoly arrived, bringing with them the electronic equipment obtained the previous morning, along with a couple of truck batteries they conveniently 'requisitioned' to provide power to test the equipment. The technicians placed the devices on the table, then took some tools out of a bag and got ready to test them.

Under the light of a couple of flashlights skillfully hung up as lamps, and with windows covered to avoid their light being seen from the outside, the technicians took apart the black boxes. While one checked the intricate net of wires, diodes, resistors, capacitors, transistors, and mini vacuum tubes, the other wrote down values in a note pad, performing the necessary calculations to make the conversion they were about to execute.

Leaving the technicians working by themselves, Mikhail tackled the sewing of the American flag. "Vanya, could you get the Union flag?"

"Yes. They gave it to me without questions," said Ivan.

"And you, Yonka? Did you bring the bedsheet?"

"Yes. I stole one from the laundry room," replied Jonas.

"Where is it?"

"Here, in this bag." Emptying the bag on Mikhail's bed, a yellowish piece of fabric fell out.

"It's dirty and full of spots!" exclaimed Vasily.

"Come on, Vasya! Don't be fastidious! That was the first one I found there. I didn't have time to search for a clean one."

"Don't worry about that, Vasya. We still can make a flag with it. The spots will not be visible," Mikhail said.

"Pavlik, give me that towel, please," Mikhail asked Pavel, who already had the blue towel in hand.

Mikhail gave the material to Yuri, the Flight Engineer, who acted as tailor for the moment.

Yuri took the bedsheet and a pair of scissors, then cut out a rectangle of about one meter by half a meter. Once he had compared the size of the red Soviet flag with the bedsheet, Yuri cut the red banner in narrow stripes. When he removed the yellow hammer and sickle, he felt a sting inside. *I'm destroying the same flag that I venerated and respected before. The flag I swore I'd defend and if necessary die for, that day when, kneeling before it, I made my military oath … But on the other hand, this flag also represents the system that betrayed me and therefore that oath has no value whatsoever.* Pushing the thoughts aside, Yuri finished the removal of the yellow star, placing the symbols aside.

While Yuri worked with the flag, Mikhail informed the other crewmen about the telegram the Flight Engineer received earlier. "… So, what do you suggest?"

"Most probably the same day Yura leaves, his replacement will arrive from Murmansk." Vasily was the first one to talk. "With him we definitely will not be able to carry out the escape plan."

"Aha. That's why we have to find a way of getting rid of him and place Yura in his stead," said Mikhail.

"Captain, I think first we have to find a way of making Yura stay here at the base. Then get rid of the replacement. Otherwise, we'll be back to square one. They'd simply send a second replacement to replace the one we made disappear," said Pavel.

"You're right … We must find a way of making Yura the replacement of the replacement. Does anyone have another suggestion?" asked Mikhail.

"How about smuggling Yura into the plane, and taking him with us to the maneuvers?" suggested Jonas.

"Yonka," Mikhail answered the question. "Don't forget that he is supposed to leave the day before the maneuvers. We must find a *legal* way of making him stay.

The same day he leaves a replacement will come from Murmansk, and this guy's supposed to fly with us to the maneuvers. Last, but by no means least, in the plane we have a stoolie that when he sees two Flight Engineers together in the same plane, he'll start asking questions and become uncomfortable. You know how uneasy Serghey gets when he sees something abnormal. However, I like that idea of smuggling Yura into the plane, before we take off. But before that, we must get rid of the replacement. Everything must be done legally, though, to avoid raising Serghey's suspicions."

Pavel interrupted the discussion: "Well, everything seems to be functioning. The parts seem to be in good working order. Now, let's see the jammers we brought."

"Khorosho," Anatoly continued. "According to the data I could gather about the TU-16P jammers, I may tentatively say that it is possible to build a frequency booster using the parts from the other equipment. It may not be as powerful as I expected, though. I'll have to increase its output enough to at least guarantee it will jam the autodestruct signal."

While the group waited for the diagnostic on the jammers, for them the most important of all the equipment they brought from the swamp, Yuri placed the red stripes on the white rectangle, already spread on the bed.

"Very well. Seven red stripes, and seven white, right?" asked the Engineer.

"Right!" said Vasily.

"Ladno. Now, give me the towel."

Vasily gave the towel to the Engineer, who placed it on the red stripes and compared sizes. "Too big. I'll have to cut it down to size."

Once cut, Yuri placed the towel on the bedsheet and cut the red stripes running under it. *"Khorosho.* Now just cut a few star-shaped holes in it, and that's it," said Alexey.

"There are fifty stars in the American flag," said Vasily.

"And you expect me to cut fifty holes in this towel? I'd spend the rest of the night just doing that! And I still have to sew it all together!" Yuri complained.

"Yura, just cut enough holes in the towel to make it look like it's full of stars. It doesn't have to be precisely fifty," suggested Mikhail.

"Aha. After all, it's not for an exhibition," said Alexey.

The Engineer was in the process of cutting the holes when Pavel announced: "Comrades, it looks like the equipment is working. After all, the crash, the cold, the snow, the ice and the rainwater did not affect it."

On hearing that, the group burst in laughs, hugs, and hand stretching. Pavel, however, remained silent, sporting a worried face. Noticing him, Mikhail stopped laughing and asked: "Pavel! What's happening! Is there any problem? Why are you so worried?"

"I think there is a problem, although I can't be totally sure."

"And what's the problem?" asked Anatoly.

"After the visual inspection, this equipment *seems* to be working, but in reality we have no sure way of knowing if it *really* works without turning it on. If we do that, here in the base they would detect the transmission immediately."

"Then that means that all those boxes would not work, and that the trip to the swamp could have been just a waste of time," said Alexey.

"No, it's not that. Everything I've checked so far seems to be working. What worries me is, how am I going to know if the jammer works as it should if I can't really test it?"

The group remained silent for a moment. Then Anatoly said: "He's right. But the worst of it all is that once we build the booster, then we *really* will have no way of testing the device. In other words, we'll have to trust that equipment *as is*, without ever testing it."

Anatoly's words were a hard reality for the group to swallow. "Besides," continues the technician, "How will we be able to simulate a signal in the same frequency of the transmitter here at the base? We have no other alternative. We'll have to escape in our plane under the constant threat and risk of an explosion. Flying as if each one of us had his personal Damocles' sword hanging over his head."

In the reigning silence they realized the enormous risk of escaping with an equipment in such conditions. Looking at each other, they silently asked themselves if it'd be worth it to go on or not. Finally Yuri, still cutting holes in the blue towel, broke the silence: "I don't care if the booster works or not. It would be used only if they push the detonator of that system. If they don't push it, we don't need the booster. If they push it, and it works, very well. If it doesn't work … Well, it's better to die trying to escape than continue living under these conditions. I take the risk."

Yuri's opinion seemed to be that of the rest of the group. One at the time, all started to nod their heads affirmatively, coming to a tacit agreement with the Engineer's words.

"*Ladno*. Make the booster. Although I hope never to use it," ordered Mikhail.

"Understood, Captain. Although I hope it works if we need to use it," replied Anatoly.

The technicians took apart the circuitry of one of the rescued jammers in order to use its parts in the construction of the booster. While they worked in the electronic equipment, Yuri finished with the towel. "Well, how do you like it?" he asked.

"Beautiful! Now we have a flag!" said Mikhail.

"*Khorosho*. Then let's sew it," said the Flight Engineer.

Taking needle and thread, Yuri started to sew the towel on the white rectangle, while Ivan tackled the sewing of the red stripes.

"Going back to Yura's problem, I think I know a legal way of making him stay the day before the maneuvers," said Vasily.

"Yes? How's that?" Mikhail asked.

"When he's in the mess hall or somewhere like that, the day of his departure, he gets violently ill, so he won't be able to leave for a day. Next day we have the maneuvers, so all we have to do is to find a way to get rid of his replacement without anyone noticing it. Then we could take Yura with us in his place."

"That looks about right. The only thing is that we'll have to get rid of the new engineer for a time long enough to be able to participate in the maneuvers. For starters, they take about seventeen hours. Besides that, add the time from the day before to take off time, plus the time we'll take to reach America. Lastly, we have to get Yura in the plane legally, so Serghey doesn't get suspicious and raise hell."

"We could lock him up in a closet, and leave him there for the rest of the day," suggested Alexey.

"Agreed. But don't forget that we need a minimum of twenty hours. Only locked up, after two or three hours there he'll be taken out of there because of the loud racket he'll make. Or perhaps he kicks the door down, sounds the alarm, and all hell breaks loose," replied Mikhail.

"That's easy to solve, Captain," said the Flight Engineer. "Let's silence him. That is, hit him in the head hard enough to keep him asleep for the next five hours, at least. Tie him, gag him, and lock him up in a closet or somewhere similar. He'll be there until he's found, and no one knows when that will be."

"Very well. That's a way of getting rid of him. But, how are you going to enter the plane without Serghey seeing you?" asked Mikhail.

"That's easy too. By that time, I should be feeling alright from my 'illness.' You'll be needing a Flight Engineer because yours 'disappeared' mysteriously and left no traces. You can't fly without an Engineer. To get another Engineer from another crew on such short notice would be almost impossible because of the paperwork involved. The only Engineer readily available will be me. You talk to Commander Degtyaryov, explain your case to him and let him know I'm the only Engineer available on such short notice, and that I'm still in the base since, because of my 'illness,' I could not leave. If he allows my stay here for one more day, I'll be able to fly with you in the maneuvers, and then 'fly south' the next day."

"Perfect! You solved your own problem," exclaimed Mikhail.

"Yes. But for that I'm counting on you all."

"And we're counting on you to get out of here," said the Captain.

"I think Degtyaryov will grant your petition, Captain. He's a sensible man," said Ivan, still sewing stripes.

"Captain, I also realize that this solves another immediate problem we're having!" Vasily said. "You see, if we take off as scheduled in the maneuvers' plans, we'll have the two TU-95s from Kipelovo flying with us down to the Atlantic," the copilot explained. "And although they'll complete their function further away from us, and from there they'll continue flying to Cuba, if we are delayed here due to the problem of the missing Flight Engineer, they will not be able to wait for us. They'll just continue flying alone, which means that we'll be *completely alone* all the way! No one around to bother us, not even the planes from Kipelovo!"

"True. I had not realized that," said Mikhail. "Fortune must be smiling on us."

"I only hope she keeps on smiling on us all the way to America," the copilot said.

At the table, Anatoly and Pavel busied themselves building the high frequency circuit of the booster, cutting wires and parts, soldering them in the jamming device when possible, otherwise, they just join them wire to wire. The other crewmen around them watched their companions working.

"Captain, I was thinking ..." said Vasily. "As soon as we turn towards Scotland, Serghey will realize it and raise a thousand hells."

"How will he know we're turning towards Scotland? Unless we tell him ..." said Alexey.

"Granted," said Vasily. "He'll not realize it if all he sees is sky and sea outside, but remember that the area around us is going to be teeming with Navy ships. As soon as we deviate from the planned return route by just a few kilometers, they'll call us, asking us what's happening, and what we're doing. Don't forget that's why we decided to go to America instead."

"I imagine that when the ships start asking, that's when the damn stoolie will ask where we're going," said Alexey.

"Exactly. That's why I was thinking that we have to find a way of getting him out of the fight while we make the escape ruse towards Scotland," Vasily finished his explanation.

"How about sabotaging the radio? That way he won't be able to hear what the ships are saying," suggested Ivan.

"No. I don't want the plane's equipment damaged," said Mikhail. "I want Serghey out of the way, not our equipment. We could need the radio later on. If we damage it we won't be able to use it."

"Well! We have to do something! We can't leave him there while we escape! What about sickening him again?" Vasily suggested again.

"I don't think it will make much of a difference," said Mikhail. "We want him out of the way until we reach America. Anyway, your idea of sickening him is not bad, just that I want to have him with us in the plane."

"Come on, Captain! Don't confuse me again! Why not sickening him again?" Vasily asked.

"Several reasons. If we sicken him, he'll get suspicious. Remember that we already sickened him once. Besides, from Intelligence they'll just send us another replacement radioman, a stoolie like him. You know they have those in quantity. So there we'd be back to square one."

"What do we do, then?" Vasily asked again.

"Put him to sleep," said Mikhail.

"Sleep? What do you mean? Hit him in the head?"

"I wish I could do that. He deserves that and more, but, no, that's not what I have in mind. I'm thinking about the same method we used on him in the mess hall, but this time we'll put him to sleep using sleeping pills we'll put in something he'll drink."

"Oh, I see! But, will he accept the drink? Usually we don't speak to him, and much less share with him what we eat or drink. Wouldn't that sudden demonstration of 'friendship' make him suspicious? He might refuse to accept or to drink it," said Vasily.

"He better drink it. Otherwise we'll have to smack him on the head, if necessary. For his own good he better drinks it, or he'll wake up with the biggest headache he'd ever had in his whole damn life as a KGB stoolie," said Mikhail.

"*Khorosho.* Now, where will we get those pills?" Alexey asked.

"The same way we got the laxative," said Mikhail.

"What laxative?" asked Alexey, surprised.

"The laxative we used to get him sick the evening we had the last party," Mikhail answered.

"Oh! So that's why he was sick that evening! He didn't get sick, but you guys sickened him! Now I understand why you said that you already 'sickened him once,'" said Alexey, laughing.

"Yes, that's what happened. Now, returning to our subject matter. One of you guys goes to the doctor, complains that he has insomnia, and asks him for some of those pills," said Mikhail.

"Sounds easy, but I think those pills the doctor prescribes them only if one *really* needs them. To determine need one has to go through a whole battery of tests and questions on why one is feeling like that. They'll try to find out the reasons for the insomnia. One may end up grounded and seeing the base psychiatrist. That takes even more time and more complications. And at the end they might not even give you the damn pills," said Jonas.

"Mmm … If that is so difficult, what about if I just make them believe I'm dying, go the doctor's office, and once there, at the first opportunity, I come flying out with a bottle of those pills?" suggested Alexey.

"It's risky, but if you want to try it, it's your call," Mikhail said.

"*Ladno.* I'll try it. Anyway, if they catch me the worst that can happen is that the nurse or the doctor there reprimand me."

"Very well. Go as soon as you can," said Mikhail.

The stripes and the towel already sewn on the bedsheet, Yuri and Ivan showed off their home made flag. "Here it is!" exclaimed Yuri.

"We'll hide it together with the booster until the day of the maneuvers. Then we'll smuggle it all into the plane," Mikhail said.

"Agreed," said both crewmen, folding the banner.

Looking at his watch, Mikhail noted the time: "0242. Almost time to go. Comrades, do you have much more to do?"

"I'm afraid so, Captain. We still have a lot to work with. I don't think we'll be finishing soon. It's late already, isn't it?" Anatoly asked.

"Yes, it's almost 0300, and in a few hours we fly. We'll have to leave the completion of the booster for the next night."

"*Ladno,*" said both technicians, pushing the work aside. Anatoly picked up the parts on the table and placed them together with the other devices. Pavel returned the tools to the canvas bag.

✳   ✳   ✳   ✳

That evening, after the long routine patrol flight, Alexey stopped by the Infirmary. Clutching his belly, he started to moan. "Someone help! I'm dying! This hurts! Help!"

The nurse there, seeing Alexey arriving in such painful state, ran to meet him, took him by his arm and had him lie on a nearby recliner. "Take it easy! Take it easy! You'll be alright," she said.

"Take it easy?! I'm half dead and you want me to take it easy?" he screamed at the woman. "Listen! You better go get the doctor right now! Move! If I die here, you'll be the only one responsible!"

"*Ladno*. Remain here while I get the doctor."

As soon as the nurse left the room, Alexey jumped from the recliner and started a frantic search in the whole room. He opened drawers, boxes and closets. Seeing a medicine cabinet on the wall, he ran towards it. Through its glass door he could see row after row of bottles filled with liquids and pills in all colors, shapes and sizes. He pulled its door, but in vain. "Damn! It's locked!" he whispered. Remembering that he saw a clump of keys in one of the desk drawers, he returned to the desk in two long steps and pulled drawers with both his hands until he found the keys. Back in front of the cabinet, he tried key after key until the lock finally yielded. He pushed the bottles to the sides until he saw, in the back row, a bottle with a handwritten label:

Sleeping pills
Do not administer without prescription!

"This is what I need!" he muttered.

Suddenly, he heard steps coming in his direction. Taking the bottle with one hand, with the other he closed the cabinet. Realizing that he would not have time to return the keys to the drawer before the nurse returned with the doctor, he took the only way out still available. Sticking his head out the window next to the cabinet, he saw the coast was clear. Gripping the keys firmly, so they made no noise, Alexey jumped out head first without even touching the window sill. He hardly touched the ground when he was already running towards the infirmary's rear.

Turning around the back corner, he stopped to catch his breath. Peeking around the corner, he looked towards the window. "Beautiful! They didn't see me," he congratulated himself. Once sure that he was not being followed, he leaned against the back wall and rested. After a few seconds he noticed that he was still holding the clump of keys. Looking around, he found next to him a box full of garbage. Throwing the keys there, he regained his composure and headed to his quarters.

*   *   *   *

"Where's the patient?" asked the doctor.

"He isn't here? Where is he?" asked the nurse, confused, looking around the empty room.

"That's what I'm asking you, Lieutenant. Don't ask me!" said the doctor, irritated.

"When I left the room, he was lying there, complaining about strong stomach aches."

"Tovarishch Leytenant! I'm a very busy man to waste my time like this!" the doctor angrily burst, amid expletives.

"But, doctor! I'm telling you, when I left the room, there was someone here!"

"Very well. I believe you," said the doctor to his confused assistant, in a calmer voice. "But next time make him go to my office. Even if he has to crawl!" The physician turned around and returned to his desk.

The astonished nurse, not knowing what to do or say, sat back at her desk to ponder the mystery.

*   *   *   *

Standing by the row of file cabinets, Senior Sergeant Sudaryev called one of his mechanics: "Ostrov! Go get the tow truck. We need to pull *Red 67* in."

"Red 67? Do we have to work on it?" asked the mechanic, surprised.

"Yes, we have to replace its radar," said the Sergeant, reading the next work order on his clipboard, the replacement of the current *'Uspekh'* targeting and control radar in the belly of the Tupolev with the newly-arrived *'Korshun'*.

"Replace its radar?" asked the mechanic once again, even more surprised this time.

"Yes, that's what I said. What now, going deaf on me?" said the Sergeant.

"No, it's that I thought that radar was going to be installed in Col. Rudenko's plane."

"That's not what's written on the work order I have here, duly signed by our Comrade Commander Degtyaryov. It clearly says *Red 67,* not *Red 57."*

"Hmmm...." not totally convinced, Ostrov opened the file cabinet drawer for *Red 57,* pulled the folder for the electronic equipment, and searched for the *'Korshun'* passport. Not finding it there, he opened the drawer for *Red 67,* pulled the folder for the electronic equipment for the latter, and found the passport stashed there.

Pulling the document out of the folder, he commented: "This is weird ... I could swear that radar was for *Red 57.*"

"I think you need a rest, Ostrov. So much work lately is making you forget things. My work order here says *Red 67,* and the *'Korshun's'* passport was in *Red 67's* drawer, so that tells me it goes on that plane," said Sudaryev.

"Could they have made a mistake?" the mechanic asked, still doubtful.

"This work order came straight from Commander Degtyaryov's office, and in our perfect Soviet Navy, Commanders do not make that kind of mistake. So, stop it, get on the truck and bring *Red 67* in," Sudaryev finalized the conversation with one wave of the work order in his hand.

The mechanic turned around and headed to the parked trucks outside the repairs hangar.

*   *   *   *

After he finished the signing of several routine orders and other documents, Col. Yakovlev's attention was attracted for a moment to the noise coming from the other side of the window. An Antonov AN-24 transport plane was taking off on its return flight back to Murmansk.

Again came to his mind the mysterious scene he saw a few days before, when he returned from Region Headquarters in that same airplane. The uncertainty of not knowing the whole truth about the matter made him try to solve it, once and for all.

His eyes focused on the airplane, he followed it in its ascent until it was just a little dot on the reddish glow of the sunset, and the reverberations of its turbo-prop engines just a soft murmur.

The airplane disappeared in the distance, but the scene in the swamps was still before his eyes, as clear as the day he returned from Murmansk. His eyes slowly drifted from the window and stopped at the air base plan next to it, on the wall.

His sight roamed the map, stopping over Runway 14A. Yakovlev stood up from his seat and unhurriedly walked towards the wall, his eyes still fixed on the map. Following a logical approach to the problem, he began at the beginning, trying to find in the map the approximate area where he saw the group.

With his index finger he followed the gliding route taken by all the planes that land on Runway 14A. This yielded no results. Soon he was at mid runway. The plan indicated only what was supposed to be there: nothing but swamps all around. Carefully he searched for any information the map could have about anything of importance there. Besides the swamps there was nothing else. The swamps weren't even named!

What could be there that could be useful to a group? he thought. The map showed nothing there, and he had to know by all means. In a few fast, long steps he returned to his desk and dialed his Deputy's extension. Nothing ... the phone on the other side rang, but no one picked up.

Suddenly, a voice came from the other side. He asked for Nikitin. "No, Lt. Col. Nikitin already left. There's no one else in the office. I was already leaving when the phone rang." Yakovlev thanked the voice on the other side and hung up.

Once again he asked himself: *Will it be worthwhile to send a whole patrol to investigate whatever could have been there?*

Even though he didn't have to give reasons to anybody but himself, he considered a waste of time and effort sending a patrol there. He would have hated to misuse his manpower that way. If he was well-known for something, it was for his efficiency.

For the first time he was happy Nikitin was not in his office to answer his call. On his part, he thought he'd be better off forgetting the whole matter and retiring to his quarters, like everyone else. It was late already, and his body screamed for a sorely needed rest he was going to make sure he'd get.

*   *   *   *

Anatoly and Pavel had already taken out the equipment from the location they had previously hidden them after the last meet. Mikhail just stood next to them, looking at the technicians work on the complicated labyrinth of electronic parts and circuits.

"I wonder how you can understand that mess of wires and parts," he said.

"Very simple, Captain. We studied all that at the Academy," replied Anatoly.

"Sometimes I wish I were young again, to learn about those things of modern electronics. During the war I could fix most of my own problems in the airplane: the engine, the radio, etc. It was convenient to know how to fix them! Especially after a dogfight, when the planes returned full of bullet holes and the mechanics and technicians could not fix them all. Then I could fix my own things using their tools. Of course, as long as the problems weren't too complicated and beyond my knowledge. So I made sure my plane would be always ready to return to the front."

Mikhail paused, gathering his thoughts, then continued: "But today matters are so different! Turboprops, I know their basic principle of operation, but I can't repair them. The same happens with the turbojets. Seeing the mechanics working on them, I see they're not as simple as the piston engines of the old propeller fighters I used to fly during the war. Those were the only ones I could repair. The same with the old vacuum tube radios we used then. About radars, detectors, identifiers, transponders, electronic jamming systems and the rest of the electronic equipment our plane carries and you guys operate today, I know only the basic principles of operation, but repairing them … Well, that's another matter altogether!"

"I understand, Captain," said Anatoly without lifting his eyes from the equipment he was working on.

Then, muffled knocks came from the door. "It looks like the rest of the guys are here," said Mikhail. After opening the door he found Ivan and Alexey standing there. Returning with the two men to the table, Anatoly thanked him: *"Spasibo,* Captain."

"What are you thanking me for?" Mikhail asked, surprised.

"For bringing the light back. When you went to open the door you took the flashlight with you, leaving me in the dark," said the technician, smiling.

"Oooh! I'm so sorry! *Izvini,* I didn't realize it!" Mikhail burst in excuses. The other crewmen burst in laughs.

That night the rest of the crew was excused from the meeting. However, the need of seeing the development of their plan come to an end ended up being more than they could take. Soon the crew of *Red 67*—except its radio operator—was complete in Mikhail's room.

Pavel and Anatoly continued their task of building the booster. Pavel had previously drawn a schematic diagram of the equipment, which simplified its interconnection. Anatoly then reviewed the circuitry.

"Good job, Pavlik. With the diagram it will be easier to assemble it, rather than picture it using only our minds. However, I see that here we must make a change."

"Where?" asked Pavel.

"This amplifier circuit here. With the specs you've given it, it will not have the necessary power. Remember, we can't use this equipment as is. We must increase its power, otherwise it will not jam the signal."

"I see. You're right. I got that diagram from a manual about those amplifiers. I copied just as it was in the book."

"Anyway. That's simple to solve. You work on the equipment. Solder all the parts and wires in the circuit as you drew it in the diagram, but don't work on the amplifier yet. I'll make all the calculations and necessary modifications to increase its power."

Following the instructions of the technician, Pavel continued working on the equipment. Anatoly proceeded to modify the amplifier circuit.

Meanwhile, Vasily and Mikhail chatted. "Once the booster is built, we'll have everything ready and on schedule. The only problem to solve now is Yura's transfer," said Mikhail.

"Aha. All we have to do now is wait for the maneuvers to start, so Icarus can take flight. Yura's matter will have to wait until then so we can start his plan," said Vasily.

"Well. Icarus has his wax wings almost done," Mikhail said, then added: "Which is great, as I was informed this morning that our plane is being retrofitted with the new *'Korshun'* radar. That will guarantee our participation in the *Okean* Maneuvers."

"Otlichno! So you guys could pull it off!" said Vasily, looking at Anatoly.

"Yes, it was not difficult. But you had to see Pavel's face when I made the switch! He looked as pale as a ghost!" Anatoly laughed at his own remark.

"Well, you'd be pale too if they had caught you doing that. You wouldn't be laughing now!" said his friend.

"What are you talking about, Pavlik! If they had caught him, they would have caught me too," said Yuri, their partner in crime. "We're all up to the hilt in this. They catch one, they catch us all. We're all in the same boat ... or in the same plane."

"The important thing is that now we'll be in the maneuvers, so all our preparations will not be in vain," said Vasily.

"How can you be so sure? Col. Rudenko could simply choose to fly in our plane, and then, it's back to square one," said Alexey.

"Not really. Knowing Rudenko, he flies *only* in his plane. He doesn't trust any other plane here," Mikhail answered Alexey's question. "Knowing him as I do, I bet he'd try other things, including getting the radar out of our plane and have it reinstalled in his, but flying our plane is not one of them."

"Very well. I hope he doesn't change his mind all of a sudden," said Alexey.

"Don't worry, he will not," Mikhail comforted the navigator. "However, I have an announcement to make: This weekend I won't be here. I'll visit my family in Leningrad."

"How many days?" asked Vasily.

"I could get a home leave pass for three days only, but that will be enough. I'll return on Tuesday, in the morning flight from Murmansk."

"Have a nice trip, Captain!" said Anatoly, his eyes still on his calculations.

"I envy you, Captain. I haven't had home leaves for a long time. I'm forbidden to have them," commented Jonas.

Thus, seeing Anatoly and Pavel work on the booster, the crew of *Red 67* spent the time. That night they went to bed as the sun rose in the horizon. They were, as usual, tired but satisfied.

*   *   *   *

In the darkness of his room, his eyes almost popped out of their orbits searching around for the gigantic figures, until he realized it was nothing more than a dream, a very bad dream. Stretching his arm, he took the small towel over the nighttable next to his bed and dried the sweat from his forehead and face. His hands were shaking like leaves in the wind, just like his whole body: uncontrollably.

The phosphorescence of the alarm clock's face announced the time: 0310. Still almost two more hours to start his day but he knew he wasn't going to be able to sleep again. He feared finding them in his dream, or should he have said nightmare? Pushing the blanket aside, he sat on the bed's edge. He turned the nightlamp on, pulled a drawer in the nighttable, and took a cigar from a box. His trembling hands made it difficult to light, but he finally got it going.

Smoking the Cuban cigar seemed to calm him. Once completely awake, Col. Yakovlev remembered that he was in his quarters at the base. As long as he had to put his plans in motion, he wasn't going to be able to see his family again. He'd have to wait until the inspection was over. Perhaps then he could visit his wife and children.

Feeling more relaxed, he thought about the dream he had. How stupid it was! Since he was not sleeping anymore, he could judge it to be so. The dream took him back to his seat in the plane that brought him back from Murmansk the day of his most recent visit there. Looking through the window to the swamps below, instead of the group of people he was expecting to see, his terrified eyes met a group of humanoids of gigantic dimensions and monstrous appearance. And they looked back at him.

One of them stretched his arms. His enormous hands grabbed the plane in mid flight and shook it violently in an attempt to get rid of its passengers. The people in the plane were ejected in all directions. He held fast to his seat as firmly as he could, desperately screaming for help, but all his efforts were in vain. He was flung out of the fuselage, falling to the ground like a rock.

Once emptied of its occupants the giants took the airplane with them, and laughing sardonically, ran towards the sea. As he fell, he saw the giants getting deeper into the water, more and more distant, until they could not be seen anymore. He landed with a loud thunder in the middle of a great hall. Here bodyless faces with no distinguishable features looked at him accusingly, holding him responsible for the appearance of the giants. Also for allowing them to take the plane.

Next he was taken to a court where he was tried and found guilty, despite his vehement protests of innocence. He was summarily sentenced to execution by firing squad. He was immediately dragged by faceless soldiers. Trembling feverishly and sweating profusely, he was taken to an old cemetery. His hands were tied to a tall post, facing a large, thick stone wall, his back to the firing squad, like a common traitor, in the same way he saw the partisans do when he was much younger, during the Great Patriotic War.

Clamping his teeth hard, grinding against each other, he closed his eyes and waited for the bullets that would put an end to his life. The loud detonations of the firing rifles brought him back to his bed, back to reality.

A revelation? A premonition? Of what? On the one hand, he was a convinced atheist. On the other hand, he was a firm believer in logic. Therefore, everything that happened must have had a logical and rational explanation. He never took a dream as a revelation of something to happen in the future. In his reasoning that was foolish.

Not finding any sense in the dream itself, he took it as a warning from his subconscious mind to investigate what he saw in the swamps. He decided to find out before he had another dream like this one, or he ended up insane. He had to do it. At least to confirm if there really was someone walking in the swamps or if he just had a vision.

Later on he'd call Nikitin and ask him about the area, what could have been there. He'd also have Nikitin ask the pilots of the morning flight from Murmansk if they got to see something that day. However, he had to have him ask them all in a casual way. Pure curiosity, no mention of visions or dreams. That would have made him look foolish.

*   *   *   *

That Friday Mikhail took the evening return flight from Kuzomen to Murmansk, spending the night at the naval base there. On Saturday morning he boarded Aeroflot's Tupolev TU-134 that would take him back home: Leningrad.

While the airplane waited for the tower's permission to take-off, Mikhail let his mind fly off once again. This time he concentrated on the immediate problem and the main reason for his visit home. If he could escape he'd necessarily have to leave his family behind in the Soviet Union. He knew his escape would only worsen their situation. His wife would lose their small apartment and his sons would lose their jobs.

Knowing this made him feel grieved. But on the other hand he also knew that escaping was better than committing suicide. He thought that if he managed to escape and somehow reach America, from there perhaps he'd be able to fight and get them all out of the Union, something he'd be unable to do if he kills himself.

The passenger plane started its take-off run. Mikhail sank deeper in his thoughts. In a few more minutes he'd see his beloved Irina, whom he married more than thirty years ago, amid the bursting of the German bombs and shells, before the Nazi blockade closed the city.

During the heroic 900-plus days the city was besieged, several times Mikhail lost contact with Irina's and his own family. Despite the war, though, he never lost hope of finding her alive. In the few letters he received from her during that grim period—usually smuggled out of the city by the trucks running on the icy 'Road of Life' on Lake Ladoga—he found out he was a proud father. Mikhail Mikhailovich Makarov—Misha—the third in the family to carry the name, had been born. Since then, day after day he dreamt about the end of the war, when he was going to be able to see his son, his first born, and carry him in his arms.

Finally, on January 27th, 1945, the German siege was broken and Mikhail could return to the city … just to find sadness and disappointment. Irina survived the siege because she was a *medsestra,* an Army nurse. Tending the wounded soldiers inside Leningrad allowed her to receive military rations, which were slightly more than those received by the civilian population of the besieged city. But she was still suffering from the wounds received in the intense and daily artillery barrage and aerial bombings the city was subjected to, courtesy of the Nazi *Wehrmacht* and the *Luftwaffe* … same which killed his first son. By war's end she had achieved the rank of Army Lieutenant in the Medical Service, and had been awarded the medal "For Distinguished Labor in the Medical Service."

The war finished and came Alexandr, their second son, then Stepan. By then Mikhail was a famous fighter pilot, hero of hundreds of dogfights, so he could afford luxuries such as a government-provided fully-furnished apartment, and access to exclusive stores where they could buy certain articles still scarce. All these were privileges available to the select few, because of the hardships caused by the war just ended. However, as his political situation worsened, gradually he lost those privileges.

Once Mikhail was demoted and transferred to the north, Irina had to give back to the State their large apartment on Nyekrasova Street, in the center of the city. This despite the fact that Mikhail was a twice decorated Hero of the Soviet Union and therefore, entitled to occupy that apartment for as long as he lived. Irina then moved in with their two children to her mother's small apartment on Malyy Prospekt, in the Vasileostrovskiy District, in the northwestern side of the city.

As his children grew up and married, they had no other choice but to remain right there with their mother. Soon the small apartment was crammed with three families: Irina and her mother, and their two sons with their respective wives and children. Eight persons in total. The sole idea of knowing that his family was living in those conditions, and not being able to do anything about it, filled Mikhail with more anger and frustration.

While his mind flew amid the clouds together with the plane, the aircraft finally reached Leningrad. The flight had ended. Mikhail was taken out of his thoughts by the stewardess' announcement on the speakers above. Minutes later, the twin engine passenger plane slowly approached the terminal at Pulkovo Airport. Its distinctive five glass towers and the name of the city written in both Latin and Cyrillic characters, imparted the building a modern look.

After obtaining his only baggage he walked to the Bus Station. Here he boarded Bus №39, which connected with the *Leningradskoe Metro,* the city's underground transportation. As the vehicle departed, from somewhere floated in the voice of a new young singer named Alla Pugachova. Her song about Leningrad poured the first stanza of Oleg Mandelstam's verses honoring the city:

> *I returned to my city,*
> *known to the point of tears,*
> *to the nerves,*
> *to the inflamed glands*

of my childhood years …
Leningrad! I still don't want to die!

There were no words that could have been a more befitting portrayal of Mikhail's most joyful feelings: *Finally home!*

At the Moscow Station of the Moscow-Petrograd metro line, he waited for the arrival of the train. He placed by his side the bag where he carried gifts for his relatives. The growing rumble of the metal snake announced its arrival. As soon as it opened its doors, Mikhail stepped inside and sat down to wait for what to him—anxious to get home as soon as possible—was a very long trip to the Central District of the city.

After stops at the Victory Park, Power Station, Moscow Gate and Frunze stations, he still had five more stations to reach home. The anxiety of seeing his family again made the short trip seem long, the stations seeming to be fifty and the train running terribly slow—at least to him. The train continued its run under the Obvodnyy Canal, stopped for a moment at the Technological Institute station, then passed under Fontanka, another of the many canals for which the city is famous, and which gives it, among others, the name of 'Venice of the East.'

Shortly after, the train stopped at the Peace Square Station. Just one more station to reach the center of the city, where he'd make a transfer. At the Nyevsky Prospekt Station, under the avenue of the same name, Mikhail got off the train and walked towards the station under the Gostinyy Dvor Department Stores, where he waited for the final train that would take him home.

Once inside the train of the Nyevsko-Vasileostrovskaya metro line, the commuter train traversed the city center, entered the tunnel under the wide and powerful Nyeva River, and reached its last stop: Vasileostrovskaya Station, in the district of the same name and where his family resided.

Crossing Sryednyy Prospekt, and after a short one-block walk through the Sixth and Seventh Line street—which seemed more a run than a walk—Mikhail finally arrived at Malyy Prospekt. He continued walking at a hurried pace, crossed the street, and stopped before the building marked with the number 15. He tackled the stairs three steps at the time, his boots echoing throughout the building.

Standing before his family's apartment door, he had to look presentable before knocking at the door. Besides, he needed to catch his breath after the hurried race to get home. Making a quick inspection of himself, he straightened his officer's cap, pulled his necktie into place and arranged his uniform. Once sure that everything looked alright and was in its proper place, he drew his typical smile and knocked at the door.

Irina's surprise, reflected in her face, became joy when she saw him standing at the door. Stretching her arms, she threw herself over him, drawing him closer to her. "Misha, you're here!" she exclaimed.

Moved, Mikhail wanted to talk, to say the many emotions he felt. The words simply refused to leave his body, bunching up and making a knot in his throat. Finally he managed to whisper a few choked words. "Irinka, Irinka, how much I missed you!"

"Misha, I'm so happy to see you here!" she said. From her tightly closed eyes tears of joy ran down her rosy cheeks.

As soon as they heard Irina shout Mikhail's nickname, his grandsons ran to receive him at the door. The happy meeting was interrupted by four little hands pulling his pants and by a couple of high-pitched voices coming from below, *"Dyedushka! Dyedushka!* Hug me too! Hug me too!"

Taking both children in his arms, he hugged and kissed them. "Misha, Andry-usha, *Dyedushka* brought you some toys!"

"Dyedushka, when I grow up, I'm going to be a pilot like you. At school they say I draw airplanes very well," said Mikhail Alexandrovich, the oldest of the two children.

"Yes, my dear. Yes!" Mikhail agreed, taking one children on each side as he walked down the hall towards the small kitchen, where the rest of his family awaited him. His sons, their wives and his mother-in-law greeted him. Alexandr, his oldest son, stood up and ran to hug him. Sonya, Alexandr's wife, took both children from Mikhail's arms.

"Papa!" exclaimed Alexandr, hugging and kissing his father on both cheeks. Stepan, behind him, repeated the warm greeting. His daughters-in-law greeted him the same way. In a corner of the kitchen, on a comfortable armchair, sat his silver-gray-haired mother-in-law, a blanket covering her legs.

"Babushka ... " Mikhail said, kneeling before her while planting a soft kiss on her hand.

"Son, don't kneel. You're going to ruin your beautiful uniform!" protested the old mother.

"Don't worry, *Babushka.* Don't worry," replied Mikhail, covering her with kisses.

Once the commotion of his surprise arrival calmed down, Mikhail looked at his Irina. Her blond hair could have been streaked by many silver lines, but for him she was the same joyful, smiling, beautiful girl he once met in the Summer

Garden. Despite all the hardships she stood during the war she was still agile, alive. She still smiled with the same happy beam. Her eyes still shone with that same sparkle she had then. For Mikhail she was the very same Irina of thirty something years ago.

"Papa, how's life at the base?" asked Stepan.

"As usual, boring. Those flights over the Atlantic Ocean are long and boring. Next month we'll have the *Okean* maneuvers again. And you, how's life treating you?"

"Hard. Still working in the same factory. Last month Andryusha got sick and that was a complete disaster. Sometimes Nadya, sometimes me, we had to take turns going to the children's hospital to take care of him."

"What about apartments?"

"The same. Still on the waiting list," replied Stepan

"Four years in that damn list, and I still don't see the day when we get an apartment!" Alexandr burst in anger.

"A friend of mine was on the list for only six months. And not only that, she got an apartment in one of the new buildings of the Victory Park complex," commented Sonya, Alexandr's wife.

"How could she do that?" asked Irina.

"Simple. She married one of the Production Managers of the Kirov Plant." Everyone understood immediately, not being necessary to offer more explanations as to how the friend was able to bypass the obligatory waiting lists, part and parcel in the life of the common Soviet citizen.

Mikhail listened in silence to the complaints of his relatives, their comments about the number one problem in Leningrad, also the number one problem in Moscow, Kiev, Minsk, and in the whole of the Soviet Union: Housing. He only regretted not being anymore in a position to help them as before.

However, he didn't have much time to ponder on those problems. His grandsons climbing on his legs quickly got him out of his thoughts. *"Dyedushka,* where are the toys you brought us? We want to play with them," said both children in unison.

Mikhail stood up and walked to the table where he had placed the bag with the gifts he brought for his relatives. The children eagerly followed him. From the plastic bag he pulled a box with a metal scale model of the Yak-3 fighter, used by the Soviet V-VS during the Great Patriotic War.

"For Misha, the youngest pilot in the Air Force, a fighter airplane!" Smiling from ear to ear, young Mikhail opened the box as fast as his small hands allowed him and pulled the plane out.

"And for me, *Dyedushka?* And for me?" Andryan repeated time and again, jumping with anticipation.

"For little Andryusha *Dyedushka* brought a paratrooper!" Mikhail exclaimed as he threw the toy in the air. As it opened its parachute in mid air, young Andryan ran to grab it in its descent.

"Come on, children, go play in the bedroom. And remember! No fighting!" Mikhail sent the children off.

"Yes, *Dyedushka,"* replied the boys as they disappeared in the bedroom, their new toys in hand.

"Irinka, I kept my word. Here's your Karelian coat," Mikhail said, showing a beautifully decorated hand-woven wool coat.

"You didn't forget! At last, my coat! But, Misha! It's so expensive! You must have paid a lot for it!" she complained, still smiling. Taking the wool, she placed it over her chest, showing it to those present.

"Don't worry about it. You know that in Murmansk one can get those things at a very low price, under certain circumstances, of course." The circumstances Mikhail referred to had to do with the broad Black Market in practically anything imaginable that could have been in demand, and which used to be a second economy in the whole of the USSR.

Even though he only had a few rubles left in his pocket, he preferred to make the sacrifice and buy the coat. That had been a promise he had made to her a long time ago. Knowing he'd leave the USSR perhaps forever, that would be one of the many happy memories she'd have of him once he were gone.

"To the girls, I brought these scarves. For you, boys, I brought these cotton shirts. I'm sorry if they look very military, but that's precisely what they are. Those were the only ones I could get at the Commissary in Murmansk."

Turning to the old lady sitting on the armchair, he showed her a colorful blanket. "For *Babushka,* this blanket, hand-woven in Azerbaijan. It'll keep you warm."

"Son! You shouldn't have bothered! God bless you and pay you back!" replied the lady stretching her arms, bringing him closer and kissing him in the forehead.

Irina placed on the table a tray with several tea cups, then brought a steaming hot *samovar.* In an ambiance of intimacy, sipping *chay,* Mikhail spent the first day of his last visit to his relatives.

*   *   *   *

On Sunday, after arriving at Mayakovskaya Station, located at the corner of Marat Street and Nyevsky Prospekt, Mikhail and his family headed to Insurrection Square Station, under the square of the same name and in the same center of the great city.

Here they boarded a car of the Kirov-Vyborg metro line, first step on the trip to the Piskaryovskoye National Cemetery. Leaving the city center, they stopped at Chernishevskaya Station, passed under the Nyeva River and arrived at Lenin Square Station, where they got off and left behind the underground system to board Express Bus №100. Getting off the bus at Bol'nitsy Myechnikova, they transferred to Local Bus №9, which made routine stops in the Piskaryovka District, where the cemetery is located.

After a short ride and walk to the Avenue of the Undefeated, they reached the gigantic burial ground, surrounded by an enormous granite wall and where rest the remains of more than 570,000 human beings, men, women, and children, soldiers and civilians, all victims of the bombs, artillery shells, bullets, cold and starvation the city suffered for more than 900 days, more than thirty years before.

Whenever Mikhail visited the city for him it was almost a ritual to visit the cemetery together with his family, in order to leave some flowers in honor of his mother, who died of starvation so his sister Natalya could live a few more days … just to die victim of the Nazi bombs during the long blockade. Here also lie his father and his oldest brother. Both fell in combat fighting against Nazism, like Irina's father and all her brothers. His own son too, Mikhail Mikhailovich, his first pride, whom he never met. Last, but not least, his friends from childhood days, from school days, from his days in the Air Force. Like the Makarovs, Sonya and Nadya also have relatives here—like almost all *Leningradtsy*—all sacrificed in the altar of the Motherland during those fateful 900 days.

The solemnity of the place stilled everyone and everything. Even the children, who usually ran all around when they strolled with their parents, remained silent.

"Mama, this is where *Dyedushka's* Mama lives, right?" Mikhail Alexandrovich asked in a whisper.

"Yes, dear. We'll visit her again," Sonya, his mother, whispered back.

Slowly walking through the Central Avenue of the cemetery they reached the foot of the colossal statue of *Rodina*, the Russian Motherland. On her hands a wreath of oak sprigs, eternal homage to her sons who gave their lives for her defense during the Great Patriotic War. Nearing the monument, Mikhail let fall at its base a bouquet of flowers. The others observed the ritual in silence.

Like Sonya and Nadya, Irina could not contain the stream of tears running down their cheeks. The solemn background music, broadcast by loudspeakers all over the graveyard, imparted an air of mourning and grief.

Mikhail turned around to see the green-grass-covered common graves bordering the Central Avenue, and where lie those who left, never to return. On the graves stood granite tombstones with engraved oak leaves and the year when they were dug: 1941 ... 1942 ... 1943 ... 1944 ... 1945. Atop, a red star or a hammer and sickle, depending if those lying there were Red Guards or workers and civilians. With his eyes he tried to see them, only to be betrayed by the tears that blurred his vision.

However, what he couldn't see with his physical eyes, he saw with the eyes of his heart. He remembered his childhood days, how happy he was when his parents, his brother and his sister were alive. The jokes and games he played with the neighborhood kids and with his mates at school. The nights of drinking and singing while in the University, and later in the Air Force barracks, after the Nazi assault on the country. All destroyed, all gone because of the Fascist monster.

"Mama, why is *Dyedushka* crying?" Andryan asked his mother.

"He cries because he has no mama."

"Oh! How sad!" replied the child in his high-pitched voice. "Mama, you'll never leave me, right? I love you very much!"

"No, son. I'll never leave you. I also love you very much," replied Nadya, pulling her son tightly against her chest, kissing him, a flood of tears pouring out of her eyes.

Seeing those painful reminders of a horrendous war, Mikhail asked himself how such a holocaust could be allowed to happen. He raised his eyes and as if answering his question, he read before him, engraved in fine Estonian marble, these immortal verses by Olga Bergholts, the famed poetess, also from Leningrad:

> "Here lie Leningraders,
>
> Here are townsfolk, men, women, children.
>
> By their sides are Red Army soldiers.
>
> With their entire lives
>
> They defended you, Leningrad,
>
> The cradle of the Revolution.
>
> We cannot enumerate all their noble names here,

So many are there under the eternal granite guard.

But know, when honoring these stones

"Nikto nye zabyt, i nichto nye zabyto—Nobody is forgotten, and nothing is forgotten."

✳   ✳   ✳   ✳

On that sunny hot Monday morning of August, Mikhail and Irina set out from Malyy Prospekt 15. Being a work day, their relatives were either at school or at work. After a short two-block walk, they arrived at the corner of Malyy Prospekt and Admiral Makarov Embankment, then followed the embankment along the Little Nyeva River. They crossed the head of the Builders' Bridge, then reached Pushkin Square and the Central Naval Museum, formerly the Saint Peterburg's Stock Exchange Building. Here Mikhail stopped for a short while at the first Rostral Column, walked toward the tip of the *Stryelka,* and silently looked at the other side of the Nyeva River, towards the Peter and Paul Fortress. Holding Irina's hand, he continued walking towards the second Rostral Column, a twin of the first, then crossed the Nyeva River via the Palace Bridge, which connects the Vasileostrovsky and the Central districts of the city.

The bridge's other end rests on Palace Embankment, which lies along the Nyeva River and where Leningrad has its most beautiful architectural jewel: The Hermitage Museum, the former Winter Palace and residence of the Romanov tsars. Unable to enter the museum, due to time constraints, Mikhail could make do only by looking at its beauty from the other side of the embankment, as Irina and him walked its *trottoir* along the winding Nyeva. Passing before the Old Hermitage building, they crossed the small bridge over the Winter Canal and reached the Hermitage Theater building. Irina had not been able to get one word out of Mikhail's mouth, despite her repeated attempts at engaging her husband in conversation.

Still walking, they passed by the Marble Palace. Approaching the Kirov bridge, to their left, Irina, unable to take one more step, complained to her husband: "Misha! I'm awfully tired! We have been walking all the way from home for almost two hours! My feet are killing me!"

Suddenly, as if coming out of a dream, Mikhail looked at his wife's deep blue eyes and comforted her: "That's alright, Irinka, just one more block, until we reach the Summer Garden. We'll sit and rest there."

Acknowledging that this was actually the best place to go and rest, Irina relented, despite her aching feet. They crossed Marshal Kutuzov Embankment and walked around the majestic statue to Field Marshal Suvorov. Here Mikhail paused to read the inscription on its granite pedestal: "Prince of Italy, Count Suvorov-Rimniksky."

Crossing Suvorov Square, Garden Street, and the small bridge over the Swan Canal, they finally arrived at the centuries-old grills of *Letnyy Sad,* the Summer Garden, Leningrad's lung.

Not being able to walk any longer, Irina sat at the very first bench she saw. Mikhail, still as if in a trance, continued walking. Irina just saw as he got further and further away from her, walking towards Fontanka, at the other end of the garden, despite her loud calls of protest.

Suddenly, he turned around and walked towards her. Without saying a word he passed in front of her bench, fixing his haze on her, but not stopping. When he was a few meters from her, he once again turned around and walked towards her. When passing in front of her he again fixed his sight on Irina.

Irina thought her husband finally lost it, but didn't say a word, just smiled at him.

Seeing her smiling, Mikhail stopped, got closer and greeted her: *"Privyet!"*

"Privyet!" Irina answered back.

"Do you come here often?" he asked.

Suddenly startled, Irina didn't know what to say at the impromptu question. But as suddenly as she was startled, she smiled even broader and replied: "Yes, I do. Almost everyday."

"Almost everyday? What for?"

"To study. I like the peace and quiet of the garden. Makes reading and studying easy."

"So do I. What and where are you studying?" Mikhail asked.

"Nursing, at the Medicine Institute."

"The one on Tolstoy Street?"

"Yes, there. And you? What and where are you studying?"

"Mechanical Engineering, at the Polytechnic Institute," said Mikhail. "May I sit?" he invited himself.

"Yes, sure! Please, do!" Irina assented, pointing her open hand towards the bench.

Mikhail sat next to her and continued the conversation.

"If you come here everyday, how come I've never seen you here before? I mean, a girl as pretty as you I'm sure I'd have noticed immediately!"

"Well, I do come here every day" Irina said, defending herself from Mikhail verbal volleys.

"Every day, or *almost* every day?" Mikhail asked once again, winking.

"Every day!" Irina said, emphatically.

"Well, me too. Anyway …"

"Misha! You little liar!" Irina said, throwing her arms around her husband. "You were the one who did not come here every day!" As she reprimanded her husband, she covered him with kisses. "Oh, Misha, you haven't forgotten! Thirty five years, and you still remember."

"How can I forget, Irinka, how can I forget …"

As he said these last words, both remained silent, remembering that day when they met for the first time. He, a young second-year student. She, a year younger, starting her career schooling. Sitting at the same bench, in the same location, and almost at the same time they met, saying the same words they said to each other then. The date, Saturday, June 21st, 1941. The next day, their lives were changed forever.

Seeing her husband once again engaged in his own thoughts, Irina couldn't contain herself anymore: "Misha, is something troubling you? I've never seen you like this before!"

"No, nothing, really. It's just that I've been assigned to fly in the *Okean* Maneuvers, on Wednesday."

"You have?" she asked, surprised.

"Yes, and that's a lot of responsibility. We'll have to conduct so many tests …"

"But, Misha, this is not the first time you're assigned to flights like that," she said, this time genuinely concerned. She had never known Mikhail to shy away from any responsibility and much less from those having to do with his military career.

"It's not that, it's that this flight will take us much further than we've ever flown …" Mikhail said, trailing his words.

"Where to? Cuba? Angola?"

"Perhaps … perhaps even further. I don't know yet. I haven't been told the flight plan. You know they only tell us right before the flight."

"But Misha, during the war you flew from here to Berlin and back. You have flown all over this side of the country. Is that flight really so serious that it has you so worried that you can hardly talk?"

"Perhaps it is … I've never flown in naval maneuvers. A lot depends on us flying according to plan. You know what they do if you don't follow the plan."

"I know ..." Irina agreed, thinking about Mikhail's unfortunate career, and how it brought them nothing more than bitter blows, due to his political views.

"Anyway, perhaps after the maneuvers life will be better for us. Perhaps we'll be able to do everything according to plan. Then we'll reap the rewards that come with that," Mikhail said, smiling and throwing his arm around her shoulder.

"It will, Misha, it will. Everything will be fine. You and your crew will make the most perfect flight of the maneuvers, and the Navy will be proud to have such a superb pilot in its roster," Irina said as she got closer to her Misha and fixed his cap and uniform.

"I hope so. We will make that perfect flight, and all our problems will be over, one way or another," Mikhail said, smiling and kissing his Irinka.

After resting for several more minutes, Mikhail stood up, offering Irina his hand. Extending her arm, she stood up, supported by her husband's strong arm.

As they walked inside the park, along the Swan Canal, Mikhail's gaze once again got lost in the distance, this time towards *Marsovo Polye*, Leningrad's Mars' Field, on the other side of Swan Canal and Garden Street. Not that this was the first time they made this walk, or the walk from home, for that matter, but she noticed that he looked intently at each and every building, street, statue, inscription, and even lamppost they found on their long walk from home. To her it was as if he wanted to intimately absorb each and every one of these sights and take them with himself back to his base up north.

Due to his silence, however, Irina couldn't help but also notice that something more troublesome, deeper than the worries Mikhail confessed to her about the maneuvers, was eating away at her husband's insides.

Why this 'curious' way of looking at the city in such a strange and attentive way? Is he leaving to never come back? He said they might send him to fly where he has never flown before ... Why is he so worried about flying 'a perfect flight'? Is he afraid his plane might have a problem and fall in the ocean? He told me that has happened already at his base ... Is he having premonitions? The very thought of losing her husband over the cold waters of the Northern Atlantic Ocean made Irina shudder in fear, especially at the thought of never seeing him again.

In order not to fall pray to such funereal thoughts, however, once again she tried to engage Mikhail in conversation.

"Where are we heading to now?"

"I'd like to walk along Garden Street," he said.

"Sounds like a stupendous idea," she said, getting closer to him, passing her left arm over his right arm and holding his hand tightly in both her hands. "And after that?" she asked.

"You might say I'm crazy when I say what I want to do next but ..."

"Whatever you say is not going to make me think you're crazy," Irina said, hoping he'd let her in on whatever was eating away at him.

"*Ladno,* I'll tell you ... I want to take the bus to go to Kronshtadt."

"What!? Kronshtadt?" Irina looked at her husband with wide-open eyes, incredulity all over her face.

"Yes, Kronshtadt," he confirmed his words.

"And why on earth do you want to go to Kronshtadt now, Misha? Don't you have to return to base today?"

"Yes, I have to return to base today, but I still have time to go to Kronshtadt and visit my grandfather's statue there."

"Admiral Makarov's statue?" Irina asked in total disbelief, not finding the reason why Mikhail suddenly dropped this bombshell on her.

"Yes, Admiral Makarov's statue. I want to go see it again."

"But, Misha, if we go there, do you think you'll have time to catch the train and then the bus to take you back to the airport? As it is, now you barely have time to catch the train. You'll be cutting it pretty close," Irina warned him.

"Mmm ... perhaps you are right, I'd hate to miss that last flight back to Murmansk."

"Right, because if you do, you'll have to wait until tomorrow afternoon for the next flight up north."

"*Ladno.* I will not go to Kronshtadt. Then let's just go down Garden Street to Nyevsky."

"Yes, we can go to Kronshtadt next time you're in town," Irina said, relieved.

"Yes, next time I'm in town ..." said Mikhail, once again letting his words trail from his mouth.

They reached the southwestern corner of the Summer Garden, crossed the small bridge over the Moyka Canal and continued their stroll down *Ulitsa Sadovaya,* Garden Street, on the same *trottoir* where lies the Engineer's Palace, one of the more than 200 palaces and museums in the city. Reaching the next corner, Mikhail detoured and entered the garden in front of the palace, where stands a statue of Tsar Peter the Great dressed as a warrior in triumph. On its pedestal, a simple inscription: "To Great-Grandfather, from Great-Grandson," placed there by orders of Tsar Paul I in 1809, the hundredth anniversary of the victory at Poltava.

While he looked at the inscription, Irina was once again surprised by his next action: Mikhail ceremoniously stood in attention and saluted the tsar, as if the real Emperor of all Russias were standing before him. The he turned around and walked towards Irina, took her hand and slowly walked towards the corner of Garden and Zamkov Streets, where he again restarted his stroll.

At the corner of Garden and Engineers Street, Mikhail made another impromptu change: Rather than walking down Garden Street, he crossed both Garden and Engineers Streets and continued walking down the latter, passing in front of the Ethnography Museum. Then reached Arts Square, walked to mid block and stopped briefly to look at the buildings surrounding him. To his right, the Russian Museum, before him, his beloved *Malyy Teatr*, the Small Theater where he and Irina enjoyed many opera and ballet performances.

Turning left, towards the statue of Alexandr S. Pushkin, the greatest Russian poet and fellow co-citizen, Mikhail slowly walked to mid square. Stopping for a short while before the statue, he continued his slow stroll down the square, towards Rakov and Brodsky Streets.

Crossing Rakov, he stopped at the corner of Rakov and Brodsky, looked up to the Leningrad State Philharmonic building, then to the other buildings on the block, his eyes fixed on their every small detail.

Finally, they reached the corner of Brodsky Street and Nyevsky Prospekt. Here Mikhail stopped once more to absorb, for the last time, a sight of the city that saw him being born, fifty four years before. Steadying his gaze on the Admiralty building, to his left, he looked at the high golden spire of the building, then he slowly turned to contemplate the old Fire Watchtower, across the street. Beyond, to his left, the yellow-white walls of the Gostinyy Dvor stores, where he and his father went so many times to buy toys. Further, the Saltykov-Shchedrin Concert Hall, location of many hours spent listening to concerts by the best composers and maestros of the Soviet Union and the world.

Mikhail ended his literal sightseeing at Insurrection Square, where Nyevsky Prospekt makes a bend which didn't allow him to see the end of the grandiose avenue. But it didn't matter, he let his mind fly and with his soul he saw what lies beyond that: The Alexander Nyevsky Monastery, in whose honor the grand avenue was named.

"Misha! Misha? Are you alright?"

The repeated inquiries of Irina at his side brought him back to reality.

"Yes, Irinka, I am alright," he said, distant.

"You sound like you're about to die!" she complained.

"Perhaps I'm about to die, having to leave once again to that damn place up north. Having to leave you here."

"You know you can take me with you up there whenever you want," she said in a soothing voice.

"Yes, I know. But that's the last thing I'd do, take you to live in that forsaken land."

"I don't mind, I never did."

"Yes, I know, you never did. But I do. I want to take you to a better place, not to a worse place. Since I cannot do it now, then I have no choice, I have to leave you here. However ..."

"... However ...?" she repeated.

"Perhaps one day I'll be able to return to take you to a better place, who knows!" he said, smiling.

"And where could that be? We're living fairly well, under the circumstances."

"I don't know, maybe right here in Leningrad, but at least in an apartment all for ourselves, like the one we had on Nyekrasova Street, remember?"

"Ah, yes. That was a great apartment, and so large!"

"Well, perhaps some day we could have one like that again."

"Yes, perhaps ..."

Mikhail looked at his watch. Knowing that they couldn't delay his departure any longer, the couple slowly walked down the entrance to the Nyevsky Prospekt station of the Moscow-Petrograd metro line, to wait for the train that would take Mikhail to Bus №39, and from there, back to Pulkovo Airport. As they waited for the train, both stood on the semi-deserted platform, tightly embraced in each other's arms.

The distant rumble of an incoming train let them know that the time to say goodbye was already there. Still unable to utter a word, Mikhail said a silent, sad farewell to Irina, not knowing if and when he'd see her again. In wordless understanding, full of ill forebodings and misgivings, Irina somehow knew she might not see him again either. These thoughts, however, she kept them in her heart, preferring not to utter them rather than trouble him more, or listen to the dreaded words she suspected might have come out of his mouth.

As the train quickly approached, came to a stop and opened its doors, to Mikhail's mind came the last stanza of the old *Poputnaya Pyesnya* or 'Traveler's Song':

> *Neither air nor grass beckon the sufferer,*
> *Like clear eyes that so brightly shine.*
> *So full of blessing the minutes of encounter,*
> *So sweet with hope the hours of departure.*

With the sweet hope of some day meeting his beloved Irinka once again, Mikhail gave her a long and tight kiss, then boarded the train. With a broken heart he left behind both his Irinka and Leningrad, returning to Kuzomen via Murmansk.

*   *   *   *

Col. Yakovlev reviewed the list of new men that were sent—albeit temporarily—for him to test his security plan. Although they were sent by Region Headquarters for that purpose, Yakovlev knew that he could deploy them in any way he saw fit. Before he deployed them to the areas he had assigned them to, that was the perfect opportunity to clear up something that had been bothering him for the last few days: What he saw by the swamps near the runway.

Grabbing his phone, he called his assistant, Lt. Col. Nikitin.

"Nikitin, Yakovlev speaking. Tell me, is there anything worthwhile around the base?"

"Worthwhile? What do you mean?"

"Yes, anything out of the ordinary that we haven't seen or heard of before?"

"Not that I'm aware," Nikitin answered his superior's question, asking himself what the Colonel was up to now.

"What about around the runways, or by the river?" the Colonel insisted.

"Around the runways? As far as I know, all that is there is just sand, swamps, trees, badgers … Is there supposed to be anything else?" Nikitin asked.

"I don't know, that's why I'm asking you. Has anyone seen or reported anything unusual around there? Movement of people or something of that sort?"

"No, Colonel. Nothing of the sort. People usually move by the roads. You know how impassable is that area around the runway heads."

"The new men from Region Headquarters, did they arrive?" Yakovlev suddenly changed the subject.

"Yes, this morning."

"How many did they send?"

"Twelve, Colonel."

"*Otlichno.* They sent me the complement I requested."

"*Da.* So it seems."

"I would like you to send them all out on their first test."

"Yes, Colonel. Will we post them by the gate area?"

"No. First, send six of them to ask anyone and everyone around the whole base if they have seen or heard of any unusual movement around the base, it doesn't matter where. Also, include the pilots of the morning and evening flights to and from Murmansk. Everyone! Don't let anyone out!"

"Yes, Colonel, and the other six? Do you want me to post them by the dispersion area?"

"No. Send them out to the area around the base."

Hearing his superior's request, Nikitin's eyes opened widely. *What? Is the Colonel going crazy? Why is he sending those men around there?* However, not wishing to contradict his order, he decided only to find the reasons behind it.

"Colonel, do you want me to post them on the inside area of the fence around Runway 14A?"

"No. Don't post them. Send them out to make a visual sweep and inspection of the area *around* the runways. More specifically, on the area around Runway 14A."

"And what should they report on?" Nikitin asked, still more surprised than before.

"They should report on anything unusual they see or find. Recent movements of people in the area, things out of the ordinary, things missing or out of place."

"Colonel, may I ask, what's the purpose of this sweep? After all, around here nothing, if ever, happens. And much less in the area you want to sweep."

"I need to start tightening up the security of this base, or of any base for that matter, making sure that there are no holes in it. And the only way to verify that is by sweeping and finding those holes, so we can plug them."

There's absolutely nothing there but sand and swamps! I wonder if being here for so long is not affecting his brains already ... Nikitin thought his CO was taking his security mania too far, but he was not in a position to countermand him either. He refused to believe Yakovlev was all of a sudden interested in an area around the base that up until then hardly deserved a second look, much less sending a whole team of men to make a thorough search of the swamps. Nikitin only hoped that this was only a temporary measure as a result of the new security plan with which the Colonel wanted to impress the *nachal'stvo* from Murmansk.

"Very well, Colonel. You'll have that report on your desk tomorrow afternoon."

"No. You'll have that report on my desk tomorrow morning. By tomorrow afternoon we have to have the security plan already delineated and ready for the inspectors' visit on Wednesday."

Blyad! Now I have to send those men in a truck and have them back here before the end of the day, so I can have time to type the Colonel's report! Despite the annoyance of having to speed up the sweep and search, Nikitin knew Yakovlev was well known for his efficiency, which would surely shine when the inspectors came from Murmansk, so he'd do his best to get some of that shine to rub off on him too.

If everything went according to his plan, Yakovlev could be promoted to Major General or more, and posted to a higher rung of the ladder, perhaps as responsible for Region Security in Murmansk, or better yet, somewhere in the south. If Yakovlev was promoted, Nikitin could be sure to be promoted too, perhaps to occupy his superior's position as Base Political Commander. Seeing a rosy future before them, Nikitin agreed to his superior's request without further delays.

"Yes, Colonel. I'm sending those men out there right now. You'll have that report on your desk in the morning!"

✳   ✳   ✳   ✳

Carrying the bags with the almost-completed jammer for the autodestruct system, Anatoly and Pavel arrived at Captain Makarov's room.

"*Dobryy vyecher, tovarishchi*. While I was out, did you make any progress with the jammer?" Mikhail asked them.

"No. Honestly, we took the time off too," said Anatoly. "All these nights working until two and three hundred, had us exhausted. So we took advantage of the weekend and blew it in town."

As they talked, the technicians worked on the jamming equipment.

"Who went? Where did you go?" asked Mikhail.

"All of us. We went to Kuzomen, to the *Kolkhoz* Club."

"What did you do, get drunk?" Mikhail asked again.

"Not really," said Pavel. "One of the reasons why we went all together was to control each other. We did not want to get drunk and start spitting our plans on indiscreet ears."

"Good, because that would have been the end of it all," said Mikhail.

"Actually, we were back in base early, by midnight. Then rested for the remainder of the weekend," said Pavel.

Suddenly, soft knocks are heard coming from the door. Mikhail went to open it. Standing at the door were Vasily, Alexey, and the rest of *Red 67's* crew except Serghey, as usual.

"Talking about the other guys, you brought them with your mind!" said Mikhail.

The crew entered and got all around the working technicians.

"So, now you're all rested and ready to complete the jammer," Mikhail continued his chat with Anatoly and Pavel. "Is there a lot to do to complete it? Remember that we have only two more days left. The maneuvers will be the day after tomorrow!"

"There's not much left to do. I think we can finish it tonight," said Anatoly. "Just connecting in series the amplifiers we boosted last time, so as to add up all their power together."

"Fine, that's one less item in our list," said Mikhail.

"There is, however, one item that we have not taken care of yet," said Anatoly.

"And that is …?" asked Mikhail.

"The matter of Lieutenant Rybakov. I have not been trained in the usage of the new radar, and he just returned from Leningrad trained. If the radar is already installed in our plane, you can be hundred percent sure he'll fly in *Red 67* instead of me."

"That's if we let him," Pavel said.

"And how can we avoid that?" Anatoly asked, worried.

"Tolya, don't worry. Just like we solved Yura's problem with the transfer, we can solve yours too. This is nothing more than another rock in our flight to freedom. Together we can get it out of the way. After all, we have been able to tackle all the other obstacles before, haven't we?" Mikhail comforted the technician.

"Yes, Tolya, don't worry," added Pavel. "Let the other guys worry about that and let's finish this thing here, because without it, it's possible we won't get to the other side either."

"Well, we could smack the daylights out of him, like we plan to do with the new flight engineer," suggested Vasily.

"Yes, they might even say he was just another victim of the frequent hold ups that happen here," said Ivan.

"No. Too much violence already. I feel uncomfortable enough by having to beat the flight engineer," said Mikhail. "We have to find another way."

"How? We can't bribe him, we can't beat him, what can we do?" asked Jonas.

"We can get him drunk, like I did with the ADS technician," suggested Anatoly, his eyes on the equipment before him.

"That sounds more reasonable. Do we have any bottles of *samogon* left?" asked Mikhail.

"Only two," answered Vasily. "We used a few of them last weekend, in Kuzomen."

"Two will not be enough to get him drunk. Not at the rate those guys drink," said Anatoly.

"I know what we could do!" said Alexey, triumphantly. All faces turned to look at the young navigator. "We could get him drunk *and* drugged. We could use some of the sleeping pills I got from the Infirmary."

"Sleeping pills and *samogon* ... mmm ... If the combination doesn't kill him first, he'll be asleep for a while ..." Mikhail said, pondering the tactic.

"Yes, he'll sleep for a long time, enough for us to get out of here," said Alexey.

"It will have to be tomorrow night," said Anatoly. "So that by morning, day after tomorrow, he's still be sound asleep ..."

"... or dead," interjected Vasily.

"Yes," Anatoly said, then continued. "And since the purpose of flying *Red 67* in the maneuvers is to test the *Korshun,* they will need an experienced radar technician available on very short notice. And who's the most experienced technician in this base, despite reports to the contrary?"

"You," replied the group.

"Not only that. Since *my* crew is the one flying that radar," added Mikhail, "I can request Commander Degtyaryov to reassign you to my team, since Lt. Rybakov is going to be 'unavailable due to illness.'"

"*Otlichno!* He'll have no choice but to do it," concluded Anatoly. "Because no one else here is experienced and qualified enough to be able to handle that radar without previous training. Fortunately, I know the *Uspekh* radar like I know my own pocket, enough to be able to correlate it to the *Korshun* system."

"*Poyekhali!*" exclaimed Mikhail. "Another obstacle out of the way!"

"And another one defeated here too," said Anatoly. "The amplifiers have been connected to the jamming equipment."

"You're done?" asked Vasily.

"Yes, all done. Now it's just a matter of sneaking the whole thing into our plane without anyone suspecting anything," said Pavel.

"I think we can do it 'as part of the *Korshun* testing'," said Anatoly, winking.

"The *Korshun* testing?" asked Mikhail.

"Yes. Who's going to say that we don't need this equipment to measure the performance of the new radar? Serghey?" asked Anatoly.

"True. He doesn't know about that. Plus, it's not that he'd care either. It's a technical matter, out of his 'political competence.' He couldn't care less about it," said Vasily.

"And the maintenance crew will care about it even less. We can bring it in and install it in our consoles," Pavel finalized the explanation.

"So, I guess all we have to do now is to wait until day after tomorrow to put our plan in motion," said Mikhail.

"Yes, and hope it all goes accordingly. Because if just one unexpected event happens, I don't know how that could affect the plan," said Vasily.

"Everything will be alright, Vasya. Don't worry," Mikhail comforted the copilot.

"*Da, byez suchka, byez zadorinki!*" exclaimed Alexey.

"So I hope, Alyosha. So I hope. Without a hitch, without a snag!" repeated Anatoly.

Having placed all their hopes and wishes on the Icarus plan, the crew began the short wait for the appointed date, two days from now, to spring into action. In less than 48 hours would start the adventure that could bring them freedom at the end of a long and arduous flight, or sure death in the air and a cold, dark and deep watery grave at the bottom of the Atlantic Ocean.

*   *   *   *

Although the plane he was sitting in was located all the way in the back of the repair hangar, Master Sergeant of the Technical Service Vyacheslav Sudaryev still could hear the howlings and the screams coming from outside.

Cracking open the pilot side window, Sudaryev tried to find out the cause of all the commotion. He didn't have to wait long, though. Coming like a desert storm, Lt. Col. Leonid Rudenko walked in long strides past all the technicians working on the airplanes parked in the hangar. Aware of the colonel's volatile temper, and wishing to keep him away from them as far as possible, the technicians pointed him to the airplane where he could find the target of his rage.

As Rudenko approached the cockpit where Sudaryev sat, the sergeant was finally able to make sense of the rush of words coming out of the officer's mouth: "*Chyort vozmyot!* Where is that *mudak* Sudaryev? Has anybody seen him?"

Knowing the colonel to be rash and prone to violence, to the point of punching in the face whoever dared to cross him, and not being afraid of anyone, not respecting even Commander Degtyaryov—or any high ranking officer for that matter—Sudaryev addressed the colonel from his high perch in the cockpit window.

"What seems to be the problem, Comrade Colonel?"

"There you are, you pederast! What the hell is that I hear my First Technical Officer saying, that the new radar has not been installed on *my* plane yet?"

The puzzled look on Sudaryev's face told the colonel that the sergeant was not understanding his words. "Get the fuck out of there and come down here,

NOW!" The colonel screamed, finishing the sentences with more curses and imprecations of all calibers and sizes, pointing his right index finger downwards.

Sudaryev's head disappeared inside the cockpit. In a few seconds his legs appeared going down the red access ladder attached to the plane's nosewheels bogie.

"Colonel, I didn't get that … The new radar … installed in *your* plane?" asked the surprised sergeant.

The sole asking of the question by the sergeant, about the required installation of the *Korshun* radar in his plane, made Rudenko's already bulging neck veins grow to the point of almost bursting, his enraged red face turned purple.

"Yes, *mudak!* The new radar, the *Korshun* that they sent from Leningrad to be installed in *my* plane. Why isn't it installed yet?"

"But, Colonel, the install orders we got from Commander Degtyaryov clearly said that radar was to be installed in *Red 67*, not *Red 57!*"

On hearing the sergeant's reply, Rudenko's eyes almost popped out of their orbits. "WHAAT? *My* radar, installed in Captain Makarov's plane? Where did you hear that, you bungling piece of shit?"

"But that's what's written in the work order!" Sudaryev defended himself as he turned and headed to the file cabinet where the work orders for the regiment's airplanes were filed.

As he walked towards the cabinets, Rudenko followed him while still insulting the sergeant, making mention of a long list of prostitutes, beggars, traitors, and vagrants in the sergeant's family and relatives, as well as putting in doubt the legitimacy of Sudaryev's birth.

Walking as fast as he could, more than anything else to stay away from the now visibly warlike officer, and also to avoid being the target of his fists, Sudaryev finally reached the cabinet, pulled the drawer for *Red 67*, and from it the maintenance folder. After a desperate search, Sudaryev found the by now much needed work order.

"Here! This is the work order, duly signed by Commander Degtyaryov himself, that authorized me to install that radar in *Red 67*, not in your airplane."

As he arrived at Sudaryev's side, Rudenko literally snatched the piece of paper from the sergeant's hand and scanned its contents. This last action only made the colonel burst anew in another long fusillade of rapid-firing curses. "Someone made a mistake somewhere, and I'm going to find the culprit. I swear that whoever it was he's going to pay for it dearly!"

"Well, it was not me nor my team, Comrade Colonel," replied Sudaryev feeling better—and on firmer ground. He had the documentation to prove that the installation was not at fault.

"*Khorosho*, Sergeant. But in the meantime have your monkeys pull *that* airplane in right now and change that radar to *my* plane! There's no way I'm going to let that stay as is. That radar is mine and it will be installed in *my* plane!"

"Excuse me, Colonel, but what's the purpose of having the radar installed in your airplane, if I may know?"

"I'm going to be the one testing it at the *Okean* Maneuvers."

"The *Okean* Maneuvers? But that's tomorrow!"

"Exactly, you smart ape! And that's why you're going to have that radar installed in my plane *by tomorrow morning!* I don't care if you and your zoo have to work the whole night on it!"

"But, Colonel, just uninstalling and reinstalling the radar may take a minimum of 48 hours! Not counting testing and calibration!" replied an exasperated Sudaryev.

"That's your problem, not mine!"

"Colonel, I can't do that. It's not humanly possible," Sergeant Sudaryev said as he braced himself for the rain of fists he was sure he was about to receive from Rudenko's already tightened hands.

"Then you'll make it humanly possible or I'll make sure you and your band of apes go finish your service time somewhere in Northern Siberia!" Rudenko said between his clenched teeth.

"Colonel, why don't you fly in *Red 67*? The radar is already installed, calibrated, and tested in it. What difference would it make?"

"I am *NOT* going to fly in that rusted bucket of flying shit!" Rudenko screamed on Sudaryev's face, saliva falling on the terrified Sergeant's eyes, nose, and cheeks. "*My* plane is the best airplane in this outfit, and there's no way I am going to spend 17 hours flying in someone else's plane, much less Captain Makarov's. I might get … infected with that shit he's always spitting at political meetings!"

"Colonel, not even if I pull all my men to work on your plane alone, I will be able to have that radar on your plane by tomorrow morning. Perhaps if you have Commander Degtyaryov assign to me more people from other departments, base telecommunications, radars, etc., perhaps, just perhaps, we could have that radar on your plane by then."

"Look, just start working on it immediately. Leave Degtyaryov to me. You'll have all the men you need to do that today, even if I have to have Degtyaryov send the guards posted at the base gate!"

Sudaryev immediately ordered his technicians to run to the hangar's ZIL truck, bring in both *Red 57* and *Red 67* and start the removal of the *Uspekh-1A* radar in one and the *Korshun* radar in the other.

Seeing that his screams got him the desired results, Rudenko turned around and headed to the Base Commander's office.

✳   ✳   ✳   ✳

"*Nyet*," was Commander Degtyaryov's terse reply.

Rudenko didn't know if he should have just blown up himself or jumped over the Commander's desk and kick him to death. "What the fuck you mean *'no'*?" asked the bewildered officer.

"'No' means just that, no. I am not going to have Sudaryev uninstall that radar from *Red 67*. I don't care if it was supposed to be installed in your plane."

"This is ridiculous! Those apes in maintenance make a mistake, and you're just going to sit on your ass and leave it like that?"

"Yes. It's going to stay like that. There's no way that they can make that change in one day. And I am not going to risk our regiment's participation in the maneuvers because of your irrational request."

"Irrational request! *Blyad!*" Rudenko exploded. "You call that an irrational request? So what is it that was done to me, 'perfectly plausible'?"

"No, a mistake was obviously made. But having that radar reinstalled in your plane is not the solution."

"*Tak,* what are you going to do about it? If that radar is not installed in *Red 57*, I will not be able to participate in the maneuvers!" Rudenko screamed at the top of his lungs.

"Lieutenant Colonel Rudenko, you'll stop your fucking screaming in my face and in my office!" Degtyaryov screamed back.

"I scream to whoever the fuck I like! That's what I am the Regiment Commander for!"

On hearing Rudenko's words, Degtyaryov stood from his chair behind his desk in one single jump and pointed an angry finger at Rudenko. "I don't care that you're the Regiment Commander! I am the Base Commander and your superior officer! You respect me or I'll have you immediately arrested!"

Degtyaryov was the only officer in the base capable of actually putting teeth to his words, so Rudenko quickly retreated to a more conciliatory position. "Colonel, all I'm asking is some way of participating in the maneuvers. Because of that 'mistake' now I can't."

"You can still fly in *Red 67*. I can sign an order to that effect right now, transferring your whole crew from *Red 57* to *Red 67*. That would solve your problem." Degtyaryov offered a solution.

"NO! I fly in my plane and in my plane alone! You know I don't trust anyone of the technicians in this base, only those assigned to mine!"

Degtyaryov remembered that, being the Regiment Commander, Rudenko hand picked each and everyone of the technicians in charge of his airplane and gave them extraordinary powers over everyone and everything related to the maintenance of *Red 57*. This went from sticking to a strict maintenance checkup routine to ordering brand new engines and electronic parts so that, at the slightest sign of trouble, the affected part or system was immediately repaired or replaced with never-used components rather than with the cannibalized parts obtained from crashed or surplus equipment as was the rule in all the other airplanes of the regiment. This punctilious care consistently earned his airplane the right to display, on both sides of the nose, the coveted red "Badge of Excellence," the figure of a stylized jet airplane in flight over a pentagon, leaving behind two streaks in its wake.

Also noteworthy was the fact that the maintenance crew of *Red 57* was under strict orders *not* to touch liquors, one of the reasons why Rudenko chose them in first place, carefully searching their personal records to verify their total abstinence from all alcohol. That was how Rudenko, knowing the drunken stupor that most of the maintenance crews happened to live in, protected himself from falling from the sky in the frequent flameouts that had plagued the aircraft serviced by them.

"*Khorosho*, that's all I can do. If you don't want to fly in *Red 67*, then stay. I can have that radar fly in Captain Makarov's plane, for all I care. As long as that radar is tested tomorrow, it's fine with me. My orders are to have that radar in the air tomorrow, and I sure do not care at all who's flying with it."

"You can not do this to me!" Rudenko screamed. "Besides, only my First Technical Officer knows how to handle it. He's the only one in the base trained in its usage!"

"*Nu, chto?*" Degtyaryov asked. "So, what? All I need is my pen and in one single stroke I can have him transferred to Captain Makarov's crew. Problem solved!"

"Then transfer him, because if you send that plane with that radar, none of those apes in Makarov's crew know how to handle it. They'll just make an ass of you!"

"That's exactly what I'll do. As for you, listen, I don't need more aggravations than I already have. You can fly in that plane, or you can get out of my face for a few days. The choice is yours."

"I'd rather get out of here. I don't want to see the fucking mess that is going to happen in this place after tomorrow."

"How many days do you want?"

"A whole week."

"A whole week? You drive a hard bargain!" Degtyaryov complained, but relented to the officer's request rather than have him scare and abuse the crews as he was used to do. "Where to?"

"Arkhanghelsk," said Rudenko, a smile finally appearing in his face. Not a bad trade off after all. A week in Arkhanghelsk all expenses paid, courtesy of the Soviet Navy, in exchange for leaving matters as they were.

Degtyaryov, for his part, agreed. It was a lot simpler to solve the problem that way rather than trying to find out who screwed up in the radar installation work order. In the 'perfect' life of the Soviet Navy Air Base at Kuzomen, screw ups of that kind never—or at least almost never—should have happened. All they did was bring undue attention from the superiors in Murmansk to the base personnel and by extension, on its officers and commanders as well.

With the recent crash of Major Ogorodnikov's plane still fresh in his mind, Colonel Degtyaryov took his pen and started signing the papers authorizing the transfer of *Red 57's* First Technical Officer, Senior Lieutenant Rybakov, to Captain Makarov's crew for the duration of the *Okean* Maneuvers flight, as well as the permit allowing Col. Rudenko to spend time in Arkhanghelsk's Navy Club.

✳   ✳   ✳   ✳

Vasily entered Yuri's room, where he found the Flight Engineer packing his belongings.

"We've got to do something about your transfer to the south. You're supposed to be leaving this afternoon and the maneuvers start tomorrow!"

"I have it all set, and I'm glad you came around. You'll be my assistant."

"Your assistant?" Vasily asked, surprised.

"Yes. Just as you suggested, I am going to 'get violently ill,' but I need your help for that."

"*Ladno.* What am I supposed to do?"

"We'll go to the Transfers Desk to get my transfer papers, etc. While there, I'm going to have 'bad, severe cramps.' You'll help me make the story convincing."

As he spoke, Yuri took a notebook, ripped out a couple of sheets and placed them on the floor. Then he took a piece of chalk, placed it on the papers and crushed the chalk to dust with his boot.

"What devil are you doing?" Vasily asked.

"As I said, you're going to help me make it all convincing," the Flight Engineer replied as he picked up the sheets from the floor, poured the chalk dust on his hands and rubbed it on his face.

"You look like a ghost!" Vasily said.

"*Otlichno!* That's precisely the effect I'm looking for!" Yuri said as he continued rubbing the chalk on himself.

"Do I look *really* sick now?"

"I'd say you're about to fall dead. I think I know how you'll do it."

"*Ladno.* Now, for the second part of the plan."

Having finished placing all his belongings in his luggage, Yuri and Vasily headed to the Transfers Office in the Administration Building of the base.

In the office, he asked the clerk in charge about his transfer papers.

"Name, rank, number!" the clerk demanded.

"Kazakov, Senior Lieutenant Yuri Yevdokimovich, 24356326263."

The clerk looked in a thick book for Yuri's information. After a short wait, he found it: "You're being transferred to the Black Sea Fleet, right?"

"Yes, I am."

"You lucky sonofabitch. You're finally getting out of this miserable swamp."

"Yes, privileges of rank and seniority. I never miss an opportunity to get out of bad situations!" Yuri replied with a groan.

"What's wrong with you?" asked Vasily.

"I have these cramps! They're killing me," the Engineer said, holding his belly and bending over, feigning pain.

"Are you feeling alright?" asked the clerk.

"In all honesty, no. I've had these horrible cramps ever since this morning, and have not stopped going to the toilet. Must have been something I ate."

"And looking at your face, you look paler than a corpse!" Vasily said. "I don't think you should fly out like that, especially if you have the runs!"

The clerk approached the desk and looked at Yuri's face. "You *do* look pale! Lieutenant, I think he's right, you can't fly in those conditions. You should go to the Infirmary and see the doctor. He'll give you something to take care of those cramps."

"Well, that sounds like an excellent idea, because the way I feel, I can hardly walk, much less fly out of here."

"Yes. The doctor has the authority to delay your flight out for a day or two, until you're back in health," suggested the clerk. "Don't worry about these papers for now. Go to the doctor, get some medicine from him, have him sign the delay papers and bring them back when you're feeling well."

"Yura, let me help you get there," Vasily said.

Yuri still holding his belly and Vasily holding him, the two men left the office and headed to the Infirmary.

*   *   *   *

... So someone was definitely in the area around the runway ... Yakovlev thought while reading the typed report Nikitin delivered to his desk just a few minutes before. Although at the moment he didn't know what to make of it, at least it did confirm his sighting of a few days before. Yakovlev continued reading the document:

> *'At the end of the truck's tracks, several relatively fresh boot tracks were found and followed for some fifteen hundred meters, to the river edge, to the location where rest the remains of a crashed TU-16. Upon inspection of the aircraft's remains, it was determined that several devices were removed from the equipment racks aboard the plane (see attached photographs), and due to the condition of the cut wiring and the holes left by the securing screws, still not corroded, the investigators could determine that the removal of said equipment must have occurred within the last few days, one to two weeks at the most ...'*

That's right, I saw those men there barely ten days ago ... However, the report only says 'several men', but not how many ... Although that's more or less what I saw, 'several men', four, perhaps five. And they used a truck to get there and, of course, carry the equipment with them ...

Yakovlev looked at the pictures of the equipment racks and the voids left by the removal of the devices contained in them. *Equipment from an old TU-16, which has been lying there for the better part of two years ... Who could have removed that equipment, and for what? Perhaps technicians went there to get it ... But, once again, for what? We don't have those planes here. I could have said that if we had*

TU-16s based here, but we don't. Anyway, I'm going to get to the bottom of this …
Taking his phone, Yakovlev dialed Nikitin's extension.

"Nikitin, Yakovlev. Get me a list of everyone given leave passes for the last two weeks. Also the manifest of all requisitioned trucks from the trucks depot, who requisitioned them, and what for. And I want them before the end of the day!"

"Yes, Colonel. Does this have to do with that report I typed?"

"Yes. There's something murky about it."

"I agree. Why would anyone need to take old equipment from a crashed airplane?"

"I don't know, but we'll find out soon."

*   *   *   *

In the base Mess Hall, Anatoly, Vasily and Alexey noted Lt. Rybakov entering the room, food plate in hand.

"Hey, Rybakov! Come join us!" yelled Anatoly.

The man neared the crew's table and pulled a chair for himself, next to Alexey.

"I heard tomorrow you're flying with us," Anatoly said.

"Yes. Cdr. Degtyaryov reassigned me to fly with you for the testing of the new radar."

"So I heard," said Vasily. "You lucky *mudak!* They sent you to the Leninets OKB for a whole week! How's Leningrad?"

"Great! One million versts away from this abandoned mudhole! Pity that I didn't stay there longer," complained Rybakov. "Even though one had to study from sun up to sun down, nights were a different story. It was from party to party almost every night! I really don't know how I managed to learn that radar system."

"Talking about parties, from here we'll go have a small 'meeting' by the hangars," said Vasily. "Want to join us?" the pilot threw hook, line, and sinker, hoping the radar technician bit.

"Tonight? … mmm … But we fly early tomorrow morning!"

"Come on, man! It's only two bottles of *samogon*! What? Afraid of two little bottles?" asked Anatoly.

"I'm not afraid of that, you know it. I would need those two and six more just to start getting dizzy."

"What is it, then?" asked Vasily.

"I don't know, perhaps it's that Col. Rudenko has us under a permanent rule of not drinking before a flight."

"But tomorrow you'll fly with us and not with him! And that, my dear friend, we have to celebrate!" exclaimed Vasily.

"Yes, and you'll see that Captain Makarov is not as strict as Rudenko," said Alexey. "He doesn't mind if we drink or not. As a matter of fact, sometimes he joins us!"

"Yes! Besides, you flying in *Red 67* means a day off for me! Testing the *Korshun* is your headache, not mine!" said Anatoly, amid laughs.

"Come with us! If you'll fly with us tomorrow, might as well also drink with us tonight," said Alexey. "Having a drink before a flight is almost a *Red 67* tradition!"

"*Ladno.* I'll go," the technician finally agreed.

Smiles on their faces, Anatoly, Vasily and Alexey looked at each other. The fish bit.

*   *   *   *

"Colonel, here are the lists you requested," said Lt. Col. Nikitin. "After reviewing it, the only name, or names, that appear in both the passes list and in the truck requisitions list are those of Captain Makarov and his crewmen."

"Makarov! ... Mmmm ..." said Yakovlev.

"Yes. And you know how problematic he has been. A whiner. Always complaining about life here in the base."

"And practically everywhere else he has been," Yakovlev agreed.

"Especially when he takes *my* weekly "Political Hour' to start venting his complaints. Sometimes I wished I could simply floor him with one single blow to the head."

"Why didn't you? You know I'd support you all the way," Yakovlev said.

"I don't want to give a bad example before the other officers. Why the devil doesn't he just remain quiet in the rear of the room, like he used to do before?"

"Well, this will surprise you, but since I told him that you had complained to me that he was disrupting your meetings, he did mellow a bit. He even offered to go pick up the special product himself at the *kolkhoz!*" Yakovlev suddenly realized what he had just said. He remained silent for a few seconds, his eyes attentively looking at his deputy's face.

"Something's wrong, Colonel?"

"Nikitin, I want you to get some of our men and search the quarters of all of Captain Makarov's crewmen. I have the feeling that there we may find what happened to the equipment taken from the TU-16."

"The *whole* crew, Colonel? Including our man in that plane?"

"Yes, including him, Lieutenant … Molotko. You know as well as I do that he has not been performing his political duties as he should. Otherwise, that crew's morale wouldn't be as low as it is. Go out to do that."

"Right now, Colonel? It's already 2300 …" Nikitin pleaded.

Looking at his watch, Yakovlev relented. "Very well. Tomorrow at first hour I want you to do that."

"Understood, Colonel. *Spokoynoy nochi!*" Nikitin said as he turned around to leave.

*   *   *   *

Sitting on some old pilot chairs in a quiet corner of the repair hangars, Anatoly, Vasily, Alexey and Rybakov continued the conversation they were holding at the Mess Hall.

"Out of curiosity, what's the difference between the *Uspekh* and the *Korshun*? Anything new and noticeable?" asked Anatoly.

"Yes, especially in the *Orbita* computer. It's capable of finer and faster target resolution," Rybakov answered.

"Interesting!" said Anatoly. "How did they manage to do it?"

"Get those bottles of *samogon* out first, then we'll talk about it!"

Alexey placed his shoulder bag on a wooden crate turned makeshift table and pulled out two bottles of the fiery home-made liquor.

"That's better!" exclaimed Rybakov as he pulled the cork out of one of the bottles, drinking the first sip straight out of it. Alexey placed on the crate four *ryumki*, the small one-shot glasses used for drinks, and poured liquor from the second bottle, one shot for himself and one for each of his other two friends.

Rybakov looked at Alexey pouring the drinks, then continued drinking from the bottle. "*Ryumki!* That's for *pederasty!* You drink *samogon* straight from the bottle!"

"Perhaps," said Alexey, "but when there are only two bottles, I prefer to go slow with it, so it lasts longer."

"Tell me. You say the *Orbita* can render finer and faster target resolution," Anatoly asked his colleague. "How's that?"

"Easy," replied the technician. "You know that the *Uspekh* radar is not capable of seeing clearly anything beyond 300 kilometers …" Rybakov began a very detailed and technical explanation of the capabilities of the new radar system installed in *Red 67,* to the glee and delight of Anatoly, who gave his colleague his full attention.

Meanwhile, Alexey let the technician continue drinking from his own bottle, while very strictly measuring the liquor poured from the bottle he held firmly in his hand.

As the technician continued his dissertation on the new *Orbita* computer, Vasily extended his hand to take Rybakov's bottle. Alexey immediately stopped him, sending a discreet negative to the pilot, while at the same time pouring more *samogon* in Vasily's *ryumka.* Although somewhat surprised, the pilot remained calm and took the drink.

Rybakov, meanwhile, continued showing the fine points of the *Korshun* system to Anatoly, although his speech had already become slurred, and his eyes were half closed.

Anatoly looked at his colleague, then looked at the bottle in his hand, noticing that it was about half full. In his mind he wondered if half a bottle was enough to get Rybakov out of kilter, as he seemed to be. On the other hand, remembering that Alexey promised to have him drugged, Anatoly didn't say a word and continued listening to the technician.

Ten minutes later, though, Rybakov was just emitting grunts and whistles as he closed his eyes. As he let go of a last stifled hiss, the technician simply fell to the side from the box he was sitting on, landing on Vasily's arms, as he rushed to trap Rybakov in his fall.

The other three men simply stood up, took Rybakov by his arms and legs and made him lie along the hangar wall. Then covered him with the same wooden boxes they used as makeshift stools and table. Before he left, Alexey took Rybakov's bottle, poured its contents on the now unconscious man's chest and head, and placed it firmly in his open hand.

The group departed to their living quarters.

"Why didn't you let me drink from Rybakov's bottle?" Vasily asked.

"*Nyet,* instead, you should have asked: 'Why Rybakov drank only from his bottle?'" said Alexey.

"*Ladno,*" said Vasily. "Why Rybakov drank only from his bottle?" he asked, smiling.

"Because I ground six sleeping pills and poured them into that bottle," answered the navigator.

"Six sleeping pills!" Anatoly exclaimed.

"Yes, six. I left six more for that *mudak* Molotko," replied Alexey.

"By now he must be dead or very close," said Vasily.

"I don't care. The longer they take to find him and wake him up …" said Alexey.

"If he ever wakes up," said Anatoly.

"Whatever. The longer they take to find him the more chances we'll have of having you onboard, and the further we'll be from this damn place," the navigator finished his thoughts.

"Fine with me, after all, tonight we killed two birds with one stone," Anatoly agreed. "We got rid of him, and I got a wealth of information about the *Korshun*. Now I know how to handle it, at least enough to test it tomorrow, so they'll have no choice but to send me in his place."

"And when they find him, he'll be so stiff, either from the *samogon* and the pills, or because he'll be long dead, that even if he ever wakes up it will make no difference. We'll be long gone," said Vasily.

PART II

▼

FREE MEN

CHAPTER 7

▼

0330. Mikhail, Jonas, Ivan, Vasily, Alexey, Pavel and Anatoly got together on the second floor hallway, by the stairs to the first floor of the living quarters building. Due to the early hour the hallway was silent and empty. After all, reveille did not sound until 0400.

Whispering, Mikhail asked his crewmen. "How did it go? Could you get rid of Tolya's replacement?"

"Yes," said Alexey. "It was easy. By 2300 he was already stone cold."

"What did you do?" asked Ivan.

"Drugged him with sleeping pills and *samogon,* as planned," said Alexey.

"Where is he now?" asked Mikhail.

"We left him behind some crates, along the back wall of one of the repair hangars. They'll take a while to find him, if ever," said Alexey.

"Oh, they'll find him, eventually," said Vasily. "Only that they should find him after we're long gone."

"Khorosho," Mikhail agreed. "Vasya, how did it go with Yura and the doctor?"

"We went to the Infirmary. The doctor there diagnosed a 'stomach virus,'" the copilot said, smiling widely. "Then he gave Yura some pills to take every six hours, with the promise that he should be alright in a couple of days, so he can 'fly out by this afternoon.'"

"Otlichno! Two down, one to go," said Mikhail. "Now we should see how to get rid of Yura's replacement."

"Captain, do you know what he looks like, the new guy?" asked Alexey.

"Yes, his name is Tugan Padzhenadze."

"Tugan Padzhenadze? What the devil is he? Tatar? Georgian?" asked Jonas.

"Georgian. As a matter of fact, his nickname is precisely *Gruzin,*" Mikhail added, referring to the way Russians call all those coming from the Soviet Socialist Republic of Georgia.

"Well, you can't deny the 'fraternal nature of our great Soviet Navy,'" said Ivan, sarcastically.

"A Georgian! You rarely see one of them up here in these northern latitudes," Vasily said.

"I'm surprised they didn't send him to the Black Sea Fleet, to Sukhumi or Batumi, or somewhere around there," said Alexey. "That's nearer to his home."

"No. He requested to be transferred up here," added Mikhail.

"He *requested* a transfer to the north?" asked Jonas, surprised.

"Yes, he said he wanted to see how life is up here," Mikhail responded.

"He must be nuts!" exclaimed Jonas.

"Does he at least speak Russian?" asked Ivan.

"Yes, he does. Heavily accented, but he does," answered Mikhail.

"Captain, how do you know all that? Have you spoken with him?" asked Ivan.

"Yes. We came in together in the same flight from Murmansk."

"Well, I don't really care if he speaks Russian or not," said Alexey. "All I know is that with him in the plane we can't put our plan in motion."

"Right, so we have to get rid of him now, before he even leaves this place. Otherwise, all we've done will be for nothing," said Vasily.

"Don't worry about that. As soon as he shows up, I'll point him to you. Then you take care of him," said Mikhail.

"*Blyad!* Will we take care of him! Honestly, I don't care if we have to kill him, but at this stage of the plan there's no way I'll let anyone stand in our way and jeopardize our escape," said Alexey.

"Right. I'll help you do that, Alyosha," said Ivan.

"Well, whatever you're going to do you better do it now, because here he comes," said Mikhail, looking discreetly to his right.

The new Flight Engineer for *Red 67* left his room, at the far end of the hallway, and headed to the stairs where the group was standing.

Having taken a good look at the man, the group immediately dispersed and headed downstairs, except Alexey and Ivan, who remained behind then walked to the other side of the hall. As the man passed by their side, Alexey and Ivan turned around and followed him.

Before he had a chance to reach the stairs, he was suddenly and violently attacked from behind by the two men of *Red 67*. While one covered his head with a pillow case, the other hit him in the head with a piece of plumbing pipe.

The sharp crack of the crushed skull bone told the attackers that perhaps the blow was too hard. Their victim slumped on their arms. The two men immediately took their unfortunate target by his arms and legs and carried him back to his room.

"What do we do with him now? We can't leave him here!" Ivan asked.

"Of course not. We'll just push him under his bed," said Alexey, kneeling. Then he turned the body around and pulled the man's wallet.

"What are you doing?" Ivan asked again.

"Taking his money and papers," said Alexey, also opening the man's breast pocket and pulling out his papers.

"What for?" Ivan asked, very surprised.

"If we take that, it will look like a simple robbery, like those that happen here almost daily, you know." Alexey took the rubles, then threw the man's wallet on his breast.

"That's right. And since he's new here, they'll think he was just cased by the robbers, attacked, and robbed."

"Exactly. And that's precisely what I want them to think when he's found. They'd never suspect that it was us," Alexey said, taking the man's legs. "Help me push him under his bed. It will be a while before they find him there."

"When he wakes up he'll raise one helluva racket," Ivan said, pushing the man under the bed.

"That's if he ever wakes up. The way his skull sounded when I hit him, it may be broken. He'll bleed to death," Alexey said, fixing the room to hide any hint of their presence there.

"Poor devil! Anyway, today we leave this place forever, so it really makes no difference to me," Ivan said as he left.

Closing the door behind them, the men headed to the stairs at the other end of the hallway.

*   *   *   *

Sitting in the back of the ubiquitous ZIL-131 transportation truck of the regiment, the crew of *Red 67*—minus a Flight Engineer and the *Korshun* radar operator—silently looked at each other. The truck waited in front of the Operations Office for the previously mentioned crewmen to show up, but they never did. Unable to wait any longer, Mikhail ordered the driver to take them to their aircraft.

"I wonder where the devil those two *mudaki* are!" Mikhail exclaimed in fake disgust. "They were not present for the preflight briefing nor to pick up their operation orders."

"Perhaps they forgot they have to fly with us today," Vasily commented.

"Whatever the reason, this is inexcusable!" Mikhail continued the charade. "First time they fly with us and they're already late! As soon as I get to the plane, Ground Control will have to locate those two *pederasty*. There's no way I'm going to take off late because of them!"

During the trip to the dispersion area the remaining crewmen discussed and wondered about the irresponsibility of the missing men.

Arriving by the flying giant's nosewheels bogey, Mikhail got off the truck's cabin before it even stopped. The plane ready for takeoff, Master Sergeant Sudaryev and his men retired their ladders from the wings and fuselage. The fuel trucks departed after having filled up the enormous plane's 71 fuel tanks with its full complement of 165,154 kilograms of T-2 aviation kerosene fuel. Here remained only a ZIL-131 truck, adapted for ground power, to provide external auxiliary power to the different electronic systems until the plane turned on its engines and relied on its own internal generators.

"Captain Makarov! *Dobroe utro!*" Sudaryev greeted, saluting.

"*Dobroe utro, tovarishch serzhant!*" Mikhail returned the salute. "Is everything ready?"

"Yes, Captain. Your plane is all fueled up and ready to go."

"I wish I could say the same about the crew."

"Why? What's wrong?" Sudaryev asked.

"I'm missing two crewmen, the flight engineer and the operator for the new radar. Both of them new. First time they fly with us."

"First time and they're already late? What a way to start," Sudaryev said.

"Right. What bothers me the most is that without either one of them I can't take off, and the maneuvers require precision to the minute," Mikhail added. "Anyway, I'll get upstairs to the cockpit and see if Ground Control can locate them." Mikhail shook Sudaryev's hand, then climbed the cockpit access ladder. "*Spasibo bol'shoye, serzhant.* I trust that, as usual, you did a good job. Especially today. I'm counting on that to perform flawlessly in the maneuvers."

"Nothing to fear, Captain. I personally did some of the work. I know how important this flight is for you," Sudaryev said.

"You do?" Mikhail asked. Surprised, he stopped at mid ladder.

"Yes, I do. The honor of the whole 364th ODRAP depends on how you and this plane perform in the maneuvers."

"Ah, yes. That is very very true. This flight of today is extremely important. Many great things may happen today," Mikhail said as he continued climbing the stairs. Behind him, the rest of the crew followed him upstairs.

The crew sat at their assigned stations, turned on their consoles and tested the different systems.

"Ground Control, Ground Control, this is *Red 67. Priyom,*" Serghey, the radio operator, called.

"Red 67, this is Ground Control, go ahead, *Red 67. Priyom,*"

"Ground Control, *Red 67* transmitting. How do you receive my transmission? *Priyom,*"

"Red 67, we receive you loud and clear. How do you receive our transmission? *Priyom."*

"Ground Control, *Red 67* transmitting. I receive you loud and clear. End of transmission."

As he finishes testing radio communications, Serghey listens to Mikhail's voice in his headphones: "Lieutenant Molotko, is radio up and running?"

"Yes, Captain. I just tested it."

"Good. I need to contact Ground Control to find out what happened to those two *mudaki*. We're already late as is," Mikhail said, switching on communications to Ground Control.

"Ground Control, *Red 67* here. Captain Makarov speaking. *Priyom."*

"Red 67. This is Ground Control. Go ahead, Captain. *Priyom."*

"I'm missing two crewmen, Flight Engineer Lieutenant Padzhenadze, and the radar operator, Lieutenant Rybakov. Both of them were supposed to fly with me today. Any news on them? *Priyom."*

"Aaah. Wait a minute on that, Captain, while we call Operations."

"Understood, Ground Control. Call back as soon as you have any news on them. *Red 67,* end transmission."

Meanwhile, both pilots turned their attention to the pre-start checklists. The rest of the crew continued the testing of their own stations. In the plane's nose, Alexey turned on his navigation radar and waited for it to warm up to operating readiness. Behind the pilots, Anatoly and Ivan did the same with their own equipment. In the tail, Pavel also turned on the '*Vishnya*' and '*Romb*' electronic equipment under his care. Jonas and Ivan tested the movement of the twin NR-23 cannons in the three tail barbettes, more out of habit than of any particular need to really use them.

Having finished the first part of their checklist, Captain Makarov once again called: "Ground Control, *Red 67* here. Captain Makarov speaking. *Priyom."*

"*Red 67*. This is Ground Control. Go ahead, Captain. *Priyom.*"

"Any news on the missing crewmen? I can't stay here the whole day until they're found! I need a Flight Engineer and a radar operator right now! *Priyom.*"

"Understood, Captain. They have not been found yet. Operations is contacting Commander Degtyaryov to supply you with a replacement crew. *Priyom.*"

"A replacement crew? I don't need a replacement crew! My crew is already here, except the two new men! *Priyom.*"

"Understood, Captain. You must understand that this is totally unexpected! *Priyom.*"

"Understood, Ground Control. How about sending me my old crewmen? Lieutenants Kazakov and Kiprenko. They're still here, ready and able to leave right now. *Priyom.*"

"Understood, Captain. We'll contact Operations again to have them relay your request to Commander Degtyaryov. We should have a reply for you soon. *Priyom.*"

"Understood, Ground Control. *Red 67*, end transmission."

Looking at Vasily, Mikhail silently made an 'everything alright' sign with his right hand, mute indication that up to now, the countless preparations for today's escape are going according to plan. Vasily acknowledged with a slight nod of his head and a smile.

"*Ladno.* Let's continue with our checklists," said Mikhail.

"It's difficult without the Flight Engineer," commented Vasily.

"Yes, but we have to make do with what we have, and redeem time. We're already behind as is ... Landing gear switch and lights!"

"Landing gear switch down, lights, on," responded Vasily.

"Propellers circuit breakers."

"Propellers circuit breakers, checked high."

The pilots continued down their list, calling and checking the status of the different systems available to them before the engines came on. Then Alexey saw through the airplane's nose glazing the lights of a truck coming to them at blazing speed. "Captain, Alexey speaking. I see truck lights coming our way. Did the new guys finally appear?"

"Not that I know of. Perhaps they did. I'm calling Ground Control right now."

"Understood. Let me know what happened," said Alexey.

Mikhail once again opened a com line to Ground Control: "Ground Control, *Red 67* here. Captain Makarov speaking. *Priyom.*"

"*Red 67*. This is Ground Control. Go ahead, Captain. *Priyom.*"

"Did they find those two? Or am I to spend the rest of the day here waiting for them? *Priyom.*"

"Understood, Captain. Commander Degtyaryov approved having your old crewmen flying with you today while the *Komendatura* searches for the new ones. *Priyom*"

"Understood. That means they have not been found yet. *Priyom.*"

"Correct, Captain. Your men are already on their way to your plane. *Priyom.*"

"Understood, Ground Control. I see a truck coming towards us. *Spasibo bol'shoye!* I was already starting to think that we were going to miss the maneuvers. Ground Control, also contact our escort from Kipelovo, and advise them to proceed without us. Inform them of our problem. *Priyom,*"

"Understood, *Red 67.* Anything else, Captain?"

"Nyet. Spasibo bol'shoye. Red 67 ends transmission."

The truck arrived and stopped under *Red 67's* nose. Anatoly and Yuri jumped from its back and ran to the cockpit access ladder. Once in the forward cabin, each crewman headed to their assigned stations. Yuri, behind Vasily and across Serghey's radio station; Anatoly, to his station by the rear bulkhead, next to Ivan's. In his hands he carried a canvas bag containing the ADS jammer and related equipment.

"Captain! It's so good to be here again for one last flight!" exclaimed Yuri.

"Yes, welcome back, Yura. Besides, what kind of last flight! The one for the *Okean* maneuvers!" replied Mikhail.

"Well, that's precisely why I'm glad to be back! It's a fitting end to a long time serving as Flight Engineer for *Red 67!*" said Yuri, pushing buttons and flipping switches on in his console.

"Right. You deserve to have your last flight with us while we're taking part in the *Okean* maneuvers," Mikhail said.

"Captain, all systems on and running on my side. You can start engines!" Yuri announced.

"Understood, Yura. Vasya, turn engine number one on," Mikhail acknowledged and ordered.

Vasily immediately pressed the button that activated the starter for engine number one. The 5.6-meter contrarotating AV-60N propellers began to turn, counterclockwise the front set and clockwise the rear set, slowly at first, until soon they were nothing but a blur. Having achieved good compression rates, Yuri ignited the NK-12MV turboprop engine's combustion chambers. The soft hum of the turbine coming to life increased in pitch as the engine achieved optimum rotational speed.

"Engine number one, on and turning at optimum," notified Vasily. "Engine number two coming on now," continued the copilot, pressing the engine's starter button.

Behind Vasily, as each engine was turned on in succession, Yuri verified their fuel consumption, oil and combustion chamber temperatures, compressor and hydraulic pressures, and all the other appropriate parameters.

Back at the radar console, Anatoly feverishly connected the ADS jammer to a power source from his console, also making sure that the unit remained off. Any stray interference emanating from it would be detected at once by both Serghey nearby, and the radio communications unit at the base. Once the device was connected, the technician proceeded to turn on his console and test his assigned equipment.

Outside, the maintenance team disconnected their auxiliary power equipment then placed all their paraphernalia on their truck. Since the enormous noise produced by all four turboprops revving at low speed made communication impossible with the men outside, Mikhail relied on the direct connection Sergeant Sudaryev maintained to his headphones via a jack on the nosewheels bogie.

"Captain Makarov, is everything alright on your side?" asked the Sergeant.

"Yes. All systems up and running normally. *Spasibo bol'shoye, serzhant!* Once again you've done a perfect job!"

"*Pozhaluysta, tovarishch kapitan!* It was a pleasure to be of service! *Udacha i dobryy polyot!*" Sergeant Sudaryev wished the crew luck and a good flight, then disconnected his headphones from the bogie jack and returned to his truck.

Sticking his head out the side window, Mikhail made a final salute as the maintenance truck departed. Closing the window, he returned his attention to the matters at hand. "Ground Control, *Red 67* here. Captain Makarov speaking. *Priyom.*"

"*Red 67.* This is Ground Control. Go ahead, Captain. *Priyom.*"

"Ground Control. *Red 67* ready to advance to take off position. *Priyom.*"

"Understood, *Red 67.* You may advance to Runway 14B. *Priyom.*"

"Understood, Ground Control. *Red 67* advancing to Runway 14B. *Red 67,* end transmission."

"Well, Vasya, this is it. Here we go!" Mikhail exclaimed, releasing the parking brakes and pushing all four engine throttles with his left hand.

The flying hulk's ten wheels began to turn, pushed by the combined might of the four turboprop engines turning all eight propellers. As Captain Makarov increased the throttle settings, the plane slowly advanced towards Runway 14B, which would take it to the beginning of Runway 32A, from where it would take off.

Advancing towards their take off position, Mikhail glanced to his right at the airplanes parked by the dispersion area, and further ahead at the various buildings of the airbase. Just like he did in Leningrad, he paid a long look at them. Only that, unlike Leningrad, it was with the firm hope of never seeing them again. The faded gray buildings of the repair hangars, the living quarters, the administration—with all its dependencies, Operations, Command, Political, the Lenin Hall, and many others, passed to their right. As they passed, Mikhail thought about the many days, months, and years of his life spent there, dull and grey, like the buildings themselves.

Red 67 finally reached the end of Runway 14B. To its left, the beginning of Runway 32A. Increasing the starboard engines throttle settings and decreasing their starboard counterpart, Mikhail pressed left rudder, turned the control wheel to that side, and entered the head of Runway 32A.

"Tovarishchi, we're at runway head," he announced to his crew. "Pre-take off checklists for everyone. *Priyom."*

Eight acknowledgements arrived in his earphones.

"Ladno. Vasya, let's start," Mikhail said, grabbing the checklist. "Wing flaps!"

"Take-off position at twenty five degrees," replied Vasily.

"Propellers!"

"Fine pitch at high revolutions."

As they went through the list, Mikhail increased the throttles to maximum to test the engines output, calling checklist points and receiving the appropriate answers from Vasily. At the flight engineer's station Yuri also went through his pre-take off checklist, like the rest of the crew.

Having finished all the checks, *Red 67* was finally ready to take off: "Ground Control, *Red 67* here. Captain Makarov speaking. *Priyom."*

"Red 67. This is Ground Control. Go ahead, Captain. *Priyom."*

"Ground Control. *Red 67,* ready to take off. *Priyom."*

"Understood, *Red 67.* You may take off from Runway 32A. *Priyom."*

"Understood, Ground Control. *Red 67* taking off from Runway 32A. *Red 67,* end transmission."

Both pilots let go of the brakes and firmly grabbed the control wheels before them. Mikhail steadily pushed all four engine throttles with his left hand.

The flying giant, feeling the surging power of its four Kuznyetsov turboprops pushing against its airframe, started to turn its wheels, slowly at first. As the engines' revolutions increased, so did its ground speed. The landing gear began to swallow meter after meter of concrete runway, ever faster.

In the cockpit, Mikhail and Vasily kept their eyes on the air speed gages before them. As their needles ran over higher and higher numbers, the airplane reached half of its take off speed, reaching also half of its take off run. As they reached rotation speed, the buildings on their left became blurs. At 1550 meters both pilots pulled slightly their control wheels, the tailplane elevators rose, the tail went down and the nosewheels went up, sliding a couple of meters over the concrete below, the aircraft approaching its take off speed.

Finally, after a run of 1800 meters the pilots pulled their control wheels even more. The airplane reached its take off speed of 300 kph, and all eight wheels of the two main landing gears jumped into the air to begin its ascent into the reddish-blue sky. The sun had already begun its daily trek across the heavens.

"Aloft at 0515," Vasily said.

"*Blyad*, forty five minutes late! Yura, Alyosha, we'll have to compensate for lost time."

"Understood, Captain," said the two men in unison.

While still ascending, *Red 67* initiated a right bank that would take it in a northwest heading, towards Murmansk and Severomorsk. As they banked, under the right wing passed the small fishing town of Varzuga, 18 kms. upstream on the river of the same name.

*   *   *   *

Having arrived at his office punctually at his customary 0500, Colonel Yakovlev diverted his attention to the noise coming from the runways. Through his window he could see *Red 67* in its take off run, the red reflections of the rising sun bouncing off its wings.

Standing up from his chair, Yakovlev walked towards the window and followed the aircraft in its run as it jumped into the air, ascended, turned, and became smaller and smaller. All this brought back to his mind the incident that had been hammering him for the last few days: Whatever or whoever he saw by Runway 14.

Despite having an incredibly busy day today—the high brass from Murmansk was due to arrive for the inspection of the base—he also had on his desk the latest report from Security: The disappearance of two men from the personnel assigned to the air crews. Whether it was due to the current crime conditions in the base— a closely held secret he and Cmdr. Degtyaryov kept carefully hidden away from the ears of the upper brass—or to other factors, that was something he'd have to investigate further, of course, but later. At that moment in time he had to have everything ready and prepared for the arrival of the Regional Inspector General and his assistant.

Looking at his watch, Col. Yakovlev expected at any second the arrival of his assistant, Lt. Col. Nikitin. Most probably he was going to assign to Nikitin the task of finding out what happened to the two lost men. After all, receiving early morning calls from Cmdr. Degtyaryov, screaming in his ears to have his men get to the bottom of that matter, was not precisely the way Yakovlev wanted to start his day. However, that was how it started, and he had all the intentions in the world not to let it end that way.

As expected, the sounds of a door opening and closing in the next office announced the arrival of his assistant. Grabbing his phone, Yakovlev dialed Nikitin's extension.

"Dobroe utro! Lt. Col. Nikitin speaking," promptly answered the voice on the other side.

"Nikitin, Yakovlev speaking. Bring me the security folders for …" Yakovlev paused, taking from his pocket the piece of paper where he hurriedly wrote the names of the two men disappeared the night before. "… Lieutenants Padzhenadze, Tugan, and Rybakov, Pavel …" Saying the names, Yakovlev suddenly noted that the second name had a certain familiarity, as if he had heard the name before. Not being able to remember exactly where he heard it from, Yakovlev left it at that, preferring to wait until Nikitin brought him the folders.

"Is that all, Colonel?" Nikitin asked.

"Yes. When you bring the folders, I'll tell you what I want you to do with them.

"Yes, Colonel. Anything else?"

"That's it for the time being." Yakovlev hung up the phone and readied his mind for the arrival of the VIPs coming in from Murmansk in just a few hours more, in the daily morning flight from that northern city.

*   *   *   *

Flying at cruising altitude and speed, *Red 67* overflew the Barents Sea. Some time ago they had already left behind the northern coast of the Kola Peninsula.

"Lieutenant Molotko, contact Major Krasnosyel'skih, he's the leader of the flight from Kipelovo," Mikhail ordered. "Tell them we're about to start the second leg of our flight. Ask them if they deem our presence necessary in order to complete their assessment of the new radar."

"Understood, Captain. Transmitting right now," said the radioman, turning to his long-range radio communication equipment.

Shortly after, a reply was received: "Captain, transmission from *Blue 54*. Major Krasnosyel'skih informs that it will not be necessary for us to be present. They'll make their own tests with their *'Uspekh'* radar. The results will be sent to Murmansk, for correlation later with our results, once we are done with our tests."

"Understood, Lieutenant. *Spasibo bol'shoye.*"

"Yura, Alyosha, you heard that. No need to hurry up to catch up with the crews from Kipelovo. Maintain present speed and altitude, same heading, same route."

Two acknowledgments sounded in the intercom system.

*   *   *   *

Standing on the tarmac in front of the main building, the same where the control tower was located, Col. Yakovlev and Commander Degtyaryov waited impatiently for the arrival of the daily flight from Murmansk. Looking at his watch, Yakovlev saw what apparently had become a normal routine for this airplane: the usual delay. The men had been waiting already for the best part of an hour when finally, in the distance, from the northwest came the muffled rumor of an engine.

Commander Degtyaryov placed his right hand above his head, as if to block the glare coming from the sun, despite it being behind him and the protection offered by the visor of his officer's cap. He squinted as he forced his eyes to look in the horizon at the small black dot that now appeared to be suspended in the air, and which seemed to be the origin of the soft drone they heard. "That's them," said the obviously disgusted officer.

Yakovlev once again looked at his watch: 0845. *"Blyad.* Forty five minutes late! One of the recommendations I'm making in my Security Plans is to finish once and for all those ridiculous delays in these flights from Murmansk," said Col. Yakovlev, remembering the last time he took this same flight.

"Go ahead. You know I'm backing you up in this. Those delays do nothing but contribute to the general lack of discipline we have been experiencing lately at the base," Degtyaryov agreed.

As both officers exchanged feelings on the flight's lack of timely arrival, the dot on the horizon grew in size. The soft drone had already become the continuous hum of the twin turboprops of the small Antonov AN-24. As the airplane approached the base it entered the gliding path to runway 14B, the one usually reserved for the utility and liaison airplanes that linked Kuzomen to the rest of the naval air bases in Kola and Arkhanghelsk.

Still descending, the tricycle landing gear extended from the underwing engine nacelles and nosewheels bay. After a few minutes sliding in its descent, the six small wheels make a soft touchdown on the concrete runway. The pilots immediately decelerated the turboprops power before applying the brakes, making the airplane lose speed. Having achieved minimal running speed, the airplane taxied to a stop in front of the control tower and of the waiting officers.

Degtyaryov—for the umpteenth time, fixed his tie and cap. Yakovlev made a cursory look on his superior, as if to assure him that he was presentable. The passenger side door opened and out of it poured Navy personnel and officers that came to the base on official duty. Finally, out stepped the object of their long wait: Lieutenant General Boris S. Griboyedov, KGB Inspector General for the Region of Murmansk, and his assistant, Colonel Arkadiy K. Morozov.

After the perfunctory greetings and hand shaking, the smiling officers walked with the newly-arrived VIPs to the Administration Building, where the inspection tour of the base began.

*   *   *   *

Northern Atlantic Ocean. In order to 'show the flag' and counter the USS Nimitz passage through the Atlantic Ocean and the Mediterranean Sea the previous month of July, the Voyenno-Morskoy Flot Sovietskogo Soyuza, the Soviet Navy, sent out the TAKr or Tyazholyy Avianosnyy Kreyser (Heavy Aircraft-carrying Cruiser) Kiev—the Soviet version of an aircraft carrier—to participate in the Okean-76 naval maneuvers. Aboard the vessel carried the Otdyel'nyy Korabel'nyy Shturmovoy Aviatsionnyy Polk or Independent Shipborne Attack Air Regiment 279, better known as the 279th OKShAP, comprising six Yak-36M (Morskoy—Naval), VTOL jet fighters, baptized "Forger A" by NATO, freshly received from the Yakovlev factories, plus a complement of 15 Kamov Ka-25 helicopters.

The month before the Kiev had sailed out of the Black Sea Fleet port of Sevastopol, crossed the Bosphorus Strait, the Mediterranean Sea, and finally reached the Atlantic Ocean, stopping at a point northeast of the Azores Islands. Here an important part of the maneuvers took place: the testing of a complex technological integration of submarine to aircraft control system known to the Soviet Navy by the Russian acronym RUS for Razvyedyvatel'naya Udarnaya Sistema or 'Reconnaissance-Attacking System.' This test involved the firing of a live missile from a submarine, guided in mid-flight by a TU-95 RTs, and finally let loose on an old target ship. All under the close eye and scrutiny of not only Admiral Gorshkov himself—aboard the *Kiev*—but also of every ship and reconnaissance aircraft of practically every NATO country that has a coast and an interest on this side of the Atlantic. From Norway and the United Kingdom in the European north to Spain and Portugal in the south, as well as Canada and the United States in North America.

About 500 kms north of the *Kiev*, the K-22 *'Krasnogvardeyets' (izdeliye 538)*, Project 675MK Series XIV, classified by NATO as an Echo II-class nuclear submarine attached to the Northern Fleet, received missile launch orders from Severomorsk. K-22 carried on board eight P-500 (4K80) *Bazal't* antishipping missiles (NATO designation: SS-N-12 Sandbox), each inside its own SM-241 canister launcher, four on each side of the sub, distributed two in front and two behind the conning tower, two almost amidships, and two in the bow, all forward-firing. Each missile was capable of carrying 1000Kg of hollow-charge armor-piercing high explosives or a 350-Kiloton nuclear warhead.

On receiving the orders, K-22's commanding officer, Captain Second Rank Valentin N. Pankovskiy ordered the sub to ascend to periscope depth in order to establish radio contact with the TU-95RTs piloted by Captain Mikhail Makarov.

Flying at 12,000 meters, midway between the K-22 and the *Kiev,* some 250 kilometers to the south of the former and to the north of the latter, *Red 67's* new *Korshun* search radar detected and tracked the general area where the intended target for the upcoming test of the radar's capabilities was anchored.

"Eagle, Eagle, Eagle, this is Sturgeon. *Priyom.*" Anatoly heard the call from Senior Lieutenant N. K. Potapov, the Missile Control Officer aboard the K-22.

"Sturgeon, this is Eagle. We receive you loud and clear. *Priyom.*"

"We're ready to receive your show. *Priyom.*"

"Understood, Sturgeon. Initiating show transmission now," said Anatoly.

The technician pushed the appropriate buttons to begin transmitting the coordinates and tracking data from the *Korshun* to the still-submerged submarine through the aircraft's *"Arfa"* signal relay and amplification system antennas, located at the end of the tail elevators.

Red 67's new *Korshun* radar had enough detection range to allow the P-500 *Bazal't* missile to be fired from maximum range. Thus, the Mach 2.5, turbojet-powered missile could destroy an enemy ship 550 km away.

"Understood, Eagle. Reception clear. *Priyom.*" Sr. Lt. Potapov confirmed the reception. On the radar screen before him small symbols represented the ships surrounding the *Kiev*, as well as the target ship. In a normal combat situation Capt. Pankovskiy would have used this display to assess the tactical situation more accurately and choose the best target for the missile strike.

Immediately Captain Pankovskiy, assisted by his MCO, analyzed the situation, picked a target and selected an old WW II veteran, the *Zheleznyakov*, an 11,300-ton *Chapaev*-class cruiser laid down at Nikolayevsk on the Black Sea in 1940. Renamed target vessel TSL-77, it sailed to the location of its last act as a useful seagoing vessel. Stationed about 20 kms east of the *Kiev*, the old ship awaited its explosive demise.

Once selected, the target's bearing and range were determined and entered into the submarine's missile control computer. The computer analyzed target lock-on and kill probability. Capt. Pankovskiy made the ultimate decision to fire on target.

Once Pankovsky gave the firing order, the sub emerged. On the conning tower a casing cover hinged back to expose the antenna for the *Argument* 3GHz S-band tracking and guidance radar (NATO designation: 'Front-Door A'). Meanwhile, one of the sub's rear hatches opened, an SM-241 launcher was promptly raised to 30 degrees, followed without delay by a loud roar. A thick cloud of acrid smoke surrounded the submarine when the solid-propellant RATO booster motor of the thin, pencil-like 11.7-meter-long P-500 *Bazal't* ignited and slid off the rails of its launcher, leaving behind a long wake of dark-grey smoke.

Thirty seconds later the *krylataya raketa*—winged rocket, as the Soviet Navy called it, better known today as 'cruise missile'—reached Mach 0.5, covered a distance of five kilometers, and ascended to an altitude of 500 meters. Then the booster, its energy spent, suddenly detonated its explosive bolts and detached from the missile. The KR-17-300 turbojet engine in the tail came to life, increasing its speed and height even more. After sixty seconds, twenty kilometers distant from the submarine, the missile broke the sound barrier and reached 2 kilometers up in the air, still accelerating and ascending.

Aboard the submarine, Sr. Lt. Potapov guided it using K-22's *Argument* tracking and guidance radar to follow the rocket in its speedy flight and ascent. The rocket devoured kilometer after kilometer in its southward journey towards the target. One hundred and twenty seconds into the flight the missile had already reached Mach 2.0, twice the speed of sound, 61 kilometers away from K-22 and six kilometers up.

Finally, after one hundred and eighty seconds, the missile reached an altitude of seven kilometers at a speed of Mach 2.5 at a distance of 112 kilometers from

K-22 and 438 kilometers from the target. Sr. Lt. Potapov pushed the appropriate buttons and switches to place the automatic guidance system in cruise mode.

Aboard *Red 67* Anatoly tracked the missile as it quickly approached the aircraft. Having flown at Mach 2.5 for four minutes, in about sixty more seconds it would reach the end of the submarine control range, some 250 kms from K-22.

"Tolya, Pavel here," Anatoly heard. "How far and from which bearing will the missile be passing by us?"

"About 3 kms away, by starboard, vector 165, in about one minute," replied the technician.

"Understood. *Spasibo,*" Pavel ended his inquiry.

Anatoly returned to the duties at hand: "Sturgeon, this is Eagle. Activating missile guidance relay on my mark ... *Tri, dva, odin,* active! *Priyom.*"

"Understood, Eagle. All relay indicators on. All systems active and functioning. *Priyom,*" acknowledged Sr. Lt. Potapov. From then on, as the distance between them increased, *Red 67* served as a mid way station between K-22 and the missile, allowing the missile officer to maintain constant control on the rocket. Using the data gathered by and transmitted from *Red 67*, the Missile Control Officer made occasional flight path corrections.

In the tail, Jonas and Pavel hurriedly grabbed their fine resolution binoculars. Jonas trained his on the wide open skies before him, alert to the appearance of the high-speed missile any second. Suddenly, to his right, a small black dot came into sight.

"I see it! I see it! It's coming by my left!" yelled the man, craning his neck in an attempt to get a better view of the rocket through the small windows of the tail position.

"Where? Where?" asked Pavel, moving his sliding seat towards the right-side blister, his binoculars trained to the rearmost part of his field of vision.

"It's slightly below us!" Jonas replied.

The rocket quickly decreased the distance between itself and the aircraft until it reached the same position the airplane happened to be in the sky.

"I see it!" Pavel yelled as the missile whizzed before him from the right. He followed it in its flight. As suddenly as it came, the small dot disappeared from his sight on the left side of the blister. *"Chyort vozmyot!* The speed of that thing! We saw it for maybe two or three seconds!"

"Don't forget it must be flying between 2000 and 2500 kms. an hour. We're flying at barely 400 to 500 kms. an hour. Compared to it, we're like suspended in mid air," said his colleague.

"Well, at least we can say we saw one of those rockets in high speed flight at 12,000 meters high!" said Pavel, a wide grin on his face.

"True. Not everyone can say that," Jonas agreed.

Five and a half minutes after *Red 67* started to relay control the missile was 490 kms from K-22. Then it started a descent to a height of 2 kms. while slowing down from Mach 2.5 to Mach 0.8. Anatoly aboard *Red 67,* and Sr. Lt. Potapov aboard K-22, followed the weapon in its quick descent. In less than a minute it reached the desired altitude.

Suddenly, Anatoly's spit a loud expletive: *"Khuy morzhovyy!* What the devil is going on?"

The radar screen before him went totally dark.

"Eagle, Eagle, this is Sturgeon … I lost all imaging from you! What's happening?" Anatoly heard the frantic call from Sr. Lt. Potapov, aboard K-22.

"I don't know, Sturgeon. I'm having the same situation here too. I'm verifying all the transmitting and receiving circuitry," Anatoly said while visually checking and inspecting the buttons, levers and switches of the panels before him.

Meanwhile, 200 kms. south of *Red 67*, the missile, now 60 kilometers from the general target area, continued flying on its own.

Anatoly desperately turned his radar console on and off, pleaded with and persuaded the malfunctioning equipment to come back to life, but his efforts were fruitless. In frustration, the technician rained powerful bangs on the sides of his console while compellingly cursing both the device and its manufacturers.

A stuck circuit breaker lever, jolted out of its state by the strong shocks of the technician's fists, dropped to the open position. Immediately, an indicator signal lighted up, telling the technician the origin of his problems. Anatoly quickly reset the wayward breaker. To everyone's relief, the screen came back to life. One second later, K-22's Sr. Lt. Potapov reported that his screen also came back to life.

Normally, at a preset range, usually in the target approach phase, the missile's onboard active radar homing system would be activated, taking over the terminal guidance to the target. For this practice, however, that system was turned off, since the K-22's Missile Control Officer was going to make this approach himself. Or at least that's how it was supposed to be.

"Blyad! A eto chto?" Abruptly, a confused Anatoly asked himself. The screen display before him, instead of showing the information provided by his own *Korshun* radar, showed him the feed from the missile's radar. "Sturgeon, this is Eagle. Why the hell I am seeing your rocket's display on my screen?"

"Eagle, this is Sturgeon. I don't know … Aah … We're trying to find out the reason," came the terse reply from K-22.

"Well, you better find out soon. Your rocket is entering approach."

"Understood, Eagle. The active radar homing system seems to be on."

"Seems to be on? It is fucking on! I am seeing it on my screen!"

"Understood, Eagle. We're seeing it here too …"

"Sukaaa!! Sturgeon, are you seeing what I am seeing?" Anatoly screamed in his microphone.

"Yes, Eagle. We're seeing it too. We're trying all possible measures to deactivate it!"

To both men's horror, they discovered simultaneously that in those critical seconds when the missile was flying blind, the onboard radar homing and target lock up system had been left on. And worse, it had locked on the wrong target: The *Kiev.* This despite the correct target having been locked earlier—at launch—using the *Korshun* data transmitted by *Red 67.*

Inside K-22, Sr. Lt. Potapov immediately pressed the abort button, but nothing happened. The missile onboard terminal guidance system had taken control. Potapov had less than one minute to blow it up or it would crash at full speed against the *Kiev.* The 4800kg missile crashing at Mach 0.8 against the target—whether it was the *Kiev* or the *Zheleznyakov*—with its 1000kg warhead was enough to cause serious damage to the ship's hull. Agitated calls began to flow from the Kiev to *Red 67* and to K-22.

"Blyad, suka, you have exactly fifty five seconds to do something about it or soon there's going to be a lot of dead people there!" Anatoly screamed once again.

"Understood, Eagle! I know! I know! We're doing all we can!" replied the exasperated Potapov, trying in vain to destroy the missile. "This damn piece of shit had to get stuck now … I … can't … get it out … I hope this will help …"

Potapov baubled incoherencies on his microphone, giving Anatoly a clear indication that the man lost control of himself just as he had lost control of the missile.

"Suka! Listen! Forget about blowing it up! Turn the guidance computer off! TURN IT OFF!" Anatoly screamed once again in his microphone at the top of his lungs. So loud that his voice could be heard by those surrounding him, despite the thunderous drone of the Bear's engines. "Turn it on again, then aim it and lock it on the target!"

Counting the remaining time to impact in short seconds, Anatoly waited for the man to comply. Hesitantly, Potapov followed Anatoly's instructions.

At just 20 kms from the target, the missile diverted from its flight path and locked on the *Zheleznyakov,* 20 kms. east of the *Kiev.* Having entered terminal approach, the missile dove to 100 meters height, turned its turbojet engine off, and slammed against the old hull of the target ship, like the *kamikaze* pilots of World War II. The impact made the heavy vessel momentarily jump into the air, only to sink once again into the cold waters of the Atlantic. On her deck and side, an enormous gaping hole appeared at the location of the missile impact. A millisecond later, a colossal blast erupted from the opening. A huge black cloud tinted with red and orange tones rose to engulf her structures, converting them into a mass of flaming and smoldering iron.

For the international observers keeping a close watch on the maneuvers, unaware of the events that had just happened, the launching of the P-500 missile from the K-22, followed by a 'flawless' flight of more than 500 kms to target, and the accuracy with which the rocket fell squarely on its predesignated target was a show off of Soviet mastery. Although to them it remained an unexplained mystery why the missile seemed to take a somewhat circuitous route to reach the target ship.

This phase of the *Okean* maneuvers concluded, Admiral Gorshkov ordered the *Kiev* northwards, towards the Shetland-Faeroes Gap, for the next phase. The vessel was followed, as usual, not only by her own support and escort ships but also by the 'uninvited guests' from several nations that accompanied and trailed the ensemble of Soviet ships.

On the bridge of his flagship, Admiral Gorshkov—like the foreign observers also blissfully unaware of how close the maneuvers were to become a disaster of colossal stature, thanks to the 'diligence' of the officers around him in hiding the magnitude of the danger—ordered his subordinates to send congratulatory messages to the crews of the vessels involved in this phase of the maneuvers.

Aboard *Red 67* a relieved Captain Makarov echoed the curiosity of everyone else aboard and asked Anatoly: "Tolya, what happened with the missile? All we could hear was your screaming, yelling and cursing, and how you banged that console so hard that for a second I thought it was going to fall apart."

"It seems that the homing system, not sensing any guidance from K-22 due to the malfunction of our circuit breaker, relied on its own internal guidance and locked on the *Kiev* rather than on the target ship," he explained.

Expletives and words of amazement exploded throughout the airplane.

"But wasn't that system supposed to be turned off?" asked Vasily.

"Yes, but for some reason it was on. Either because it was left inadvertently on, or it came on on its own when it felt no guidance from Sturgeon," Anatoly explained.

"Lieutenant Kiprenko, how did you know he had to turn it off?" asked Serghey. "As far as I know, you have not been trained in those systems."

"It's a matter of common sense. Logically, if you can't get control back, turning it off and then on should restart the whole thing and bring it back to a state where you can regain control once again."

"Very well done, Lieutenant! I'll see to it that this shows up in your papers," replied Serghey. Anatoly almost fell from his seat when he heard the radioman sing praises to him. His surprise was so great that he only managed to thank him. *"Spasibo, spasibo bol'shoye!"*

Vasily wondered about Serghey's sudden change of attitude as far as his treatment of Anatoly was concerned. The answer came a few seconds later, when Serghey hand-delivered to Mikhail a copy of the message Admiral Gorshkov had telexed to the crew of *Red 67* a few minutes before.

For the sake of his own service sheet, Serghey knew it was to his advantage to show the recently accomplished deeds of the radar technician in the best possible light. A perfect crew service record meant more praises and even money prizes from the *nachal'stvo* in Murmansk.

Mikhail read the message aloud in the intercom, for the benefit of all aboard: *"Tovarishchi, vnimanie!* Attention everyone:

To the commander and crew of the reconnaissance airplane *Red 67*:

> *Pozdravlyayu!* You have performed admirably and demonstrated a true Communist spirit, worthy of the appellative 'Leninist.' In the name of the Soviet Navy High Command, I congratulate you for achieving a perfect score in the performance of your duties in these *Okean* Maneuvers.
> Gorshkov, Serghey G., Admiral of the Soviet Fleet, aboard the *TAKr Kiev.*

There you have it guys, straight from the big old man himself," Mikhail said.

The storm over, Captain Makarov continued to the next step in his flight orders: "Well, Vasya, our job here is almost done. All we need now is an in-flight refueling, isn't it?"

"That's right, Captain. There's a meeting with an M-4 tanker," said the copilot.

"Commander to Flight Engineer. What's your status, Yura?"

"Fuel down to 20%. Obviously that's not enough to return to base, but the fuel transfer will raise that to approximately 85%. No problems to report, except a few minor problems with stuck gages in the main tanks, as usual, and the pressure for compressor in engine №3 is too weak for my taste, but nothing to worry about."

"Commander to Navigator. Where is that refueling going to be, Alyosha?"

"Refueling scheduled at 1430 hours local time. Coordinates: fifteen degrees west, sixty degrees north. Altitude: seven thousand. At hour present speed we should be there in about two hours and a half. Local time: 1200. Time in flight: eleven hours, sixteen minutes."

"*Otlichno!* Right on time! Despite the delay when taking off and the problems with the missile!" Exclaimed Mikhail, beaming with pride. "*Tovarishchi,* this time we'll sure get what we want out of Commander Degtyaryov and Colonel Rudenko: Money, day passes, and promotions for everybody. And the 'Excellence Award' for our crew! That's the value of team work, for the good of all in the plane. Take a break guys, you deserve it, you earned it."

After the short pep talk everyone aboard the plane stood down. Having two and a half hours for rest and relaxation, only the essential personnel needed to remain on duty.

Turning to Vasily, Mikhail suggested: "Vasya, take a nap. Go lie on the belt. One hour for you and one hour for me. I'll watch everything from here."

"*Ladno, kapitan,*" said the copilot. Then he left the cockpit and stepped on the corridor between the compartments for the Flight Engineer and the Radioman. Here Vasily placed a pair of parachutes on the conveyor belt leading to the escape hatch, sat on them, and stretched his frame over the two chutes.

Anatoly and Ivan, not being needed for this final phase, simply stretched themselves on their seats, closed their eyes and submerged their tired minds in a sorely needed break.

In the tail, Jonas turned off his oxygen valve, signaled Pavel—behind him—to do the same, and showed him a cigarette. Pavel complied and shut off his oxygen valve. While Jonas lighted up his cigarette, Pavel placed a parachute in one of the blisters by his sides, sat sideways and stretched his aching body, his head over the parachute, his back and buttocks on the seat, and his legs on the opposite blister. Having accommodated himself, the man simply fell asleep in a few minutes. Jonas whiled the time looking at the clouds in the blue, bright summer sky surrounding him, amid puffs of his cigarette.

✳   ✳   ✳   ✳

Since their arrival at the air base early that morning, Cdr. Degtyaryov and Col. Yakovlev showed Lt. Gen. Griboyedov and his assistant, Col. Morozov, each and every corner of the military installations.

"The Committee for State Security is very proud to have men of your caliber in our cadre, Konstantin Denisovich," Lt. Gen. Griboyedov congratulated Col.

Yakovlev. "You can be certain that our report is going to be very positive. The improvements you have made to the security of the base are stupendous!"

"I agree with the General," added his assistant. "Achieving a 98% decrease in the rate of delinquency incidents in a 12 months period is something to be genuinely proud of."

Of course, especially if 88% of those incidents are never reported to your office, thought Cdr. Degtyaryov. *And there's no way they'll be reported. Our promotions and perks depend on that. I know it, Konstantin Denisovich knows it, and you know it, so we'll all maintain those numbers as they are, since they make us all look good in Leningrad.*

"*Spasibo bol'shoye, tovarishchi,*" replied Col. Yakovlev. "You know it's the constant improvement of our State Security that keeps foreign enemies at bay and internal discipline in our bases. We can't let our guard down for one second!"

"And now, *tovarishchi,* allow me to invite you to a round of drinks with the rest of the officers of this fine 364th Regiment," said Cdr. Degtyaryov, pointing his distinguished visitors to the Lenin Hall, where the officers of the regiment, including crew commanders and sub commanders, navigators, flight engineers, radiomen and radar technicians, all dressed up in parade uniforms, already awaited for the entrance of the Regional Inspectors.

As the officers entered the room, Lt. Col. Nikitin approached Col. Yakovlev and whispered on his ear: "Colonel, can I speak to you in private for one minute?"

Assenting with a nod of his head, Yakovlev stayed behind the entourage and detoured to a corner of the building's foyer.

"What's going on? Have you found the two missing crewmen?"

"A lot, Colonel, a lot. We found one of them, Lt. Rybakov, Pavel Alexeyevich."

"Rybakov … The name sounds familiar … Isn't he in Colonel Rudenko's crew?"

"Yes, the same. He was drunk beyond all hopes. Two bottles of *samogon* on him. I suppose he drank them both."

"As usual. Where is he?"

"I have him locked up in the *Komendatura* right now. But he's still asleep."

"When he wakes up, tell him he's under arrest for a week, and fine him 50 rubles for dereliction of duty … No, make it two weeks and 100 rubles. That will teach him not to get drunk before a flight."

"Even if it's with our own *samogon,*" said Nikitin.

"Even if it's with our own *samogon*." repeated Yakovlev. "What about the other man, what's his name?"

"Lt. Padzhenadze, Tugan."

"Yes, him, the Georgian."

"We have not found him yet. I requested the *Komendant* to lend us some of his men to assist us in the search."

"Very well. Anything of importance on Makarov and his men? Have you searched their quarters?"

"Well, the reason why I requested the *Komendant's* men to help us in the search for the missing man is because I have all our men searching Captain Makarov's crewmen's quarters."

"Very well thought, Nikitin. But, what has that to do with Makarov?"

"Colonel, have you noticed why Cdr. Degtyaryov himself asked you to find those two men this morning?"

"No, not really. Unusual that the Commander placed so much emphasis on finding two missing men, but not totally out of the ordinary."

"Right. Usually that's something he'd send directly to the *Komendant,* not to us. Unless it's something grave."

"Anything grave about it?" Yakovlev asked, surprised.

"Ground Control called him this morning to notify him that Captain Makarov's plane could not take off, because it was missing *two* crewmen ..."

"Don't tell me," interrupted Yakovlev. "Rybakov and Padzhenadze."

"Exactly. Both of them were assigned to fly in *Red 67* today. So, since they disappeared, Cdr. Degtyaryov had no choice but to authorize the two previous crewmen to fly with Makarov this morning."

"And? What's so extraordinary about that? One was found drunk, and the other probably is AWOL, most probably also drunk in town. Happens everyday. At least Rybakov got drunk here."

"Well, yes. But I think it's too much of a coincidence that both men, from the same crew, disappear the day before a flight," Nikitin expressed his concerns.

"Listen, I have to go back with our visitors. As soon as they leave, I'm going back to my office. Have a report ready there about everything you've told me so far and about anything found in Captain Makarov's crewmen's quarters."

"Yes, Colonel. I think I'm also going to have a reception committee waiting for Makarov's return."

"Do what you must," Yakovlev said, then he headed to the Lenin Hall, where a banquet was already awaiting the guests of the base and the political commanders.

Inside the building the honored visitors were shown a table full of a variety of foods, pastries, fine black caviar from the Caspian Sea and other delicacies. All was complemented by vodka, Soviet *shampan'skoe* and Georgian *Tsinandali* wine. A private, tray in hand, approached the officers and offered each one of them a crystal drinking cup which he promptly filled with the bubbly Crimean champagne.

Cup in hand, General Griboyedov raised his own and proposed a toast: "To our glorious Soviet Motherland, our Great Soviet Navy, our heroic sailors, and to the *Okean* maneuvers!" All those present raised their cups and shouted in unison: "*Na zdrov'ye!*"

Apparently happy, Col. Yakovlev congratulated himself on the start of the Regional Inspector General's inspection. To his mind came an old Russian saying: *Vsyo khorosho, chto khorosho konchaetsya* ... 'All's well that ends well.'

*   *   *   *

"*Pelikan* to *Oriol, Pelikan* to *Oriol. Dobryy dyen'!* We see you, *priyom,*" said the pilot of the Myasishchev M-4-2 tanker.

"Understood, *Pelikan. Dobryy dyen'!* We also see you. ETA in five minutes," Mikhail answered the call from the flying gas tank.

Having descended to 7,000 meters and positioned *Red 67* about two kilometers behind the tanker, Mikhail slowly increased speed until the aircraft was behind and slightly below the tail of the large aircraft before him—as large as his own TU-95 RTs—matching its speed to the meter.

Once in position, Mikhail alerted the refueler, who immediately opened the hatches of what used to be the bomb bay of the Myasishchev M-4 bomber, occupied by the fuel tanks and refueling system of the bomber-cum-tanker. A long, snake-like hose began to unreel from the belly of the aircraft towards the tail, where *Red 67* awaited. At the end of the long hose, a large 300 kg drogue cone opened up to facilitate the insertion of the 2m-long 'cannon' or refueling probe, part of the *'Konus'* inflight refueling system, located at the nose of the Tupolev, above the navigator's position.

Once the drogue cone stopped and stabilized before the thirsty Tupolev, Mikhail, assisted by Vasily, carefully advanced and moved the aircraft's nose towards the awaiting conical drogue, using the superb skill and mastery obtained in so many years of flying. As the probe slowly entered the drogue, both pilots maintained a firm grip on their control wheels, moving the 200-ton aircraft in a centimeter by centimeter creeping ever deeper into the cone, until the long cylinder finally latched inside the hose.

"*Oriol* to *Pelikan*, we got connection! *Priyom,*" announced Yura to his colleague on the M-4.

"Understood, *Oriol*. We got it here too. How much do you need?" asked the refueler.

"*Oriol* to *Pelikan*. As much as you can give us. We can take it all. You have here a very thirsty machine. *Priyom.*"

"Understood, *Oriol*. I can give … you … 25 to 30, no more. *Priyom.*"

"Understood, *Pelikan*. We'll take 30. Ready to initiate transfer on my mark. *Priyom,*" Yuri replied. The refueling system was ready to receive the thirty tons of fuel.

"Understood, *Oriol*. We're ready whenever you are. *Priyom.*"

"Understood, *Pelikan*. Initiate … transfer … now!"

On receiving the command, the refueling engineer aboard the Myasishchev turned on the powerful pumps and started the transfer of high-octane aviation fuel, at the rate of one ton a minute.

Meanwhile the pilots, still maintaining a firm grip on the control wheels, kept the flying giant steady, beneath the similarly large flying tanker. Two giants of the air, flying at only scarce meters from each other. All done by hand, without any assistance from automatic pilot systems. Due to the strain, after thirty minutes in this endeavor both pilots were bathed in sweat, despite the light summer flying suits they wore.

"*Oriol* to *Pelikan*. My gauges show the transfer completes in one minute. *Priyom,*" said Yuri.

"Understood, *Oriol*. My gauges verify that. *Priyom.*"

"Understood. You may stop transfer on my mark … *tri … dva … odin … Stop!*"

The refueler stopped the pumps and initiated the separation of the hose and drogue from *Red 67's* probe. Free of the probe, the drogue cone went on wild gyrations while the rolling motors aboard the M-4 reeled in the long hose back to the aircraft's belly. Once the hose was secured inside the airplane, the hatches closed.

"*Oriol* to *Pelikan. Spasibo bol'shoye za zapravku! Udacha i dobryy polyot! Priyom,*" Mikhail thanked his colleagues aboard the tanker for the refueling just received.

"Pozhaluysta, kapitan! It was a pleasure! Good luck and good flight to you too!" replied the commanding pilot aboard the M-4. His airplane then ascended and increased its speed to optimum cruise.

As the tanker got lost in the distance, Mikhail ordered: "Vasya, raise it up to cruise altitude and speed." Vasily increased power to the engines while slightly pulling the control wheel in order to initiate his aircraft's ascent to cruise height. The Captain then contacted the flight engineer: "Yura, do you still have some of that tea?"

"Yes, Captain. I haven't touched it. Now is the perfect time for it," said the flight engineer.

"Could I have some, please."

"Konyechno, kapitan. Anyone else?" asked the crewman.

"Yes, Yura. Me too, please," said Vasily.

"Yura, Alexey here. Could I have some too, please."

"Understood. Tolya, Vanya, want some tea?" Yuri asked his colleagues in the technical department, behind his station. Two negatives came from that side of the aircraft.

"Seryozha, want some tea too? There's enough for everyone."

Serghey remained silent for a moment. He had been taken off guard by the unexpected question, since this was the first time he could recall being addressed by his nickname instead of his rank and last name, plus being offered tea by a crewmember for the first time in memory. Remembering, however, the general feeling of wellbeing and elation generated by the great performance in the maneuvers, together with the message telexed by Admiral Gorshkov two hours before, and wishing to maintain those same feelings going on, the radioman relented and acquiesced to the offer.

"Yes, please," he said, dryly.

Tea bottle in hand, Yuri stood up from his seat to deliver the drink to his friends. Reaching the cockpit, Yuri poured the drink in the cups already in the pilots' hands. Crossing the short tunnel between them, he then poured some tea in Alexey's waiting cup, but instead of capping the bottle, left it open before the Navigator, while pointing with his index finger at the mouth of the container.

The navigator immediately understood the silent signal, pulled a small envelope from his shirt pocket and poured all of its powdery contents into the open steel bottle. Yuri hurriedly capped the bottle, shook it vigorously several times and returned to the cockpit.

Before returning to his own station, behind Vasily, Yuri stopped at Serghey's station and poured the last remaining tea in the radioman's cup. Without saying a word, the man took the cup, drew it to his lips and sipped a first draught. After savoring it for a few seconds, all the while looking at the flight engineer before him, the man then drank a larger gulp.

Having seen Serghey ingest the drink, Yuri returned to his station, verified the gages on his panels and annotated in his logs, among other things, the fuel transfer just completed. His chores finished, he contacted the cockpit.

"Captain, we received thirty tons of fuel, enough to reach our destination at normal cruise speed and altitude. Just continue as planned to complete the flight. It should be uneventful, that is, if the pressure in compressor №3 continues holding, although right now it's at minimum."

"Understood, Yura. You think it will hold?" asked Mikhail.

"Unknown at this point, Captain. But if it decays even more, I'll be forced to shut off that engine."

"Understood. Let's hope it remains where it is." Mikhail then addressed the whole crew: "Well, guys, we're all done. Let's fly out of this maze and head home. Like Icarus!"

Hearing the codename, the plotters in the crew understood that the moment for which they had been working so arduously, and preparing themselves for weeks, was only scarce minutes away. Everyone knew his assigned role and everyone's heart started beating with trepidation as the initial action was already set off.

Keeping a steady eye on the radioman to his right, Yuri patiently waited for the moment to let Icarus fly. For this, however, the flight engineer did not have to wait long. Soon Serghey began to nod and close his eyes. The drug started to have its sedative effect on the man.

Yuri blasted at full lung in the cockpit: "Captain, pressure in compressor №3 dropping! I'm shutting that engine off!"

Hearing the alarm, Mikhail ordered the copilot: "Vasya, feather that engine!"

Vasily immediately actioned the indicated levers to increase the propellers pitch to the position of least aerodynamic resistance. The loss of power from the engine was promptly felt in the consequent reduction in speed. To compensate for the lost engine, Mikhail increased power to engine №4.

At his station, Yuri increased compression and fuel consumption for the starboard engine, which alone carried the weight of that side of the aircraft.

"*Chto chyorty ...*" exclaimed the Flight Engineer. "Captain, engine №4 is dying!"

"What do you mean 'dying'?"

"It just had a flameout!"

"Flameout? What the devil is happening?"

"That's what I'm asking myself. I think the damn engine could not take the added pressure!"

"Vasya, compensate with the port engines! Yura, give me everything you have on that side!" Mikhail then called for Serghey's assistance: "Radioman!"

Nothing but silence came from the radioman's station.

"Radioman!" Mikhail repeats, louder.

"Yes, Captain!" Serghey replied in a stupor, as if drunk.

"Immediately initiate a transmission in all international emergency frequencies."

"Captain, no Soviet airplane does that. If we need assistance, we get it from our own ..."

"Lieutenant! Don't give me this patriotic shit speech now. We're going down and need all the assistance we can get!" Mikhail screamed.

"Captain, flameout in engine №2, and compressor pressure is dropping in №1!" Yuri's voice interrupted both men.

"Lieutenant Molotko! Begin that transmission now, while we still have enough height and time!"

"*Ladno ... kapitan ...*" said the radioman, his voice sounding tired and sluggish. The knobs and levers before him began to turn and dance as he tried to set them to the appropriate frequencies for the ordered broadcast.

"Captain, engine №1 just died! Flameout in all four engines! We're going down!" Yuri screamed in his microphone.

At his station, Serghey desperately tried to make sense of the jumble of levers, buttons and dials in the panels before him.

"Mayday ... Mayday ... Mayday ... This is ... airplane of ... Navy of ... Soviet Union ... *Red sixty seven* ... we have emergency ..." Albeit in English, these last words came out of Serghey's mouth almost inaudibly. As the drug got a firmer hold of the man's body and mind, the latter ceased to function in anything other than Russian, so he just repeated in the clear, ever slower and more slurred: "*Sovietskiy ... samolyot ... krasnyy ... shestdesyat syem' ...*"

As he sank deeper into unconsciousness, Serghey collapsed on his station. His last thoughts echoed in his mind: *I don't want to die like this ...*

"Captain, the bird is sleeping!" Yuri announced.

"*Otlichno!* Let's get this thing down to thirty meters and get lost! Yura, give me full engines back. We'll need all the speed we can get out of them! Vasya, restart and unfeather №4, and call the altitude and rate of descent every minute. Alyosha, indicate the planned heading." Each called crewmember immediately got engaged in the assigned task.

"Altitude: Five thousand eight hundred. Rate of descent: Five hundred a minute. Unfeathering and restarting engine №4 now," Vasily said.

"Captain, turn to new heading two-four-zero. That will take us straight to Canadian airspace, in the vicinity of Newfoundland," Alexey said.

"Newfoundland?" Mikhail asked, slightly surprised.

"Yes, approximately by Gander. It has a runway long enough to allow us to land there." Alexey answered.

"Well, fine. I don't care where we reach America, as long as we reach it safely."

As the plane descended, Mikhail slowly banked it to port, pointing to the new heading.

"Alyosha, how long will it take us to get there at combat speed?" Vasily asked.

"At combat ... about three hours," said the navigator.

"Captain, all engines performing normally," Yuri informed. "But I suggest reducing to at least fast speed as soon as we are out of this area. Flying at combat speed at this height will more than triple our fuel consumption."

"Right," Vasily agreed. "Captain, remember that we already discussed that. You know how difficult it is to fly this monster at combat speed only thirty meters above the water. The wheel will feel like concrete! Altitude: five thousand three hundred."

"Agreed. As soon as we're comfortably far from here, reduce speed to fast," Mikhail ordered. "After all, we want to give the impression that we *fell* around here not that we literally *crashed* here."

"Half hour at combat speed and the rest of the trip at fast will place us in Gander in about four and a half hours," Alexey informed the new flight data.

"Perfect, we'll have to fly longer but at least we won't get there on empty tanks," said Yuri.

"Not only that. I honestly think that flying this thing at more than 900 kilometers an hour, at just 30 meters high, is simply suicidal! Fast is not ideal but at least is more bearable," said Vasily.

"How about raising altitude to at least three hundred meters? When we're far from here, of course," suggested Yuri. "Once we're at a safe distance, it's not much they could do to stop us. Besides, they'll be looking for us around here, not there."

"*Ladno. Tak ustrayvaet,*" Mikhail agreed. "Let's go at combat speed for half hour, then raise altitude to three hundred and reduce to fast speed."

"Understood, Captain. Altitude: four thousand eight hundred," Vasily continued calling the height.

"Svoboda, nakonyets ty budyesh' nasha!" exclaimed Alexey.

"Yes, freedom will be ours, at long last!" Mikhail agreed.

"That reminds me of something my father always used to say," said Jonas.

"What was that?" asked Vasily.

"Jūs pažinsite tiesą, ir tiesa padarys jus laisvus," Jonas said.

"Which in Russian means …?" Vasily asked, again.

"I poznayte istinu, i istina sdyelaet vas svobodnymi," replied Jonas.

"And you will know the truth, and the truth will make you free … I like the sound of that!" repeated Alexey. "Where did he get that from? I never heard it before. And I've read a lot, mind you!"

"I believe he got it from the church Bible. I remember that he used to read it a lot at home. He always went to church, every Sunday, despite the dangers. Many were arrested by the KGB for doing that, my father included," Jonas remembered his childhood days in Kaunas, Lithuania.

"The Bible … no wonder I never heard that. I've never even seen one Bible, much less read it," said Alexey.

"Religion …" said Anatoly. "Although I don't believe in gods or spirits or whatever, I still think that those who want to believe it should be allowed to do so. That's a personal matter the state should not meddle with."

"Don't worry about that," Mikhail intervened. "In America you can believe whatever you wish to believe. The state does not interfere with that."

"How do you know, Captain? You've never been there," asked Alexey.

"Yes, I've never been there, but I spoke with both American and British pilots during the war. Almost all of them were believers in some religion. In fact, I never met one that did not believe."

As *Red 67* continued its fast descent, slowly increasing its speed to combat, the crew continued their conversation, savoring with anticipation their forthcoming freedom. Serghey, asleep as he was, couldn't hear the frantic calls offering assistance and requesting more information, sent by all the other Soviet and foreign vessels and aircraft, produced as a result of his earlier call for help. The farther *Red 67* got from the general area of the 'accident,' the more sparse and faint the calls became.

*   *   *   *

Surveying the displayed evidence spread all over his desk, Col. Yakovlev could not avoid arriving at the most logical conclusion: Something big had to be afoot with the crew of *Red 67*. The collection of drawings, timetables, navigation charts, maps, and similar documents found in the quarters of *Red 67's* crewmen gave him that impression. Examining in detail the information on them, Yakovlev could not help but to arrive at the inescapable conclusion that perhaps the crew was attempting something never done before in an aircraft the size of a TU-95: Defection.

Of especial importance to Col. Yakovlev was a copy of the navigation chart used in the *Okean* Maneuvers already in progress on the Northern Atlantic Ocean and which, according to Navy protocol, should have been delivered to the crews of the involved aircraft only at the preflight briefing. The fact that it was found in the Navigator's quarters, already full of annotations and time schedules, gave the indication that the chart had been in his hands for a while.

"Nikitin, by the looks of this, the whole crew had been planning this flight for some weeks already," said Yakovlev.

"Right. And it seems their intended destination is Scotland. Look at this line," Nikitin agreed. His index finger followed a line going from a refueling point northwest of the British Islands to British airspace.

Yakovlev looked at his watch. "It's already eighteen hundred thirty hours. By now they should have initiated the return flight back to base. We have to know their present position," said Yakovlev, then grabbed his phone's handset.

"Control tower, please," he requested.

After a few seconds waiting, Yakovlev inquired. "Colonel Yakovlev speaking. Lieutenant, what's the actual position of *Red 67,* and its estimated time of arrival at base?"

Still holding the handset to his ear, Yakovlev's eyes grew in size until they almost popped out of their orbit. "What? When did that happen?"

On hearing the question, Nikitin pushed the button for the loudspeaker next to the phone set. "… about twenty minutes ago. *Red 67* transmitted an emergency distress signal in the international distress frequency. It was seen falling very rapidly towards the sea."

"Where did that happen, do you know?" Yakovlev asked again.

"Approximately by coordinates 15 degrees West, 60 degrees North, Colonel."

On the chart before him, Yakovlev placed his index on the indicated coordinates, then followed the line extending from there towards Scotland.

"Has Cdr. Degtyaryov been informed of this?" Yakovlev asked once again.

"Yes, Colonel. As soon as it happened."

"Ochen' khorosho, Lieutenant. *Spasibo bol'shoye,"* said Yakovlev, then hanged up the handset.

"Did they transmit a real emergency distress signal, or was that the beginning of their defection plan?" Yakovlev asked Nikitin.

"Hard to say, but I lean towards the beginning of the defection ... Perhaps we should call Cdr. Degtyaryov and ask him what he thinks about this 'incident,'" Nikitin said.

"Yes. That way we'd know what he knows about this, but I also believe it would be good to let him know of our findings," added Yakovlev.

"I agree," said Nikitin. "Then he'd be able to alert others about Makarov's intentions."

Yakovlev lifted his phone's handset again and dialed Cdr. Degtyaryov's extension.

"Boris Rodyonovich, Yakovlev speaking ... What have you heard about Captain Makarov's airplane?"

"They transmitted an emergency distress signal roughly half hour ago, shortly after they met with our tanker," Degtyaryov said. "Then they were seen falling towards the ocean," his voice sounded disembodied, due to the effect of the loudspeakers on both ends of the line.

"Has anything else been heard from them?" Nikitin asked.

"No, nothing. Admiral Gorshkov has suspended the maneuvers and directed all available ships and airplanes towards the general area of the accident, to help in the search for survivors."

"Is Leonid Ivanovich still here in the base?" asked Yakovlev.

"Yes, I'm here," answered Col. Rudenko. "They called me back to the office before I could leave for Arkhanghelsk."

"Leonid Ivanovich, you were the one supposed to fly in the maneuvers, weren't you?" Yakovlev asked.

"Yes. From our regiment, only me," Rudenko responded.

"And yours was the only one of the Regiment's airplanes to fly by itself and return to base, right?" Yakovlev asked again.

"Yes. The two airplanes from the 392nd in Kipelovo went straight to Cuba. The other two from the 997th in Olenyegorsk went straight to Angola. Mine was the only one supposed to fly by itself, to test the new *Korshun* radar, then return here."

"So, what happened, why didn't you?" Yakovlev asked again.

"Sudaryev and his monkeys made a mistake and installed it in Captain Makarov's airplane instead of mine …"

"Why didn't you have them uninstall it from his plane and reinstall it in yours?" asked Nikitin.

"I found out yesterday. There wasn't any time left to uninstall it, reinstall it and test it."

"So, why didn't you fly in *Red 67*?" Yakovlev asked.

"*Nikogda!* You know I only fly in *my* airplane! Precisely to avoid what happened to *Red 67* today. By now they must be food for fish, three kilometers under water."

"So, they were supposed to fly unaccompanied and carrying the prototype of the new *Korshun* radar …" said Yakovlev.

"That is right," Rudenko confirmed.

Yakovlev and Nikitin looked at each other with immense fear and distress. The tension could be felt even across the phone.

"Konstantin Denisovich, is there something wrong?" Cdr. Degtyaryov asked Yakovlev.

"Well, Nikitin and I … made some findings that we think you should know about."

"And what is that?" Degtyaryov asked once again.

"I think it's better if you and Leonid Ivanovich stop by my office and take a look at what we found."

"Very well. We'll be there right away."

Yakovlev hanged up the handset. In sepulchral silence both KGB officers awaited the arrival of the two Navy officers.

After the naval commanders reviewed the available information, Degtyaryov asked: "Konstantin Denisovich, why are you so sure that they are on their way to Scotland and not at the bottom of the Atlantic Ocean?"

"Just look at the evidence before your eyes, Boris Rodyonovich! *Okean* navigation charts, flight schedules, refueling timetables. Information that is supposed to be top secret, only available to them on the day of the flight, found in their quarters. Plus, it's information they somehow got *out of your own office!*"

"But even if they're running towards Scotland, as you say, they must do it at sea level to be able to evade our radars," added Rudenko. "If they're flying at sea level, someone must have seen them. Remember that the area is teeming with our ships as well those of the foreign navies watching the maneuvers. Plus, Konstantin Denisovich, as pilot of a TU-95, I can tell you, flying that beast at 30 meters over the waves is a job in itself. The controls usually are hard at cruising height. At sea level they feel like concrete!"

"We must call Murmansk," said Degtyaryov.

"What for?" asked Col. Yakovlev. "To tell them that we have evidence that *Red 67* is defecting to the British?"

"No, just to confirm or verify the situation with *Red 67,*" said Degtyaryov.

"With your permission, *tovarishchi,*" Nikitin interjected. "I agree with Cdr. Degtyaryov. Murmansk can tell us if they have found anything in the search area. If they *really* fell, by now they must've found something, debris, pieces of the airplane, flotsam, anything that might indicate that an accident happened to them."

"*Ladno.* Let's call Murmansk. But make no mention of defections or anything similar," Yakovlev agreed.

"*Tovarishchi,* it is bad enough as it is," Degtyaryov commented. "That they could plan this defection right under our noses ..."

"Over my dead body you'll tell them about this!" Rudenko exploded, interrupting Degtyaryov in mid-sentence. "Do you realize that telling them that is like signing our own death warrants?"

"Boris Rodyonovich, Leonid Ivanovich is correct. You can't tell them that! I'd rather just blow my brains out myself than have them shoot me for gross incompetence!" Yakovlev screamed.

"But if they're really defecting and we withhold this information from the *nachal'stvo,* we'll be seen as part of Makarov's plot, which is even worse!" Degtyaryov screamed back.

"*Blyad!* I can't believe this is happening to me! Damn Makarov and his band of *mudaki!*" Rudenko flew into one of his trademark ill-tempered rages.

"It's your fault!" Rudenko suddenly pointed his finger at Yakovlev. "What the fuck you have people from your department in our planes for, if they don't do what they are supposed to be doing? What was that *mudak,* what's his name? ... Molotko, doing in Makarov's plane? Smelling his own ass?"

"My men are very disciplined and do what they're supposed to do!" Yakovlev stood up and retorted at Rudenko's accusations. "The inspectors that came today gave me high marks and commendations for our work here! I'll not allow you to tarnish our name and our reputation!"

"Are you threatening me, Colonel Yakovlev?" Rudenko asked, leaning over Yakovlev's desk.

"I do not threaten anyone, Colonel. The KGB has no need to do that. Our reputation is well known!"

"I am not afraid of your 'KGB reputation,' Colonel. Yours or anyone else's! I fear no one and you know very well I don't care to break anyone's face if I have to!" Rudenko screamed just centimeters from Yakovlev's face.

Tempers flaring, Cdr. Degtyaryov intervened and separated the angry men before the situation escalated to the point of physical aggression. *"Tovarishchi, tovarishchi, khvatit!* Enough of this! Arguing and fighting among ourselves is not going to solve our problem! We must find a solution, and fast, before it reaches the *nachal'stvo's* ears and becomes an even worse crisis!"

The two men, still throwing killer glimpses at each other, separated their faces.

Despite the heated argument and August's warmth, the silent atmosphere in Yakovlev's office was so cold, hard and thick that it felt rather like the Siberian tundra frozen soil in winter. Yakovlev behind his desk, and Rudenko by the office door, both men paced back and forth in the small office. The other two men simply leaned against the office walls, their minds immersed in a thousand and one thoughts about their dilemma and its immediate and long-range consequences.

Finally, after several tense minutes, Yakovlev broke the silence: "Leonid Ivanovich, if we're going to tell them about Makarov's plans, at least let's do it in the best light possible, with the best person that right now could be in the best disposition to receive such a news from us."

"And who's that?" asked Rudenko.

"General Griboyedov. He must have arrived in Murmansk by now. He gave us glowing marks about our job here. I got a lot of goodwill accumulated with him today. Might as well use that goodwill to our advantage."

Rudenko digested Yakovlev's suggestion, then replied: *"Ladno.* But I know all hell is going to break loose when they find out about this ..."

Not having a better option, the other two men consented to Yakovlev's proposal with nods of their heads. Yakovlev lifted his phone's handset and requested a direct line to Lt. General Griboyedov's office in Murmansk.

*   *   *   *

Aboard the *TAKr Kiev*, steaming at full speed towards the area of the reported accident suffered by *Red 67*, Admiral Gorshkov was suddenly approached by one of his officers.

"Admiral, urgent call from Leningrad Headquarters."

"Urgent? Who's calling?" Gorshkov asked, surprised.

"The Commander of the Northern Fleet, Admiral Yegorov."

"Admiral Yegorov?" Gorshkov asked again, even more surprised than before, as he took the handset from the officer.

The Admiral listened intently for several minutes to the high-ranking officer on the other side, then asked: "Are you sure? Who provided you with this information?" Gorshkov's face became more and more agitated as he listened to the detailed information provided by the Commander of the Northern Fleet.

"Has Mironenko been advised?" Gorshkov asked, referring to the Commander of the Naval Aviation.

"*Khorosho* ... No. I will notify *towarishchi* Ustinov and Brezhnev myself. This is a private matter of the Soviet Navy and we will solve it ourselves. No need to get others involved in it ... *Spasibo bol'shoye, Admiral.*" Gorshkov returned the handset to the attending officer standing next to him. With a tired sigh, the 66-year-old Admiral looked at the officers around him. Then, without saying a word, he got up from his seat.

"Something wrong, Admiral?" asked Captain First Rank Sokolov, Commander of the *TAKr Kiev*.

"Yes, *tovarishch komandir*. It is of the utmost importance that we go to your ready room and contact Moscow."

"This way, please, Admiral," with a gesture of his hand, Sokolov indicated to Gorshkov the way to his ready room.

Seated at the Commander's desk, Admiral Gorshkov asked for direct lines to the office of the Minister of Defense of the Soviet Union, Marshall Dmitriy Fyodorovich Ustinov and to the office of the Prime Minister of the Soviet Union, Premier Marshall Leonid Ilich Brezhnev. After several minutes waiting, Captain Sokolov informed: "*Tovarishch Admiral*, Marshalls Ustinov and Brezhnev are on the line, in conference."

"Dmitriy Fyodorovich, Leonid Ilich ... I have news of extreme importance to tell you ..."

"Yes, we've heard, Serghey Gheorghievich," Ustinov cut off Gorshkov's words. "One of our reconnaissance airplanes crashed today in the Atlantic Ocean. I've already ordered ..."

"No, Dmitriy Fyodorovich, it's worse than that. I wish it had been that it had just crashed into the ocean."

"What do you mean, Serghey Gheorghievich?" asked Premier Brezhnev, in his thick Ukrainian accent.

"Leonid Ilich, I have received reliable information from both Murmansk and Leningrad ... That the crew of the airplane in question ... is trying to defect."

"What do you mean 'to defect'?" Ustinov asked, in a concerned tone of voice.

"According to the information I received from Admiral Yegorov, in the quarters of that plane's crewmen was found material that leads them to suspect they're flying towards Scotland."

"Are you *absolutely sure* of this, Serghey Gheorghievich?" Brezhnev asked again.

"Yes, Leonid Ilich. My sources have confirmed all the data."

"Serghey Gheorghievich, have your search parties found anything?" Brezhnev asked once again.

"No, nothing at all. I've ordered every available craft in the area to scour the ocean's surface, especially in the area they were when they sent their distress signal," Gorshkov responded.

"If they went to Scotland, they must be landing somewhere in Britain by now," said Ustinov. Irritation made his voice quiver in anger.

"Did they say what was wrong with their aircraft?" Brezhnev asked once again, as if trying to hold to the hope of a crash rather than an embarrassing defection.

"No. All that was heard was that they had an emergency, nothing else after that," Gorshkov said.

"*Ladno.* Dmitriy Fyodorovich, Serghey Gheorghievich, we need to handle this situation ourselves. We cannot and should not allow foreigners to intervene in this matter," Brezhnev said, very authoritatively.

"I agree, Leonid Ilich. We're capable of conducting this search ourselves. We don't need assistance from foreign navies," Gorshkov added.

"Serghey Gheorghievich, instruct your ships to refuse all offers of assistance," Brezhnev said. "If the foreign ships around you see you searching, they'll offer assistance, namely because they'll want to know what you're searching for."

"It makes no difference, *tovarishchi*. The distress signal was sent in the open, using the international emergency frequency. Everyone here knows that one of our airplanes is in distress," Gorshkov informed.

"That's more of a reason to keep foreigners away from us, Serghey Gheorghievich," Ustinov added once again. "If one of your airplanes crashed or its crew defected, either way it is an incident that may become an embarrassment to the prestige of the Soviet Union. We have to expand the search to determine as soon as possible if they really crashed or if they defected. The reputation of the Soviet Union is at stake now."

"*Khorosho.* I will do everything in my power," Gorshkov agreed.

"Very well," said Ustinov. "In the meantime, Leonid Ilich, I think it would be convenient if you contact our ambassador in London as well as our intelligence network in the United Kingdom. Obtain as much information as possible from them, in case this 'accident' becomes an international quandary involving defectors."

"Agreed, Dmitriy Fyodorovich," said Brezhnev, then addressed Gorshkov: "Serghey Gheorghievich, keep us informed of anything your ships and aircraft find out. We'll do everything in our power to find that airplane, whether it's at the bottom of the ocean ... or in Great Britain."

*   *   *   *

"Alyosha, how long to reach Canadian airspace?" Mikhail asked Alexey.

"At our present speed and course ... about 2 hours, more or less," answered the navigator.

The words seemed to come distant, as if from another world. At first, all Serghey could do was just hear the words, although they made no sense to his drugged mind.

... Canadian airspace ... Canadian airspace ... Why Canadian airspace? Why are we flying towards Canada? Serghey asked himself time and again.

"Vanya, Yonka, have you heard anything about us in the radios?" Mikhail asked his two crewmen in charge of monitoring radio transmissions.

"Nothing so far," said Jonas. "I've been monitoring all the frequencies within my range. No foreign crafts, on the sea or in the air, have said anything. Ever since we left the area around Scotland, I have not heard a thing."

"The same for Soviet crafts," added Ivan. "When Serghey sent the distress signal, I received a flood of requests offering assistance and asking for more information. But right now, nothing. It's as if they have no idea where we are."

"*Chudno!* The plan is going as if on wheels ... or on wings, in our case," exclaimed Mikhail, a wide grin illuminating his face.

"Yes! Finally we'll be able to leave behind that horrible life in Kuzomen," said Vasily.

The surprised Serghey, still slumped immobile on his radio console, tried to digest and understand the words coming to his ears through the airplane's intercom system.

Arriving in Canada in two hours ... When I blacked out, the airplane had an emergency, falling like a brick ... but now it's on its way to Canada ... Why Canada? Canada is not the nearest land to go in an emergency, that is—or was—Scotland ... If they had a real emergency, they'd have flown there, not Canada, still two hours away ... unless ... unless that had been their intention from the very beginning ...

And now, as they said, no one knows where we are, and 'the plan' is going like on wings ... A plan to fly to Canada ... What for? Canada is not a friendly country, but an adversary ... What can we do there? Nothing ... except ... to defect? YES! Otherwise, why the emergency, which obviously was fake? Otherwise, why heading there? It has to be that ... I wouldn't expect anything less from these betraying swines ... Betrayal, betrayal of the worst kind, pure and simple ... That explains the crew's odd behavior whenever I was around them. Their evasiveness, their secrecy ... leaving me out of their meetings and outings ... And now making me black out, drugged, most probably, with that damn tea they gave me! Fortunately I never trusted them, especially after all of a sudden they start being 'nice' to me and share their tea with me, when before they could not even talk to me in a decent manner ... I'm glad I did not drink the whole concoction they gave me ... well, the horrendous flavor it had did not help either. If I had, they'd have been able to carry their plan to fruition ...

As he slowly emerged from the drug-induced stupor, Serghey tried to get movement back to his limbs, which felt like lead. He opened his eyes, only to see cobwebs before them. His mind was the first to return to him, then his body gradually returned to normality.

... All this time they were planning a escape towards Canada ... but not while I'm aboard ... No, they will not ...

The radioman slowly, quietly and stealthily lowered his arm to his right leg. His fingers felt the hard metal tightly tied against his calf. *Otlichno! They did not discover it. It's still there ...*

Pulling up his right pants leg, Serghey pulled a hidden Makarov PM 9mm pistol out of its holster. Slowly still, pistol in hand, he raised his right arm to his radio console. At eye level, he visually inspected the gun, carefully moved the safety latch down, and with his left hand silently pulled the slide, inserting a round in the firing chamber. Once sure the pistol was ready to fire, Serghey cocked its hammer, to ensure an accurate first shot, if the need arose.

Sitting directly behind the pilot, Serghey was at a disadvantage, since he didn't have a clear line of sight to the crewmen around him. Slowly and quietly he stuck his head out of the bay where his station was located and looked towards the rear of the airplane, to the stations occupied by Ivan and Anatoly.

Ivan, perched on his high seat, one meter above the airplane's floor, looking aft, whiled his time listening intently at the radio transmissions around him, searching for any sign of discovery by anyone outside.

Serghey cursed his location. From there he couldn't see what Anatoly, who sat directly behind him, was doing. Then he turned to look towards the nose of the airplane, where the pilots, the navigator and the flight engineer sat. From there he was also unable to see the pilot or the flight engineer sitting at their station, so he wasn't sure whether the men were awake, dozing, or totally asleep. Directing his gaze to the copilot, he could see the man just dozing on his seat.

One out of action! That means Captain Makarov is handling the flying right now. Looking further forward towards the nose of the plane, he could see Alexey, the navigator, looking into his navigation radar.

Gun in hand, the radioman disconnected his helmet from his station and quietly stood up, making sure his boots stepping on the metallic escape belt on the floor made no noise whatsoever. Then he turned around and stood at the opposite wall of the airplane's narrow corridor between stations. From his new location he could see much better. Looking to his left, he saw Anatoly. The technician, not needing to stand watch on his radar, was simply dozing off on his seat.

Otlichno! One less to worry about. He thought, drawing a smile on his face. Looking to his right he could see Captain Makarov, his hand on the control wheel, completely absorbed in the piloting of the airplane. Further, in the plane's nose, Alexey still looking to his navigation radar.

Not having been noticed by anyone, and despite not knowing what Yuri, the Flight Engineer, was doing, and with the rest of the crew behind him, Serghey decided to risk it by first tackling the crewman closest to him: Ivan. Slowly he approached the man, still absorbed in his listening of radio emissions, his back to the approaching Serghey.

Ivan felt fingers tapping his hip's left side. Thinking it's another one of his companions, Ivan turned around, only to see the now fully awake radioman placing his left index finger on his mouth, as a signal to keep quiet and silent while menacingly pointing and pushing his 9mm Makarov pistol at him.

Taken completely by surprise, the startled Ivan slowly turned around on his seat, then looked down to where Anatoly was sitting, only to see the man completely submerged in his dreams.

Serghey, still pointing his gun at him, hand signaled Ivan to come down from his high seat. Complying, the man descended slowly. Once at eye level, Serghey, always pointing his gun at Ivan, signaled him to go to his right.

"One word out of you and you're a dead man! Now, move!" Serghey ordered in a whisper.

As he passed before Serghey, Ivan looked at the gun, noticing its hammer already cocked, then at Serghey. Both men saw each other eye to hateful eye.

"Now, sit!" Serghey ordered Ivan once more, still whispering.

Ivan complied silently and sat on a small foldable seat on the corridor's escape belt, always under Serghey's watchful eye.

Having already successfully eliminated his first opponent, Serghey then tackled the second menace to his overtaking of the crew. Approaching the still sleeping Anatoly, Serghey touched his arm with the tip of the barrel, his eyes darting back and forth between the sitting Ivan and the sleeping Anatoly.

Anatoly, suddenly brought out of his sleep, just managed to open his eyes widely at the sight of the gun pointed at his face. Once again, Serghey placed his left index finger on his mouth, indicating absolute silence.

Waving his weapon, Serghey ordered the startled Anatoly to move out of his seat and walk to where Ivan sat. As the radar technician stood up, he lunged towards Serghey, arms thrown forward, intent on getting a hold of the man's gun.

Suddenly Serghey jumped back, slamming himself against the wall opposite to Anatoly's station. One sharp crack thundered inside the airplane. Anatoly slumped to the floor, blood oozing from the left side of his head, falling on the exit hatch. Ivan quickly jumped from his folding seat and headed towards Serghey, only to be stopped cold by the sight of a barrel pointing straight to his face.

"I don't care to kill you too, Lieutenant!" Serghey screamed, having lost the advantage of silence and surprise he enjoyed up until now.

Behind Ivan, four extremely surprised faces looked at the scene developing before their stunned eyes. The loud shot heard inside the airplane, despite the engines deafening noise, was enough to get everyone's attention.

Anatoly's crumpled body lied on the floor, a small pool of blood beginning to form under his head. Standing before him, Serghey had his gun firmly held in his right hand, pointed straight at Ivan's head. Ivan stood in the corridor, his hands up in the air, his eyes fixed on the gun's barrel. Behind him, Yuri, startled by the shot, got up from his seat and stood by his station, looking at Serghey's face, now a mask of pure hate. From their seats both pilots, and Alexey between them, all looked back at the situation developing in the corridor.

"So this is what you have been planning to do all these months, *predatel'nyye sobaki!*" Serghey screamed at the top of his lungs, both out of the wrath he felt inside as well as to be heard over the engines drone. "To run like cowards towards the enemy! You thought you could plan your betrayal right under my nose! Well, you failed! You failed miserably, and now you're going to pay dearly for it!"

"Lieutenant ... Molotko. Anatoly is badly hurt. He could die at any moment," Ivan pleaded, hoping that his friend were not already dead from the bullet wound to his head. "Let me take care of him."

"He got what he deserved! And it's the same you'll all get, betraying dogs! You'll all be executed for betraying our Motherland. I'll make sure of that!" Serghey continued barking his wrath on *Red 67's* crew.

"Lieutenant Molotko, you really have no need to do this. To you, we're worth more alive than dead," said Yuri, still standing behind Ivan. "Remember that the more there are of us, the better you're going to look to the *nachal'stvo.*"

As Yuri talked, Ivan, his hands still up in the air, slowly started to kneel as he got closer to Anatoly's slumped body.

"Stand up, or I'll shoot you too, *sukin syn!*" Serghey barked.

"You might as well shoot me now. I am not going to let Tolya die!" Ivan said, lowering his arms. Then he took Yuri by his armpits and straightened his body lengthwise, feet towards the plane's tail. As he was pulled, Anatoly left a long trail of blood on the floor conveyor belt.

"I wouldn't worry about him. He's already dead!" Yelled Serghey.

"That's to be seen," said Ivan, taking Anatoly's left arm and trying to feel his pulse.

"Vanya, is he alive?" asked Yuri, standing behind Ivan. "Perhaps he's just unconscious."

"I hope so, Yura, I hope so ..." For a few seconds Ivan remained silent, his fingers trying to find a sign of life on the wounded radar technician.

"Never mind ... I think he's dead already. I feel no pulse in him," said Ivan, disappointment and pain marking his face.

"And that will be your fate too if you don't obey my orders!" Serghey yelled at the discouraged crew. "You, stand up and go back to that seat!" he yelled at Ivan. "And you too, go back to your station!" he yelled at Yuri.

Ivan stood up and sat again on the small folding seat in the corridor. Yuri returned to his seat.

Having eliminated the opposition, his eyes and his gun still pointed at Ivan, Serghey returned to his station.

"Lieutenant Krylov, don't move from your seat, and don't look back at me! You look, you die!" Serghey barked at Ivan. His left hand fumbled looking for the connector to plug his helmet back into his radio station.

Once connected, Serghey was able to talk to the rest of the crew through the plane's intercom: "I don't know where we are right now, but I'll soon find out.

And from wherever we are, you will fly this airplane back to the Soviet Union, Captain Makarov. Your plan to defect to the adversary failed!"

The crew of *Red 67* listened in silence.

Serghey then accessed the external communications system and transmitted in the radio frequencies common to all Soviet Navy vessels: "This is Lieutenant Serghey Molotko, aboard Tupolev TU-95 *bortnomer Red 67*, transmitting to any Soviet vessel or aircraft that can hear this message. Please respond. *Priyom.*"

After repeating his message several times, Serghey finally hears a response: "*Red 67*, this is the Soviet ship *Faddey Bellingsgauzen.* We hear you. Please, state your present position and altitude. *Priyom.*"

"At this moment I am unable to provide that information. I don't know where I am. I just wrestled control of this airplane from its crew. I need all possible assistance to establish my position, and to return this aircraft to our nearest friendly base. *Priyom.*"

"Understood *Red 67.* You do not appear in our radar. Perhaps you're too far, but we could use your transmission as a way to triangulate your position with other ships in this general area."

"*Otlichno!* I also would like to reach any one of the vessels participating in the *Okean* maneuvers. It's urgent that I transmit the situation of the events happening aboard this aircraft!"

Suddenly, a third transmission broke in Serghey's ears: "*Red 67*, this is the Soviet cruiser *Admiral Makarov!* We hear you. You seem to be about one thousand kilometers southwest of us."

"This is the *Faddey Bellingsgauzen.* We confirm that bearing. Your transmission comes from about six hundred kilometers southeast of us. We just need one more station to transmit your bearing, so we can obtain a fix on your position. *Red 67*, repeat your transmission again, so any other Soviet vessel in the area can locate you. *Priyom.*"

Serghey once again clicked in his radio equipment and sent his identification number: "This is Tupolev TU-95 *bortnomer Red 67*, transmitting to any Soviet vessel in the area. Do you hear me? *Priyom.*"

A fourth faint incoming voice burst in the radioman's ears: "*Red 67*, this is Tupolev TU-95 *bortnomer Blue 36.* We hear you. You're coming approximately one thousand five hundred kilometers northeast of us ... *Bellingsgauzen*, can you use our transmission and locate *Red 67's* exact position? *Priyom.*"

"This is the *Bellingsgauzen.* Understood, *Blue 36.* We're triangulating its position at this moment ... *Red 67* seems to be ... at approximately latitude 40° 15' West, longitude 51° 50' North ... That's odd, you're outside the normal flying routes for Soviet aircraft … *Red 67,* are you having problems with your navigation equipment? *Priyom."*

"No, the situation is much worse than that … *Admiral Makarov,* do you hear me? *Priyom."*

"Understood *Red 67.* We hear you. Please go ahead. *Priyom."*

"I need a direct relay to Admiral Gorshkov's quarters aboard the *Kiev.* Can you connect me? *Priyom."*

"Understood, *Red 67.* Relaying transmission now. *Admiral Makarov* ends transmission."

Aboard the *TAKr 'Kiev,'* Admiral Gorshkov listened intently at the detailed explanations given by *Red 67's* radioman about his takeover of the defecting aircraft and its crew.

"Lieutenant Molotko. I commend you for your successful actions," said Gorshkov. "You've performed a great service to our Soviet Navy and to the Soviet Union. I'll make sure you receive your deserved dues for what you've done. Now, I'm told by my personnel here that you're flying too low, and still towards Canada. They suggest you have the pilots raise their flight level to at least 3,000 meters, and make a 180 degrees turn, so our radars can track you."

"Understood, Comrade Admiral. I'll have the pilots do exactly that. We should be appearing in your radars momentarily. *Priyom."*

"Otlichno, Lieutenant Molotko. I also have ordered Major Krasnosyel'skih, the commander of *Blue 36,* to take a new heading in order to intercept you and accompany your airplane in its return flight back to the Union. Please keep contacting our vessels periodically, so they relay your position at all times."

"Understood, Comrade Admiral. Senior Lieutenant Molotko, Serghey Gheorghievich, carrying out your orders as given, Comrade Admiral. End transmission."

Turning his attention to the crew aboard *Red 67,* Serghey immediately started barking orders again: "Captain Makarov, you will take this airplane up to three thousand meters and make a 180 degrees turn, towards the Soviet Union. This is the end of your foolish attempt to deliver our airplane to the enemy."

"Lieutenant Molotko, you're making a grave mistake …" Mikhail said.

"YOU are the ones making a grave mistake!" Serghey barked back. "Betraying our Soviet Motherland in such a dirty, underhanded way! You and your henchmen thought you could get away with it, but you forgot that we're always prepared for situations such as these. Now we'll return home, where you'll get your just reward for your betrayal, and I will get mine for discovering it!"

Not having another choice, Mikhail began the slow climb to three thousand meters. At the same time, he turned the control wheel to reach the new heading towards the Soviet Union.

Seeing his orders carried out, Serghey sat at the position previously occupied by Ivan, under the cupola, one and a half meters above the floor, like on a throne, and from where he was able to gaze on all the crewmembers of the overtaken aircraft.

As *Red 67* climbed, its signal appeared in the radars nearby.

*   *   *   *

USNSKEF, the United States Navy Station Keflavík, located in the Reykjanes peninsula, in the southwest portion of Iceland, suddenly became an anthill of activity as a strange blip suddenly appeared at the extreme range of their radars. To make matters worse, the sudden appearance of the blip, seeming to come from a southwesterly direction, made the radar operators ask themselves why that 'bogie' had not been tracked before.

Previous reports coming from the Soviet *'Okean'* Maneuvers indicated that one of their airplanes had suffered a catastrophic failure and was presumed lost at sea, northwest of Scotland. The passage of two Soviet TU-95 Bear D by Keflavík radars a few hours before was nothing out of the ordinary. After having participated in the maneuvers they continued their flight, presumably towards Cuba, duly escorted by F-4C II 'Phantom' jets of the 57th Fighter Interceptor Squadron.

What was becoming extraordinary was the sudden appearance of this 'bogie' which IFF identified as 'foe,' and which had all the appearances of being *a third* Soviet airplane. Where did it come from? The US military personnel at NS Keflavík was determined to find out.

Three F-4Cs, ID numbers 63-7529, 63-7534 and 63-7589 were immediately dispatched to the area where the 'bogie' was reported to have appeared. As they took to the air, their Radar Interception Officers, better known by their acronym RIO, received the intercept coordinates.

*   *   *   *

The excruciating pain caused by the huge, smashing hammer-like pounding in his head, plus the throbbing, seeming almost as if his brain was about to explode, were the only feelings Anatoly had. What happened before, where he was, or why he was in this predicament, he simply couldn't remember. All he knew was that the horrendous ache in his head barely let him think, much less discern his present condition. However, despite it all, he made an effort in order to think and find out what happened.

Unable to open his eyes, or to move for that matter, the technician only managed to hear his surroundings. The constant, loud drone of the four Kuznyetsov engines told him he was still inside the airplane. The ribs of the conveyor belt pressing on his back made him aware of his position. He could feel he was on the floor of the plane. Trying to get more information on his surroundings, the man—slowly at first, opened his eyelids, but his vision was totally blurred. Gradually he began to discern what he could see: the green color of the boxes and tubes covering the ceiling, the switch boxes on the left and right walls, with the many cables and tubes protruding from them. Curiously, his vision field felt incomplete. Soon, though, he discovered why: his left eyelid was closed shut. He tried to open it again, but it remained shut, so he stopped his feeble and painful efforts. The throbs in his head did not let him do anything else.

Anatoly returned to his ears, trying to hear anything that could have given him a clue as to why he was lying on the floor of the airplane, with a horrible headache, and unable to see much beyond the ceiling, or move. Besides the drone of the engines, however, he could hear nothing else. Desperate for more information, he attempted to move his head. At the first attempt the immense wrecking ball he felt his skull to be just threatened to explode right then and there. The pain was so overwhelming that he only managed to remain immobile on the floor, waiting for the hard blows to subside.

After a few minutes of rest, the poundings died down. He attempted once again to lift his head. This time the wrecking ball made his head explode. The pain was so great that he couldn't help moving his arms to his head, letting a moan escape.

"He's still alive!" a voice echoed in his head.

Alive ... Was I dead? ... I guess not ... At least I know that's true. If I were dead I wouldn't have this horrible pain! Opening his good eye, Anatoly once again tried to see his surroundings and localize the origin of the voice he just heard.

"Tolya, are you alright?" The voice reverberated inside his head. Within his limited, blurred vision field, Ivan's familiar face got into focus, above and behind him.

"Tolya, talk to me, are you alright?" the crewman repeated.

Suddenly, another harsher, louder voice came from above and before him: "Lieutenant Krylov, one more word and you are a dead man!"

Anatoly immediately recognized Serghey's raucous, raspy, guttural voice. Looking towards the origin of the voice, the wounded man saw the radioman jump from his seat under the cupola and approach him, pistol in hand.

"Lieutenant, if Anatoly is not taken care of now, he'll die!" Yuri pleaded.

"Let him die! One less traitor to execute later," Serghey barked back, pointing his pistol threateningly at both crewmen.

Suddenly, Serghey got closer to the wounded crewman on the escape belt, and astride on him, pointed his gun at Anatoly's head. "Better yet, let's execute him right now and solve this problem once and for all!"

As Serghey leaned to aim better, Anatoly suddenly grabbed Serghey's gun and directed it away from him, at the same time raising his left leg. His boot's tip smashed squarely against the man's crotch.

Taking advantage of the momentary distraction created by the growing surge of pain in Serghey's lower abdomen, Ivan sprung from his seat and threw his body and both his arms on him. Ivan's left arm embraced the man's head, his right hand on the Makarov 9mm gun, still held by Anatoly, away from his head.

Hearing the commotion, Yuri jumped over both Anatoly and Ivan, and joined the fray, landing his boot squarely on Serghey's jaw. The impact of Yuri's heel crashing against his jaw was enough to send Serghey reeling back the full length of his body, his head finally crashing against the base of Ivan's usual seat, under the cupola. The radioman remained immobile.

The commotion over, Yuri and Ivan carried Serghey's unconscious body to his own station, where they tied him securely to his seat using adhesive dressing and gauze from the plane's First Aid Kit, and even his own boot laces. Meanwhile, Vasily and Alexey attended to Anatoly's injured head.

"AAAAGH! THAT HURTS! That *mudak* almost kills me, but I made sure he'll not have children!" Anatoly complained loudly. "I only wish I could have castrated him with my bare hands!"

"Shut up and don't move! Cutting your hair is difficult enough as it is!" Vasily shot back, slowly cutting Anatoly's hair, stuck with caked blood to his leather helmet, in an attempt to remove the latter from the injured man's head.

The helmet removed, and the injury cleaned and bandaged, the crewmen returned to their stations.

"How does Tolya look?" Mikhail asked Vasily.

"He's alright. Fortunately the bullet only grazed the left side of his head. Naturally, being a head wound, he bled profusely. That's why he was all drenched in his own blood, which made it look worse than it really was," said the copilot.

"Can someone tell us what the devil is going on over there?" Jonas' loud, almost angry voice came from the tail through the intercom.

"Ah, Yonka! Forgive me! We were sort of busy here, solving a situation," Vasily responded his friend's question.

"About time! This must be at least the tenth time I call you! What happened?"

"Tolya woke up and Serghey wanted to kill him, but he could grab the gun away from Serghey. Vanya and Yura then jumped him and took him out." Vasily resumed the latest events for the benefit of his friends in the tail.

"Potryasayushchiy! And where's the *sukin syn* now?" asked Pavel.

"He's dreaming about the broken jaw Yura gave him, all tied up on his seat," Vasily said.

"Tovarishchi, is everyone alright? Tolya, do you feel up to it?" Mikhail asked.

"Yes, Captain. My head just hurts a bit, but I'm alright," responded Anatoly.

"What about everyone else?" Mikhail asked once again.

Six positive answers sounded in the intercom.

"In that case, let's return to our previous route. Alyosha, tell me the new heading towards Canada."

"I have it calculated already. Make a 170-degree turn to port. Descend to 30 meters, so as to disappear from all radars," said the Navigator.

"Understood. Vasya, lets descend to 30 meters, increase speed to combat. We must put as much distance from here as we can," Mikhail ordered the copilot as he pushed and turned the control wheel, thus initiating the turn and descent towards the indicated heading and altitude.

*   *   *   *

"Captain, what do you mean that 'it disappeared'?" Asked a very irritated Admiral Gorshkov.

"Yes, Admiral. *Red 67* is no longer showing in our radars. None of our vessels reports its position any longer," answered Captain First Rank Sokolov.

"What is the last known reported position for *Red 67?*" asked Gorshkov.

"Approximately 700 kilometers southwest of Iceland, as reported by the *Admiral Makarov,* Admiral."

"And after that, what?"

"It was at the extreme range of the *Admiral Makarov's* radar, so the information was not very precise. It was seen descending rapidly, then disappearing from the screen."

"How long ago did Lieutenant Molotko make his last report?"

"About forty minutes ago."

"So how come nobody bothered to contact him again?" Gorshkov asked, his face showing the immense annoyance he felt at what he perceived to be the incompetence of his subordinates.

"We could track his progress in our radars, plus his next report was not due until ten minutes after his disappearance," Captain Sokolov defended himself and his crew.

"Have you tried to contact Lieutenant Molotko after that?" Gorshkov asked again, the tone in his voice rising.

"Yes, Admiral. Several times. And still no response."

"Perhaps this time it really fell into the sea. Captain Sokolov, order battle regime, turn your battle group towards the last known position of *Red 67*, combat speed. I want to make sure it did fall into the sea this time!" Gorshkov ordered, authoritatively.

Battle alarms sounded aboard the *TAKr Kiev* and its accompanying destroyers and cruisers. Soviet *matrosy* ran to their assigned posts while the speed of their vessels increased to the maximum their powerplants allowed.

Keeping the secret hope that *Red 67* was by then reaching the bottom of the Atlantic Ocean rather than being once again in the hands of the defectors, Admiral Gorshkov and his entourage now headed northwest, towards *Red 67's* presumed watery tomb.

✳   ✳   ✳   ✳

Aboard the *Akademik Kurchatov* and the *Faddey Bellingsgauzen (Nikolay Zhubov*-class), two oceanographic and hydrometeorological survey ships officially attached to the Soviet Academy of Sciences, anchored at a point northeast of the Labrador Peninsula and due south of Greenland. Although both ships were dedicated to scientific research, and therefore had no offensive weapons, and the crew of the *Akademik Kurchatov* was entirely civilian, strangely, that of the *Faddey Bellingsgauzen*, although she had some seventy scientists and technicians onboard, was entirely military, in order to hide her secondary function.

Most of the air lanes usually traversed by civilian passenger aircraft lie to the south, towards the Gander (Newfoundland) airport, where these kinds of airplanes make their fuel stopover on their way to Europe and back. Stationed further up north, these two Soviet ships were perfectly positioned to spy on the B-52, C-5, C-141, KC-135, C-130, Avro Vulcans, and similar military airplanes of the USAF, RAF, Luftwaffe, and other NATO air forces flying out of Canada to Europe and back, keeping track of their number, flight times, time of departure from, and time of arrival at CAF Goose Bay AB, in the Labrador Peninsula.

After the excitement caused in its radio room because of the intercepted transmission from *Red 67*, for the last hour and a half nothing eventful or significant had happened. Everything returned to normal, despite the flurry of activity generated in the adversary forces by the *Okean* Maneuvers.

For radar operator Pyotr Bogdanov, in the radar control room aboard the *Akademik Kurchatov*, the constant watch on his radar screen was painfully boring. The sweeper constantly turning at regular intervals had an hypnotic effect on him. His eyes felt heavy and his eyelids droopy, intermittently closing and opening in step with the turning of the radar sweeper.

In one of these eye nappings, Pyotr's tired eyes simply did not notice the small blip appearing at the extreme range of his screen. As the sweeper turned, it showed the blip quickly advancing towards his vessel.

Pyotr finally opened his eyes at the time the blip dissolved. Not sure of what he had seen, he kept them open, waiting for the sweeper to reach once again that same position on his screen. He didn't have to wait long. The sweeper passed over that position, and the blip once again reappeared. Something was coming towards them at very high speed, *and very low*. So low, in fact, that it was barely tracked by the *Kurchatov's* radar.

"This is the Soviet vessel *Akademik Kurchatov* transmitting to the aircraft approaching by vector two-four-zero. Please, identify yourself," Pyotr broadcast his message in English.

After repeating his message several times and obtaining no response, and with the aircraft at just 50 kms from them, Pyotr feared an attack, so he sounded a general alert throughout the ship. The crew standing on its decks with binoculars pointed in the general direction of the approaching aircraft, Pyotr continued transmitting his message.

*   *   *   *

Aboard *Red 67*, the only person who could have listened to the *Kurchatov's* message, radioman Lieutenant Serghey Molotko, was lying tied up on his chair, unconscious. Since they didn't have much to do until their arrival in Canadian airspace, and especially after the recent ordeal at the hands of Serghey's brutality, the technical complement of the crew turned off their radio and radar equipment. The former in order to avoid any kind of tracking by anyone outside, the latter because of its uselessness at the low altitude they were flying. So they rested.

Only Vasily and Mikhail at the controls, and Alexey and Yuri at their navigation and flight engineering posts were still awake, keeping tabs on the developing situation. The pilots, flying the thunderous beast at almost 900 kph, barely 30 meters above the water, showed signs of exhaustion. The heaviness of the controls plus the tension of not being able to deviate one hair from their assigned height—under penalty of instant destruction—had both of them sweating profusely. Behind them, his eyes fixed on the fuel, pressure, oil, temperature and voltage gages, Yuri was having a similarly troubled look. He feared that at the rate the engines were consuming fuel, not even the thirty tons of the liquid they received from the flying tanker was going to be enough to reach Canada. He wished he could tell Captain Makarov to ascend in order to conserve the precious fluid, but he also understood that flying low was the key to slip under all radars and reach their intended destination.

In the nose of the airplane, Alexey kept track of the distance and time flown, meticulously annotating his charts at exact intervals, in order to reach Canada in the shortest flight path. This would conserve the fuel Yuri so many times had told him may not last if they took another route. Grabbing his sextant to make another reading of the sun, Alexey looked ahead.

What the devil is that? he thought, letting go of the sextant and grabbing his powerful binoculars instead. Placing the instrument before his eyes, he hurriedly adjusted its focus until he got a clearer view of the object he'd discerned a few seconds before.

"Captain, Alexey here! We have two ships straight in front of us! At this speed and height we'll crash into them!" The sudden crackling of Alexey's voice in their ears startled not only the tense pilots, but the whole crew as well.

Preoccupied as they were flying their aircraft low and fast, and their forward vision impeded by the clutter of instruments on the panels before them, allowing mostly side vision, the pilots did not see the fastly approaching wall of the two ships, side by side, bow to stern.

Alexey, Mikhail and Vasily see open-mouthed crewmen on the deck and superstructures of both ships, looking at the flying giant charging towards them at combat speed, 30 meters above and two kilometers before them. Realizing the danger before them, and counting their reaction time in scarce seconds, both pilots pulled their control wheels in unison, hoping the maneuver would allow them to clear the tallest structures of both ships. The sailors on the upper decks, seeing the aircraft approach, began a mad run towards safer places, some of them jumping to the safety of the lower decks in the lower sections of the ship.

Flying almost over the ships, both pilots continued pulling their control wheels as far back as they could. Because the wheels felt like solid concrete, they placed their boots on the instrument panels before them, coaxing more pull out of their bodies.

As the ships flashed under them, the crew aboard *Red 67* let go a single scream of terror, caused by a sudden, loud bang coming from starboard. As fast as the vessels appeared before them, likewise they were left behind.

"Status report! What the hell was that bang I heard?" Mikhail asked his crewmen.

"The right wing tip neatly clipped the antenna of the ship on the right," Jonas reported from the tail. He followed the sliced tall mast in its fall towards the upper superstructure, bringing down the radio antenna with it.

"I think that whatever that ship is, it has no radio now," Jonas continued, seeing the cables lie by the vessel's funnel.

"Fortunately Alyosha saw them coming, otherwise, we'd have flown straight into them!" said Vasily.

"And that would have been the end of our escape," Mikhail agreed.

"That's strange, this area is usually empty of ships. Most of them sail further south," noted Alexey.

"More important than that," Mikhail said. "I wonder what nationality they are. If they're western ships, then there's nothing to worry about."

"Captain, I'm sorry to be the bearer of bad news, but I think they are Soviet ships," said Jonas.

"Soviet ships? How do you know?" Vasily asked.

"I saw red Soviet flags on them," said Jonas.

"They're Soviet, I saw the flags too," Pavel added.

"*Blyad!* So many damn ships in this vast ocean, and we have the damn luck of almost crashing not on one but on two Soviet ships!" Mikhail exclaimed.

"I bet you that by now the whole Soviet Navy knows where we are ..." Vasily said.

"Perhaps, but, what can they do to make us return? We must be at least 500 kms from the nearest Soviet Navy vessel that can be a danger to us," said Mikhail.

"True. As a matter of fact, there's no need to fly this fast," said Vasily.

"... or this low," interjected Yuri. "If we keep on flying like this, I can not guarantee there will be enough fuel to reach Canada."

"How much fuel do we have?" Mikhail asked.

"For about one more hour. Two if we fly higher, at cruise speed and altitude, and carefully manage what we have," answered the Flight Engineer.

"Very well. Vasily let's go up to 10,000. Once at cruise altitude, decrease speed to cruise. I want to reach Canada in one single piece, not after being fished out of the Atlantic by the Canadian Navy," Mikhail ordered.

*   *   *   *

"Admiral! We received the following message from the *Faddey Bellingsgauzen:* 'Soviet aircraft, presumably type TU-95, overflew us at 60 meters high. Wingtip cut the antenna mast of the *Akademik Kurchatov*. Damage negligible. Aircraft was following a heading of 240 degrees. Await instructions,'" Captain First Rank Sokolov read the message to Admiral Gorshkov.

"Flying on a heading of 240 ... So the *mudaki* got control of the airplane and are still flying towards Canada. Probably they, being six in the forward area of the airplane, were able to overcome Lieutenant Molotko ... Captain, what are our chances of intercepting them?"

"With our Yak-36s, Admiral, very slim. They might not have the range to reach the given coordinates," said Sokolov.

"Still, I'd like to intercept them. They're not going to slip from our hands and into the adversary's hands right under my nose!" thundered Gorshkov. "Captain, if you extend their range using additional external fuel tanks, can those airplanes reach them?"

"Perhaps, but that would be at the very limit of their range. Their usefulness would be very limited. Plus, they'd only be able to carry—perhaps—bullets in their cannons, nothing else. Not even one single missile," Sokolov said, not fully convinced of Gorshkov's intentions.

"Do that, Captain. Have your men strip all your fighters of all the unnecessary weight, add external fuel tanks, and arm their cannons. That's all we'll need to stop them," Gorshkov ordered.

"Yes, Admiral. Immediately," Sokolov said, then added: "Admiral, may I suggest also ..."

"Yes, Captain. I'm listening. Any suggestion is welcome," Gorshkov said, now in a more paternal, soothing voice. He encouraged independent thinking in his subordinates, something seldom seen in the regimented, hierarchical environment of the Soviet Navy, where such thinking was mostly discouraged.

"The Admiral should remember that we're carrying *Izdeliye 48*, which has a very long range, and is ideally suited for such operations," Sokolov said.

"Izdeliye 48?" Gorshkov asked, surprised.

Izdeliye 48, better known by its military designation as Yak-41, the prototype for the next generation of Soviet carrier-based VTOL jet fighters, was the Yakovlev Design Bureau's answer to the requirements of the Soviet Navy for a replacement for their short-range, slow Yak-36Ms. The *TAKr Kiev* carried the prototype of the aircraft to test it under actual seagoing conditions.

The 'accident' suffered by *Red 67* precluded this testing phase of the *Okean* Maneuvers, but when a more powerful deterrent was urgently needed to avert *Red 67's* defection, the prototype could be once again brought into scene and used for that purpose. It was the hidden 'ace in the hole' kept under wraps by Admiral Gorshkov and the Soviet Navy.

"That's right, Captain. So much in my mind with the problem we have at hand, that I forgot all about it," Gorshkov agreed.

"That airplane may have the range to intercept *Red 67*. And that while carrying at least two missiles," Sokolov reminded the Admiral.

"Captain Sokolov, order the immediate preparation of that airplane, so it takes off together with the others. It's going to be our last resource to bring that other airplane back … or to destroy it. One missile in the engines, that should be enough," Gorshkov commanded with resolve.

The technicians for the Yak-41, ensconced in a corner of the hangars below deck, off-limits to all but a few select personnel, removed the tarpaulins covering the fighter, armed it with a complement of one *Vympel* UR R-23T infrared and one *Vympel* UR R-23R radar-guided air-to-air missiles and replenished its GSh-301 30mm cannon's magazine with 120 rounds. The maintenance team then topped all its fuel tanks, both internal and external, to allow it to reach its maximum flying range.

Quickly armed and readied, *Yellow 75,* the single example of the new fighter, was taken to one of the carrier's elevators and raised to the deck, where the other six Yak-36Ms of the 279th OKShAP were already ready and waiting to take off.

In that interception mission, the first and only one ever performed by the 279th OKShAP, its Commander, Colonel Vladimir Ivanovich Kolyesnikov flew the prototype Yak-41 *Yellow 75,* while his deputy, Lt. Col. Vasily Nikolayevich Ratenko piloted the Yak-36M *Yellow 71.* They got ready to take off together with the rest of the pilots of the regiment.

When the Yak-41 reached the flight deck, Lt. Col. Ratenko, already seated in his Yak-36M, started its two RD-36-35FV liftjet engines and its single R-27V-300 main engine. Fully laden with 3,350 kgs. of aviation fuel in its internal tanks and in three external drop tanks, plus a single GSh-23L 23mm cannon slung inside an underwing UPK-23-250 pod, the Yak-36M started a short take off roll, rather than the fuel-gobbling vertical take-off. At the end of the roll it got airborne at maximum weight, its tail clearing the bow.

Immediately after, with short intervals between them, the other five Yak-36s jumped into the air in the same fashion. As soon as the last Yak-36 left the deck, the Yak-41 initiated its own take off roll and quickly joined its escorting fighters in the air. The fighter squadron then headed to the interception coordinates transmitted by the Control Center aboard the *TAKr Kiev.*

∗   ∗   ∗   ∗

"Cruiser *Kiev* calling *Red 67* … Cruiser *Kiev* calling *Red 67* … Please respond, *Red 67* …" The radio operator aboard the *Kiev* repeatedly called the missing airplane's call sign, attempting to reestablish communication with its crew.

"Cruiser *Kiev* calling *Red 67* … Please respond, *Red 67* … It's useless, Captain. They haven't responded for the last twenty minutes. They must have switched their radio off," said the radio operator.

"Keep trying! I have orders from the Admiral himself to raise them up in the radio!" ordered Captain Sokolov.

Aboard *Red 67,* still in a southwestern heading towards Canada, the insistent calls from the *Kiev* finally achieved their intended purpose. They aroused Ivan from the stupor in which he had been submerged since their escape from Serghey's clutches. Hearing the calls crackling in his earphones, Ivan jumped on his seat and immediately pressed the button for internal communication.

"Captain, Ivan speaking. I'm receiving a call from the Cruiser *Kiev!*"

"The *Kiev?*" Mikhail asked, surprised.

"Yes, Captain. Do you want me to put it through?" Ivan asked.

"Yes. Please."

Ivan flipped a switch. In the crew's earphones the relentless calls from the *Kiev* repeated several times.

"Captain, I think we should not respond," said Vasily.

"I agree, Captain," said Anatoly. "They're trying to contact us in order to find out where we are and try to stop us."

"But … What can they do to stop us?" asks Mikhail. "We're at quite a distance from them. The Soviet vessel nearest to us are those two we overflew some time ago."

"That's right," said Alexey. "The area is clean of Soviet vessels. Only a few foreign ships have appeared in my radar. And no airplanes."

"Therefore, there's nothing they can do to us, even if they try. They have nothing out there they can use to stop us now," said Mikhail. "I think we should respond and find out what they want. Most probably they'll try to talk us into returning. However, responding is not a decision I want to take on my own. *Tovarishchi,* you decide if we respond or not."

"I say we respond," said Alexey.

"I agree," added Ivan.

"Pavel and I have decided already. Whatever you out there in front decide, we'll go for," said Jonas, from the tail.

Yuri, who until now had been silent, listening to the opinions of his friends, cast his vote: "Why not? Even if they order us to return to the Union, we can't. We don't have enough fuel to go there, so their only choice is to let us continue flying towards Canada."

"Well, it seems that only Anatoly and I are against," said Vasily. "Majority wins. Let's respond."

"Vasya, Tolya. Even if most of us are for it, I want to be sure of your feelings," Mikhail said. "Remember that we're in this all together, unanimously. Are you sure of your decision?"

"Yes, Captain. I am," said Anatoly. "After all, like you said, what can they do to stop us now?"

"Right. They can't do anything. Responding to them is not going to do any harm," said Vasily.

"*Ladno.* Agreed," said Mikhail. "Ivan, open a line to the *Kiev.* We'll respond and see what they have to tell us now."

"More of their lies, most probably. Like they have been doing always," said Vasily.

"Line is open, Captain. Go ahead," said Ivan.

"Captain Mikhail Makarov, of *Red 67,* responding to Cruiser *Kiev. Priyom.*"

The sudden, unexpected response from *Red 67* caused a small commotion in the bridge of the *Kiev.* "Captain Sokolov! It's *Red 67* responding!" yelled the radio operator.

Captain Sokolov immediately approached the radio station, grabbed a headset and transmitted: "*Red 67,* Captain Makarov. This is Captain First Rank Sokolov, aboard the Cruiser *Kiev.* I have an urgent communication from Admiral Gorshkov for you."

"Understood, *Kiev.* We're listening," Mikhail said.

Shortly after, Admiral Gorshkov's tired, raspy voice buzzed in the crewmen's ears. "Captain ... Makarov. This is Admiral of the Fleet of the Soviet Union Serghey Gheorghievich Gorshkov. Do you hear me? *Priyom.*"

On hearing Gorshkov's voice, Mikhail was greatly surprised. Pressing the intercom button, he addressed the crew: "*Tovarishchi,* did you hear that? It's the old man himself. He wants to talk to us!"

"I wonder what he's going to tell us ... *Vernites' domoy, pozhaluysta,*" said Alexey, sarcastically.

"Yes, 'return home, please!' As if we were going to return to that hellhole!" said Pavel, amid laughs.

"Yes, I'd rather die here than return there," added Alexey.

"*Tovarishchi,* let's hear what he has to say. Silence, please," Mikhail ordered, then pressed the external communication button. "Yes, Admiral. We hear you clearly. *Priyom.*"

"Captain Makarov, you are aware that you have stolen property of the Soviet Union in order to commit your unholy deed, are you?" Gorshkov said.

"With all due respect, Admiral, this airplane was not stolen, it was merely *borrowed* to reach our destination," Mikhail said.

"And what destination is that, Captain? The adversary?" Gorshkov asked.

"No, Admiral. It's anywhere we can find freedom. Freedom to follow our hearts and minds," Mikhail said.

"Are you saying that the Soviet Union is not a free country, Captain Makarov?"

"Yes, that's exactly what I am saying, Admiral. I speak for my crew when I say that we want to live in a place where our minds are not controlled by the twisted politics of the almighty Communist Party of the Soviet Union."

"Your whole crew thinks like that, Captain? It seems to me your radio operator, Lieutenant Molotko, does not think like that."

"That was his choice, Admiral. We made ours. So we decided to leave the Soviet Union forever."

"And in order to do that, you have to betray your country and your glorious navy. A navy of which your own grandfather was a proud member."

"*Your* country and *your* navy, Admiral! My country is Russia and my grandfather was an admiral of the Imperial Russian Navy, not of that abomination of yours, which pretends to control the lives and minds of everyone in the world!"

"Captain Makarov, those are realities of politics that do not concern either one of us at the moment. What is also a reality is that you have exactly *ten minutes* to initiate a return to the Soviet Union, or I will employ stern methods to force you to return or destroy your aircraft. Anything within my means to avoid that airplane falling in enemy hands," said Gorshkov.

The Admiral's threat took Mikhail by surprise. *What can he do to make us return or destroy us, as he says?* ... Mikhail immediately pressed the intercom button: "Tolya, turn on the ADS jammer, now!"

"Captain, The ADS jammer is busted!" said Anatoly, alarmed.

"Busted? What do you mean 'busted'?" Vasily asked.

"Yes, busted. The bullet Serghey shot only grazed my head but it also ended up lodged in the jammer's main control. It's totally blown apart," Anatoly explained, looking at the remains of the device.

"In other words, the Admiral can make good on his threat to make the plane explode in mid air," said Yuri.

"Yes. And there's nothing we can do about it from here," said Ivan.

"Captain Makarov, are you there? Your time is running short," Gorshkov's voice sounded again in all the crewmen's ears.

"*Blyad!* After all of this planning and running he got us by the balls now!" said Alexey.

"Not so fast, Alyosha. Remember that there's always an open door before you when one closes behind you," said Mikhail. "Tolya, think. That night, when you spoke with the technician in charge of that system's receiver, did he tell you where it's located?"

"In general terms, yes. It's somewhere back there," said Anatoly.

"Back where, exactly?" asked Vasily. "Because if it's in the bomb bay section, *nas poyebali!*"

"I don't know where it is exactly, but it must be somewhere easily accessible, perhaps even while in flight," said Anatoly.

"Captain Makarov! You have exactly eight minutes to signal your agreement to return!" Gorshkov's voice once again crackled in the crewmen's ears.

"Tolya, Vasya, *tovarishchi,* find that damn receiver, wherever it could be, and disable it," said Mikhail. "Meanwhile, I'll agree to whatever the Admiral says. That'll buy us time for you to do that. Agreed?"

"Agreed, Captain," said Vasily.

"Admiral Gorshkov, this is Captain Mikhail Makarov speaking ... We would agree to return, under several conditions."

"Conditions, Captain Makarov? Conditions? Do you think you are in a position to ask for conditions?"

"Yes, conditions, Admiral. You want this airplane back in the Union, don't you? After all, many millions of rubles were spent making it, right?"

"Yes, I would like to have it back. I would do almost anything to have it back, even listen to your conditions, Captain. But I would also destroy it with my own hands, if need be, before I let you deliver it to the enemy."

"Very well. In that case, perhaps we can reach an officers' agreement. You're known to be a very honorable Navy man, who keeps his word," Mikhail said.

"And what conditions are those, Captain Makarov?"

"That you yourself head a commission to investigate our grievances, Admiral. They're the main reason why we decided to leave the Union."

"And what grievances are those, Captain? Are they so serious that they pushed you all to commit such a heinous crime against the Union?"

"Yes, Admiral. As you justly said, they are serious enough to push us to do exactly that. Starting with the intolerable conditions under which we have to live in the bases of the north."

Mikhail recited a list of grievances—both real and imaginary—against the Soviet government, the Soviet Armed Forces in general, and the Soviet Navy specifically. Vasily and Anatoly joined minds in order to find the possible location of the ADS receiver and its deadly cargo of plastic explosives.

"If it's in the bomb bay, there's no way we can reach it from here," said Vasily.

The bomb bay—where the main *'Korshun'* radar and its related antenna and peripherals were located—and the forward cabin were separated not only by their respective bulkheads but also by several of the TU-95's seventy one fuel tanks. This made passage from one section to the other all but impossible. As far as the crewmen in the front cabin were concerned, anything there could have been on the far side of the moon.

"I agree," said Yuri. "Even if there were a way, a hatch, or something we could use to reach that part of the plane, we can't do it at this height. That area is not pressurized. We'd have to descend to about 2000 meters before we could get there," said the Flight Engineer.

"Then we descend to 2000 meters! We can start the descent right now!" exclaimed Vasily.

"What if it's in the equipment bay?" asked Jonas. "I know we can access it from here. Perhaps there's even a way to go to the bomb bay from there."

"That's if the receiver's located there. What if it's not? What if it's located in the wings?" Said Ivan.

"I doubt it. I clearly remember Pyotr Davidovich saying that it's somewhere in the fuselage," said Anatoly.

"Well, then let's start searching. Sitting on our butts is not going to do us any good," said Pavel, then he turned around and faced the bulkhead behind his seat.

"This section here must be pressurized. Is that right, Yura?" asked Pavel.

"Yes, it is. The tail and the equipment bay section between you and the bomb bay is pressurized," answered the Flight Engineer.

"I thought so. After all, the only thing separating us from that section is this wall made out of polyester, felt and insulation," said Pavel, touching the greenish felt.

"Yes, that's right," Yuri confirmed. "It is polyester."

"Then it's easily breakable," said Pavel. Pulling his knife from its scabbard, he plunged it twice into the material, making a large X-shaped cut.

"It's dark like hell there!" said Pavel, looking into the open cavity before him. Then asked: *"Tovarishchi,* is there a way I can access the intercom there?"

"Yes. There should be a communication outlet back there. The repair technicians use it to talk to the ground crews," Ivan said.

"Then I'm going in!" Pavel said. He disconnected his helmet's headset from the intercom system, then crawled his way from his seat by the observation bubbles towards the equipment bay portion of the airplane.

Meanwhile, Mikhail continued his negotiations with Admiral Gorshkov. "… Admiral, I knew I could count on you to listen to the problems of the common Navy man, despite your high rank and position!"

"Spasibo bol'shoye, tovarishch Kapitan Makarov! And I know you are a reasonable man. So, that taken care of, you and your crew agree to return that airplane to the Union?"

"Yes, Admiral. Now that I have your solemn word as an officer and Admiral of the Soviet Navy, my crew and myself feel free to return. However, we have a problem here."

"And what problem is that, Captain?" Gorshkov asked.

"The Flight Engineer tells me we have enough fuel to reach, perhaps, Iceland. No more. Realistically, we cannot reach the Soviet Union with the available fuel."

"We can contact the Soviet Embassy in that country and arrange to place you and your crew under Soviet protection, as soon as your airplane lands there," Gorshkov suggested.

"That would solve this immediate problem satisfactorily. You could also arrange to have our plane refueled. That would expedite our departure from there and continue our flight back to the Union, Admiral," Mikhail continued his negotiations.

"Captain, landing in Iceland? Refueling there? Returning to the Union?" An incredulous Vasily interjected his questions in Captain Makarov's ears through the intercom system.

Momentarily closing the external communication, Mikhail addressed his copilot's question. "Yes, Vasya. Landing in Iceland, or wherever. I don't care what I tell this *mudak*, as long as I can stall him long enough for the guys to find that damn receiver. What's the status? Have they found it already?"

"Pavel is in the rear section of the fuselage, searching there," Anatoly said.

"Any luck?" Mikhail asked.

"Not yet. He's searching in almost total darkness," said Jonas.

"Notify me as soon as he finds anything. I'll keep the old man busy so he doesn't get jittery," Mikhail ended the internal communication and returned to his negotiations with Admiral Gorshkov.

"… and I'm sure, Captain Makarov, that you would not mind having some of your colleagues escort you until you land in Iceland. Just to make sure you're not disturbed by foreign aircraft," said Gorshkov.

"Not at all, Admiral. Not at all. Their support is welcome!"

"Very well, because I've ordered Major Krasnosyel'skih, Commander of *Blue 36*, of the 392nd ODRAP, to fly back from his present position and join you."

"Will he land in Iceland with me?" Mikhail asked.

"No, he will simply return to the Union," Gorshkov responded.

"What was his original destination?"

"Our base in Cuba."

"*Otlichno*. Admiral, my navigator has just plotted our flight path back to Iceland. We're changing heading in that direction," said Mikhail.

"Captain Makarov, once again I promise you and your crew will be treated justly by the investigation committee. You have my word on that," said Gorshkov. Closing his side of the communication, he immediately ordered: "Captain Sokolov, I want confirmation that he's indeed turning towards Iceland! Vector your jet fighters to intercept that airplane at once!" Gorshkov thundered.

Attentively looking to the radar screen before him, Sokolov confirmed. "Yes, Admiral. He seems to be changing his heading northeastward."

"I don't mind agreeing to whatever he wants to hear, as long as he returns the airplane in one piece. Once he's in the Union, fulfilling that agreement, that's another story altogether. However, if he plays tricks with me, I swear they'll end up at the bottom of the ocean, whether by my own hand or by means of the fighters. One way or another that airplane will return or sink, but it will not fall in enemy hands!"

As *Red 67* slowly made a turn towards its new heading, the six Yak-36M and the lone Yak-41 of the 279th OKShAP also changed their heading to intercept the giant of the air at a point southwest of Iceland.

*   *   *   *

"*Posmotrim* ... these are the channels for the rounds for Yonka's guns ... and these are the ammunitions boxes ..." Pavel talked to himself as he crawled his way inside the equipment bay. He slowly patted each square centimeter of the darkened bay's interior, seeing with his hands the shape of each and every box and piece of equipment there.

"... These are the oxygen bottles ... This is ridiculous! At this rate we'll be back in the Union before I search this whole place! That damn box could be anywhere! Or not be here at all! It's like looking for a black cat in a dark room ... Without knowing whether it's there or not!" Pavel's complaints resounded in the bay. Fortunately for his companion behind him, Jonas couldn't hear him due to the extreme noise in the airplane.

Feeling the bay's walls and floor, Pavel made use of his memory to discern what his hands were touching. "These two must be the transmitter and the receiver for the *'Argon'* system ..." He identified the first box he found on his way towards the front of the aircraft, referring to the system used to relay information to the missiles in flight.

"Now, what is this?" he said. His path was blocked by an enormous barrel-like object bolted to the floor. In the surrounding darkness he was barely able to distinguish the shape of the drum containing the 800 rounds for the lower barbette NR-23 Nudelmann-Rikhter 23mm twin cannons and their guidance mechanism.

Having identified the weapon installation, Pavel went around it and continued his search for the ADS receiver, trying to visualize the purpose of the other boxes contained in the bay. "*Posmotrim* ... These are the transmitters for the *'Romb'* and the *'Vishnya'*..." he continued his identification, referring to the ELINT system and the SIGINT equipment which he himself used for communications interception, the antennas of which are immediately outside the fuselage.

In the claustrophobically dark enclosed space Pavel continued his inspection of the equipment bay. Suddenly, before him emerged another large-sized object. Straining his eyes to distinguish its features, he noticed that this one was bolted to the upper side of the fuselage. By its large size and round shape, he could identify it as the drum containing the 700 rounds for the upper barbette NR-23 Nudel-mann-Rikhter 23mm twin cannons and their guidance mechanism.

Knowing that this latter weapon installation was near the end of the equipment bay, and that beyond there was only a bulkhead, Pavel began to feel discouraged. *"Blyad!* I checked this whole damn bay for nothing! That means the damn receiver is in the bomb bay. And there's no way we can reach it there!" he exclaimed aloud.

As he was about to turn back to his seat in the aircraft's tail, his boot bumped against something on the fuselage floor. Surprised, he looked down.

"I wonder what the devil this is ..." he said to himself, then knelt before the object. Feeling its shape, Pavel determined its approximate size. *"Posmotrim* ... one meter long, by half meter wide, by twenty centimeters high ... What the hell is this? I'm not aware of any other equipment, technical or otherwise, being stored here ... Well, after all, I'd never been in this part of the airplane before. Not that I wanted to be working here either, for that matter ..."

Feeling the shape of the box, he also found its lock. When trying to open it, it was firmly secured. *"Khuy morzhovyy!* It's so damn dark here I can't even see what it says on top, or if it has any markings whatsoever!" He cursed.

Undoing his way back to the tail, Pavel returned to his seat, connected his helmet's communication jack into the intercom system, and conveyed his findings to the crew. *"Tovarishchi,* I found something back there. I have no idea what it is. I can't identify it because it's too dark, but I'm not aware of anything similar being stored there."

"What does it looks like?" Vasily asked.

Pavel described to the listening crewmen the metal box's shape, dimensions, and location.

"It doesn't look like anything I know," said Anatoly.

"Where did you say it's located?" asked Yuri.

"Against the first bulkhead of the equipment bay, right under the drum for the upper barbette," responded Pavel.

"Mmm ... That's bulkhead number 50. On the other side of that bulkhead we have fuel tanks N4, N5, and N5a ..." said Yuri.

"That's a splendid location to put a bomb if your want to maximize its explosive power. Right next to a bunch of fuel tanks!" said Vasily.

"Could you see any markings on it, any letters, anything to indicate what it is?" asked Alexey.

"No. It was too damn dark. I could hardly see anything there," Pavel responded.

"Pavlik, go back there with some lighting and verify what it is," said Mikhail.

"Yes. There's a good probability that's what we're looking for," said Vasily.

"*Ladno.* I'll go back. I'll have to use my cigarette lighter to see there, though."

"Take mine too, in case yours dies while there," Jonas said.

Pavel once again entered the small opening behind him and crawled, then walked his way back to where he found the mysterious box.

Kneeling by the box, Pavel flicked his lighter. By the dancing light of the small flame he examined the dark box, looking for any letters or markings that could tell him its purpose. Not finding anything other than its dark color, Pavel carefully inspected its twin locks in order to find the most expedient way to open it and access its contents.

"This damn thing seems to be made never to be opened ... But I must open it if I hope to know what it is, or what's inside ..." He carefully lifted the locks clasps. Once up, they lifted the securing bars from their cradles and fell down, freeing the box's cover.

"Let's see what this box holds so tightly that they can't afford to put not even a word about it on the outside ..." He slowly lifted the metal sheet that functioned as a cover.

Before him, by the flickering flame of the lighter, a jumble of cables, wires, electronic devices, gages, meters and batteries betrayed their intended purpose. On the far side of the box, wires sank into a grey plastic square container marked with the red letters 'V. V.'

"*Evreka!* Found it!" he exclaimed loudly. However, realizing the monumentality of his discovery, he immediately lowered the cover very slowly and carefully, making sure he didn't disturb too much the jumble of cables and gadgets in the box.

Standing up, he hurriedly headed again to his seat. "*Tovarishchi,* I found it. It's that damn box I told you about before!"

"And how do you know it's that box?" asked Ivan.

"Well, besides the obvious wires, meters and batteries, on one side it has this gray block with the letters *V. V.* on it. What do you think they mean?" Pavel asked, sarcastically.

"*Vzryvchatoe Veshchestvo!*" said Anatoly.

"Exactly. 'Explosives!'" Pavel agreed.

"*Otlichno!* Now, what do we do?" asked Alexey.

"Disarm it, of course!" said Anatoly.

"Well, that's great, but, how do we do it? I certainly don't know how," said Pavel.

"Don't worry, Pavlik. I'll tell you how," Anatoly said.

"Tolya, are you sure you can do it?" Mikhail asked.

"Yes, Captain. First, all receivers are the same, and second, I can use the explanations Pyotr Davidovich gave me about the system to have a pretty good idea how to disarm it," said Anatoly.

"*Ladno. Tovarishchi,* let's get to work and get rid of that thing. It's the only obstacle between us and freedom," said Mikhail.

"How am I going to talk to you?" asked Pavel. "The only jack to plug in a helmet is about two meters from the box. If I plug my helmet there, I won't be able to reach it."

"Pavlik, I can go back there with you, plug my helmet there, and relay you Tolya's instructions," said Jonas.

"Good idea, Yonka! But you'll have to scream. You know how noisy it is there," said Pavel.

"Don't worry, I have very good lungs!" said Jonas, amid his friends laughs.

Both men crawled into the equipment bay. Pavel knelt next to the metal box containing the ADS receiver and explosives. Jonas remained behind him, his helmet connected to the intercom jack used by the maintenance and repair technicians.

Pavel once again inspected the metal box, describing in a loud voice his findings to Jonas, who relayed them to the rest of the crew. *"Posmotrim* ... Outside, on the right side, it has several wires coming into one single connector, most likely for power and the receiver's antenna ... That's all there is outside ..."

Then he opened the box's locking clasps and proceeded to describe its contents. "Inside, on the side near me, a device that obviously looks like a miniaturized receiver. On it, a dial measured in volts and another in hertz ..."

"The power and frequency meters," added Jonas, for the benefit of his friends in the forward area. Here, Anatoly and Ivan penciled a sketch of the box and its contents as Pavel and Jonas described it to them.

"Covering the right side, a device with several lights, most of them on, a meter in DC volts and two connectors, one going to the receiver, the other going to one set of two batteries ..."

"That could be the power supply. The batteries are the power backup," Said Anatoly.

"I agree," said Jonas.

"Between the batteries and the power supply there's a small box with connectors from the batteries, the receiver, and the power supply. The box has one single dial with two hands ... seems to be a chronometer, measured to ... ten minutes!

Over that, at the top, there is the gray container with the letters *V. V.* There's one single connector going from the small box to the gray box."

"The small box is the detonating relay box …" said Anatoly. His tone of voice betrayed the importance he attached to this last piece of the puzzle.

"Very well … We have to find a way to disarm this box without triggering its arming mechanism," said Anatoly.

"Which could happen if we disconnect practically any wire," said Ivan.

"Correct," Anatoly agreed.

"We must find which ones can be taken out of the circuit without triggering anything," said Ivan.

"Correct again," Anatoly said. "Let's work this puzzle like an equation, from the explosives back to the relay box, back to the receiver, back to the power supply …"

"Can't we just cut the wires going into the explosives?" asked Jonas.

"If it were so easy, they wouldn't place such a system here," said Anatoly. "Has Pavel looked inside the explosives container?"

"No. He'll do that now," said Jonas.

Pavel opened the cover for the gray container. Inside, wrapped in brown cardboard, 2 two-hundred-gram bars of plastic explosives, marked

SEMTEX
VCHZ Synthesia
Pardubice, ČSSR

Each of the bars was penetrated by two short pencil-like cylinders, which acted as detonators. The detonators were linked to each other by a wire, then all the wires bifurcated and went to the connector on the cover, and to another unseen connector which attached to the relay box, but internally.

"The whole damn thing is booby-trapped!" exclaimed Pavel. "If you cut any one of the detonators' wires, the system senses it and detonates the whole thing!"

"How can you determine that?" asked Jonas.

"It has a hidden connector from the plastic to the relay box," said Pavel.

"So it is if you eliminate any one of the power sources too," said Anatoly. "The other would trigger the mechanism to explode immediately."

"*Blyad!* How are we going to disarm this bitch?" asked Jonas.

"Calm down, Yonka. There must be a way to go around its traps," said Mikhail. "We just have to put our heads together and find it. We've done it before, we can do it again."

"The Captain is right," said Vasily. "We've been able to get this far, right?"

"Let's think this over ..." said Anatoly. "If the system receives the trigger signal, it activates the relay box, which turns on the arming mechanism, which starts the countdown ..."

"Captain, how long is that countdown?" asked Alexey.

"About ten minutes. Enough to abandon the airplane," Mikhail said.

"I don't know ... I don't think I trust that 'countdown.' I have the feeling there would not be any. The plane would just blow up the second that button is pushed. You wouldn't know what happened.... What a way to die!" Alexey exclaimed, expressing the distrust they all felt about the autodestruct system.

"Tolya, any way of killing all power to it?" Mikhail asked.

"That would be the ideal solution, Captain," responded the technician. "The problem is that it relies on two, possibly three power sources."

"Three? Pavlik mentioned only two," said Ivan.

"I don't count on that. It could have an external power source too ... That's what I would do if I were them ..." said Anatoly. "Yonka, ask Pavlik to tell me how many wires there are in the external connector of the box."

"One thick, insulated cable and four smaller wires," Pavel's reply came through Jonas.

"Just like I thought. The thick one is from the antenna, and the smaller ones is the external power for both the power supply and the relay box," said Anatoly.

"Can't we just cut the antenna cable? It wouldn't be able to receive the signal," suggested Yuri.

"They thought of that too. Systems like that are usually designed to sense a radio signal coming on through the antenna. If the signal is suddenly lacking, the damn thing is immediately armed, or worse, detonates," explained Anatoly.

"Khuy morzhovyy! How the hell are we going to deactivate that cursed box?" asked Vasily.

"I don't know, but we'll find a way, Vasya. I promise we will!" exclaimed Anatoly.

"Tolya, what about using one of the three sources of power to supply energy to the sensing circuits for the other two, thus eliminating them from the circuit?" suggested Ivan.

"That's a suggestion we could use," Anatoly agrees.

"Then it's just a matter of knowing which one to use as supplier and which ones to eliminate," added Jonas, then he informed Pavel about the suggestion.

"I agree," said Pavel. "I lean towards using the batteries as supplier, and eliminating the external power and the power supply."

Jonas relayed his friend's thoughts to Anatoly and Ivan. After visually examining the sketched circuit before them, both technicians reached an agreement and relayed it to Pavel.

"Running a length of wire from the batteries positive to the positive wires in both the power supply connector and the external power connector should take care of those two," Pavel suggested.

Both technicians in the forward area put their minds to think about their friend's suggestion, following the new addition on their sketch of the circuitry. "Very well, Pavlik. Go ahead. Jump the power supply first, then cut it out of the circuit … and let's hope for the best," said Anatoly.

The crew collectively holds its breath as the technician carefully inserted a wire from the batteries positive poles to the connector going from the power supply to the relay box.

"Done! Well, at least it didn't short or blow up …" Jonas exclaimed, relieved.

Having succeeded in the first operation, Pavel attempted the second. He held the wire providing power from the power supply to the relay box between his left thumb and index finger. With one flip he closed his lighter and placed it on the floor. Now in darkness, Pavel pulled his knife, and in one single and swift stroke cut the wire.

"AAH!" he exclaimed in a loud voice.

"Pavlik, what happened?" Jonas asked, concerned.

"Nothing. I thought this damn thing would blow up. It didn't," Pavel said.

"Yes, we're still here," Jonas agreed.

"Now, let's cut off external power," Pavel said. Shunting another piece of wire from the batteries positive poles to the connector for external power, the technician repeated the previous maneuver, isolating the power feeds to the relay box. The system remained depending solely on battery power.

Having informed the rest of the crew of the procedure, Jonas waited for their collective thoughts to be gathered again in order to continue disabling the system.

"Very well. The receiver is still on, and the relay box too. That guarantees the radio signal is sensed by the relay box. The power sensing circuitry is receiving its feed too, so there's nothing to fear on that side," Jonas said.

"*Otlichno.* Going back to my original thought, that is, explosives, relay box, signal receiver, power supplies, we have eliminated the latter. That leaves us with only the other three," said Anatoly.

"I believe we should eliminate the receiver now," said Ivan.

"I disagree," said Anatoly. "Remember that this system *must* sense a radio signal at all times, otherwise, it arms. Besides, that was more or less the purpose of the jammer we constructed back at the base."

"And which now lies useless, thanks to that *sukin syn* ... " said Yuri.

"I would prefer to cut all connections between the explosives and the relay box, so even if it arms, nothing would happen. It would have no explosives to detonate," suggested Anatoly.

"Good idea, but how?" asked Pavel, after having been informed by Jonas.

"I don't know," was Anatoly's short reply.

"What about cutting *all* the wires to the explosives?" suggested Ivan.

"If that were possible to do in one single stroke, yes. Unfortunately, for that you would need ... one, two, three, four, five, six hands and six cutters, all cutting at the same time. One fraction of a second delay, and that's the end. Back there Pavlik and Yonka have only four hands and at most two knives. I don't see how that's physically possible."

"Ladno ... " Ivan said, disappointed.

"And if we cut only the main and backup wires from the relay box to the explosives, what would happen?" asked Pavel.

"Good question ..." said Anatoly, observing the effects of such a cut in the sketched circuit before him.

"Perhaps that is our solution," said Ivan.

"I agree," said Anatoly. "But it will have to be done using our available four hands and two knives."

"Tolya, what do you mean?" asked Jonas.

"You and Pavlik will have to cut both those wires at the same time. There can be no delay! If one is still alive while the other is cut, the system may detonate immediately."

"The risk is very high," said Mikhail. "Tolya, Vanya, is there any other way, less risky?"

"Perhaps there is, Captain. But right now that is a real possibility to disable that damn thing," said Ivan.

"Tovarishchi, it's up to you to make the decision of cutting those wires and hope for the best," said Mikhail.

"If anyone disagrees, say it now," said Vasily.

A heavy, thick silence comes from the intercom. Not even the roaring thunder of the engines drowns it.

"Very well. Pavlik, Yonka, cut the wires," said Mikhail.

"*Tovarishchi,* remember that while we do this, I will not be able to talk to you. My helmet will be disconnected," said Jonas. "Also, we'll have to make the cuts in darkness, back here. For us to be able to cut those wires we'll have to place the lighters on the floor, hold the wires with one hand and the knives with the other."

Once again, silence came from the cockpit. The whole crew understood what their two friends had to go through and do back in the equipment area. No words were necessary.

"Yonka, you cut the main wire from the relay box. I cut the backup wire," Pavel said. "Let's prepare them for cutting, so that when we close the lighters, we can find them. Also have your knife ready to find and cut."

"*Ladno,*" Jonas agreed.

Having prepared the wires, both men closed their lighters and in almost total darkness, prepared themselves for the outcome of their actions.

"Yonka, on the count of three we cut. Here we go ... *raz, dva, TRI!*"

Having made the cut, only the engines' drone sounded all over the airplane.

"Are we still here?" asked Jonas.

"I guess so. I still hear you, and those damn noisy engines!" exclaimed Pavel.

"Bravooooooooooooooooo!" exclaimed Jonas in a very loud scream.

By the light of his relit lighter Pavel examined the cut wires. "Yes! The explosives are all cut from the relay box!" he said, then continued his examination of the rest of the system. "This is weird ..." he said again.

"What is weird?" asked Jonas.

"The relay box is armed, even though the wires going to the explosives are all cut off."

"Well, remember that it's designed to do just that," said Jonas.

"Yes, but, why bother to arm it when there's nothing to detonate?" asked Pavel.

"Unless there really *is* something to detonate ... How many minutes before it gets to zero?" asked Jonas.

"Not even the customary ten minutes. It advanced all the way up to one minute!" said Pavel. The chronometer on the relay box had its hands set one over the number nine, the other, thinner, moved once a second towards the zero mark.

"Is there another power feed to the relay box?" asked Jonas.

"There's only one way to know!" said Pavel, desperately pulling the two Semtex bricks from their box. Holding the explosives in his hands, he could see their underside: "*Blyad!* They were both live all the time!"

To his horror, protruding from each brick, two detonators, already wired to the relay box, showed up like deadly fangs, ready to strike. The thin hand on the chronometer quickly and inexorably moved closer to zero.

"*Chyort vozmyot!* Only ten seconds! Yonka, cut them off, CUT THEM OFF!" Pavel screamed at his friend.

Jonas dropped his lighter still lit. With one hand he took the two wires, with the other hand grabbed his knife and in one single, forceful stroke cut both wires simultaneously.

In an act of pure reflex, Pavel sent the two plastic bricks flying across the bay, falling harmlessly by the ammunition drum of the lower gun barbette.

"Yonka! Yonka! Yonka?" Pavel called his friend, but received no reply. Pavel took his lighter and flicked it. The dancing light held in his hand revealed the reason for Jonas's silence: The man lied unconscious against the airplane's wall. Grabbing him by his shoulder, Pavel woke him up.

"Yonka, we did it! We did it!" Pavel gave his friend the news.

"We did? WE DID IT!?" Jonas at last reacted to the news.

"Yes, let's tell everyone!" Pavel immediately stood up in one single jump and ran to the intercom jack, where he plugged his helmet.

"*Uspekh!* Success!" he screamed in the intercom.

The six crewmen in the forward area, who—although still in one piece, had not heard from their friends by the plane's tail in more than 5 minutes, broke in one single scream of relief, followed by hugs to each other by Mikhail and Vasily in the cockpit, and among Ivan, Anatoly, and Yuri, behind the cockpit, as well as handshakes to both pilots from Alexey, kneeling at the mouth of the tunnel leading to his post. All this amid more screams, laughs, and yells.

Once the mayhem returned to normal, Mikhail called the crew back to order. "Yura, what's the fuel situation?"

"We have fuel for about one and a half, perhaps two more hours flying time," said the Flight Engineer.

"Alyosha, where are we?" Mikhail asked his Navigator.

"We're about two hours away from Iceland," replied Alexey.

"And how long to Canada?" asked Vasily.

"About two hours and a half," said the Navigator.

"I really don't like the idea of continuing flying to Iceland," said Mikhail.

"Neither do I," Vasily agreed.

"Yura, do you think we could, perhaps, reach Canada?" Mikhail asked again.

"Well, there's barely enough fuel to reach Canada, but I think we can make it, if we are frugal with it," said the Flight Engineer.

"And if we don't?" asked Alexey.

"Then we'll have to ditch," responded Yuri.

Suddenly, a cacophony of voices burst on the intercom. All the crewmen wanted to make their opinions heard at the same time.

"Tovarishchi! Tovarishchi! Khvatit! Molchites'!" Mikhail commanded in a firm voice. Silence and order were once again restored. "Let's decide what we'll do. Continue flying to Iceland or head back to Canada?"

"Head back to Canada!" said Vasily. "In Iceland the KGB is already waiting for us."

"Yes, that's true. In Iceland we'll be all handed to the KGB as soon as we land. I don't believe we'll refuel there. So I vote we head back to Canada," agreed Yuri.

"Canada! That's our original destination," said Alexey, the navigator.

"Canada!" was Anatoly's single word.

"Ladno. Those in favor of heading back to Canada, say so now," said Mikhail. Seven positive answers come in quick succession through the intercom.

"I also vote for heading back to Canada," said Mikhail. "By unanimous vote of the crew of *Red 67*, this airplane returns to its original heading. Alyosha, plot a new heading back to our original one," Mikhail ordered the Navigator.

"Ponyal, tovarishch kapitan!" replied Alexey.

∗   ∗   ∗   ∗

"Captain! Are you sure that airplane is still flying?" Admiral Gorshkov asked, incredulous of the answer he heard.

"Yes, Admiral. *Red 67* is still flying and once again in a heading of 240 degrees," responded the technician in charge of the ADS aboard the *TAKr Kiev.*

"Push that damn button again!" Gorshkov yelled. "Those dogs are not going to escape from my hands just like that!"

"I'm sorry, Admiral. I've pushed it three times already, and the airplane is still flying," said the technician. "They must have done something to the system to disable it."

"Predatel'stvo!" Gorshkov screamed, angrier than before. "Betrayal of the worst kind! Lots of heads are going to roll because of this! That I promise!" Turning to the 279th OKShAP controller, Gorshkov ordered a quicker pace and immediate interception.

"Sokol, Matka calling. *Priyom … Sokol, Matka* calling. *Priyom …"* called the controller.

"Matka, Sokol speaking. *Priyom,"* responded Col. Kolyesnikov.

"Krolik has turned to a new heading. Change your heading now to intercept. *Priyom,"* said the controller.

"Matka, can you confirm that change of heading? *Priyom,"* Col. Kolyesnikov asked.

"Confirmed, *Sokol.* They're once again on a heading of 240," said the controller.

Although still several hundred kilometers away from the defectors' airplane, Kolyesnikov understood that only he and his escorting fighters could intercept it and force it to return, or destroy it in the air. However, with *Red 67* still outside the range of his radar, Kolyesnikov had to rely on the information provided by the controller.

"Sokol, our radars are tracking uninvited guests heading towards you," informed the *Kiev* controller.

"Guests? Who are they, *Matka?"* asked Kolyesnikov.

"They seem to be American fighters. They're by your vector 045. Intercepting you in about five minutes."

"Blyad! Amerikosy! I detest when these *mudaki* put their long noses into matters that clearly are not their business!" Kolyesnikov exclaimed aloud.

"Understood, *Matka. Sokol* ends transmission," Kolyesnikov then informed his escort. *"Sokol* to *Burevestnik, Sokol* to *Burevestnik.* Stay on the alert. We're having guests. Repeat, we're having guests. Please receive them accordingly while I go follow our charges. *Priyom,"*

"Understood, *Sokol.* We'll entertain them. You may proceed to your assigned duties. *Burevestnik* ends," Lt. Col. Ratenko responded, then proceeded to instruct his fliers. "Maestro to musicians, Maestro to musicians. American interceptors coming our way, vector 045. Let's intercept and block. Warning: Under no circumstance we'll make use of weapons, unless we're shot first. Maestro ends transmission."

Col. Kolyesnikov sped up and accelerated his interception of 'Krolik,' the defectors' airplane. Lt. Col. Ratenko and the rest of the squadron turned and changed heading towards the three American F-4C interceptors flying from Keflavík.

All six Yak-36M fighters followed a heading that took them to meet the American interceptors head on. Their purpose was not so much to intercept the F-4Cs as to actually block and make them change heading.

Aboard 529, the leading F-4C, Capt. John Starrett, call sign 'Starsky,' and his RIO, Major Stephen Hutchinson, call sign 'Hutch,' coincidentally put together in the same airplane like the famous couple of the TV show then in vogue, continued flying their interception course towards the coordinates previously transmitted by Keflavík Control.

"Captain, six Soviet bandits are coming our way. A seventh one has detached from them and is heading southwest, towards 'Bogie One,'" Hutch informed the pilot.

"They're all 'Forgers', aren't they?" asked 'Starsky.'

"Correct, from the *'Kiev.'* They've been flying this way, seemingly to intercept 'Bogie One," said the RIO.

"We gotta find out what's going on. Why they're so interested in meeting that plane," said 'Starsky.'

"The funny part is that after 'Bogie One' changed heading, all seven 'Forgers' sped up," commented 'Hutch.'

"What's their position now?" asked 'Starsky.'

"Six of them are approximately seventy clicks from us in a heading that is directly in front of us, by 12 o'clock! The lone 'Forger' is still advancing towards 'Bogie one,'" said the RIO.

"What do you mean 'by 12 o'clock?" asked the pilot.

"Exactly that, Captain. All six 'Forgers' are going to meet us head on!" responded the incredulous Radar Officer.

"Let's go after the lone 'Forger,'" said the Captain. "After all, we seem to have the same interest."

"Its speed is much too high to be a 'Forger.' It's flying almost as fast as we are!" said 'Hutch.'

"That makes it even more interesting," said 'Starsky,' then he pushed the twin throttles and increased his speed.

"Captain, I suggest we start evasive maneuvers. The six 'Forgers' have not changed heading," 'Hutch' informed the pilot.

"Roger. I see them coming." In the cloudless afternoon sky of the North Atlantic the small dots approached the trio of F-4Cs, growing in size by the second.

"The 'Ruskis' think that because they're more we're going to change heading?" asked 'Starsky.'

"Oh no. I hope they're not playing 'chicken' this time," said Hutch.

"Well, if they are, they're gonna have one helluva surprise!" said 'Starsky.' "One of the two groups is going to change altitude, and that's not going to be ours!"

Major 'Hutch' began to feel nervous. Ever since his Vietnam stint, Captain 'Starsky' was known to be a hothead, having already caused a few flaps because of his overflying of Soviet 'Bears' passing by Iceland, sometimes flying too close to them. This in turn generated a flurry of formal protests from the Soviet Embassies in both Reykjavík and Washington.

The two groups of airplanes got closer and closer. The danger of a head-on collision became more and more real as their combined speeds—exceeding fifteen hundred kph—shortened the distance and time between them. In a matter of seconds they would meet, unless one of them changed its course. However, neither Captain 'Starsky' nor his Soviet counterpart, Lt. Col. Ratenko, budged one meter from their flying paths.

In the rear seat, Major 'Hutch' diverted his eyes from the open sky to the radar screen before him. The nine little blips that formed the two fighter groups were about to become one. Again looking outside, chills ran down his spine as the small black dots he saw before became distinguishable airplanes, and growing larger.

"Captain, perhaps we should evade now," suggested the nervous 'Hutch.'

"Evade my ass! And show the 'Ruskis' we are the chickens? Over my dead body!" said 'Starsky.'

Dead is what we'll be if we don't get out of their way ... thought Major 'Hutch.' He respected Captain 'Starsky' but at the same time he hated his hotheaded and impulsive behavior, especially in situations when their own lives were in danger. On the other hand, 'Hutch' understood him. Ever since he returned from Vietnam 'Starsky' exhibited a strong dislike for anything and everything Soviet and Communist, hence his crazed antics whenever he intercepted the 'Bears.'

As the 'Forgers' approached, the drop tanks slung under their wings became clearly visible. 'Hutch' could not help but to close his eyes and brace himself for the high-G maneuver that would involve an upward or downward evasion.

Flying the leading Yak-36, Lt. Col. Ratenko followed the three American fighters in their flight towards him, not deviating one meter to either side. Wishing to really put American resolve to the test, but also knowing that he had no authority to endanger the lives of his pilots nor cause the destruction of the fighters entrusted to them, Lt. Col. Ratenko instructed his men. "Maestro to musicians, Maestro to musicians. On my mark, we go up ... *Raz, dva, tri, navyerkh!*"

Like one single body, all six Yak-36s deflected their exhaust nozzles to point downward while at the same time pointing their noses upward. Thanks to the slower speed of the Yaks, plus the added maneuverability of their VTOL design, the sudden change of course made the incoming American F-4s simply slide and pass unharmed just scarce meters under their fuselages. Fortunately for the former, had this been a real combat encounter, the latter would have dispatched all six of them long before they managed to come this close.

"HA! Fucking Russian chickens! I don't care to die as long as I take a few of you with me down to hell!" screamed 'Starsky' when the fuselage of one the Yaks showed him its blue underbelly, so close that 'Hutch' felt he could just extend his arm and touch it.

Ascending and putting some distance between them and the F-4s, the Yak-36s initiated a quick turn that placed them behind the former, as if they were going to attack from the rear. The slower Yaks could make tighter turns than the much faster F-4s.

"Captain, evasive action, now! They're turning by our 5 o'clock!" 'Hutch' screamed as he followed the Soviet fighters on his radar screen.

"Like hell they're gonna get on my ass!" said 'Starsky,' pulling a tight turn to port.

Outside, the other two F-4s similarly avoided the Yaks' attempts to stay behind them, the perfect position to take a shot. In a few minutes all nine airplanes engaged in a dogfight-like mêlée equal to those fought in Korea or Vietnam, turning and gyrating in a huge, angry ball all over the sky. The pilots from both sides tried to latch to each other's tails in order to scare their opponents. The two groups were somewhat equal. Although the six Yak-36s were qualitatively inferior, they compensated by having numerical superiority. The three Americans, flying superior machines, had to contend with their aircraft having to evade two or three Yaks at the time. Fortunately for all parties involved, not a single bullet was shot in this cat-and-mouse demonstration of piloting skills.

"Hey, 'Hutch', did you notice? They have no rockets, only fuel tanks!" said 'Starsky.'

"Yes, I noticed. Three fuel tanks and one cannon pod."

"Right! But, why don't they use it? Bastards! I dare you to shoot at us, if you can!" screamed 'Starsky,' turning and weaving his way in the sky.

"It would be suicidal of them to shoot, and they know it … I think they just want us to stay away from 'Bogie One'!"

"Why is that, 'Hutch'?"

"Because the single 'Forger' is getting closer to it," the RIO responded. The small blip on his radar screen appeared at just 30 kms from 'Bogie One.'

"Well, if that's the case, let's see what's so important about it!" said 'Starsky,' then he addressed his escort. "Black Knight Leader to Black Knights. Follow me! Engage full burners!"

Pushing his throttles, he engaged his powerful General Electric J-79 turbojet engines full 17,000 pounds of afterburner, leaving the much slower Yaks behind.

"Kiss my ass! Assholes!" 'Starsky' screamed. His Mach meter quickly approached the 1 mark. Behind him, the other two F-4s repeated the maneuver.

Lt. Col. Ratenko, having been left behind by the faster American jets, just saw them widen the gap between his squadron and the still accelerating trio of F-4s. Having accomplished his mission of delaying the American planes in their interception of *Red 67*, Ratenko ordered a prompt retreat. "Maestro to Musicians, Maestro to Musicians, let's return home, let's return home."

Five acknowledgments reached his ears. With their fuel tanks holding just enough fuel to return to their awaiting floating base, the six Yaks reduced their speed back to cruise, turned and took a heading that got them to land on their aircraft carrier less than thirty minutes later, almost at the end of their flight endurance.

*   *   *   *

Aboard the Yak-41, Col. Kolyesnikov—enjoying a clean and free time and distance advantage over the Americans, and knowing that he alone could intercept *Red 67* and destroy it—contacted Mikhail and his crew to afford them one last chance to return to the USSR or face destruction. *"Sokol* calling *Red 67, Sokol* calling *Red 67.* Please, respond." Kolyesnikov repeated his call time and again, without success. He received no reply from the defectors.

Khorosho, khvatit! If they don't want to reply, then let's see what we can do to wake them up ... Kolyesnikov armed his single radar-guided *Vympel* R-23R air-to-air missile. *I can't illuminate them well at this distance, but at least this will call their attention* ... The target set, Col. Kolyesnikov pushed the firing button.

Aboard *Red 67,* alarms went off in Jonas' panels. "Captain, Jonas speaking. Missile fired! Right behind us!"

"What type? How long before impact?" asked Mikhail.

"Radar-guided! Less than four minutes!" was Jonas' terrifying answer.

"Vanya! Yonka! Fire upper and lower guns as soon as it registers within range!" Mikhail ordered.

Ivan in the forward area, and Jonas in the tail, immediately actioned all the buttons and levers that turned on the radar targeting system for both the upper and lower cannons. The barbettes emerged from their enclosures and their twin 23 mm Nudelmann-Rikhter cannons sprang to life.

As soon as the targeting radar notified the system that the rocket was within range, at only 5 kms. behind *Red 67,* the cannons automatically let loose a barrage of fire, each DOS-15 23 mm *PRLS* round exploding just 2 kms away, generating large balls of chaff behind the aircraft. The rocket's guidance system, fooled by the wall of chaff, got confused and detonated inside the clouds of aluminum strips. The tremendous blast caused by the explosion made Jonas and Pavel think they were dead men. Fortunately, their tail position survived.

"Yonka! Pavlik! Are you alright back there?" Mikhail called his crewmen.

"Da, kapitan. A bit shaken but unharmed," said Jonas.

"Very well," said Mikhail. "The *mudak* behind us, whoever he is, he's wrong if he thinks he'll make us go back to that hell."

"Captain, *Sokol* is calling again," informed Ivan.

"Ignore him. I'd rather die trying to escape than to be shot in an unknown jail cell in Moscow."

"Captain, *Sokol* says that the first missile was just a warning. The next one will be for real," Ivan said again.

"Chepukha! Gavno! He's only bluffing. If he intended it to be a warning, he'd not have launched it from so far," said Anatoly.

"Tochno. That's why I think he's bluffing too. And he's desperate!" said Vasily.

"Well, desperate or not, he says we have one minute to acknowledge, or he'll fire again," said Ivan.

"Let him fire!" said Mikhail, defiant. "Even if he shoots us down now, it was worth it. Better to die with dignity than to cow in slavery."

"Well, if he fires another radar missile, we're dead. All we have is *PIKS,*" said Jonas, referring to the heat-generating rounds shot by the twin cannons before him.

As soon as Jonas finished talking, once again the terrifying shrill of the missiles fired alarm shrieked in the panel before him. "Captain, missile fired! One, heat seeking!"

"I knew it!" exclaimed Mikhail. "Yonka, you know what to do!"

The rear gunner immediately prepared the automatic targeting system to detect the incoming rocket and destroy it using the appropriate means. Since the rocket was fired from a shorter distance, it came much sooner within radar range. The two cannons fired almost as soon as they came on, the rounds exploding and forming a wall of fire barely 1000 meters behind them. The wall, however, was successful. When the rocket slammed against the fireballs, their heat fooled it into believing they were the Tupolev's engines. The warhead exploded.

The second explosion, much closer to the tail, strongly jarred Jonas and Pavel. Jonas' head slammed on the side of the narrow cabin he sat in, causing a small cut by his temple. Fortunately for him, the padded helmet he wore protected him from more grievous harm.

"Yonka! Pavlik! Anybody alive back there?" Mikhail asked for the third time.

"Uuuunh! Pavel speaking, Captain. Yonka I think is still groggy from the shock wave. This time I thought we were goners," responded the crewman.

"Never mind me!" said Jonas. "All I have is a small cut, nothing serious. What is more serious is that now we're defenseless. All rounds have been used up. The guns are empty. If they use more rockets, we're dead men."

"Don't worry about it," said Ivan. "If they had them, they would have used them already. If they have not launched yet it's because they have no more."

"Right. Plus, it's only one airplane following us," said Pavel, "the IFF identifies only one aircraft around here as 'ours'."

"True, but most probably it has a cannon, so it can shoot us down, and we won't be able to do anything against it," said Jonas.

"Yonka, a while ago you mentioned God ... Do you know how to pray?" Mikhail asked the tailgunner.

"Yes, Captain. My mother taught me to pray when I was a child," replied the crewman.

"Then now is the time to do it in earnest," said Mikhail. "Ask God for all of us, to get us out of this mess. Because if a miracle doesn't happen now, we'll simply die here."

Jonas closed his eyes and for the first time since childhood he tried to remember the long-forgotten prayer his mother had him say every night, while praying before their little home altar: *Tėve mūsų, kuris esi danguje. Teesie šventas Tavo vardas ...*

"Captain! I'm seeing more aircraft approaching!" Anatoly's words in his ears interrupted Jonas' silent prayer. "Approaching from vector 160, behind the Soviet fighter."

"IFF identifies them as 'adversary,'" said Ivan.

"They must be American interceptors from the American base in Iceland!" exclaimed Vasily.

"Perhaps, but what makes you think they'll intervene in this fight?" said Alexey. "They'll see it as a Soviet fighter escorting another Soviet aircraft."

"Not really," said Mikhail. "They must've seen the two rockets that *mudak* fired at us, so they must figure that something big must be going on between us and him,"

"Yes, like we want to defect and they're doing everything in their power to stop us," Vasily added.

"*Tochno!* Otherwise, why shoot rockets at us? That's not 'escorting'!" said Jonas.

"Agreed, but what can the Americans do? Even if that *mudak* decides to shoot us down, they won't intervene," said Pavel, discouraged.

"Don't think so," said Mikhail. "The Americans are a just people. When I met them in Germany they usually intervened whenever they saw any injustice being committed. That struck me very deeply then. I never forgot it."

"Well, then I hope for our own sake that they do something now," said Jonas. "I can see the Soviet fighter behind us, and the three Americans coming behind it."

"Can you identify the Soviet aircraft?" asked Anatoly.

"No, never saw it before," said Jonas, inspecting the Yak-41 through his binoculars. "It's a bit far but I can distinguish ... it has ... twin tail ..."

"Twin tail? Like the MiG-25?" asked Alexey.

"Correct, but it can't be a '25.' There's no way that plane can be here! There's no Soviet base in more than three thousand kilometers around!"

"Could it be an F-14? They have twin tails too," asked Alexey.

"Yes, they have twin tails, but they don't fire Soviet missiles, their pilots don't speak Russian, and they don't identify themselves as 'Sokol'," said Ivan.

"This definitely is a new type of airplane. I can not identify it," Jonas said when the Yak-41 got closer and was therefore more identifiable.

"Can you identify the Americans?" asked Vasily.

"Yes, they seem to be the usual F-4 'Phantoms.' Most probably from Iceland," informed the crewman.

*   *   *   *

The American fighters flew closer to the airplane before them. "What the hell is this? Never seen this plane! Hey, 'Hutch,' have you ever seen this plane before?" Capt. 'Starsky' asked himself and his RIO when he saw the Yak-41 prototype before them.

"Negative. I can't identify it either. I'm surprised no one has seen it before," said the RIO.

"You were right when you said it was too fast for a 'Forger,'" 'Starsky' said, then immediately called on his companions: "Black Leader to Black Knights ... Cover me while I go check on 'Bogie One.' I gotta find out what is so important that they were shooting rockets at it … And while you are at it, take some pics of that plane. New one, you know."

"Roger, Black Leader. We'll keep an eye on the bandit," replied his wingman.

F-4C 'Phantom' 529 sped up. Overtaking the Yak-41, it passed over and to starboard of the Soviet. Still from afar its crew could hear the rumble of the four Kuznyetsov engines, caused by the tips of the enormous blades of the eight AV-60N propellers turning at supersonic speed. Closer to *Red 67,* 'Starsky' made a preliminary inspection. "Let's see … 'Bogie One,' as suspected, is a 'Bear D.' Nothing new there, except that I wonder where it came from. It's not one from the pair that flew around here earlier today, is it, 'Hutch'?"

"Negative. Those two continued flying down the Canadian coast … This one is a regular 'Bear D' alright … But, why is it flying around here? Isn't this out of their regular flight paths?" asked the RIO.

"It is. It's too much to the north. Is it lost?" asked 'Starsky.'

"Doubtful. Those planes can navigate all the way down to Cuba and Angola for this one to get lost and fly so much out of its way," said 'Hutch.'

"Perhaps that's why the bandit was shooting at it?" asked 'Starsky.'

"To blow it out of the sky because it got out of its regular flight path? That makes no sense," answered 'Hutch.'

"Well, it's obvious the bandit didn't blow it up. It's still there," said 'Starsky,'

"However, the Soviets are known to do that with runaways," said 'Hutch.'

"Runaways? Could this be a runaway? A defector?" asked 'Starsky.'

"It's possible. Otherwise, why shoot two rockets at it? And it looks like they managed to avoid them too. That shows they are good and intent on getting away."

"We must find out these guys' real intentions, whether they're defecting or what," said 'Starsky.'

The F-4C approached *Red 67,* cautiously inspecting its crew, beginning with Jonas and Pavel by the tail. As they got closer, the smiling face of the rear gunner peered from his side window. When they passed by the starboard bubble, Pavel made a V-sign to the passing American pilots.

As the F-4C continued advancing parallel to the fuselage, 'Starsky' and 'Hutch' reached the forward area. Here Yuri's face peered out of his side window, smiling and waving his hand. Finally they reached the cockpit, where Vasily was also smiling and waving at them.

"Well, they seem friendly enough," said 'Hutch.'

"That doesn't mean anything. They always do that whenever we meet them, you know," said 'Starsky.'

Behind him, still followed by Black Knights Two and Three, Col. Kolyesnikov in the Yak-41 also maintained its distance from *Red 67*.

Aboard *Red 67,* Mikhail asked Jonas: "Yonka, is the Soviet plane getting any closer?"

"No. He's staying some two kilometers behind us," responded Jonas.

"I thought so. He's going to shoot," said Vasily.

"He can't shoot at us with the Americans all around!" said Alexey.

"Why not? He already launched two rockets at us. What makes you think he'll not shoot his cannons now?" said Jonas.

"Do you think the *nachal'stvo* cares about a Soviet fighter shooting down another Soviet airplane?" said Vasily.

"Vasya's right," said Yuri. "I see it already: 'Terrorists steal an airplane from a naval base. Fortunately, due to the rapid intervention of our very efficient Armed Forces, they were shot down before they could fly the aircraft to the adversary's territory.'"

"That's if they go that far," said Mikhail. "Most of the time events like these are just ignored and quickly swept under the rug by the *nachal'stvo.* I'd be surprised if they even acknowledge it happening."

"The Captain is right," said Anatoly. "I remember the rumors going around saying that sailors of the Baltic Fleet mutinied, took control of their ship and then tried to take it to Sweden. They were simply blown out of the water by V-VS bombers. To this day, I have not heard anything concrete about that anywhere."

"And you never will," said Vasily. "Don't think we're going to be treated any differently. That fighter back there is going to shoot us down, and there's nothing the Americans can do to prevent it."

"Vasya's right," said Ivan. "This is the end of the road for us. After all, they don't have to give the Americans or anyone else an explanation as to why they did it. And if they do, they'll not tell the truth, of course. To them we're nothing but terrorists, like Yura said."

"Enough of this defeatist nonsense!" Mikhail burst. "We did not do all this or came all the way here just to be shot down now, so stop it!"

Suddenly, streaks of light flashed by his left side. "Captain, the Soviet fighter is shooting at us!" said Jonas.

"Captain, it's *Sokol* again," said Ivan. "He says that was a warning. If we don't return immediately, he'll shoot to kill."

"*Blyad!* Where are the Americans?" asked Mikhail.

"They are still behind us, by vector 160!" responded Jonas.

"Do you think they'll intervene, Captain?" asked Vasily.

"I don't know, but there is one thing we could do," said Mikhail. "Vanya, use the international frequencies. Transmit our intentions!"

"Understood, Captain." Ivan tuned his radio to the frequencies normally used to transmit distress calls, and started a broadcast: "This is Tupolev 95 *Red 67* to American aircraft, please respond. Over." Ivan said, speaking in English.

Aboard F4-C 529, now flying behind and on the starboard side of *Red 67*, 'Hutch' couldn't believe his ears. "Captain, the Soviet Bear is calling *us!*"

"What? Are you sure?" asked a shocked 'Starsky.'

"Yes, Captain. They're repeating their call," said the RIO. "They want us to respond."

"They want to *talk* to us?" asked 'Starsky,' now even more shocked than before.

"That's what it seems, Captain," said 'Hutch'.

"Very well, open a line. Let's see if we can get some insight about what's going on. Why they're being shot at so fiercely," said 'Starsky.'

"Line's open, Captain," informed 'Hutch.'

"Soviet airplane, this is US Air Force Black Knight Leader. Please, state your intentions. Over," 'Starsky' responded.

"Black Knight Leader, this is Tupolev 95 *Red 67*. The Captain of this aircraft and the crew want to land in America, Canada. We request your permission to land. Over."

Ivan's transmission fell on the stunned pilots of the American trio of fighters like a bolt from the blue.

"Whaaaaaaaaaaaaaaaaat? They're defecting?" asked an incredulous 'Starsky.'

"That's what it looks like, Captain. That's why they were so friendly to us when we approached them," 'Hutch' agreed.

"*Red 67*, aah, did you say you want to *land* in Canada?" 'Starsky' asked for confirmation of the request, still refusing to believe what he heard.

"Yes, Black Knight Leader. We request permission to land in Canada," confirmed Ivan.

'Starsky' decided to get closer to the tail. Once there, he could not believe his eyes: "'Hutch!' Look at that sight! I never thought I'd live to see something like it!"

Behind the starboard blister, Pavel unfolded an American flag.

'Starsky' slowly advanced his fighter, remaining parallel to the larger airplane. As the two American jocks flew past, each in turn saluted Old Glory.

"Well, I guess that confirms it," said a very stunned 'Starsky.' "Never in my fucking life I thought I was going to be around when someone from the other side was trying to get to our side. And a whole Bear crew at that!"

"That explains why they're being shot at, but, what can we do? We're in international air space, just like they are," said 'Hutch.'

"I don't know, I certainly don't want to see them being shot down like that for trying to defect ..." said 'Starsky.'

Aboard the Yak-41, Col. Kolesnikov was losing his patience. Not only he didn't have the luxury of a lot of fuel but he also had to count on the only means available to him to force the defectors to return: his cannons. Having already spent one fourth of his ammo on the first barrage, he had to make the remaining ammunition last. He carefully aimed for a second short burst, this time much closer to the Tupolev's port engines, and let loose a wave of fire on the hapless TU-95.

"The bastard is shooting at them again!" screamed 'Starsky.'

Not wishing to be in the Yak's field of fire, 'Starsky' pulled his fighter's nose, ascended and occupied a perch several hundred meters above and behind the TU-95, midway between the larger airplane and the Soviet fighter behind.

In their headphones burst another desperate call from *Red 67*: "Black Knight Leader, we request your assistance. We are disarmed ... Please ... help."

Hearing the request, 'Starsky' realized that they got caught in the middle of a dilemma that could blow up into a major international predicament, with serious repercussions to all the involved parties, and perhaps even start a war.

"We know those guys there want to defect, but they're not in American or Canadian air space. That is a Soviet airplane, and the fighter shooting at them is another Soviet airplane. They could be hijackers, for all we know ..."

'Starsky' pushed his airplane's throttles, banked and sank its wing to port. "... But one thing I know: Whether they're defectors, hijackers or whatever, I am not going to allow a Soviet fighter to shoot down another airplane, Soviet or otherwise, with an American flag inside."

The F-4C followed a trajectory that placed it directly in the line of fire of the Yak-41 behind it. A stunned 'Hutch' just managed to ask: "Captain, what are you doing?"

"I'll place myself between them and the fighter. I doubt very much he'll dare to shoot at me. He knows that would mean instant destruction for him," said the pilot.

Suddenly, as he finished his flight trajectory, multiple tracers flew by his left. "He shot at us? That Russian bastard is dead meat!" 'Starsky' screamed at the top of his lungs.

He immediately banked to starboard, pointed the plane's nose down, losing altitude. Then made a hard turn to starboard, initiating a wide 180-degree turn.

"Black Knight Two to Black Knight Leader, the Soviet plane shot at you! Permission to fire back!" His companion confirmed his initial suspicions.

Finally having a reason to retaliate, 'Starsky' replied: "Permission granted. Fire at will. Blast that bastard out of the sky!"

Having missed with the third volley when he tried to avoid hitting the American fighter, after its surprise appearance before his line of sight, Col. Kolyesnikov prepared to fire a fourth barrage of rounds. Pushing throttles, he came closer to the Bear, just 500 meters behind it, to make sure he'd not miss at that distance. He had to make this one count. All he had left was enough ammo for one last burst, enough to spray and ignite the engines on the starboard wing.

Placing engine number three in his sight, he was about to press the trigger when, unexpectedly, his airplane was struck by multiple blows coming from the back.

With one single spit from its cannon, Black Knight One disabled the Yak, neatly cutting off the starboard tailfin and elevator and chewing up the engine exhaust. Thick smoke began to pour out of the struck engine. A second later, a loud explosion. A huge ball of yellow-reddish fire occupied the place in the sky where the Soviet fighter used to be. Orange tongues of flame leaped out of the fireball, which for a moment seemed as if suspended in mid air, then slowly fell towards the ocean below, picking up speed as the furiously burning remains of the airplane plunged downwards, leaving in its trail a thick, black wake.

Curiously, at that same moment, a distress transmission was received by all the radios in the area: "Mayday! Mayday! This is Tupolev TU-95 *Blue 36.* We're experiencing stall conditions. Our plane is falling down! Any Soviet vessel in the immediate area, please assist!"

Aboard *Red 67,* another alarm voice rang out. "Captain, Ivan speaking. *Sokol* was blown apart by the Americans!"

"Well, he deserved it!" said Vasily.

"I'm also receiving a distress transmission from *Blue 36!*" said Ivan.

"*Blue 36?* Isn't that Major Krasnosyel'skih's plane, the one Gorshkov sent to escort us back to Iceland?" Mikhail asked.

"The same," said Ivan.

"Are they stating the reason for the distress?" Mikhail asked again.

"It's falling due to stall!" Ivan replied.

"Any reason for the stall?" Mikhail asked.

"No. The transmission is breaking up. I can hardly catch it. They're still about three or four hundred kilometers south of us," Ivan responded.

"Yonka, what's *Sokol's* status?" Mikhail asked.

"Still falling," Jonas answered. His eyes followed the spiraling burning wreck.

"And the Americans?" asked Mikhail.

"Still behind us, and getting closer," responded the crewman.

All three Black Knight fighters approached the Bear, two on each side, the other behind.

"'Hutch,' call Base Control; let them know what's going on here. They'll never believe us! Also tell them to contact the Canadians. I know they will not believe this either."

The RIO called his base in Keflavík and informed them of the events just happened. After several minutes, a reply arrived: "*Red 67,* we have notified the Canadian Government about your request for landing permission in that country," Captain 'Starsky' informed Ivan, who translated for the benefit of his friends. "Permission has been granted. Interceptors from their Armed Forces are coming to escort you."

Hearing the news, the crew of *Red 67* let go a collective scream heard all over the airplane, despite the loud drone of the engines. "*Rah-ger,* Black Knight Leader. On behalf of the Captain and the crew of this aircraft, I thank you. *Spasibo, spasibo bol'shoye!*" Ivan replied.

"You are welcome! We hope here you find what you came for!" replied 'Starsky.'

"Yes, we will. I am sure we will!" was Ivan's heartfelt answer.

"Roger to that! Good luck to you all, and have a safe landing! We're returning to base! Black Knight Leader out." 'Starsky' closed communication.

"*My ochen' vam blagodarny! Udacha i dobryy polyot vam tozhe!*" Ivan replied. All three F-4s initiated an ascent and 180 degree turn that would take them back to Keflavík.

"Well, there we are, finally made it!" exclaimed Alexey.

"Yes! It cost us a lot of sacrifice, but it was worth it!" Vasily agreed.

"Unbelievable! It's like a dream come true!" exclaimed Anatoly. "After so much planning and running, we're on our way to Canada!"

"Yes, even when *mudaki* like Serghey, still clinging to his twisted KGB ideals, tried to stop us, and old buzzards like Gorshkov tried to blow us up, we still made it," said Ivan.

"Well, my head still hurts, but that's a small price to pay for what I got in return," said Anatoly, patting the bandages on his head.

"I guess now it's just a matter of waiting for the Canadian airplanes to escort us to a landing place," said Mikhail.

Amid recounts of their sacrifices and fears during the last four weeks of planning their defection, the crew of *Red 67* spent the time. Then a thrilled voice was heard in the headphones: "Captain, Anatoly speaking. I see three aircraft coming in our direction, vector 350," announced the radar technician.

"Yes, those are the Canadian escort fighters," Mikhail confirmed. "How long until we meet?"

"About ten minutes," responded Anatoly.

Shortly after, like Anatoly informed, glistening in the sunset sun, three small specks appeared before them, leaving behind black contrails. Growing in size as they got closer, the Canadian CF-101 'Voodoo' jet fighters of 416th Squadron, based at Chatham-Miramichi, New Brunswick province, appeared to port and above the giant Tupolev.

"That is a welcome sight!" exclaimed Mikhail. "For the first time in I don't know how many years, I can say I feel really free!"

The 'Voodoos' made a wide turn, ending one on each side, and one behind *Red 67.*

When *Red 67* crossed the geographic bounds marking the beginning of Canadian air space, the pilot commanding the escorting interceptors burst in their headphones: "*Red 67*, welcome to Canada!"

"Well, *now* I say we're finally there!" said Mikhail.

"Not me, Captain," said Yuri. "We have enough fuel for about 45 more minutes flying. So, either we get some place nearby where we can land quickly, or we'll have to ditch."

"Vanya, transmit that information to our hosts," Mikhail ordered the radioman. "The fuel situation is critical. We need to land *now!*"

Ivan immediately set to the task. "Canadian fighters, Canadian fighters. This is *Red 67*. Over."

"Roger, *Red 67*. We read you loud and clear. Over," came the reassuring voice of the Canadian Squadron Commander.

"Our bort engineer says we have enough fuel for flying forty five more minutes. We must land before that time or we will have to surely land our aircraft in water. Over," Ivan explained the situation the best that he could.

"Roger, *Red 67*. We're contacting our base momentarily. We should get you to land safely before you have to land your aircraft in the water. Over." the Canadian pilot responded with a chuckle.

After a few minutes, a reply came. *"Red 67*, you are authorized to land at Goose Bay airbase. It's the closest one with a runway long enough to allow you to land. However, I must inform you that it is approximately forty to fifty minutes flying time from our present position. *Red 67*, do you want to risk a landing there? Over."

Ivan translated the authorization and the question. The crew of *Red 67* was once again at a crossroads, the latest in the series of life-and-death decisions they had to take on this fateful day.

"Blyad! Decisions again!" Complained Alexey.

"Yes, but decisions that must be made, nonetheless," said Mikhail. "What do you think, Yura, do we have enough fuel to make it there?"

"It's like a fifty-fifty chance. We could make it ... or we could not," said the flight engineer.

"Yes, but only you can answer that question," said Vasily.

"I'd trust our good luck and go. I think if I nurse the fuel and scrimp and save as much as I can, we'll make it. I say let's go."

"Khorosho. Does everyone agree?" Mikhail asked.

Seven positive responses settled the matter.

"Vanya, tell the Canadians we will go to their base at *Gus Bey*. Hopefully the fuel will be enough to reach it, or so says our excellent flight engineer!" said Mikhail, the joking tone felt through the intercom.

"Gus Bey ... what a funny name!" said Vasily. "Vanya, does it have anything to do with the Turkish beys?"

"Of course not! It just means *bukhta gusyev* in English," explained the radioman. "'Bay' is *'bukhta'* and 'goose' is the same in Russian too, *'gus'!"*

After 23 hours in the air, having covered more than sixteen thousand kilometers, and with tanks almost empty, *Red 67* reached Goose Bay airbase. Late in the long summer day, with the sun finally setting in the western horizon, common for the higher northern latitudes where the air base is located, *Red 67* readied for landing. Flaps out, propellers pitch to fine, all three landing gears out.

Suddenly, all four engines died in succession. Different from the previous alert by Yuri about all four engines dying, this one was for real. There was no more fuel for the extremely thirsty Kuznyetsov turboprops, so they died one after the other.

Propellers windmilling, Mikhail lets the flying giant use its final momentum to glide the last meters to the runway, quickly losing both height and speed in the fall. However, unfortunately for the crewmembers, the height loss is much higher than the speed loss, so the rate of descent is not only too high, but also the angle of descent is too steep. Mikhail and Vasily fly the airplane in its barely controlled fall the best they can, combining their strength to handle the usually heavy wheels, now feeling twice as heavy.

As the flying giant just about reaches the runway head, Vasily yells: "Captain, landing speed, three hundred twenty!"

Mikhail worries. He knows this speed is still much higher than a TU-95's normal landing speed of 270 kph. However, his tone of voice hides his preoccupation. *"Nye bespokoys', Vasya.* Be calm. We'll land alright." Turning to the rest of the crew, Mikhail announces: *"Tovarishchi,* we're landing, but it's going to be rough!"

The hard bump of the Bear's main eight wheels hitting Goose Bay's concrete runway is felt from the nose to the tail as if a locomotive just hit them from below. Fortunately for them, the plane's rugged landing gear was built to withstand landing its 200 tons not only on normal concrete runways but also on the semi rough runways found throughout the Soviet Union. The screeching and smoking coming out of the squealing tires show their discomfort at having to suddenly turn at a speed much higher than the usual. The landing, although rough and bumpy, and despite the high speed, did not cause any damage. The nose gear falls violently on the runway but the aircraft continues running.

Not having a working engine, however, means not having any one of the plane's power generators working, which means having no hydraulics either. No hydraulics means no brakes. No brakes means letting the giant run its course on the 3600 m long runway and hope it gets to stop before the concrete belt comes to an end.

As they quickly traverse the runway, the safety and rescue equipment assigned to the airbase run behind them, their sirens ululating and their lights blinking, to the amusement of the crewmen in the tail. Amused as they are, though, this amusement is not shared by the pilots.

"Captain, we're at mid runway and still running at two hundred fifty!" Vasily yells. The airplane has already swallowed half of the runway and they barely reached slightly less than their normal landing speed. Unless something happens between the middle of the runway and the end, they'll reach the latter and just continue running over the rough terrain beyond.

"Captain, I'm seeing the end of the runway!" Alexey calls.

"Yes, Alyosha. We see it too," Mikhail responds calmly, not wishing to reveal his real worry. To his consternation, 300 meters beyond the end of the runway, he also sees the tree line. Either the airplane slows down and stops before it reaches the trees, or that will be the *real* end.

As they leave the runway itself and enter the runway end, its white-painted surface zooming below announces the few remaining meters of concrete. Beyond that, the rough terrain.

"Captain, speed, one hundred fifty!" Vasily calls again. They are reaching the end of the runway, and the airplane is just half its landing speed, good if they were still on the runway, bad because they're now entering the rough terrain beyond.

"*Tovarishchi*, it's going to get rough again!" Mikhail announces as they reach the end of the concrete and enter the rough terrain.

The change in surface is readily apparent, however. Instead of the proportionately increasing rumbling they were expecting, they feel a sudden but perceptible deceleration.

Fortunately for the crew of *Red 67,* their good luck held to the end. The local rains of the night before made the usually rough terrain soft and muddy. The landing gear makes deep streaks in the mud, sinking the heavy aircraft ever deeper, helping to slow it down.

From his station behind the nose glazing, Alexey sees the tree line getting closer and closer. Mikhail, in one last desperate attempt to stop the airplane before they reach the tree line, makes a sudden decision. "Vasya, on my mark turn to port!" Mikhail screams. "*Raz, dva, tri,* turn!"

Both pilots turn their control wheels to the left. The huge airplane almost jumps out of the ruts it's cutting in the mud as it forces its way towards the side, and along the tree line, running for several meters along it, then turning further more to the left, decelerating enough to smooth the run, becoming a soft run, until it finally comes to a complete stop.

For several seconds there's only silence in the airplane. Then, as if on a prearranged signal, pandemonium breaks in. Everyone's talking, yelling, screaming, shouting and cursing together. Alexey shoots out of his station's tunnel and falls headfirst on both pilots, while behind them Yuri, Anatoly, and Ivan embrace and kiss each other, jumping like children in a schoolyard. In the tail, the scene is repeated by Jonas and Pavel, despite the close quarters they're in.

The upheaval continues for several minutes until it is stopped by the ululating sirens of the rescue vehicles outside, coming to their assistance.

Despite the physical exhaustion of the long flight and its accompanying personal ordeal, and even despite his head wound, Anatoly grabs the exit hatch handle, turns it, and in one single pull opens the door to the right side. Without even bothering to see who or what is outside, he jumps feet first through the entrance, flies the three and a half meters down, and sinks his boots deep in Canadian soil.

Ivan, not wanting to be left behind, jumps feet first, but grabs the rear edge of the entrance with both hands, swings to the rear of the airplane, and also lands on both his feet.

Not to be outdone by his companions, Alexey slides on the conveyor belt on the floor, sticks his head out of the entrance, and in an extraordinary display of physical agility, jumps out *head first*, holds the rear edge of the entrance, and somersaults the distance to the ground, also falling on both his feet.

Yuri, calmer, simply sits on the edge, and from there he jumps to the ground.

Fortunately for Mikhail and Vasily, the firemen from the rescue team bring a ladder and attach it to the nosewheel bogie. Vasily slowly descends the steps, then turns around and waits for Mikhail to descend.

Pavel and Jonas, five meters up in the tail, open their exit hatch, jump from their station to the top of a fire truck parked beneath, then descend to the ground using the fire truck's side ladder. The crewmen from the tail compartment, seeing their friends on Canadian soil at last, run towards them, under the forward exit hatch, where they hug each other tightly, kissing each other on both cheeks, while rivers of mutual congratulations flow in all directions.

Finally, Mikhail makes his appearance at the airplane's entrance. Regally, although tired, Captain Mikhail Mikhailovich Makarov starts a slow descent, stopping on each rung of the ladder. As he descends, his crew stands at attention on each side of the ladder, their right hands touching their foreheads in a martial salute.

When he finally touches ground—and to their surprise—the Canadian personnel surrounding them bursts in applauses. As if it were contagious, the wave of applauses extends to the crew of *Red 67* too. Only that this time they applaud their Captain, not themselves.

"*Tovarishchi*, we made it," says Mikhail, raising his hand in salute.

A Canadian Armed Forces officer comes forward and stands in salute before Mikhail. "In the name of the Canadian Government, I'm very happy to welcome you to Goose Bay!"

The other Canadian personnel mix with the crewmen of *Red 67*, shaking their hands and hugging them. The crewmen, in turn, in typical Russian fashion, kiss each one of them on both their cheeks.

Another officer approaches Mikhail and asks him something. The Captain, not remembering much of the self taught English he spoke during his WWII days, has to call Ivan for help understanding what the officer is asking.

"He wants to know if we're the whole crew," translates the technician.

"Ah, no. Tell him that there's one more upstairs, sleeping," says Mikhail, smiling.

Ivan translates the Captain's response, and the officer orders two soldiers to go up the ladder and into the airplane. Minutes later, two more soldiers go up the ladder carrying a stretcher.

Securely tied to the stretcher like a salami, to avoid him falling to the ground, Serghey—still unconscious—is lowered to the waiting arms of two medical service nurses, who place him in an ambulance.

As the crew boards the bus that will take them to the air base terminal buildings, Mikhail, the last one to climb aboard, turns around and takes one last look at *Red 67*, then says a silent *spasibo* to the airplane that for many years was his working vehicle, at the end of this flight to liberty.

THE END ♦ КОНЕЦ

EPILOG

▼ ————————

Immediately after debriefing in Canada, the crew of *Red 67* asked for political asylum, except Lieutenant Serghey Molotko. Today, 30 years later, most of the crew of *Red 67* lives comfortably in the United States.

Captain Mikhail—Misha—Mikhailovich Makarov, Commander of *Red 67,* settled in Virginia and worked as a consultant on Soviet Naval Aviation matters for the US Navy until his retirement in 1987. In 1992, after the collapse of the Soviet Union, he finally returned to Saint Peterburg, the old Leningrad, met Irina once again, and brought her and their sons and families out of Russia to the US. During this trip he did visit the statue of Admiral Stepan Osipovich Makarov in Kronshtadt.

Senior Lieutenant Vasily—Vasya—Aristarkovich Chkalov, Deputy Commander of *Red 67,* settled in Florida and still works as a transport pilot for a well known international parcel delivery company.

Senior Lieutenant Yuri—Yura—Yevdokimovich Kazakov, the flight engineer, settled in Texas, where he works as flight engineer for an airline.

Senior Lieutenant Alexey—Alyosha—Andreyevich Kocherghin, the Navigator and operator of the *"Rubidiy MM"* radar, settled in New York City and went to work for a large map-making company in Midtown Manhattan.

Senior Lieutenant Anatoly—Tolya—Filippovich Kiprenko, operator of the *'Uspekh-1A'* and later of the *'Korshun'* main target acquisition and missile control and guidance radars, settled in Chicago, where today he operates a successful Radio Shack franchise.

Junior Lieutenant Ivan—Vanya—Petrovich Krylov, the second radio operator and IFF/TACAN/DMS/ILS System operator, settled in Boston, MA., where he opened a seafood restaurant.

Junior Lieutenant Jonas—Yonka—Tulauskas, the Firing Stations Commander stationed at the tail of *Red 67,* also settled in Chicago, among the large Lithuanian community in that city, where he worked in an agency dedicated to help the plight of his Lithuanian countrymen until the collapse of the USSR. After Lithuania regained its independence, he returned to his beloved native country and now holds an important position in its government, helping it by means of the extensive contacts he acquired throughout his years in America.

Junior Lieutenant Pavel—Pavlik—Pavlovich Tsipov, operator of the *"Vishnya"* and *"Romb"* SIGINT equipment, settled in California, where he directs a small electronics company repairing radars at a local airport.

Senior Lieutenant Serghey Gheorghievich Molotko, the radio operator, elected to return to the USSR. He was delivered to the Soviet Embassy in Ottawa, which quickly sent him out of the country in an Aeroflot jetliner. Shortly after his arrival in Moscow he was arrested by KGB agents. Fate unknown.

As soon as they landed on the deck of the *TAKr Kiev,* all six pilots of the Yak-36Ms of the 279th OKShAP, including its Deputy Commander, Lt. Col. Vasily Nikolayevich Ratenko, were summoned to the presence of Admiral Gorshkov and sworn to secrecy about the events that happened with the American fighters, as well as the fate of the regimental commander, Col. Vladimir Ivanovich Kolyesnikov, and that of his aircraft, the prototype for the Yak-41. The maintenance crew of the Yak-41 signed documents to the effect that they were in charge of the maintenance of the Yak-36s of the OKShAP, then were forbidden to even mention the existence of the former airplane.

Immediately after Captain Makarov's defection, the 364th ODRAP was disbanded. Its Tupolev airplanes were distributed to other Naval Aviation regiments throughout the USSR. The AV-MF airbase at Kuzomen was closed. Its CO, Col. Boris Rodyonovich Degtyaryov together with his secretary, Sr. Lt. Arkhip Nikolayevich Dubov, were arrested by the Soviet GRU and transported to Moscow. Fate unknown.

Col. Konstantin Denisovich Yakovlev, Lt. Col. Ghennady Ivanovich Nikitin, and Lt. Col. Leonid Ivanovich Rudenko, Political, Deputy Political, and Military Commanders respectively of the 364th ODRAP, were all arrested by KGB men and transported to Moscow. Fate unknown, except for Col. Yakovlev, who in chilling premonitions had seen his own downfall in his frequent nightmares, committed suicide while still incarcerated.

Newspiece as it appeared in the British magazine *Aviation International* of June 1987:

> *In early August 1976, two TU-95 Bear D maritime surveillance aircraft of the Soviet Naval Aviation took off from an airbase in the Kola Peninsula to participate in the Okean 76 multi-ocean exercises of the Soviet Navy, rounded the North Cape, crossed the Norwegian Sea, overflew the Soviet naval forces exercising in the Iceland-Faeroes Gap and proceeded on Southward to Cuba. This flight of more than 10,000 km took the airplanes to the airbase of the Fuerza Aérea Revolucionaria Cubana (Cuban Revolutionary Air Force) at San Antonio de los Baños, Cienfuegos, from where they could fly ELINT missions along the entire American Eastern seaboard.*

In 1989 The Soviet Navy acknowledged that on August 4th, 1976, a TU-95 RTs piloted by Major A. I. Krasnosyel'skih, of the 392nd ODRAP, based at Kipelovo, Vologda, crashed in the Northern Atlantic Ocean, some 230 kms. SE of St. John's, Newfoundland, on its return flight from Cuba to the USSR. The reported reason for the accident was stated as uncontrollable spinning due to horizontal stall at 9000 m.

On December 25th 1991, the Union of Soviet Socialist Republics officially ceased to exist, victim of its own corruption, under the onerous weight of a gargantuan military system that consumed approximately between 15% and 20% of its Gross National Product, according to Western sources.

In 1996 the Russian magazine *Aeronavtika Mira* (World Aeronautics) published a series of articles called "*Hot Skies of the Cold War*," by Aleksandr Kotlyarovskiy and Igor Sedov. In article number 3 of the series, published in December 1996, appeared the following excerpted paragraph:

> *Another Soviet reconnaissance (aircraft) type TU-95RTs, flying over the Norwegian Sea and further into the Atlantic Ocean, fell on August 4th, 1976, in the region around the island of Newfoundland. In a patrol flight over the Atlantic, the TU-95 was subjected to interception by a trio of US Navy F-4 Phantom fighters. One of them, completing a risky approach under the wing of the Soviet airplane, cut part of the wing of the TU-95 with its tail. The crew of the F-4 catapulted out of the airplane, but the Soviet crew with difficulty controlled the ill-fated airplane*

in an attempt to return to base and land, but to no avail. The airplane stalled, went out of control and crashed in the sea. There were no survivors.

Every year, on the anniversary of their daring escape from the Soviet Union, the crewmembers of *Red 67* meet in a different city of the United States, in order to keep the camaraderie alive, and to remember that fateful day when they finally became *Free Men.*

GLOSSARY OF RUSSIAN AND ENGLISH TERMS AND ACRONYMS

A eto chto? (А это что?)—And what is this?

Alghidras alkogol' ghidravlicheskoy sistemy (Алгидрас, **ал**коголь **гидрав**лической **с**истемы)—Alcohol for the hydraulic system

Amerikosy (Америкосы)—Americans (derogatory term used by the Soviets)

Apparatchik (-ki) (Аппаратчик(-ки))—Member(s) of any organization

AV-MF (Aviatsiya Voyenno-Morskogo Flota) (АВ-МФ, Авиация Военно-Морского Флота)—Naval Aviation

Baba (Баба)—Farmer's wife

Babushka (-ki) (Бабушка (-ки))—Grandma(s)

Blat (Блат)—Pull (in the sense of having influence in a situation)

Blyad! (Бляд!)—Damn!

Bogie—Unknown object in radar

Borshch (Борщ)—Beets soup

Bortnomer (Бортномер)—Number used for aircraft or vessel identification

Borzhomi (Боржоми)—Mineral water from the Republic of Georgia

Bumaghy (Бумаги)—Papers, documents

Burevestnik (Буревестник)—Petrel (bird)

Byez suchka, byez zadorinki (Без сучка, без садоринки)—Without a hitch, without a snag (exp.)

Chay (Чай)—Tea

Cheka (Чека) The first Soviet Secret Police. From *'CHe-Ka'* the first letters of its Russian name: *CHrezvichaynaya Komissiya* (Чрезвичайная Комиссия)—Extraordinary Commission

Chekist (Чекист)—Member of the *Cheka* (predecessor of the NKVD). Any secret agent.

Chepukha! (Чепуха!)—Nonsense!

Chyort vozmyot! (Чёрт возмёт!)—Devil take (it/him)!

Chyort! (Чёрт!)—Devil!

Chto chyorty? (Что чёрты?)—What devils? (excl.)

Chudno! (Чудно!)—Wonderful!

ČSSR (Česko Slovenská Socialistická Republika)—Czechoslovak Socialist Republic

Da (Да)—Yes

Do svidaniya (До свидания)—Good bye

Dobroe utro! (Доброе утро!)—Good morning!

Dobryy dyen! (Добрый день!)—Good day!

Dobryy vyecher! (Добрый вечер!)—Good evening!

DOSAAF *(Dobrovol'noe Obshchestvo Sodyeystviya Armii, Aviatsii i Flotu)* (ДОСААФ, Добровольное Общество Содействия Армии, Авиации и Флоту)—Voluntary Society of Assistance to the Army, the Air Force and the Navy

Dyedushka (Дедушка)—Grampa

ECM—Electronic Counter Measures

ELINT—ELectronic INTelligence

ETA—Estimated Time of Arrival

Evreka! (Эврека!)—Eureka!

Gavno! (Гавно!)—Shit!

Great Patriotic War—The war between the USSR and Nazi Germany (1941-1945)

GRU (Glavnoe   Razvedyvatel'noe   Upravleniye) (ГРУ,   Главное Разведывательное Управление)—Main Directorate for Intelligence

Icarus—Character from Greek mythology

IFF—Identify Friend or Foe

Izdeliye (Изделие)—Product

Izvini (Извини)—Forgive (generally used to mean 'excuse (me)')

KGB   (Komitet   Gosudarstvennoy   Bezopastnosti) (КГБ,   Комитет Государственной Безопастности)—Committee for State Security

Khorosho (Хорошо)—Well

Khuy morzhovyy! (Хуй моржовый!)—General exclamation (lit. 'Walrus dick!')

Khvatit! (Хватит!)—Enough!

*Kolkhoz (**kollektivnoe khoz**yaystvo)* (Колхоз, **кол**лективное **хоз**яйство)—Collective farm

Komandir (Командир)—Commander

Komendant (Комендант)—Head of the Military Police

Komendatura (Комендатура)—Military Police

Konyechno! (Конечно!)—Of course!

Kopek (Копек)—One hundredth of one Ruble

Korshun (Коршун)—Kite

Krolik (Кролик)—Rabbit

Ladno (Ладно)—OK

Leningradtsy (Ленинградцы)—Leningraders, citizens of Leningrad

Leytenant(y) (Лейтенант(ы))—Lieutenant(s)

Luftwaffe—German Air Force

Matka (Матка)—Little Mother (when referring to an aircraft carrier—*aviamatka* авиаматка—in Russian)

Matros(y) (Матрос(ы))—Sailor(s)

*Medsestra (**Meditsinskaya** sestra)* (**Мед**ицинская **сестра**)—Nurse

Molchites'! (Молчитесь!)—Shut up!

Mudak (Мудак)—Asshole

Muzhik(i) (Мужик(и))—Farmer(s)

My ochen' vam blagodarny! (Мы очень вам благодарны!)—We're very grateful to you!

Nachal'stvo (Начальство)—Top (military) brass

Nas poyebali (Нас поебали)—(They) screwed us

NATO—North Atlantic Treaty Organization

Navyerkh! (Наверх!)—Upwards!

Nikogda! (Никогда!)—Never!

NKVD (Narodnyy Komissariat Vnutrennikh Dyel) (НКВД, Народный Комиссариат Внутренних Дел)—People's Commissariat for Internal Affairs

Nu, chto? (Ну, что?)—So what?

Nye bespokoys' (Не беспокойсь)—Don't worry

Nye za chto (Не за что)—For nothing (you're welcome)

Nyet (Нет)—No

OKB (Opytno-Konstruktorskoe Byuro) (ОКБ, Опытно-Конструкторское Бюро)—Experimental Design Bureau

Ochen' khorosho (Очень хорошо)—Very well

Ochen' tebye blagodaren (Очень тебе благодарен)—Very grateful to you

ODRAP (Otdyel'nyy Dal'nyy Razvedyvatel'nyy Aviatsionnyy Polk) (ОДРАП, Отдельный Далный Разведывательный Авиационный Полк)—Independent Long-range Reconnaissance Aviation Regiment

Okean (Океан)—Ocean

OKShAP (Otdyel'nyy Korabel'nyy Shturmovoy Aviatsionnyy Polk) (ОКШАП, Отдельный Корабельный Штурмовой Авиационный Полк)—Independent Shipborne Attack Aviation Regiment

Oriol (Орёл)—Eagle

Otlichno! (Отлично!)—Perfect!

Papirosa (-sy) (Папироса (-сы))—Hand-rolled cigarette(s)

Pederast(y) (Педераст(ы))—Pederast(s)

Pelikan (Пеликан)—Pelican (bird)

PIKS (Protivo InfraKrasnyy Snaryad) (ПИКС, Противо ИнфраКрасный Снаряд)—Anti Infrared Projectile

Pirozhok (-zhki) (Пирожок (-жки))—Pastry(-tries)

Ponyal (Понял)—Understood

Posmotrim (Посмотрим)—Let's see

Potryasayushchiy! (Потрясающий!)—Fabulous!

Poyekhali! (Поехали!)—There we go!

Pozdravlyayu! (Поздравляю!)—Congratulations! (I congratulate!)

Pozhaluysta (Пожалуйста)—Please

Predatel'nyye sobaki! (Предательные собаки!)—Betraying dogs!

Privyet (Привет)—Hello

Priyom (Приём)—Roger (communications call sign for acknowledgment)

PRLS (Protivo RadioLokatornyy Snaryad) (ПРЛС, Противо РадиоЛокаторный Снаряд)—Anti Radar Projectile

RATO—Rocket-Aided Take-Off

Raz, dva, tri (Раз, два, три)—One, two, three

Razvedchik Tseleukazatel' (Разведчик Целеуказатель)—Reconnaissance and Target Indicator

Rodina (Родина)—Motherland

Romb (Ромб)—Rhombus

RUS (Razvyedyvatel'naya Udarnaya Sistema) (РУС, Разведывательная Ударная Система)—Reconnaissance-Attacking System

Ryumka (-ki) (Рюмка (-ки))—Small, one-shot glasses used for drinks

S udovol'stviem (С удавольствием)—With pleasure

Samogon (Самогон)—Moonshine (liquor)

Samovar (Самовар)—Russian-style tea maker

Serzhant (Сержант)—Sergeant

Shampanskoe (Шампаньское)—A variety of Soviet-made champagne from the Crimea

Sibiriak(i) (Сибиряк(и))—Siberian(s)

Sokol (Сокол)—Hawk

Spasibo (bol'shoye) (Спасибо (большое))—Thank you (very much)

Spokoynoy nochi (Спокойной ночи)—Good night

SRS (Stantsiya Razvedki Svyazi) (СРС, Станция Разведки Связи)—Reconnaissance and Communication Station)

Suka! (Сука!)—Bitch!

Sukin syn! (Сукин сын!)—Sonofabitch!

Tak (Так)—So

Tak ustrayvaet (Так устрайвает)—So it's convenient

TAKr (Tyazholyy Avianosnyy Kreyser) (ТАКр, Тяжёлый Авианосный Крейсер)—Heavy Aircraft-carrying Cruiser

Tochno (Точно)—Exactly

Tovarishch(i) (Товарищ(и))—Comrade(s)

Tozhe (Тоже)—Also

Tri, dva, odin (Три, два, один)—Three, two, one

Trottoir—Sidewalk (French)

Tsinandali—Wine from the Republic of Georgia

Tyshto! (Тышто!)—General exclamation

Udacha i dobryy polyot! (Удача и добрый полёт!)—Good luck and good flight!

Uspekh (Успех)—Success

Vernites' domoy (Вернитесь домой)—Come back home

Vishnya (Вишня)—Cherry

Vnimanie! (Внимание!)—Attention!

Voyenno-Morskoy Flot Sovietskogo Soyuza (Военно-Морской Флот Советского Союза)—Navy of the Soviet Union

VTOL—Vertical Take Off and Landing

VTUZ *(Vysshee Tekhnicheskoe Uchebnoe Zavedenie)* (ВТУЗ, Высшее Техническое Учебное Заведение)—Technical College

V-VS *(Voyenno-Vozdushnyye Sily)* (ВВС, Военно-Воздушные Силы)—Air Force

Vyedomyy (Ведомый)—Led airplane

Vyedushchiy (Ведущий)—Leading airplane

Vympel (Вымпел)—Pennant

Vzryvchatoe Veshchestvo (Взрывчатое Вещество)—Explosives (lit. 'exploding thing')

Wehrmacht—German Armed Forces (pre-1945)

Za tvoyo zdorov'ye! (За твоё здоровье!)—To your health!

Zdrastvuy! (Здраствуй!)—Be healthy! (used as informal greeting)

ZIL (Zavod Imeni Likhachova) (ЗИЛ, Завод Имени Лихачёва)—(Vehicles) Factory named Likhachov

СОВЕРШЕННО СЕКРЕТНО *(Sovyershenno Sekryetno)*—Top Secret

TECHNICAL APPENDIX

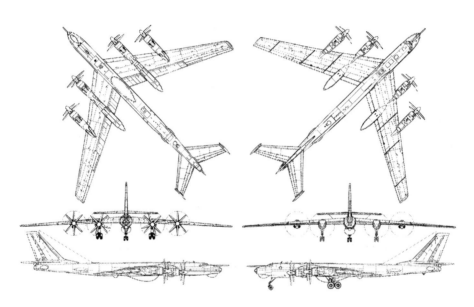

Tupolev TU-95 RTs (NATO Bear D)

Designer: Andrey Nikolayevich Tupolev. Manufacturer: OKB Tupolev.
Length: 47 m. Wingspan: 50.5 m. Height; 12.5 m. Powerplant: 4
Kuznyetsov NK-12MV turboprops rated at 14,795 ehp, each turning 2
eight-blade contra-rotating reversible-pitch 5.6m diameter AV-60N
propellers. Max. speed: 925 kph. Cruise speed: 430 kph. Cruise altitude:
12,000 m, Max. altitude: 14,000 m. Range (unrefueled): 13,500 kms.
Fuel capacity: 90 tons. Endurance: 20 hours.

In the sixties, as part of the modernization plan started by Premier Leonid I.
Brezhnev and pushed by its Commander-in-Chief, Admiral of the Fleet of the
Soviet Union Serghey G. Gorshkov, the Soviet Navy built new airbases in several
small towns across the width and breadth of the Soviet Union, in order to base its

Naval Aviation regiments. Among these were Kipelovo, near Vologda, 400 kms. north of Moscow; Mongokhto, near Sovyetskaya Gavan', Far Eastern Siberia; Khorol', in the Vladivostok area, also in Far Eastern Siberia; Olenyegorsk, 92 kms south of Murmansk; and Kuzomen, 350 kms south of Murmansk, and near the small town of the same name, both in the Kola Peninsula, Northern Russia.

From these airbases the *Bears* flew regular reconnaissance patrols down the western European coast, from Murmansk to Ireland and down the eastern coast of the North American continent, from Canada to Cuba, where they landed at the *Fuerza Aérea Revolucionaria Cubana* (Cuban Revolutionary Air Force) air base at San Antonio de los Baños, province Cienfuegos. Also to other airbases in friendly countries such as Guinea, Angola, Mozambique, Ethiopia, or Vietnam.

Here in Kuzomen was stationed the 364th *Otdyel'nyy Dal'niy Razvedyvatel'nyy Aviatsionnyy Polk,* ODRAP in its Cyrillic acronym, or Independent Long-range Reconnaissance Regiment. The 364th ODRAP received the newly-produced TU-95 RTs *Razvedchik Tseleukazatel'* or Reconnaissance and Targeting platform *(izdeliye* VTs), known as *Bear D* by NATO, serial № 66MRTs307, *Bort № Red 67,* flown by Captain Makarov, from Aviation Plant №18 of the Tupolev OKB-156 in the city of Kuibyshev, Russian SFSR, on March 24th, 1966, being the seventh aircraft from the third batch, and number 37 out of a total production run of 53 which started in 1963 and ended in 1969.

In Kuibyshev the aircraft was equipped with the accoutrements that allowed it to perform the mission for which it was designed as part of the Soviet Navy's *"Uspekh"* (Success) naval electronic reconnaissance and submarine-based air-to-air and ground-to-ground guided missile target acquisition and control complex, in coordination with the "Project 651" (NATO Codename: Juliett) and "Project 675" (NATO codename: Echo II) submarines. These submarines carried four and eight V.N. Chelomey-designed P-500/4K80 *"Bazal't"* (NATO codename: SS-N-12 Sandbox) nuclear antishipping missiles respectively, controlled by the PRS-1 *"Argon"* ranging control system operated jointly with the TU-95 RTs.

The TU-95 RTs thirty-two bladed propeller tips, when turning at supersonic speed, produced an incredible noise, heard by NATO pilots while still 3 kms away from the *Bear.* Closer, at one kilometer away, the pilots said the reverberations of the propellers could be felt in their chests as if they were before a powerful loudspeaker. It was even said that some western jet fighters had difficulty keeping up with the *Bear* when it accelerated to top speed.

In a forward pressurized compartment extending from the plane's nose to fuselage former №13, there were several stations. Like an enormous unicorn horn, the 2m long *'Konus'* refueling probe sat atop the nose, over the navigator station, to be used when refueling from a Myasishchev M-4-201 (NATO codename: *Bison A)* flying tanker, which could top its tanks with an additional 30 more tons of fuel. This, of course, also increased its already impressive flight endurance of 20 hours in the air to an amazing 26 hours. More than a whole day flying!! Such was the extraordinary range and endurance of this flying giant, the fastest propeller airplane in the world.

In an undernose fairing was located the antenna for the *"Rubidiy-MM"* (NATO codename: Short Horn) four-PRF (Pulse Repetition Frequency) range J-band circular and sector scan navigation radar, the same one used in the bomber version of the TU-95. *Red 67's* Navigator, Senior Lieutenant Alexey A. Kocherghin operated this radar. His station was located in the nose of the plane, accessible through a short tunnel between the pilot and copilot seats.

Immediately after were located the stations for the Commander on the left, and that of his Deputy on the right. Captain Mikhail M. Makarov and Senior Lieutenant Vasily A. Chkalov were the leaders of *Red 67*.

After the flight deck, in a compartment behind the pilots and separated by a bulkhead, sat *Red 67's* technical team. On the fuselage starboard or right side, behind the copilot, facing aft, sat the Flight Engineer, Senior Lieutenant Yuri Y. Kazakov. To his right, on the fuselage port or left side, at the station behind the pilot, facing forward, sat the Radio Operator, Senior Lieutenant Serghey G. Molotko.

After the Radio Operator's station, on the port side and facing forward, sat the Tactical Officer, Senior Lieutenant Anatoly F. Kiprenko, operator of the MTsRS-1A *'Uspekh'* (NATO codename: Big Bulge-A) I-band Search and Missile Acquisition and Guidance Radar.

On the floor, to the right of the Tactical Officer's station, was located the cockpit exit hatch. On this section of the floor, from the navigator's tunnel to the cockpit exit hatch, a unique conveyor belt system extended about two meters in length and allowed the rapid evacuation and escape of all crewmembers sitting at the nose and the cockpit. This system was operated by pneumatic compressed air and was actuated only after the nosewheels bogie was lowered.

After the exit hatch, sitting in a position about 1.5 meters higher than the rest of the crew, his head below the transparent upper cupola that allowed him to see the whole upper hemisphere, sat the second radio operator and forward gunner, who was also the operator for the different ECM and tactical systems such as the SRO-2 *"Khrom-Nikel"* (NATO codename: Odd Rods) IFF, A-321 ADF,

A-325Z and A-321B TACAN/DME/ILS, and the A-322Z Doppler radar. Lieutenant Ivan P. Krylov occupied this station.

From former №13a up to former №49, where the unpressurized bomb bay was located in other versions of the TU-95, the RTs version carried the *'Uspekh-1A'* radar. It was used for reconnaissance and to provide data on potential targets to the launching submarines via a PPI link to the launching vessel. The TU-95 RTs were easily distinguished by the bulbous cover for this radar's antenna under the fuselage.

From former №50 to №87 there was a second pressurized section containing one of the three gun stations carried by this aircraft: Six Nudelmann-Rikhter NR-23 23mm cannons, two in a barbette at the top (fired by the forward gunner from his cupola) with a provision of 700 (350 per cannon) DOS-15 23 mm type *PRLS (Protivo radio lokatornyy snaryad*—anti radar projectile) chaff-dispensing rounds, which usually exploded 2 kms behind the aircraft. Here were also located nitrogen and oxygen bottles, hydraulic system gear, and other miscellaneous equipment for maintenance and support.

From former №87 to the tail was located the rear pressurized section. This section had, in lateral fairings on the fuselage, the *Stantsiya Razvedki Svyazi* or SRS-4 *'Romb-4a' (Izdyeliye-30)* ELINT system, and the SRS-5 *'Vishnya'* SIGINT equipment for communications interception. At the base of the rudder there was a PRS-4 *'Kripton'* (NATO codename: Box Tail) gun-laying radar, which sent its input to the gun stations, and an SPO-3 *'Sirena-3'* I-band (NATO codename: Bee Hind) radar warning and detection system. In this section were also located the second and the third gun barbettes, each containing one pair of Nudelmann-Rikhter NR-23 23mm cannons. The bottom barbette contained a provision of 800 (400 per cannon) DOS-15 23mm type *PRLS (Protivo radio lokatornyy snaryad*—anti radar projectile) chaff-dispensing rounds, and another pair of guns at the tail with a provision of 1000 (500 per cannon) *PIKS (Protivo infra krasnyy snaryad*—anti infrared projectile) heat-generating rounds. All the TU-95 RTs armament was used purely for defensive action against attacks from the rear. This section was accessible through port- and starboard-side camera ports, where the AFA-42/100 high resolution long-range cameras were on the ready.

Lastly, separated by a canvas and polyester felt panel, here also were located the stations for the rear gunner and for the operator of the *'Romb-4a'* and *'Vishnya'* communications interception equipment, Senior Lieutenant Jonas Tulauskas and Lieutenant Pavel P. Tsipov, respectively. This section of the airplane, under the tailfin and rudder, was accessible only through a hatch under the tail.

To his right and left Pavel had teardrop-shaped observation blisters of about 2m long by 1.5m wide, used during the photographic missions *Red 67* was sent out. At the end of the tailplane stabilizers were located the cigar-shaped transmitting and receiving antennas for the '*Arfa*' signal relay and amplification system for missile guidance.

Curiously, despite the long, twelve- and sixteen-hour flights carried out by the *Bear* crews, none of the TU-95RTs were provided with toilets or similar facilities for the benefit of the seven men cramped in the forward pressurized compartment and the two men in the tail.

Each member of the crew received a stainless steel bottle, used for the relief of the corresponding organ. For more serious matters both compartments had a container shaped like a cooking pan, with a resin membrane inside and a hermetically sealing cap, located under the seat of the flight engineer. No one, however, ever used it, not even once. Just one look at the device and imagining oneself sitting at it, before the eyes of the rest of the crew, or worse, in the tail, behind the huge observation blisters on both sides of the fuselage, before the eyes of any foreign pilot who happened to fly by, was enough for the total disappearance of all feelings of need.

For years, in the long-range reconnaissance regiments circulated the story of the unfortunate crew that ate something that got some of them sick. The commander of the crew in question got fed up of the foul smell and of having to look after them, so he lowered the airplane to 2000m, ordered decompression, opened the exit hatch, expelled the offending party to the forward landing gear well, closed the hatch, and did not let them get out until they had bowel movement and poured the whole concoction on the well doors.

It was not unusual for the crews to go on their long flights and hold their needs until they returned to base. According to the recommendations of aviation doctors, one has to drink more liquids before a long range flight at high altitude, at least three times more. But because of the absence of toilets, crews drank or ate less. As a result, soon entire crews started to have problems with their teeth and bones.

Another point of contention for *Bear* crews was the difficulty—almost impossibility—of jumping out of a TU-95 RTs in flight, especially for the crewmen in the forward compartment of the airplane. They only had two means of egress. The main exit hatch, which could be used only after the nosewheel bay doors had been opened and the nose landing gear lowered. Also the upper exit hatch, located on the roof, behind the cockpit, between the stations of the Flight Engineer and the Radioman, and placed there by the designers in case of forced landing in water.

However, what constituted the biggest danger to the crew was not so much the difficulty of exiting the airplane using either one of these two hatches, but reaching a prudent distance from the airplane *alive*. If a crewman managed to jump out of the airplane—while still flying at over 350kph—using the lower hatch, he still had to contend with the main radome under the fuselage, which he might or might not hit on his way down and aft as he was carried away by the slipstream, depending on how heavy he was and how lucky too. If he hit the radome, the consequences to his body were predictable. If he did not, he could consider himself fortunate.

On the other hand, if he managed to reach the outside using the upper exit hatch, the unfortunate jumper then had to contend with not one but two dangers as he was brusquely grabbed by the strong slipstream: The rudder fin and the tail elevators, which would hit him equally hard whatever side of the fuselage he happened to take on his fall, breaking every bone in the impacted area. That was if he managed to avoid hitting any one of them square on, in which case they would just slice his body like a hot knife through butter, each part of his severed body simply fluttering away in the wake of the airplane. If he was so fortunate that he could escape unharmed, then he could open his parachute and float down to earth. In both of these scenarios the crews considered the chances of the latter happening usually nil.

The only crewmen who were able to leave the airplane in one piece were those in the tail, provided the air cylinders used to open the exit hatch on the floor worked as designed, and overcame the external pressure of the slipstream, in which case the hatch also worked as a dam against the fast onrushing air.

When TU-95RTs crews complained to the Soviet Navy about the practical impossibility of leaving the airplane alive, the Navy put together a special demonstration team to show them techniques to jump out of the airplane using parachutes. The demonstrations usually occurred flawlessly, and the team went from air base to air base demonstrating the techniques. Of course, the Navy never told the spectators that the team members were all expert paratroop jumpers with thousands of jumps under their belts.

After having it in storage for several months, the Canadian government offered to return the purloined TU-95 to the Soviet Union, with the proviso that they had to come pick it up themselves. Since the Soviet government did not even acknowledge the presence of their airplane in Canada or that the event even happened, the offer was ignored. As far as the Soviets was concerned, the plane crashed in the deep waters of the Northern Atlantic Ocean, near Newfoundland. After the Soviet rebuff, the Canadian government transferred the airplane to the USAF, which flew it to Edwards AFB for testing. At the end of the tests the airplane was flown for one last time to the Davis-Monthan AFB for storage.

On Thursday August 1st, 1996, almost twenty years later to the date, after spending several years mothballed in a remote, far away corner of the airframe cemetery at Davis-Monthan AFB, Tucson, AZ, TU-95RTs Serial № 66MRTs307, *Bort № Red 67*, was finally scrapped and chopped to pieces by the same giant cutters that had previously cut so many B-47s, B-58s and B-52s, airplanes belonging to the forces opposing its frequent flights over the naval vessels target of its relentless maritime searches.

As of March 1995, all TU-95 RTs were grounded due to cracks in the wings. By 1999, 18 airframes had been chopped and sold for scrap at the Engels AFB, near Saratov, Russia.

The *Korshun* radar carried by *Red 67* was a dismal failure, becoming obsolete even before it reached operational use. The USAF technicians, after seeing the outdated miniature vacuum tubes populating the radar circuitry, could do nothing but stand in amazement at the backwardness of then-current Soviet radar technology. Due to its extreme unreliability, the Soviet Navy soon replaced it with the more advanced *Korshun-Kaira* or *Korshun-K,* which was later installed in all its TU-142 (Bear F) antisubmarine warfare airplanes.

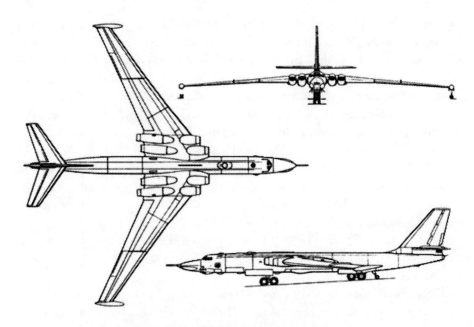

Myasishchev M-4-2 'Molot' (Hammer) (NATO 'Bison A')

Designer: Vladimir Mikhailovich Myasishchev. Manufacturer: OKB Myasishchev Plant No 23, Moscow. Length: 47.67 m. Wingspan: 50.53 m. Height: 11.5 m. Powerplant: 4 Mikulin RD-3M-500 turbojets rated at 9500 kg. Max. speed: 930 kph. Cruise speed: 800 kph. Max. Altitude: 12,800 m. Cruise altitude: 12,500 m. Range: 8,100 kms. Total Fuel-carrying Capacity: 34 tons. Armament: None.

The *'Molot'* was the flying tanker version of the Myasishchev M-4 bomber.

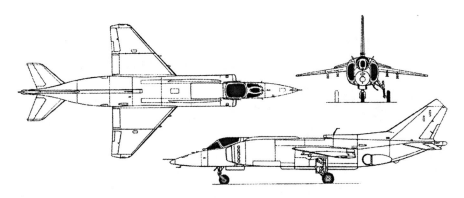

Yak-36M (NATO 'Forger A')

Designer: Alexandr Sergheyevich Yakovlev. Manufacturer: OKB
Yakovlev. Length: 16.3 m. Wingspan: 7.5 m. Height: 4.25 m.
Powerplant: 1 Tumansky R-27V-300 turbojet rated at 6100 kg. and 2
Rybinsk RD-36-35FV turbojets rated at 3000 kg. Max. speed: 1020 kph.
Cruise speed: 850 kph. Cruise altitude: 12,200 m. Range: 380 kms. Total
Fuel capacity: 3,350 kgs. Armament: AS-10, UV-32-57, FAB-250 and
-500 bombs, AA-7 Missiles.

The first prototype of the Yak-36 flew in 1971 and first appeared to the West
in July 1976 when the *TAKr 'Kiev'* deployed with a developmental squadron of
Forger-As and traveled through the Mediterranean Sea and the Northern Atlantic
Ocean. The normal complement for the Kiev-class through deck aircraft carrier
was a dozen single-seat Forger-As and one or two twin-seat trainer Yak-36U
(Uchebnyy) 'Forger-B's. The primary roles were fleet defense (particularly against
shadowing maritime surveillance aircraft), reconnaissance, and anti-ship strike,
but was never used in combat. A total of 231 aircraft had been built by the time
production ended in 1988. The 'Forger' was removed from front line service in
1992-93, although a few remained in the Russian Navy inventory for another
year as limited proficiency training aircraft.

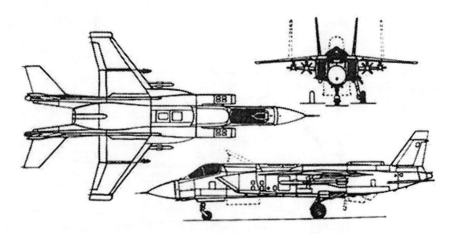

Yak-41 (NATO 'Freestyle')

Designer: Alexandr Sergheyevich Yakovlev. Manufacturer: OKB
Yakovlev. Length: 18.36 m. Wingspan: 10.11 m. Height: 5 m.
Powerplant: 1 Soyuz R-79-30 augmented turbofan jet engine with
vectored exhaust and 2 Rybinsk RD-41 lift turbojets. Max. speed: 1800
kph (Mach 1.7). Cruise speed: 1,250 kph. Cruise altitude: 11,000 m.
Max. altitude: 15,000 m. Range: 2100 kms. Fuel capacity: 4,400 kg.
Empty Weight: 11,650 kg. Maximum Weight: 19,500 kg. Maximum
External Load: 2600 kg. Armament: One internal GSh-301 30mm cannon
with 120 armor-piercing rounds; 5 hardpoints.

Conceived by the Yakovlev Design Bureau as a supersonic single-seat Short/
Vertical Take-off and Landing aircraft, the Yak-41 (designated 'Freestyle' by
NATO) started life in 1975, after the design bureau received a contract for its
development. Since the Yak-41 was based somewhat in its previous design, the
Yak-36, the design and construction of its prototype was not as protracted as that
of similar airplanes. Besides, in order to expedite the design of the prototype,
Yakovlev not only made use of the enormous resources at its disposal—courtesy
of the Soviet Navy—they also threw in all their resources and their best minds in
the resolution of the immediate problems such a type would create.

After studying more than fifty different configurations, Yakovlev settled on an
airframe powered by three powerplants, two small engines, rated at about 2 tons
each, mounted in tandem behind the cockpit, their thrust pointing downwards at
85 degrees, and one main engine, rated at 7 tons with its thrust aft, but with a
movable round nozzle, which diverted the jet efflux downwards up to 90 degrees.

Years later, after the collapse of the Soviet Union, the Yakovlev Bureau would
construct another, more advanced prototype of the Yak-41, resurrecting it as the

Yak-141. However, development of the same seems to be halted due to a lack of funds.

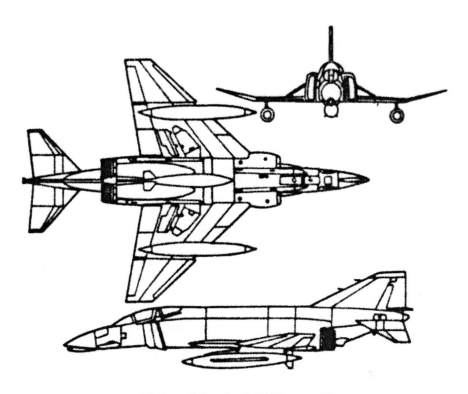

McDonnell Douglas F-4C 'Phantom II'

Manufacturer: McDonnell Douglas Corporation. Length: 19.2 m.
Wingspan: 11.7 m. Height: 5 m. Powerplant: 2 General Electric
J79-GE-17A axial compressor turbojets. Max. speed: 2370 kph (Mach
2.23). Cruise speed: 940 kph. Cruise altitude: 12,190 m. Max. altitude:
18,300 m. Range: 680 kms. Fuel capacity: 7,549 l. Empty Weight:
13,757 kg. Maximum Weight: 28,030 kg. Armament: One 20mm M61
Vulcan cannon with 639 rounds; 9 hardpoints.

First flown in May 1958, the Phantom II originally was developed for U.S. Navy fleet defense and entered service in 1961. The USAF evaluated it (as the F-110A Spectre) for close air support, interdiction and counter-air operations, and in 1962 approved a USAF version. The USAF's Phantom II, designated F-4C, made its first flight on May 27, 1963. Production deliveries began in November 1963. In its air-to-ground role the F-4 could carry twice the normal bomb load of a World War II B-17. The USAF's F-4s also flew reconnaissance and "Wild Weasel" anti-aircraft missile suppression missions. Phantom II production ended in 1979 after more than 5,000 had been built—more than 2,800 for the USAF, about 1,200 for the Navy and Marine Corps, and the rest for friendly foreign nations.

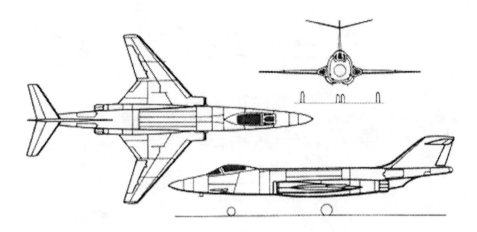

McDonnell Douglas CF-101 'Voodoo'

Manufacturer: McDonnell Douglas Corporation. Length: 20.55 m. Wingspan: 12.09 m. Height: 5.49 m. Powerplant: 2 Pratt & Whitney J57-P-55 afterburning turbojets. Max. speed: 1963 kph (Mach 1.7). Cruise speed: 1,250 kph. Cruise altitude: 15,545 m. Max. altitude: 17,800 m. Range: 2494 kms. Empty Weight: 18,097 kg. Maximum Weight: 21,171 kg. Armament: Two MB-1 'Genie' missiles and two GAR 2A 'Falcon' missiles.

The McDonnell Douglas F-101 Voodoo was acquired by the RCAF as a replacement for the CF-100 fleet used by the Air Defence Command. After the cancellation of the Canadian-designed CF-105 'Arrow' aircraft just two years before, the nuclear-capable CF-101 'Voodoo' was acquired by the RCAF in the United States. As a supersonic, all-weather interceptor, the twin-engine, two-place 'Voodoo' provided high speed, excellent climb performance and a very good combat radius and ceiling plus additional flexibility as a replacement for the CF-100. Used almost exclusively in the NORAD defense role, the aircraft type proved to be a safe and reliable weapons platform until replaced by the McDonnell Douglas CF-18 'Hornet' in the mid-eighties.

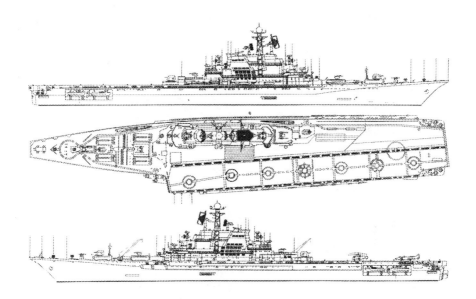

<u>*Tyazholyy (Taktycheskiy) Avianosnyy Kreyser*</u> *(Heavy (Tactical) Aircraft-carrying Cruiser) 'Kiev'*

Designer: Nevskoye Planning and Design Bureau. Builder: Chyornomorsky (Nikolayev South), Crimea. Displacement: 36,000 tons standard; 43,000-43,500 tons full load. Speed: 32 knots. Dimensions: 249.5-257.0 meters long waterline, 273.0-274.0 meters long overall, 32.6-32.7 meters waterline beam, 53.0 meters flight deck width, 9.5 meters draft standard, 12.0 meters draft mean full load. Propulsion: 8 turbopressurized boilers, 4 steam turbines; 200,000 shp 4 shafts. Crew: 1,200-1,600 (including air group). Armament: Missiles: Two SA-N-3 Goblet twin launchers (72); two SA-N-4 Gecko twin launchers (40); eight SS-N-12 Sandbox tubes (16); Guns: four 76.2-mm/59-cal AA (2 twin), eight 30-mm/65-cal AK-630 close-in (8 multi-barrel). Torpedoes: ten 533mm torpedo tubes. Aircraft: 12 or 13 Yak-38 Forger VSTOL Fighters and 14 to 17 Kamov Ka-25 Hormone or Kamov Ka-27/29 Helix Helicopters.

The 36,000 ton *TAKr 'Kiev'* was the prototype for the second class of Soviet carriers. Assigned to the Northern Fleet, the *'Kiev'* passed the Bosphorus Strait on 18 July 1976, despite international protests about possible infractions of the Montreux Convention, which prohibits the transit of aircraft carriers through that strait. After decommissioning from the Russian Navy in 1995, the *TAKr Kiev* was sold to a Chinese company in May of 2000 for 70 million Yuan

(US$8,630,000). Presently it's anchored in Tianjin, PR of China, following its conversion to a theme park for tourists.

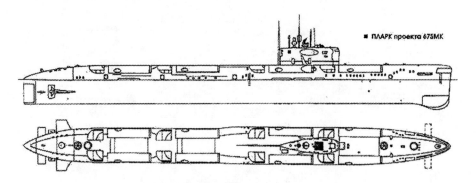

K-22 'Krasnogvardeyets' (NATO Echo II)

Designer: P.P. Pustyntsev of the Rubin Central Marine Design Bureau (SKB-18), Leningrad. Constructed at Factory 538, Komsomolsk-na-Amur, Far Eastern Siberia. Displacement: 4500 tons surfaced, 5760 tons submerged. Speed: 23kts surfaced, 29kts submerged. Dimensions: length: 115.4m, beam: 9.3m, draft: 7.8m. Working depth: 240m. Maximum depth: 300m. Propulsion: Two 70MW VM-A pressurized-water nuclear reactor steam turbines; 25,000 shp 2 shafts, 5-bladed propellers. Crew: 137. Endurance: 50 days. Armament: 8 SS-N-3 or SS-N-12 rockets, six 533mm torpedo tubes forward, four 406mm torpedo tubes aft, 36 mines. Radar: MRP-25 (NATO: 'Snoop Tray') I-band surface search radar; *Argument* (NATO: 'Front Piece/Front Door') fire control radar; *Nakat* (NATO: 'Stop Light') 10GHz ESM radar. Sonar: *Feniks* low-frequency. Called *Podvodnaya Lodka Atomnaya Raketnaya Krylataya* (Cruise Missile Atomic Submarine) or *PLARK* in the Soviet Navy. The US Navy gives it the hull classification SSGN.

On August 8th, 1976, while on her way to the Mediterranean, the K-22 '*Krasnogvardeyets*' Echo II submarine took water when the hatch for the second launcher developed a leak. The malfunction was promptly repaired by the personnel onboard while she was still underwater. On August 28th, 1976, while performing a fast dive in the Mediterranean, 244 kms south of Souda Bay, Crete, Greece, K-22 collided with the US Navy destroyer escort DE 1047 *USS Voge*. In the collision the *USS Voge* sustained serious structural damage in the port quarter below the helicopter hangar, split bulkheads, buckled plating, and a damaged propeller, losing propulsion as a result, necessitating towing by the US Navy ships *USS Monester* (FF 1097) and *USS Preserver* (ARS 8) and later drydocking at Toulon, France.

K-22 suffered a damaged №1 rocket launcher, several moving mechanisms, some hull, sail, and deck rail structures and superstructures. Water ingressed into the hull through a hole in the raising mast for the *'Argument'* radar mechanism at a rate of 2-3 tons an hour. K-22, assisted by Soviet Navy ships but sailing under its own power, reached a Greek port off Kithera Anchorage. On September 7th, 1976, the US State Department announced that the US and the USSR had exchanged notes, each blaming the other for the collision. On July 7th, 1994, K-22 was given the tactical number "B-22" by the new Russian Navy. A week later she was struck from the Russian Navy's active submarines list. Finally, in November 2000, K-22/B-22 was placed in permanent storage at the Ara Guba Naval Storage Base for nuclear submarines in Vidayevo, near Murmansk.

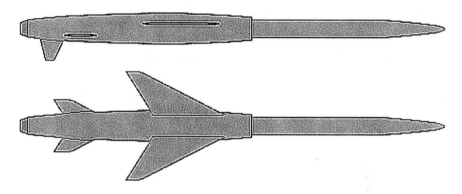

P-500/4K80 'Bazal't' (NATO SS-N-12 Sandbox)
Designer: Vladimir Nikolayevich Chelomey. Manufacturer: KB
Chelomey. Designation: P-500 (4K80). Guidance: Mid-course autopilot;
terminal active-radar seeker. Warhead: 1000-kg High-Explosive armor
piercing or 350-kiloton nuclear. Propulsion: liquid-fuel rocket. Range:
550 km. Speed: Mach 2.5. Length: 11.7 m. Body Diameter: 88 cm.
Wingspan: 2.6 m. Launch Weight: 4800 kg. Date Operational: 1975.
Platforms: Project 675 (Echo II) submarines, Project 1164 *(Slava-*class)
cruisers, and Project 1143 *(Kiev-*class) aircraft carriers. Users: USSR,
Russia.

The P-500 was a long-range, supersonic cruise missile. Its development started in 1963 as the P-350 (4K77) program, which was canceled but subsequently evolved into the P-500 (4K80) project. It was accepted to service in 1973 and became operational two years later. It had a cylindrical body with a slim front ending in a sharply pointed nose. Almost by mid-fuselage it bulged before tapering toward the rear. The missile was powered by a turbojet fed by a small air intake about halfway along the body. The missile featured command or inertial guidance with the option of mid-course updates. Aircraft such as the Tupolev Tu-95RTs Bear D, the Kamov Ka-25 Hormone B, and the Kamov Ka-27 Helix B helicopters were used for over-the-horizon (OTH) targeting. Terminal-phase guidance was either by an active-radar seeker or by passive radar homing. The payload consisted of either a 1,000-kg high-explosive warhead or a 350-kiloton nuclear device, but the latter was usually removed. It could be launched from surface ships or submarines, although the latter first had to surface in order to launch. Associated radars were the H/I-band *'Argument'* 'Front Door' or the 'Front Door C' system, which provided mid-flight updates to the missile if required. The former was a missile-guidance radar with a multiple antenna system and was intended primarily for submarine use. The latter was used by surface vessels and featured a "hidden" antenna that hinged out when needed.

The test of the Chelomey-designed P-500/4K80 *Bazal't* missile system, although successful during the *Okean 76* Maneuvers, did not progress any further since the missile was already at the end of its useful design life. It was promptly replaced by the P-700/3M45 *Granit* system (NATO designation: SS-N-19 'Shipwreck') using a satellite-link guidance system which dispensed with the need to use relay-station aircraft such as the TU-95 RTs.

978-0-595-42558-7
0-595-42558-5

Printed in the United States
105313LV00005B/177/A